SHADOWS
OF MALLIN

SHADOWS OF MALLIN

DRAKA BOOK ONE

AvaritiaBona

Podium

SHADOWS OF MALLIN

CHAPTER ONE

Falling

My body was on fire. Every muscle strained as I fought to keep my hold on the slick rocks, damp and slimy from trickling water and whatever lichen or algae could grow on them in the total darkness. Stupid! I was so stupid! Going into these caves alone, without letting anyone know where I was? Just texting Andrea that I was "going out"? What was I thinking? And then, when I found a new crevice that wasn't on the map, I blithely crawled in there. Sure, the cam that I used to fasten my rope should have held, but perhaps—and this is just a thought—I should have tested it properly before putting my full weight on it?

I'd been rappelling into a cave that opened a short way into the crevice when my cam failed. Rappelling off a cam in the first place wasn't the brightest idea I'd ever had. It had always worked before, but that was no excuse. I dropped . . . I couldn't tell how far. It was quick. Two or three meters, maybe. I didn't break anything, but I also couldn't move for a while.

Everything hurt.

When I realized that my rope had come down with me, I did my best not to panic. Both my headlamp and my backup worked and had plenty of battery left. The cave continued into the depths. The entrance to the passage was oddly symmetrical, and even with the danger I was in, it tickled my curiosity, but going in wasn't an option. I had to get out.

I searched the walls under the ledge I'd come down from. After a while, I found a route back up that looked climbable for a good boulderer, and I wasn't good—I was fucking great. It was my life. I was an instructor, and my gym used me to grade walls. Ten or twelve meters with decent holds? No problem.

I was so close to the top that I could taste it—when I slipped. My feet came off the wall and I dangled, held by only my fingers, as I tried to find something that would let me put some weight back on my legs. I was still not panicking. I was strong, and I had endurance, and I had trained for something like this because I knew that I was reckless and arrogant enough to take risks that might put me in a situation like this. I secured one foot and tested the hold. Then the other. Taking a deep breath, I relaxed a bit, just a tiny bit, and reached for the handhold that would let me reach the top.

My other hand slipped, and the wall fell away. That's when I panicked.

I woke in darkness. My lamp must have shut off or broken in the fall. I was in pain, but the second fall didn't seem to have done any more damage than the first. My back ached, and I think I landed on my ass because my tailbone hurt, but nothing felt broken. Two falls and no breaks. I was quickly running out of luck.

It's possible I was concussed or something. That's the only way I could explain the confusion of the next half hour or so. I couldn't find my gear anywhere, which was extremely weird. I groped around the floor for several minutes before I gave up, but I was knocked around enough that I decided to just go by feel. I'd always had a good memory for holds, and I figured I might be able to make it without my gear. Dumb and cocky. That was me, and I was at peace with it.

My neck was stiff, so I stretched it a bit. It felt strange, like it'd turned too far, which was never a good sign. But that was a problem for once I got out. I was rewarded for my efforts by a dim light, high up, which I suspected was where I'd come in. I didn't remember leaving a light there, but I must have. There was no other explanation. I got up stiffly and made my way to the wall right below the light. Feeling around, I found my first handhold. Great! A little higher than I remembered, but I found it, and then the next, and then my footholds. Everything was a little higher than I could recall, and a little farther apart, but I stretched easily enough and found them.

With painstaking slowness, I made my way up the wall. I felt strong and confident, sure that I'd make it this time. I gripped my holds tightly, and I could swear that sometimes it felt like my fingers actually locked in to the stone, leaving me rock solid for the next stretch.

The hardest part was right at the top. I didn't want to risk using the treacherous hold that I'd slipped on, so I had to hunt around for several agonizing minutes until I found one that would serve. But I made it. Goddamn right, I made it. An eternity after I began the climb, I had both hands on the edge, then both elbows, and then I was up, panting and laughing hoarsely. My voice sounded weird, but I figured it was just the cave throwing the sound back oddly.

"Fuck you," I growled at the darkness. "I win."

Squeezing my way out through the crevice was easier than I thought, though my back kept scratching against the rock. Getting out was a huge relief, and the farther I got from that damn pit I'd fallen into, the better I felt. But I was a little weirded out when I noticed that the light wasn't shining from anything I'd left there. Instead it was something growing on the wet stone that gave off an extremely weak greenish-white glow, like the glow-in-the-dark stars I'd had on my ceiling as a kid. By now, the pain was catching up to me, and I didn't stop to wonder about it. I had to make it out of the cave and get some help.

I'd known the way out, but things were different now. There were rocks in the wrong places, stalagmites and stalactites that were unfamiliar. The general twists and turns of the cave were the same, but some passages were wider or narrower than I remembered, and everything felt a little too big. Even so, I made my way up and out toward the surface. My legs burned and my hips hurt, and after a while, I had to drop to my hands and . . . not knees. Feet. I walked on all fours, and it immediately felt much better, the burning in my hips receding.

I must have really hit my head, because I could swear that I kept banging my butt on something, even when there was plenty of room. But it didn't matter. As long as I made it out, I could find people, or a road, and then I could get to a hospital, and everything would be all right. I wasn't dumb enough to try to ride my bike out, not with the way I was feeling. Then I realized that I could just call someone to pick me up and that I should check if my phone had made it. I went to open my padded belt pouch and . . .

What the hell? Was I naked? My hand touched rough, bare skin. Why had I taken my clothes off? What the hell had I been thinking? Just how hard had I banged my head, anyway?

Now I had another problem. What if I made it to a road and a lone guy stopped? Should I trust him or run? I'd never had what you'd call a classically feminine figure, but there were probably plenty of bastards who wouldn't care about that if they saw a naked, injured woman walking by the side of the road. Most guys would probably want to help, but was it worth the risk?

Dammit! *Okay*, I told myself. *Plan for it.* If I saw a group of men stop for me, I'd just run away and try again once I lost them. If there was a woman in the car, I'd have to take the chance. *Fine. Plan made.*

I saw more light up ahead. Proper light, trickling in from outside. I sped up, reflexively falling into a pretty comfortable all-fours gait, eager for it all to be over and sure that I'd be back in a few weeks anyway. I saw a tall crack in the rock that led to salvation, the light blinding me as I approached. I passed through, blinking, and didn't understand what I was seeing.

Between the high walls of the crack that led to the cave entrance, I could see a vast, rolling forest stretch out before me. The signs and parking lot that should've been outside the cave were nowhere to be seen, and neither was the road. Instead I stood on a deep ledge above a steep cliff, a small, stubborn tree and some hardy weeds my only companions. There was no way down. No easy way, at least. The cave I had entered was in the hills, sure, but there had been a forested plateau right outside it, with a road and all. This was high on a steep mountainside. I blinked, stupidly hoping that the bright sunlight was messing with my vision, and then sat down hard, taking my weight off my hands. That just made my butt hurt, and no wonder. I was naked, wasn't I? I looked down at my legs and feet and . . .

Scaly black hide. Four toes per foot, each with a curved claw coming out of the end. No, wait. Five toes. One was set so far to the side that I missed it at first. *This little piggy went . . . what?* I looked at my hands. Four fingers and a thumb, each one clawed. Thick hide on the palms and pads of my fingers. Scales like little black shields on the back and running up my arms to my shoulders, down my chest . . .

Huh.

Again, I never had much in the way of curves, and I was fine with that, but what little I'd had was gone. In their place I saw scales covering bulging muscle, and lower . . . no hair. I started to bring a hand down, then remembered the *claws.* So instead, I bent forward, way too easily, and took a look. This confirmed that, yeah. No nothing. *Okay. Oh, wow.* I twisted to look at my back and saw more scales, but more importantly, *I twisted my head all the way around and looked at my back.* My neck was longer and let me turn my head far enough that I could just casually inspect my own butt, which might have been funny if not for the long, tapering *tail* growing out of it and the two folded *wings* coming out below where my shoulder blades should be.

"What the . . . What is this . . . ?" I stammered. It was all I could do. My voice was lower than I was used to, but richer and with a slight hiss to it. Still feminine, though. Kind of smoky. *They'd love this on Insta or TikTok,* I thought and started to laugh. Gently at first, then louder and more and more violently. I couldn't stop myself. I was screaming hysterically with laughter, retching and hiccupping as I touched the snout extending from my face and the dumb little stubby horns growing out of my head.

After a long time, out of breath and my stomach cramping, I started to calm down. My laughter slowly petered out, and then I felt the top of my head and realized that I had no hair there either.

"No more bad hair days!" I announced triumphantly to the vast, open sky before me, mad snickering taking over again until I collapsed onto the ground, shaking first with laughter, and then with tears.

I woke up. It was too hot. My scales were black. My scales. And I was lying in the sun. I got to my feet, all four of them, and crawled back into the cave to sleep and be miserable in the darkness and maybe wake up somewhere better.

When I woke up properly, the sun was rising above the forest, and I was thirsty. I was pretty sure that this wasn't the next day. I dimly remembered waking, then going back to sleep many times. Sometimes I'd cry a little, or a lot, before I slept. But now I was thirsty, thirstier than I could ever remember being. I dragged myself out of the cave and looked across the forest. There were breaks in the trees; small ones with rising smoke that could hold villages, but also large, wide ones where there might be lakes and narrow ones where there could be rivers. Far in the distance, right on the horizon, was the shimmer of something that might be a sea. Water. I desperately needed water.

I wasn't sure if I'd died and this was hell, or if I was in a coma somewhere and this was all a dream, but I was not going to just give up and die. I looked at the mountainside. It was steep, but it wasn't vertical. I should've been able to climb down it, maybe even do a controlled slide near the bottom. I carefully found a hold, then immediately slipped as I stretched out my leg. I felt weak from hunger. Luckily, I instinctively spread my wings and lashed my tail for balance and managed to stabilize myself before I slid or fell. *My wings.* The two giant leathery things on my back.

If I call myself dumb enough times, I told myself, *it might stop being true.*

I got back on the ledge. I looked over the edge and decided that if what I was about to try worked, great. If not . . . I wouldn't be any worse off than I already was. Not a great thought, but it seemed true. Then I spread my wings. It felt completely natural, almost like a second set of arms, and my body knew exactly what to do. I flapped them experimentally, and nothing much happened. Then I tried again, harder, and felt the weight on my limbs lessen. Deciding that I might as well go for it, I bent my legs and lifted my wings high. I took a deep, only somewhat-shuddering breath. Then, before I could lose my nerve, I jumped and flapped hard at the same time, and *I took off*!

Of course I started to fall immediately, but reflex and instinct knew what to do. In a moment, I was beating my wings, almost lazily, hanging not at all stationary in front of the ledge. I was swerving all over the place, but I was flying. I was *flying*! With a scream of triumph, I turned and dropped, locking my spread wings so I could glide. I swooped across the treetops, reveling in the glorious feeling of it all until I hit one of the trees with my wing, lost control, and smacked face-first into a tall spruce. Or maybe a fir. Some kind of giant Christmas tree. I tumbled, crashing through the branches until I hit the ground.

That was three falls now, this one with a high-speed collision. I was still alive, and still nothing was broken, except my pride.

I decided that was enough flying and started limping toward the nearest break in the trees. I had a pretty good idea about the direction, and in my experience, you would usually come across brooks and streams here and there in a forest. I heard birds singing and the occasional animal crashing or sneaking through the underbrush, and sometimes I thought I smelled something on the wind, but nothing bothered me. Being a giant winged lizard had that effect, I supposed. I still hadn't put a name to what I was, though it was pretty obvious. I just hadn't accepted it.

What I found when the trees broke was not a river, or even a stream. It was a road. To my right, it crested a small rise, long, wide, and slightly curved, with two tracks and some sparse grass and the occasional brave sapling growing down the middle. The road showed signs of recent use—even I could figure out that the hoofprints and wheel tracks might disappear before too long. That meant people, and people meant help! But first I needed water. I knew that the road was here, and I could find it again easily. I would get some water, and then, once that was taken care of, I'd find some people. I wasn't sure what I would do once I did, considering my new look, but I would have to take it one step at a time. Even getting stuck in a lab or a zoo was better than dying alone.

I was no longer sure where to find water, so I decided to give flying another shot to give me a better vantage point. The trees grew thick and tall around me, so my best bet seemed to be to use the road as a runway. I found a stretch where the trees didn't crowd in above it, then got into a sprinter's stance—well, kind of. I had four legs now—and started running, hoping that the speed would give me some extra lift. When I was going as fast as I could, I leaped and beat my wings, and it worked! One beat had me gliding above the road, another few brought me above the trees, and then I was speeding along just above their tops, birds scattering in panic and me having learned absolutely nothing.

CHAPTER TWO

Here Be People

Flying was, in a word, glorious. I had always loved climbing for the sense of freedom that it gave me, the feeling that I could go anywhere, but this was on a whole other level. I had gone hang gliding once, and it was brilliant, but the instructor was the one doing the flying. I'd just hung there, enjoying the view. Now I was in complete control, and it was such a wholly visceral thing! I changed the angle of my wings slightly, flapped a little harder, and I felt the acceleration in my guts as I climbed. I folded up, plummeting toward the trees with a dizzy joy that beat any roller coaster, and then opened up and locked, turning all that speed into a racing glide that made the trees beneath me look like green blurs and my eyes water until I . . . *blinked* would be the wrong word. Rather, a membrane slid into place from the corner of each eye, protecting them from the wind.

Circling back the way I had come, I looked at the now-distant mountains. I had come so far already! I didn't know exactly how fast I could fly, but it seemed damn fast. The mountains were a wall of blues and grays stretching roughly from north to south, some of them smooth and others jagged, with low wooded valleys and high naked ones cutting between the peaks and long spits running out into the forest. They were like nothing I'd ever seen and absolutely breathtaking.

I blasted past a flock of small birds that scattered, chirping indignantly in my wake, and I roared a laugh of pure, unbridled joy. This was worth every moment of horror and every tear I had shed. If death was the price for another few minutes of this glory, I would pay it without hesitation.

Or maybe not. I needed water. I could see a lake shimmering out from behind the trees ahead and slowed down, preparing to land. But this proved difficult. Taking off and staying in the air had been instinctive, but landing took more planning and experience. The problem lay in getting close to the ground and staying stable enough that I could actually land instead of smashing into the dirt. Whenever I got close, I was too fast and got cold feet, and then I'd flap my wings to slow down and either go too high, sideways, or backward. The solution, I determined, was to let the water cushion my landing.

I pushed myself out over the edge of the lake, not too far, and braked as best I could without flapping. Then I folded my wings and let myself drop. I did not consider that my new body was very different from my old one. It was clearly not adapted to swimming, at least not in the way I was used to. I was much denser, and sank like the proverbial stone, water rushing into my nose as I hit the muck of the bottom. I quickly realized that my limbs couldn't move enough water to propel myself with any speed, and that I was in big trouble. I tried to open my wings, but the water resisted too much, and I was too tired from my aerial frolicking.

But I understood, very suddenly, that there were worse things than being a big, flying lizard. Being a big, drowning lizard was one of them.

I desperately dug my claws, then my fingers and toes, into the bottom of the lake. Success! I was moving, albeit slowly. I could see, barely, which way the bottom sloped toward land, so I started making my way there, stretching my neck up high every so often and hoping to break the surface of the water.

Something moved. Out of the corner of my eye, I saw a huge shadow snake fast through the murky water in my direction. My fear of drowning was quickly replaced by something deeper: the bone-deep terror of knowing I had a predator's undivided attention. I also felt . . . anger? No, not mere anger. Full-blown, fiery rage! A wild and bloody fury that this *thing* would challenge *me*, that it thought that I, *in all my glory*, was prey! I stopped thinking. Death and pain did not scare me as long as I showed this bastard what it was messing with!

In a surge of speed and teeth, it was on me. A snout long enough to bite me in half tried to catch me, but I caught its nose in one hand and let it push me backward, toward the shore. The maw snapped shut, catching nothing and letting me wrap my forelimbs—arms?—around it to keep it from opening its jaws. It tried to roll, then dove and pushed me against the bottom of the lake, trying to scrape me off, but I was strong. Damn, I was strong!

As the thing flailed its head, I began to kick, my clawed feet raking through its skin and flesh. The water became black with its blood, and then, with a powerful jerk of both my feet, I tore it open halfway down its abdomen, its guts spilling out and floating hideously around it. It still fought, but the outcome was decided the moment I had closed its jaws.

Snorting and gasping, I broke the water's surface, sweet air filling my lungs as I dragged my kill ashore, relishing the taste of its blood in the water. I panted heavily until my heart stopped racing, then roared in triumph, warning everything in close range of what would happen if they dared challenge me. The dead thing smelled delicious. I moved in to feast . . .

Then my conscious mind took over, remembering what had happened and seeing the steaming carcass of the crocodilian creature I had killed. I retched, my empty stomach cramping in futile spasms, and collapsed onto the grass.

I lay for a while, collecting myself. My new body clearly had urges and reflexes that were completely unfamiliar to me, and I wasn't sure how to feel about that. But I was still desperately thirsty. I heaved myself to my feet and moved away from the mess of torn meat on the shore and the muck I had whipped up, hoping to find some cleaner water. In moments, the thirst, while I was so close to water, became overpowering, and I shoved my face in, not caring about how dirty the water must be. I drank, gulping down sweet, cool water until my stomach cramped and I stopped with a pained moan. Then, once the cramp passed, I drank more and more, until I had filled my stomach to bursting and felt like I might throw it all up again. I sat back on my hindquarters, exulting in the feeling of finally having slaked my thirst. It felt almost as good as flying.

Soon I started to doze off in the afternoon sun, when a sound caught my attention. I'd been getting used to the birds, the wind in the trees and the sloshing of water, but this sounded like a cough. My mind cleared, and I listened carefully. It came again—an unmistakably human sound! I looked toward the trees in the direction of the sound, but I didn't see anything. I carefully moved closer, and the wind shifted, bringing a cloying metallic scent to my nose. My sense of smell must have gotten much sharper, because I could swear that I could tell where the smell came from. I heard the cough again, and then a soft groan that was quickly choked off. It came from behind the thick stem of an old tree, something like a fig, and as I approached it, I saw that the bark and the ground were stained a dark, glistening red. Blood. The dirt was deeply scuffed around the base of the tree, as though something had been dragged around it . . . or someone had dragged themselves.

I was filled with a horrified curiosity. I had to know. Keeping my distance, I circled the tree, climbing over its thick, reaching roots. A leather boot came into view, then a leg and a torso, and then I locked eyes with a man, sitting in a hollow between two buttress roots. I couldn't place his ethnicity, but that didn't mean much. His hair was a deep brown and curly, his skin almost ashen, even through his dark tan complexion. His eyes were green, and they were full of fear as they followed me. I kept circling, not getting any closer, and was filled with a sickened sympathy at what I saw. He had a deep gash through his left shoulder, his arm hanging limp and blood trickling down his chest.

Beyond him was carnage. I took it in with stunned silence, seeing everything and wishing I hadn't. A few trampled tents and a still-burning campfire were surrounded by still bodies, all stabbed or hacked apart. There were blood and flies everywhere. A little ways from the living man lay a dead one, a sword through his chest. I looked back to the survivor, and you didn't need to be a crime-scene investigator to get a good idea of what had happened. There had been a fight—no, a battle. One where people had hacked each other apart with swords and axes. I didn't need to think about that. The survivor had killed the man in front of him but had taken a bad wound in doing so. A trail of smeared blood and dirt led to the tree. Had he dragged himself there so the lake could be the last thing he saw? I looked at him again and felt a deep, aching sadness.

"How can I help you?" I asked, but the man's fear didn't lessen. He was kicking his leg out, trying to reach the sword that had killed the other man. He was trying to defend himself, even though he was clearly dying, and I realized what this must look like to him. He'd probably seen me crash into the lake, and now instead of peacefully bleeding out, he was about to be torn apart by some horrible monster.

After a while, he stopped struggling. He closed his eyes, took a few deep breaths, and said a few words in a language I'd never heard before. It looked like he was forcing himself to relax. It looked like he was preparing to die.

I didn't know what to do. I had to help him somehow. I could see, and somehow even feel, that he was dying, but I had to try. I knew what to do about a cut, even a deep one. I looked at the guy's wound again and suppressed the thought that there was no way a bandage could help with that. But *You don't get to make that call* was what had been drilled into me in the gym's mandatory first aid training. You always had to try.

I needed something to dress his wound. I turned and raced through the camp. Two forlorn horses stood at the edge of the camp and bolted into the trees when they saw me. I ignored them. I was trying not to see the bodies, trying not to think about how good the blood smelled, and started looking in the tents. There were sleeping bags of some sort, boots, helmets, people's personal things. Lots of bags. I tore them open and found mostly clothes, gear, dried food, and keepsakes. No bandages. Then I got to a tent that was untouched. An old man in a robe lay dead outside, his neck hacked through almost completely and his head lolling in a terrible way, but inside I found a bag, and in the bag: bandages! Clearly, obviously bandages, cut rolls of soft, clean cloth. There were other things in the bag as well, so I took the whole thing in my teeth and raced back on all fours to the dying man.

He was still sitting where I'd left him. It wasn't like he could go anywhere. He had his eyes open again, and there was a hope there that quickly faded as I approached. He looked tired, near passing out. That was very bad. The blood loss might already be too much. I got close enough to drop the bag within reach of his good arm, and he drew back, pressing himself into the tree to get as far away from me as possible. That hurt, but I couldn't blame him. I was used to most men enjoying it when I got close to them, and this was a painful reminder of what had happened to me. I was a monster. An awesome monster that could fly and kill crocs, but still.

"I'm trying to help you," I told him, knowing that he wouldn't understand. I opened the bag, showing him the bandages, and his eyes got a little wider. I took out one of the bandages, but my hands now—I didn't like to think of them as talons—were not nearly as dexterous as my human hands had been, and I fumbled when I tried to unroll it.

Now a growing comprehension tinged with wonder and disbelief was growing on his face. He whispered a question to me, but I didn't understand. He seemed reluctant to take his eyes off me but pointed to the bag and repeated his question. Not sure what he wanted, I pushed the bag closer, and he dug his hand in, rooting around, then froze with a look of cautious hope as he found something. Very slowly, as though it was the most precious thing in the world, he took out a green glass bottle, corked and sealed with wax. I couldn't see the color of the liquid, but there was a distinct shimmer to it, almost a glow. My best guess was that it was some kind of fancy alcohol.

Liquor? Was that what he was looking for? I felt a little annoyed, then looked at his injury and decided that if he wanted to take the edge off the pain and fear, then he could do whatever he wanted. Carefully, he brought the bottle to his mouth, using his teeth to tear the wax. He slipped and almost dropped it, then became very, very still when I brought my hand up to steady it. After a few breaths, he continued, and after some jiggling, he got the cork out. He very carefully brought the bottle to his lips and drank in tiny sips, making sure not to spill anything. When about half the bottle was gone, he poured the last of the liquid over his wound, hissed with pain, gasped once, and slumped against the tree.

When the guy collapsed, it felt like I'd been punched in the gut. I genuinely thought that he'd died. Maybe the liquor sent him into shock, or maybe the liquid was actually a quick-acting poison, meant to put a permanent end to his pain. So I was surprised, and more than a little relieved, to see that he was still breathing. It was labored and shallow, but he was definitely still alive, and the bleeding seemed to have slowed enough that I didn't think he'd die as soon as I turned my back.

I fetched a small pot I'd seen in the same tent as the bag and filled it in the lake. It wasn't clean at all, but it would have to do. I put it straight on the coals of the fire, and after an eternity, it had boiled for long enough.

The guy was wearing something like a thick jacket of hard leather—armor, I guessed—and I needed to be able to see the wound. I really didn't want to move his left arm, but I didn't have much choice, so I boiled a bandage, let it drain and cool a bit, and then pressed it onto the wound while I used my other hand to clumsily get his armor and shirt out of the way. The armor was held together with straps, and my messed-up fingers couldn't work them, but I quickly found out that my teeth were sharp enough to cut through them with some effort. There was no way I was getting his shirt over his head, and I had to tear it, scratching him more than once with my claws in the process, but I didn't cause any real damage that I could see.

Once I had his armor open and his shoulder free, I took another boiled and wadded-up bandage and started wiping off the blood so I could see the wound. To my surprise, it was less deep than I'd thought, and when I had a third bandage prepared to act as a compress, I was shocked to see that it was shallower still. I looked at the wound, red and ragged, and almost didn't believe my eyes as I saw the flesh slowly, ever so slowly, pulling itself together.

"What the fuck?" I whispered to myself. "What the fuck, what the fuck, what the fuck . . . ?" I stared at the wound as it closed before me, and soon there was nothing left but a centimeter-wide strip of smooth scar tissue. I picked up the empty bottle and stared at it. No wonder Guy had been so happy to find it. An actual, real-life healing potion? If I hadn't already been half-convinced that this was all a coma dream, I'd have doubted my own sanity.

Guy's breathing had gotten better, as had his color. He still looked like hell, but behind that, I could tell that he was pretty, well . . . pretty. Nice chin bones, a strong jaw, light brown skin, and rich, curly hair. The strong, slightly soft build of someone who does a lot of exercise because he has to. Not my type at all, but I could recognize an objectively good-looking guy when I saw one.

Being this close to him, and having a moment to relax, I also realized that he was bigger than I'd thought. Everyone here was bigger than I'd expected. I wondered about that for a while, and then the most likely explanation struck me. They weren't bigger. *I* was *smaller*!

That caught me completely by surprise. I got close to Guy again and compared myself to him. He didn't seem much taller than any of the other dead men, so if he was average . . . I'd always been happy that I was a bit taller than most girls. I could look most guys level in the eye. Now my best guess was that I was a bit bigger than something like a German shepherd, which hardly seemed fair. Sure, if you included my tail and longer neck, I could stretch to a bit less than two meters, and my wingspan was impressive, but I still obviously wasn't the awe-inspiring apex predator that my new instincts told me I was.

It was that moment, when I was flat on my belly on the ground, trying to stretch as much as possible, that Guy chose to wake up. First a cough, then a groan. I quickly got to my feet and hoped that he hadn't seen me. Then his hand went to his wound, and when he found nothing, he tried his left arm. He winced, but it seemed to work fine. He looked at me, gave me a tired smile, and said something, hopefully expressing his thanks. Then he got halfway to his feet and promptly keeled over again, falling to his hands and knees. I started forward to help but stopped when he crawled over to the dead man. My breath caught, and a knot of dreadful anticipation grew in my stomach when he grasped the hilt of the sword impaling the man, braced with his foot, and pulled the thing out with a wet, meaty sound.

I'd helped him. He would have died if not for me, and he'd thanked me, hadn't he? Surely he wouldn't . . . ? But my fears were unfounded. Using some of the spent bandages, Guy cleaned the sword and then sheathed it in the scabbard on his belt. After that effort, his reserves were apparently spent, and he sat back heavily, arms hugging his knees.

He spoke to me. I told him that I didn't understand, and he smiled wryly. Then he mimed eating and drinking and looked at me hopefully, and I understood that easily enough. Apparently coming back from the dead takes it out of you. I remembered seeing dried food and bottles in the tents, so I went off to gather some. In one tent, I emptied a bag and collected in it what I could in the way of food and drink, carrying the bag in my mouth.

I was getting ready to go back when I noticed a tent I hadn't searched. When I got there, I smelled something. It must have been there before, but I was too distracted to notice. It was absolutely wonderful, sweet and savory and metallic all at once, to an almost intoxicating degree. I sniffed the air, hunting around the tent until I found a small locked box under a neatly folded pile of clothes. I had to have it. I couldn't get it open, so I put it in the bottom of the bag and headed back to Guy.

My patient gratefully tucked into the bread, dried meat, and cheese that I had found and opened a bottle of what smelled like sweet wine to wash it all down. Seeing him eat made me realize that I was hungry as well. I hadn't eaten at all since I had woken up like this, and now that water had expanded my shrunken stomach, I was ravenous. The bread didn't smell appetizing at all, but I started bolting down meat and cheese at such a rate that Guy began to look worried. At one point, he reached for a hunk of cheese at the same time that I went for it, and a warning rumble came unbidden from deep in my chest. Guy wisely chose a heel of bread instead. I felt slightly embarrassed, but I'd already saved his life, fed him, and brought him booze. He could damn well let me eat my fill.

Once we'd eaten, and he'd finished off one whole bottle of wine and half of another, the sun was starting to get close to the mountains. Guy had found a shirt and put some more wood on the fire, but I could see that he was avoiding looking at the dead people. Many of them had probably been his companions, or even friends. I couldn't imagine what was going through his head. I didn't even know anyone here, and I felt almost sick with grief just knowing that they were all dead. Guy . . . Well. I'd lost my nan to cancer. She was the only person I knew who had ever died. I couldn't imagine.

Guy didn't want to sleep in the tents, I guess, because he found a sleeping bag somewhere and brought it out near the fire. He had long since accepted that I was intelligent and seemed more comfortable around me, if pretty confused as to why I was helping him. We weren't talking. There was no point, unless it was just to hear a voice. But it was thanks to that silence that I heard the rumble of hooves before the literal cavalry arrived.

Guy got unsteadily to his feet, a hand on his sword, and I was ready as well on the opposite side of the fire when a large group of men riding horses and carrying spears thundered into the camp along a path that presumably led to a larger road. Well, they were mostly men. One of them called out in a bright feminine voice full of pain mixed with relief. She rode almost all the way up to Guy, vaulting off her horse and throwing herself at him, nearly knocking him off his feet. He caught her as best he could, and they embraced so warmly that I started to feel embarrassed. Then the newcomers saw me.

There was pandemonium. The woman had discarded her spear, but her sword hissed out of its sheath. Guy was shouting, trying to hold the woman back and calm the others down. The men, still on their horses, were yelling, and one, deciding to take initiative, lowered his spear and charged at me with a yell.

I had a second to think, and thank God for that. From the moment I'd heard the horses, I'd been wary and focused. While my body roiled with fury and wanted to stay, to fight and kill all of these fools who dared come for me, my human side knew that fleeing was the only option. I threw myself to the side, saving myself from getting pinned to the ground. Then, without thinking, I grabbed the bag of food in my teeth and exploded into a sprint—a gallop, really—and launched myself into the air. I would later remember this as one of the smoothest and most graceful takeoffs I'd ever made.

I was halfway back to the cave by the time I started to process what had happened. Grief and loss and a sense of extreme injustice kicked in, and silent tears began to flow.

CHAPTER THREE

Greed Is Good

I had cried more in those few days than I had in the months leading up to them. I had connected with someone, but how the hell would I find him again? And even if I did, the others who showed up had confirmed my fear: I was a monster. Guy had only given me a chance because he had nothing to lose. Either I would eat him or he'd bleed out any minute anyway. But what about people who weren't completely powerless? Would everyone react the way his companions had? What was I supposed to do about that?

I slunk off into the cave, deep enough that only a bit of sunlight would reach me in the morning, and tried to sleep. In a way, I was worse off than I had been before. The same thoughts kept roiling in my head. I had met someone, and I'd been chased off. What if that was the only chance I got? Everyone had reacted the same way to me, even Guy at first. With fear, immediate and violent. If he hadn't been literally broken and dying, I have no doubt that he would have tried to kill me too. But he'd seen that I didn't mean any harm. He'd understood that I wasn't a monster. I just needed a chance—just a goddamn chance!

The disappointment and frustration were exhausting, and finally, too tired to even feel anymore, I slept.

Eventually, I woke up on the stone floor of the cave with my tail curled over my snout, wings half-spread to form a canopy above me. It was surprisingly cozy. The sun was peeking in and disturbing my rest, so I angled a wing to shade myself. That was a thing I could do now. The wings were simply a fifth and sixth limb, and using them came completely naturally to me, no different than making complex movements with my arms or legs. Or perhaps a hand was a better comparison; the wings were batlike, and bat wings were really just long, flappy hands. Either way, the movements needed for flight were extremely precise, and I performed them without thinking, no matter what else I was doing at the time.

I wanted to cry a little, but I wouldn't let myself. It might make me feel better, but it wouldn't help. I needed to figure things out. I was still a little hungry, but this time I had something to eat! And possibly to drink, but wine seemed like a particularly terrible idea when I relied on flight to get myself out of the cave. The bottles would probably be a pain to open anyway.

There was only a little cheese and dried meat left, and I ate them. I looked skeptically at the bread, then ate that as well, hoping that it wouldn't make me sick. Then I got to the bottom of the bag and found the little box.

I had almost forgotten about it, but the instant I saw it now, I was filled with desire to get it open. I knew there was something wonderful inside. I could literally smell it.

The box rattled mutedly when I shook it. I tried prying it open with my claws, but that didn't work. Then I tried my teeth, but, long and sharp as they were, they couldn't break the hard wood of the box, and I didn't want to risk cracking a tooth—it wasn't like I could visit a dentist to have them fixed. So I settled on using a rock. Tools were, after all, what separated man from beast, and I needed to feel a little bit human. After placing the box on the ground, I found a loose, heavy stone. Then, like a raging ape, I smashed the box until it cracked open.

There was gold inside. Nine gold coins, glimmering in the morning sun. On one side was a woman's head in profile and some weird letters. On the other side was the stylized head of a dragon, which felt very right.

They were the most beautiful things I had ever seen. I would never let anyone take them from me. I would defend them with my life.

I picked up the coins and rolled them between my hands. They clinked, and I giggled at the sound. I was so caught up in it that I nearly didn't hear the voice that spoke softly in my ear. My old voice. My real voice. It spoke in a way I never had, full of lazy satisfaction and power. I screamed in surprise and whirled around, but there was nothing there.

"Your hoard has grown," my voice purred. *"A minor threshold has been reached."*

"What?" I exclaimed into the empty cave. "Hello? Who's there?"

"How will you increase your power?" the voice demanded, and I instinctively knew that I had to make an irrevocable choice, here and now.

"Strength, to overwhelm your enemies. Fortitude, to shrug off harm. Physical greatness, to increase the power of your body in all ways—at a cost. Stealth, to strike unseen. Tongues of men, to understand and manipulate those beneath you. Choose." The voice sounded impatient now. Okay, that was a little more like me, but I was still freaking out. Hearing disembodied voices is not a good thing, but I had been through a lot. I hadn't snapped, had I?

"Please," I said into the emptiness. "Show yourself. If someone's here, just come out!"

"Strength! Fortitude! Greatness! Stealth! Tongues! Choose now!"

The voice was agitated. It was angry now, and a pain like the worst headache I could imagine shot through me. It was like a hammer of liquid fire had smashed into the base of my skull, beating me down to the ground, writhing and groaning.

"*Choose!*" the voice roared.

"Tongues!" I gasped. It was the only real choice. I didn't need to be stronger. I didn't want to die, but if the alternative was to be alone forever . . . Well. If it happened, it might be a relief. I scolded myself for thinking so. *That's a destructive idea. You're in a bad place right now. Let that one go.*

Physical greatness? I knew instinctively that this meant size. I was not happy with the size I was now, but being bigger came with a cost. I'd need more food, and it would be harder to get into some places or hide when I needed to. That was out of the question for now.

Stealth was enticing. I'd rather avoid conflict than have to fight or flee. But tongues? This option would let me understand and speak all human languages. I didn't understand how, but I knew that it would. If I had been able to speak to the people who came for Guy the day before, maybe things would have gone differently. Maybe not, but being able to communicate would have surely made a world of difference.

As soon as I made my choice, the headache vanished. I was on the floor, the dust turning to mud where I'd smeared drool on the dirty stone. I didn't bother questioning what had happened. It was neither the worst nor the strangest thing that had happened to me in this hallucination, or altered reality, or whatever this was. I had to accept it and try to use it to my advantage.

I wanted to get up and felt that I had my hands closed, clasped tightly to my chest. Protecting my treasure. My *hoard*. I looked at the gold coins in my hand, rich yellow with a fiery tint to them. I wasn't sure if they were pure gold, but they were beautiful, felt wonderful in my hands, and smelled like nothing else. I was overcome with an urge to protect them, to hide them away where no one could stumble upon them and take them from me. The cave seemed like a good place to start. It was high up and hard for any creature that wasn't a bird or a particularly ambitious mountain goat to reach. Still, I couldn't leave them near the entrance. They needed to be safe.

I looked around and found the box. The lid was cracked and the hinges were broken, but it would do for now. I gently placed the coins inside and closed the lid. It took a lot of willpower, since I didn't want to stop looking at the coins. I didn't want to stop touching them. But I couldn't stay in the cave forever, and so

I powered through. I knew just where to hide the box too, a place that only I knew about. I descended past the light and the fresh air to the depths from where I had come. The slime on the walls still shone, but it took a while before my eyes adapted to the faint light and I could continue. Soon I reached the crevice. This wasn't even halfway to the deepest explored part of the cave system, but the crevice and the cave beyond were mine.

I squeezed through, which was easier than last time now that I knew that I could splay my wings out to the sides, and reached the ledge inside. There, around the corner from the crevice, I placed my treasure. I couldn't see it in the darkness, but I could smell it, and I knew that it was there. I knew that if I opened the box I'd just start playing with those wonderful coins again, and then who could know how long it would be before I got out, so I stroked the cracked lid one last time and then returned to the entrance.

It felt like leaving a loved one, not sure if I'd ever see them again.

I had never been materialistic. I earned enough money as an instructor at my gym to make a living. I lived in a tiny apartment, mostly full of old and second-hand stuff, which I shared with my best friend, Andrea. I paid my bills, got groceries, and put a little bit away each month for emergencies. Everything else got spent on stuff for climbing, taking care of my bike, and enjoying life. Most of my accessories were cheap shit that I wouldn't be sad about losing, though I did have a nice set of silver and sapphire earrings with a matching necklace that I loved because my nan gave them to me for my graduation. But overall, money came and went. That was how I had always lived my life.

Now I had a small box of fewer than a dozen gold coins, and I wanted more. I knew that it was crazy, and I didn't care. The pleasure that I got from touching those little bits of beautiful yellow metal, from seeing them, smelling them, *having* them—there was nothing that could compare to it. It was better than ice cream, better than a hot bath after a long, cold day, better than cuddling in the afterglow of good sex. It was plain better, better than anything, *and I wanted more.*

I looked out from the cave, across the forest. There were people out there. People with swords and spears, but gold and other treasures as well. If I could find them, and if I played my cards right, then those treasures could be mine. I didn't particularly want to steal from anyone, but I'd figure something out. I had a bad habit of calling myself dumb, but that was rashness more than anything. I wasn't *dumb* dumb. I was smart, and strong, and now I could talk to people. And I knew what I was. I'd known deep down ever since I woke up like this and stepped into the light, but when I'd seen the image stamped into the gold coins, I had begun to truly accept it. And why shouldn't I? I was glorious.

Dragon. I let the word simmer for a while as I stepped out into the full sunlight. Transparent, nictitating membranes slid into place over my eyes, cutting the glare and protecting them from the wind.

"Dragon," I said to the world, letting the word roll off my tongue. There were dozens, maybe hundreds of words for what I was in all the languages spoken, but I liked the English one best.

"I am dragon! Hear me roar!" The open sky swallowed my words, and I leaped forward, caught the air with my wings, and soared.

CHAPTER FOUR

From the Mouths of Babes

For the first time since I woke up in the cave, I wasn't just reacting to my circumstances. I had a long-term goal, and while it felt petty to my human mind, the dragon in me saw it as natural and noble. What else was there to life but to grow one's hoard? But first thing's first. I needed to survive, and for that, I needed food, water, and shelter. I had the cave, so shelter was taken care of for now. Water was easy, and if I didn't have anything to eat, I could at least fill my stomach with it—a little trick from my younger, less confident days. What I drank from the lake hadn't made me sick overnight, so it was probably safe, but I'd rather drink something clean. If I could find a spring or a stream nearby in the mountains that would be ideal, but I didn't want to spend time searching right at that moment. I could find the lake, and where there's a lake, there are streams feeding into it, so that was where I headed.

I stayed low and quiet over the treetops, wary of people. For all I knew, the forest was crawling with archers hoping to kill me, and I would rather they didn't see me coming.

When I reached the lake, I quickly located the clearing where the camp had been. I made two quick flybys and found no sign of people. I took my time with the landing, making many attempts before setting down on the grass much harder than I would have liked. My hips and knees ached, having taken the brunt of the force, but at least it was better than almost drowning myself again.

The croc-like thing I'd killed the day before was gone. I felt slightly miffed by that. I didn't want it, but it still felt like someone had stolen it from me, and I assumed that those were reptile-brain predator instincts making themselves known.

I cautiously made my way to what had been the camp. The tents were gone, as were the bodies, and the fire had been covered with dirt, though the large stones marking it remained. The whole place still reeked of blood, and I caught a smell, rank and bitter, that I could only think of as death. I followed it. To my surprise, it . . . didn't make me sick. In fact, once I got used to it, it was a smell like any other. Not pleasant but neutral. It simply was.

The blood, though . . . That was almost pleasant.

I found the source of the death smell about a hundred meters away from the camp, among the trees. There was a grave there, long and wide enough for three people lying head to foot. Assuming that whoever dug it had buried the bodies decently deep, it didn't look big enough for all the corpses I'd seen, but that made sense. They probably would have taken their companions with them for proper burials.

In any case, there was nothing for me there. I went back to the lake, made sure that I had some trees between me and the water, and then snuck along the shore until I found a quick-flowing stream. I followed it upstream for a good while until I found an opening in the trees. There, I drank my fill, and the water tasted much better than what I'd had at the lake. Then I practiced taking off and landing with limited room. Flying was pretty easy, but taking off and landing vertically without hurting myself was very, very hard. When I tried to take off, I kept going too far forward, then I overcompensated and went backward into a tree. I'd drift sideways and hit the tips of my wings, which hurt like hell. After many attempts, broken up by resting when it hurt too much or my flight muscles got too tired, I finally got to the point where I could consistently take off without hitting anything, as long as I started at one edge of the clearing. On the upside, I got good enough at landing in all my attempts that I didn't hurt myself anymore. I accomplished this through small, frantic flaps as I got close to the ground rather than the graceful glide-and-brake maneuver that birds usually used. I was sure that it looked ridiculous, but it worked.

With that taken care of, my next concern was food. I'd worked up an appetite with all my practice, and I had nothing left over from the day before. I could probably forage something, but my last meal had told me that what I really needed was meat. I had no idea how to get that, unless I wanted to try to catch another one of the crocs using myself as bait. However I did it, I wasn't looking forward to eating anything raw.

In books and movies, dragons would usually hunt by incinerating their prey with their fiery breath. I was, as far as I could tell, severely lacking in that department. Feeling around my mouth with my tongue, I found two large glands running along my jaw, then made an absolute fool of myself trying to blow flame or express some kind of chemicals that would ignite when mixed. All I managed was a pitiful spray of bitter spittle. My pride was sorely tested, and I had no way to cook anything. I had a vague idea of how to make fire with dry wood or flint and steel but wasn't sure if my new hands were up to the task. I could maybe see myself eating raw fish, but didn't they freeze the fish first for sashimi or something? So eating fish without being able to prepare it was just asking to get sick.

Eggs, maybe? It seemed like the right season for it, and as far as I knew, salmonella and other food-borne illnesses were mostly a problem with factory-farmed eggs due to overcrowding and the overuse of antibiotics. I could handle raw eggs, and if there was one thing I was good at, it was climbing. I'd been bloody brilliant as a human, and if anything, this body was even better at it. I felt vaguely bad about the idea, but I resolved to raid some birds' nests in the hope of finding unhatched eggs.

It took a while, but I finally located a nest near the top of a tall tree. Some kind of crow, perhaps, judging by how it was built. I looked around, a little anxious and reminded of psychotically swooping magpies, but I didn't see anything.

There were no branches within reach, and I considered using my wings to get up, but then I remembered my claws. Like a big cat, I dug my claws into the bark and heaved myself up, and it worked! I barely needed branches at all, quickly getting to the top. Unfortunately, when I got the nest, there were no eggs, only a bunch of screaming chicks, and no matter how hungry I was, I didn't have the heart to eat them. Seeing them made me aware of a problem with my plan, though. If I did find any eggs, they were almost certain to be fertilized, meaning that there may be half-formed chicks inside.

That thought made me sick enough to put me off eggs for a while, and I slunk back down to the ground. I was still hungry, though, and sooner or later, I might have to put my feelings aside and eat some bird babies. I prayed it wouldn't come to that.

As I rested by the stream I became aware of a thin, high-pitched noise. I looked up and snorted with irritation, and it came again from upstream. With nothing better to do, I gave in to my curiosity and followed it. The sound got louder the farther I went until it became recognizable as a girl screaming her head off. I did what I had always imagined I'd do in a situation like this. I ran toward it.

When I got close, I slowed down and crept forward. In the distance I saw a giant pig, a wild boar of some kind, circling and butting its head against a young tree. In the tree, screaming in terror and holding on for her life, was a girl in a faded green dress. She had the same light brown skin and black hair as most of the people I'd seen, with features that tended more toward Southeast Asia, like the woman who'd hugged Guy. Guy had looked noticeably different from this girl and from the other people, living and dead, at the camp. I wondered if he was a transplant from some other region, then scolded myself. Not the time. The boar looked determined, and the tree looked like it couldn't take much more. I could guess what would happen if the tree went down—pigs eat anything.

I roared, rushed forward, and realized my mistake in the span of a few heartbeats. The girl saw me and started screaming even louder, which I hadn't thought possible. The boar saw me and didn't get scared. It got pissed off. I saw the boar up close and nearly pissed myself. The thing was more than twice as tall as me, and it must have been at least ten times my weight, a small hill of angry muscle and bristles sporting four wicked tusks. The dragon wanted to fight, of course, but when the thing let out a thundering squeal and charged at me, I didn't think. I used my wings and leaped into the nearest tree, hanging on by my claws.

The boar raged, its tusks stripping bark, but my tree was sturdier than the girl's and didn't seem likely to fall. I might have been able to get out, but I didn't want to leave the girl to her fate. Again, instinct and reflexes came to the rescue. As the boar savaged my tree, I turned my head toward it. What I wanted to do was to scream at it, something useless like *Piss off!* What came out instead was a hiss accompanied by a narrow spray from those big glands in my mouth.

The spray hit the pig fully in the face, and it immediately began to squeal in pain, throwing its head around and dragging it through the leaves and needles of the forest floor. I hissed and sprayed again, catching it on the side of its head, and this time the beast turned and ran, plunging through the stream and disappearing into the distance.

"Yeah!" I called after it, bodysurfing a wave of adrenaline. "Ya better run, ya wanker!"

The girl was still screaming.

I dropped out of my tree and sat down a few meters away from hers. I wanted to tell her to come down, but she was terrified and unlikely to listen. Besides, even though I should be able to understand and speak any language, I had no idea what language she might speak. Screaming is not a language, and my new ability didn't work retroactively. I had no idea what Guy and his people had been saying the day before.

I could have left her, but she was a kid, and I didn't want to leave her alone. She had nearly died once today, and I wanted to be sure that she'd get back home safely. After an eternity, the girl was finally all screamed out and just cried instead. I took the relative silence as my cue to speak up.

"It's okay," I told her in my most soothing talking-to-kids-and-animals voice. I spoke English, so she probably wouldn't understand a word, but I hoped that the tone would get my message across. "You're safe now. You can come down."

The girl looked at me but kept crying. All I needed were a few words from her, so I kept trying, telling her that it was okay, that nothing would hurt her, and that I wasn't going to eat her.

After a while, she sniffled and looked at me accusingly. "You're talking," she stated, and I finally had something to latch on to.

"Thank you!" I exclaimed in the same language. I didn't spend much time thinking about how weird yet completely natural it was to be able to speak a previously unknown language. My patience had worn thin enough to read through. "Two words, that's all I needed. Oh. Oh no, don't cry!"

The girl was crying again. It took another couple of minutes before she calmed down enough to talk. "Are you going to eat me?" she asked between sobs.

"No." I sighed with exasperation. "I'm not going to eat you. I just want you to come down so I can help you get home."

"You look like a demon," the girl said, her puffy eyes narrowing with suspicion. *Ouch.* "My uncle says that if I see a demon, it will promise me things, but it will all be lies."

"I'm not a demon," I said defensively. "Come down!"

"If I come down, you'll eat me," she squeaked, close to tears again.

"Look," I told her. "If I wanted to eat you, I'd come up there. See?"

I leaped back into my tree and climbed even higher than she was to drive the point home.

"I'm very good at climbing, and I don't want to hurt you. I don't want anyone to hurt you. That's why I don't want you to be all alone out here."

The girl considered this. "What's your name?" she asked after thinking for a while. "My uncle says that a demon will never tell you its name."

I was about to answer but realized just in time that my real name sounded like some crude slang in this language. Unable to think of a good name on the spot, I simply replied, "I'm . . . *Dragon.*" I said the last part in English. I was doing pretty well and didn't want to scare her again.

"Dra-ka?" she tried, not quite managing the unfamiliar word.

"Sure, kid. Draka. I'm Draka. Pleased to meet you. What's your name?"

"My uncle says . . ."

"Look, kid, I just told you my name, so I'm not a demon, yeah?"

She accepted my unassailable logic. "I'm Lahnie. If you're not a demon, why can you talk? You're a big lizard."

"I'm a magic lizard," I told her. That was even almost true.

"Are you a boy lizard or a lady lizard?"

"What do you think?"

"You sound like a lady."

"Good guess. Got it in one. Hey, why 'boy or lady'? Why not 'boy or girl'? I don't sound that old, do I?"

"My sister says that all girls are ladies, but most boys are dogs or pigs, and only some are men." She stated this as though it were an objective and indisputable fact.

"Sure, she's not all wrong . . ." I muttered. "Hey, Lahnie?"

"Mm-hm?"

"Can you come out of the tree, Lahnie?"

"I'm too high," she said. "I'm scared to jump."

"More scared than being stuck up there until it gets dark?"

"Yeah."

I vacillated for a while, and then sighed. "Lahnie, I'm going to climb up the tree, okay?" I said to her, trying to sound reassuring.

"Okay," she answered, sounding not the least bit reassured.

"I'm not going to try to eat you."

"Okay."

"I'm going to climb up there, and I want you to get on my back."

Lahnie paused. "Okay," she finally answered.

"Okay. Here I come."

I walked up to the tree, reached as high as I could, and sunk my claws into the wood. The tree shuddered and leaned a little as I put my weight on it, but it held. Lahnie went rigid, but there was no going back now. I climbed up, my eyes on the girl, until my long neck brought us face-to-face. Her eyes were huge. Then she wrinkled her nose.

"Your breath is stinky," she declared.

"That's not very nice," I told her.

"We have a dog whose name is Soldier, and your breath is worse than his."

"Just get on my back," I said, wilting under her scorn.

It was slow and took some careful maneuvering, but the girl managed to get onto my back, knees locked around my hips and hands holding on to the base of my wings. Climbing down backward was not much harder than climbing up, thanks to my claws, and in a moment, we were on the ground. Lahnie clambered off and stood up, then looked down at me.

"I thought you were bigger."

My shoulders were about chest-high on her, so I sat back and raised my neck up to be able to look down on her. It was petty, but I did not feel right about being shorter than a little kid.

"Yeah," I told her. "So did I until yesterday. Where do you live?"

"Pine Hill."

"Where is that?" I asked flatly.

"There's a road and a bridge if you follow the river," she explained. "Then if you go over the bridge, you get to Pine Hill."

"Okay." I sighed. "Let's get you home."

"Wait!" she exclaimed, and suddenly took off into the forest. Caught completely off guard, I squatted there for a moment, then ran after her. I realized very quickly that I was not built for running any distance. Keeping up with Lahnie was hard, and talking while I ran was nearly impossible.

"Why . . ." I panted. "Where . . . are . . . you . . . going?"

"I need my basket!" she shouted as she ran. Sure enough, when she finally stopped and I could catch my breath, I saw that she had picked up a basket. She was gathering spilled mushrooms off the forest floor and putting them in the basket.

"Picking . . ." I panted more. "Picking mushrooms, huh?"

"Yeah!" she exclaimed, beaming with pride as she held up the brimming basket.

"All right." I was tired. I was hungry too, but I didn't want to steal a little girl's mushrooms. Besides, they may be deadly poisonous to dragons for all I knew. "Now let's get you home."

"Okay!"

Her harrowing experience with the boar seemingly forgotten, Lahnie happily walked by my side as I led her back toward where the road should've been. She chattered happily about things her mother cooked with mushrooms and funny things her dog Soldier had done and how dumb and unfair her older cousin was.

"I wish Lalia still lived with us," she told me. "She was always nice to me."

"Yeah?" I asked, only half listening. This road was far away. "Lalia, huh?"

"Uh-huh," Lahnie said. "She's my sister, but she's all grown up and moved to the city and she met a boy and she has a horse and a sword."

"A sword, huh?"

"Mm-hm. She let me hold it once when Mama and Papa weren't home, but it was too heavy. Her horse is named Windfall because he's really fast or something."

"Imagine that." I'd finally caught sight of the road, and we turned onto it, heading toward the stream and the bridge Lahnie had mentioned. The bridge was short but made of stone and looked pretty nice as far as I could tell. Lahnie proudly told me that there was a family of stonemasons in her village, and their great-great-grandfather or something like that had built the bridge. We continued like that for another minute, her chattering, me walking, until I heard voices calling in the distance.

"Lahnie! Lahnie!" There were multiple voices, male and female of different ages. Lahnie seemed to hear them too.

"Oh," she said, stopping. "Mama and Papa are going to be mad."

"Why is that?" I asked, already knowing the answer.

"Because I went in the forest alone." She hung her head, looking ashamed.

"And you're not supposed to."

"No."

"And what happened?"

"I found mushrooms and met you!" she said, brightening.

"And before you met me?"

She hung her head again, scuffing the dirt with her shoe, the picture of contrition. "I got chased by a big pig."

"Yeah. Listen, Lahnie."

"Yeah?"

"I think your mama and papa are going to be very happy that you're safe. But be careful, okay?"

"Okay."

"I think they'd be scared if they saw me or if you told them about me. So don't tell them, okay? You don't have to lie, just . . . don't say anything unless they ask."

"Okay."

"Good. Now go home."

Lahnie looked down the road, toward the voices, and then back at me. Then, without warning, she threw herself at me, wrapping her arms around my neck.

"Thanks, Draka," she whispered into my scales as I choked. "You're not a demon."

Then she was gone, running down the road and calling for her parents.

CHAPTER FIVE

Apex Predator

On the one hand, I had just saved a little girl's life and brought her back home to her parents. That felt really, really good, and I was rather pleased with myself. On the other hand, I had been repeatedly insulted by an overgrown toddler, it was getting late, and I was still hungry. I was no closer to solving that, and I would obviously need a long-term solution.

I needed to take stock of what I had available. I hadn't properly done that so far, being too caught up in everything that had been going on, so I found a decent spot where the moss grew thick and plopped myself down to check myself out. A mirror would have helped, but I hadn't even been able to find a reflective pool. I had to rely on my hands for what I couldn't see.

Carefully starting from the top, I felt two stubby horns on my head. No external ears, though I could hear fine, and there were two thick flaps of skin that I could move with some concentration to open and close my earholes. That might be useful. My face was kind of doglike, I guessed, with a snout full of sharp, curved teeth and a long tongue. My eyes were set farther apart and to the sides than I was used to, but I hadn't noticed a problem with that. On the contrary, my field of vision was wider, which should help with detecting anything moving to the sides without sacrificing any ability to focus on things in front of me. I also had a great sense of smell compared to humans. My head sat on a long neck so that when I stretched it out as far as I could, I could only just still reach my horns with my hands. It could turn far enough for me to look at my own back, which took some adjusting to. All these things should make it easy to find and eat animals smaller than me. The only problem with that was that I really didn't want to.

My torso wasn't that different from before. I had wings and some big, beefy flight muscles, of course, so that was new. Other than that, my hips were set a bit wider, and I wasn't as comfortable standing or moving on two legs as I had previously been. I could balance on my feet, but my ankles, hips, and knees got tired pretty quickly. I still had opposable thumbs, so my hands could grasp things, but my motor control was way down. On the bright side, I had some pretty savage claws that I could partially retract, and my feet were built for grasping too. Probably to carry off prey. I was a predator through and through.

To finish off, I had a fairly narrow, tapering tail. I couldn't do much with it other than swing it around, but it did help with balance. And under the tail . . . I didn't want to use my hands for that, so I bent at the waist and used my long neck to have a look. Yep, like I'd concluded before, I was all reptile. Just one smooth slit, the combined functions of which were easy to guess. As far as I was concerned, I was still female, but to be honest, I had no damn way to tell what my body really was. And all that had no bearing at all on the problem at hand: Food.

I had good senses. I was strong, I had sharp teeth and claws, and I could fly and run pretty fast in bursts on all fours. I could also spray something, come to think of it, either venom or acid. Trying to remember the feeling from when I'd driven off the boar, I tried to do it consciously but only managed an embarrassing dribble. Still, it didn't seem to do anything to the moss, so it was most likely venom. I also had most of my body covered in overlapping shield-shaped scales, which proved very hard when I tested them with my claws. My belly and the inside of my joints had flatter scales that didn't overlap, to allow for a better range of motion.

I was an apex predator. That was the only conclusion. I had fought and killed a croc on its home turf and come out fine. As long as I could find and catch something that wasn't too much bigger than me, I could probably kill it. The issues lay in the finding and catching something and the fact that I didn't want to tear apart some poor animal and eat it raw. However, I was pretty sure that I had to eat meat to survive. Like a cat. I'd read that cats couldn't even taste sugar because they were so dependent on meat for a bunch of nutrients. Judging by the tastes my body had displayed, dragons were the same, and it wasn't like I could get farmed meat from a butcher.

I wasn't happy about the obvious: it came down to survival. I needed meat, and I had no access to fire, at least not yet. I was going to have to learn to hunt and then get over myself and get used to eating some raw meat. Mentally, I felt disgusted. Physically, I got hungrier, just a gnawing in my belly.

Hungry as I was, I still didn't have it in me to start hunting today. I filled up on water, then got airborne and flew back to my cave, resigned to going to sleep hungry. I'd find food in the morning.

When I got back to the cave, the first thing I did was check on my hoard. It wasn't a conscious decision, but I didn't question it. The feel and smell of the gold settled my nerves, and after a few minutes, I returned to the cave entrance. I sat on the ledge, watching birds fly and trees move with the wind until the sun dropped beneath the mountains behind me, drowning everything in shadow. It was peaceful. No highway noise or airplanes passing by, just the wind and the birds. A few small patches of slight brightness must have been villages, with something larger to the far southeast. I probably wouldn't have been able to see them with human eyes, but my new body saw much better in the dark. Not perfectly by a long shot—there was little in the way of color—but instead of straight darkness, I saw a million shades of gray and a thousand subtle shades of black, and above me there were so many more stars than I remembered.

It was beautiful.

As I lay there, relaxed and looking out, I felt my eyelids getting heavy. I slunk back inside my cave to my sleeping spot, curled up with my wings covering me, and went to sleep.

Morning came and I woke, resigned to hunting for my breakfast. The most likely strategy was clear. I had wings, claws, and a long, agile neck. There must be reasons for all these things. Every predatory bird that I knew of hunted by swooping down from above and either surprising or outflying their prey. Maybe there were some flightless predatory birds, but I didn't know of them, and it didn't matter. Why couldn't I do the same? I'd fly around until I saw a likely target, then swoop down and grab 'em. Easy.

As it turned out, it was not at all easy. Everything I knew about my new body told me that I was set up for success, but putting that into practice seemed impossible. I found a small herd of mountain goats and just went for it, but they scattered. When I picked one to follow, it turned out that even though I was faster than it while flying, it was so much more agile than I was that there was no contest. By the time I gave up, I suspected that the damn thing was having fun and messing with me, standing still until the last second and then popping out of the way while I ate rocks. I decided to take my bruised ego and battered flesh and try the forest instead, hoping for a boar or even a rabbit, but I couldn't see anything there because the canopy was too dense. While hunting goats, though, I did find a stream in the mountains near my cave, so that was nice.

I tried going after birds but didn't have any more luck there. Every time I went after one, they'd spot me and either outmaneuver or outfly me as I got close. By the time the sun started to get close to the mountains, I was far past frustrated; I was famished and more than a little upset with myself for not being able to do the one thing my body seemed made for. Besides, I was getting genuinely worried. I'd been doing a lot of flying, and I knew that I must have spent many times more calories than I'd gotten from the meat and cheese I'd eaten. I was in very real danger of starving. Soon I'd start getting too weak to fly, and once that happened, I'd be done for, wouldn't I? I'd just have to curl up with my treasure and die.

Was that how people in comas died? Did they die in a dream and just go? I still didn't know if everything I'd been experiencing was a coma dream or whatever, but I really, really didn't want to die. I could fly. I could talk to people. I had sort of made a friend, maybe? It didn't seem fair that I should die because I couldn't do the one basic thing that every hunting animal in the world could.

Maybe I could find Lahnie and beg her for something to eat.

It was with those cheerful thoughts that I headed back to the mountains for another hungry night's sleep. I'd go to the stream and fill up on water, and then I'd wait for morning to come around so I could try again. My next plan was to use myself as bait in the lake. Croc didn't taste so bad, and I'd already proven that I could kill one.

One hungry night became two, then three, then four. I'd go out, come back as the light failed, check on my treasure, and sleep. On the second day, I tried baiting crocs, but they were either rare or smarter than I gave them credit for. On the third and fourth days, I was desperate enough to dig for worms and search for carrion, flying as little as possible and trying to use updrafts to glide when I did. I raided a few nests for eggs, swallowing them whole, but it did little for my hunger.

It felt like the dragon got stronger the hungrier I got, making me angrier and less inhibited. When I curled up to sleep at the end of the fourth day, I could hear the voice, my voice, whispering to me. Not an intrusive thought, but an actual voice telling me that there was one place I knew of that was full of prey. Pine Hill was small. Surely they didn't have any warriors. And there were little ones there that liked to wander . . .

I would rather die. The dragon would not.

On the morning of the fifth day, my life and possibly my soul were saved by a stroke of luck. Beautiful and heart-wrenching all at once, I saw a mountain goat. It must have slipped or been knocked off a cliff, because one of its hind legs was badly broken, and the other was pretty banged up as well. It was trying to move but barely making any progress, and a horribly sad mewing sound escaped from its mouth.

I landed in front of it. It scrambled back in terror, trying to get away but falling over and over again as it tried to support itself on its broken leg. The scene was . . .

I had a certain image of myself. I thought of myself as fairly calloused. Shit happened, and you dealt with it. Sometimes people got hurt, and you helped them if you could, and if you couldn't, that was too bad. Thinking about this made me want to cry. I felt so bad for this poor goat, and I knew that there was only one thing I could do for it, but it would be hard. The dragon didn't care at all, of course. It wanted to pounce and start tearing, whether the goat was living or dead, but I held back. I tried to rationalize. The thing was as good as dead. Its leg would never heal, and if infection or blood loss didn't kill it, some predator would. No reason that predator shouldn't be me.

I closed in.

"It's all right, little goat," I lied. I guess I was trying to deal with my own guilt for what I was about to do. "It'll be over soon. No more pain."

I wasn't sure how to do it, though. Not safely. I didn't think that I could break its neck. It looked pretty sturdy. Lots of animals killed their prey by crushing the windpipe with their teeth, but I didn't think that was a good idea because the thing was bigger than I was, and it might do some real damage to me if I hung on to it until it suffocated. I decided that cutting the big veins and arteries in the throat with my claws would probably be the quickest, kindest way.

I was trying to get in a good position to lunge, do the damage, and get out when the goat went on the attack. *It* lunged at *me*, horns first and broken leg be damned. In one reflexive motion, I leaped back, hissed, and sprayed venom at its face, a dense mist that I couldn't seem to replicate on command. It got in the goat's eyes, nose, and mouth, and the thing went mad, screaming and tossing its head around. I stood back, horrified at what I'd done, and the screaming got softer and turned into a wheeze, and then nothing at all. The goat still moved, scrabbling with its hooves on the stone and tossing its head. It couldn't breathe, its mouth opening and closing, its eyes bloodshot and rolling madly in their sockets.

"I'm sorry," I whispered. Then I sprang forward. I extended my claws fully, dug them into the goat's neck, and raked them along its throat. Blood pumped and spurted, quickly pooling on the ground. The poor thing kicked weakly a few times, and then it was still.

I had tears in my eyes as I used my claws to strip the skin from the goat's flank and finally got to eat my fill.

CHAPTER SIX

People Watching

I learned a few things from killing that mountain goat. I learned that I, the thinking me, could kill if I had to. I learned that raw meat and blood actually tasted pretty good, at least to a dragon—I had no experience as a human to compare, not counting sushi. And I learned that I could eat what felt like my own weight in meat. Once I got started, I just kept going. I think the dragon took over. I stripped one of the goat's legs, then another, and then I got into the abdomen and started tearing things out and scarfing them down without chewing. There was still some meat left for the scavengers when I was so bloated that I physically couldn't eat any more, but not much.

I also learned that one meal like that could last me a long time. After washing the gore off in the stream, I made my way back toward my cave. I walked most of the way, feeling heavy and drowsy, and I had a terrible worry that I wouldn't be able to fly. My belly was visibly distended to a worrying degree, and I might be too heavy for my wings to carry me. I made some attempts and concluded that while taking off from the ground was not going to work, if I jumped off from something, I should be able to glide, so I risked it when I reached the cliff above my cave and made it down without incident. The landing was rough, but I was so blissfully stuffed that it didn't bother me.

I was so tired and weighed down that I didn't even go check on my hoard. I barely made it to my sleeping spot before lying down and curling up, and there I stayed for an uncertain number of days. I think I went into some kind of torpor while digesting my meal. I'd wake and see sunlight, and then it would be dark, and then there would be sunlight again.

So it went.

The next time I woke fully, my stomach was mostly back to its normal size. I had a powerful need to do what one does after eating thirty or forty kilos of meat, so I flew off a good distance from my cave and dealt with that. It was . . . an experience. What I left behind didn't at all explain where all the mass and volume had gone, but I decided not to question it. Other than some lingering guilt about the mountain goat's last moments, I felt great. I felt strong, alert, and healthy, ready to take on the world and find some treasure.

Of course, that was the next step. While I was figuring out basic survival, I had been thinking about how to get more gold, where to find it, and how to make it mine. The dragon very unhelpfully suggested finding a village or town, laying waste to it, and taking anything shiny. The human didn't want to hurt anyone and wondered if there was some way I could earn money. I didn't have any expenses, so if I could get paid, it would all go to the hoard. That idea, however, seemed difficult or impossible to put into practice. I was a terrifying vision of scales, teeth, and claws, and I had no idea what the market for freelance work looked like in this place—especially as a dragon. Still, I could talk, which meant I might be able to work something out anyway, so I didn't reject the idea completely.

I briefly considered trying to just find some gold. This didn't rely on interacting with people, and the fact that I could smell the stuff was a big advantage. Gold could be found lying around, even in my world. Maybe I could scour the mountains and try to find it by smell? I was pretty sure that native gold was usually found in tiny pieces, though, and usually in streams or rivers. Panning for gold was an option, though a weak one since it required equipment. Pans, probably. But again, I didn't reject the idea.

Finally, I thought I could take gold from those who didn't deserve it. The dragon was of the opinion that this included everyone but me, but I was thinking more about bandits and corrupt nobles. This was a medieval world as far as I could tell, and both in fantasy literature and in history, that time period always sounded like it was full of bandits and corrupt nobles preying on the common folk. Why shouldn't I make their ill-gotten gains mine? It would likely mean I'd have to fight for it, but this body was very capable, and I might be able to scare them off. I didn't have a philosophical problem with hurting bad people, but I'd rather not risk getting hurt myself.

The other problem with this idea, besides the risk of violence and bodily harm, was that finding a bandit lair or a corrupt noble would probably be as hard as finding gold in the mountains. I'd need information.

Needing information meant that I needed to find people. I was wary of direct contact, but I could be sneaky if I needed to be, and my hearing was good. Since I was fed and feeling good about the near future, I decided that some patient observation was in order. As I saw it, the safest place for doing this was the road. Judging by its size and state, it was well trafficked, so I'd start there and see where it led me.

Since I knew that the road ran close to the lake, I headed there first. The previous few desperate days that I could remember had forced me to learn a lot about efficient flying, and after dropping off my ledge, I managed to glide almost half-way there using only momentum and updrafts, which was very satisfying. Slower and less exhilarating, sure, but it also gave me more time to look around and think.

I figured that there would be more people moving near settlements. At night I could see villages in the dark, so I knew that there were quite a few dotted around the forest. I hadn't really memorized their locations, but I could find Pine Hill if I had to, and there had been a glow in the southeast that I thought to be a large town or city based on how much brighter it was than the villages. Logically, there should be more traffic closer to a larger settlement, so I decided that I'd go south along the road until I reached a town or something interesting happened.

At the lake, things were much the same as how I'd left them. The smells of blood and death were fainter but still there if you knew to search for them. It didn't look like anyone had used the campsite since the battle. Of course, I didn't know how commonly used this place was; I only assumed that it was an established campsite because it was a large, clear area, and the firepit was lined with large stones that looked like they'd been there awhile. Not wanting to waste time, I didn't look any closer and instead followed the path that led away from the lake.

Like I'd guessed, it brought me to the road. I kept well into the trees, where I could still see and hear anyone on the road while staying hidden. As long as I was careful about my movements and kept to the shadows, I should be fine, with my low profile and matte-black scales. For the next several hours, I slowly made my way south along the road, stopping whenever I picked up someone by sight, smell, or sound. Mostly these were people traveling by foot or by horse, alone or in pairs. Many of them were transporting things. Most carts—the most advanced piece of technology I saw—seemed to be pulled by hand, which I found very impressive, but I also saw a few wagons drawn by horses or oxen.

I got a pretty good idea of what the people here looked like during those hours. Everybody I saw was darker than I had been, with Lahnie's somewhat-Asian features and wavy or curly hair being the norm. But while I didn't see a single truly pale face or blond head of hair, there was clearly some movement of people here. I saw one more person, a woman, with Guy's lighter skin tone and sort of Middle Eastern features, and a few people who were a little darker than others. Still, Lahnie and the people who had come to Guy's rescue were by far the majority.

When it came to dress, they wore a mix of ren faire and Spartacus-type attire, with lots of tunics, vests, laced shirts and blouses, loose trousers, shorts and skirts, and dresses in different styles. The people here loved their greens and yellows, that was clear enough. There were other colors, but green and yellow were by far the most common when the clothes weren't just made of undyed cloth.

The most interesting group that I saw were what I could only assume to be mercenaries or adventurers. They were four men and one woman, all carrying arms and armor as well as large packs and joining the road heading south from a smaller side road. I stayed with this group for a while, feeling a bit like a creep but enjoying just listening to them. The woman and one of the men were a couple, or were about to be, hanging back from the rest of the group and exchanging whispers and hidden smiles and glances. It was sickeningly sweet, and I envied them deeply. My last relationship had ended months ago, and I was out of the "happy to be single" phase and starting to think about dating again when it was suddenly not an option anymore.

The group as a whole was in high spirits, laughing and joking constantly with each other. They carried a big, wet sack with them. Apparently, they'd killed some dangerous beast in the woods and were expecting to get paid well for doing so. I'd have liked to have known what exactly it was, but they just called it "the beast" or "the thing," and since they all knew exactly what they were talking about, they never described it. Very inconsiderate of them, but I couldn't really come out and ask.

Unfortunately, at one point, I got careless, and the man I'd come to think of as Lover Boy stopped the group.

"What is it?" another man, Big Beardy, called back.

"Quiet, please," Lover Boy replied. "I heard something."

"Yeah, we scared a deer is what I say," said Short-and-Wide.

"We'll put that on your tombstone," said Awesome Curls. That was the woman. She had great hair. Like, shampoo-commercial great. She had no business walking out of the forest with hair that lively and lustrous. "If Baran thinks he heard something, he probably did."

This decided things, and the group fell silent. I was pressed into the ground, playing dead, keeping completely still and barely breathing. I could see them through a small break in the bush I was hidden behind. They had their hands on their weapons, and while the swords and spears were bad enough, Big Beardy had strung a bow that was bigger than anything I'd ever imagined. The damn thing must have been two meters long with the string on. He had a long, thick arrow with a broad head ready, and I really didn't want to test if my scales could stop something like that.

Lover Boy, or Baran, I supposed, was scanning the forest along the road, though he seemed unwilling to go among the trees. After a while, he slowly bent down and picked up a stone, which he threw into one of the bushes near me. When nothing happened, he grabbed another stone and chose another bush. I stayed still and silent, even when a rock the size of a small apple bounced off my shoulder. Finally, Lover Boy ran out of bushes and got the group moving again, but now they were silent and wary, so there didn't seem to be much point in following them anymore. I decided to stay where I was for a while and then call it quits.

This was the beginning of a new pattern for me. Hunger wasn't an issue for now, and I could get by on water once in the morning and once in the evening, so I'd stay out all day, keeping an eye on the road and stalking interesting groups of people. I came across more armed groups and deduced that they came in two types: adventurers, who were usually ragtag groups with whatever equipment they could get their hands on, and soldiers, who I later learned were actually mercenaries and who were much like the adventurers but wore some kind of uniform or distinguishing piece of equipment that showed that they belonged together. The mercenaries seemed to be patrolling the road rather than going somewhere, and if I stayed in one place long enough, I'd see the same group going north in the morning and coming back in the evening.

However, most of the people on the road were travelers, farmers, or merchants, traveling between villages or to or from the city, usually for the sake of the market there. No matter who they were, I learned some interesting things from listening to their conversations. For example, the city was called Karakan, and it had a harbor and was home to at least a hundred thousand people, possibly more. Additionally, there was a large group of bandits in the area who robbed travelers and villagers and had attacked a mercenary camp recently. Presumably, Guy and his friends belonged to the mercenary company, and it was his camp that people talked about. The bandits could operate here because there was talk of war, and most of the soldiers had been sent to the border with another country, or duchy, or something. That was also why the mercenaries were here; with the soldiers away, the mercenaries had been hired to keep the bandits in check.

The adventurers dealt with smaller, more localized problems. Apparently, monsters were a thing, and when they got too close to a village or a road, they needed killing. Adventurers would either be contracted to deal with a specific problem or they would just go out and look for trouble and hope that whatever they killed had something valuable or that someone would be willing to pay them for their trouble. The fact that this was a viable way to make a living suggested that monsters were a very real and very common problem, and from what I'd heard, it had been getting worse the last couple of years. I thought back to the boar that I had saved Lahnie from. Was that a monster? It was certainly many times larger and more vicious-looking than any wild pig I had ever heard of. I wondered where it had gone and hoped that Lahnie and Pine Hill were still okay.

There was no talk of a dragon being spotted in the area. That would have been a relief if there weren't a decent amount of talk about an unusually large wyvern, which I could only assume referred to me. I was less than pleased with that. The word *dragon* had connotations of power, majesty, and cunning. Wyverns, from what I gathered, were stupid, cowardly beasts that stole small livestock and might only be a threat to particularly small children. The differences were stark. Adventurers as a group seemed ambivalent about the idea of hunting a wyvern; they were a pain to track down, and the reward for killing one was rarely more than decent.

I should have been relieved that no one was likely to be too enthusiastic about coming after me. But instead, I was mostly offended, and my pride was badly wounded.

At least it all gave me an idea. Could I hunt monsters? If they had treasure, I could take it. If you could get paid for killing them, and if no one would get paid much for killing me, perhaps I could create some kind of partnership with one or more people. I had friendly relationships with two people already, although both of those had sprung from special circumstances. Would it hurt to try again? I wondered. And so, I began to hatch a plan.

CHAPTER SEVEN

Onward to Adventure!

The next morning, I got as close as I dared to the city. The last few kilometers before the city were all fields and pastures, and I didn't want to leave the cover of the trees. I was waiting for a particular type of group, and after two or three hours of following several groups, I found a likely target—or three: two women who stuck out to me for being the first truly dark-skinned people I'd seen, probably sisters by how alike they looked, and a man with a shaved head. One of the women was half a head taller than him, while he was a head taller than the other woman. They were all armed and wearing leather armor, each with a sizable pack on their back. The short woman had a spear in her hand, the taller one an unstrung bow, and the man had a shield strapped to his pack. They all had swords and daggers among the various bags and pouches on their belts. Textbook adventurers, I figured.

Three was a perfect number. A lone adventurer or a pair of them were unlikely to be on an interesting job, and a larger group would be too much of a threat to me if things went sour. But the deciding factor was the vibe I got from them. These three put on brave faces, but they had a smell of desperation about them, and their equipment looked old and worn. That should make them more likely to take a job that they couldn't handle. Sure enough, the main topic of conversation was whether this was a good idea and how much they needed the money. They were tight-lipped about what the job actually was, however. I guessed that the risk made them anxious enough to not want to talk about it, and that was understandable but also annoying. If they were this scared, the job must be really hard, and if that was the case, I would have liked to know something about what we were walking into.

I'd been following them north for a couple of hours when they stopped to rest. There was no discussion beforehand; the man simply pointed into the forest and said, "Here. A good spot. Looks nice." He looked to the shorter of the two women, who followed his hand.

"Yeah, good find," she said, and the group left the road, entering the trees on the side opposite me.

Since I had to be careful not to be seen, I backtracked a bit, made sure no one was coming, and then rushed across the road. When I got close to the group again, they were set up in a small, sunny glade, still in sight of the road. I settled in to watch and listen, keeping low and quiet. They had their packs off and were eating from wrapped bundles of food. At first they ate in silence, but they soon returned to the same running conversation they'd been having since I'd first spotted them.

"Are you sure there were no safer jobs?" the taller woman asked. She seemed to be the most cautious member of the group and was the one I had to be most careful not to be spotted by. She got the same answer as always.

"Not that paid enough quickly enough. Not for sure. It has to be this," said the shorter woman. I thought of her as the leader. She looked and sounded like she was the older of the sisters, and her two companions deferred to her.

"One job, sure, but—" the younger sister interjected, but her male companion cut her off.

"Makanna is right," he said, clearly tired of the argument. "One hundred and twenty eagles are needed, three nights hence. Other jobs were offered, but they paid little or were far away. Or"—he raised his hand to forestall the younger sister, who had looked ready argue—"they paid only per head. Too risky. These gremlins are sure. We will reach the mine tonight. Tomorrow we do the job. Overmorrow we receive two hundred eagles and pay Tamor's jailors. The fine is paid, Tamor has his license, and he is free."

"But the risk—" the younger woman cut in.

"The risk is acceptable. I will die before Tam is sent away. If you will not, turn back," the man said. There was no anger in his words, but they were final. He would not be swayed.

"Mak?" The young woman—and she was young, likely still a teenager—turned to her sister. She looked small and miserable, and the name was spoken like a plea for support and understanding.

The older sister, Makanna, looked away. Her expression was just as grim and determined as that of their male companion. "If we don't pay on time, we'll never see Tam again." The group was silent for a moment, and Makanna looked at her sister. "I'm with Val. You asked to come, but if you truly don't think that you can do this, go back to Karakan. Nobody will blame you. I know this is a big step up from the other jobs you've helped out on, but—"

"No!" the younger sister exclaimed indignantly, standing up from the log she'd been sitting on. Scraps of food hit the forest floor as the cloth in her lap fell. "Tam is my brother too! I'm not leaving you two to get killed only to see him shipped off to gods know where!"

"I know you won't," Makanna said, reaching out for her sister's hand and pulling her down next to her. She put her arm around her sister's waist and brought her in close for a while, then spoke. "Time to go. We want to be at the mine before it gets dark."

The others agreed. They packed up and got back on the road. Soon they turned onto another well-made road that led toward the mountains, which I thought made sense. They had been talking about a mine, and that seemed like the place to find one.

Most of their conversation clearly revolved around keeping the younger sister's courage up. They talked about happy memories, jobs that had gone well, and things like that, and I got their general story. The two women were indeed sisters. In addition to their dark skin, they had straight hair, waist-long on the older sister and shoulder-length on the younger one, where most other people I'd seen had wavy or curly hair.

I had already gotten the older sister's name, Makanna, and I heard the man call the younger one Herald, as in the literal word in their language for *herald*. I wasn't sure if that was her name or a title, but neither of her party members called her by anything else that I heard. The sisters had a middle brother named Tamor, who was in trouble with the law for doing something without a license, and they needed to bail him out before he got "shipped off." Judging by how they talked about it, being shipped off was a terrible thing, thus their desperation for money.

The man was called Val, which sounded like a nickname. Val had a serious, vaguely handsome face, though his jaw was perhaps a little too square. I didn't see him smile much, even compared to the sisters. Otherwise, he was of average height, with a shaved head and big shoulders. He, Makanna, and Tamor had apparently been an established group for a few years, with Herald joining for a few easier, safer jobs in the last year or so. While they all seemed to get along well, I got the impression that Val's real connection to the group was Tamor. I couldn't tell if they were a thing, but Val, at least, was clearly smitten with the other man. I didn't know if same-sex relationships were generally accepted or not, but the sisters were evidently aware of Val's feelings and didn't seem at all uncomfortable about them.

By late afternoon, I was invested and rooting for them. I also felt like a creep again, following them and listening to what was supposed to be a private conversation, but I had a plan to stick to, and there really wasn't much else to do.

I got a lot of practice sneaking through the forest, but other than that it was a choice between creeping on them or being bored. There were supposed to be bandits and monsters in the forest, and I stayed alert for any sign of those, but as far as I could tell, there wasn't anything threatening around. I smelled some animals but couldn't tell what they were, and sometimes a rabbit or another small critter would burst out of a bush and run away from me.

That was it. A nice, long walk through the forest with my unwitting friends. The most excitement I got was when they passed through a large village. They didn't even slow down, but I had to find a way around without being seen, dodge a few villagers who were out cutting wood, and then sprint like hell to catch back up with the group. Trying to find an optimal mix of speed and stealth when running on all fours was educational, but it was not by any means easy.

I did at least get a lot of time to think about my surroundings. Everything was . . . wrong. It didn't match up. I'd seen rabbits, foxes, boar, deer, squirrels, and other animals that belonged in Europe or America and a lot of birds that I didn't recognize. But the trees were more like what I'd expected back in Australia. They weren't quite right, and most of them were too tall, but a lot of them were close enough to gums, pines, and figs that if I didn't look too closely at them, they might have fooled me.

As we made our way west toward the mountains, the road began a slow, winding climb. The vegetation changed, with most of the leafy trees disappearing, replaced by pines and other conifers. The ground between the trees also became steadily more open, making sneaking around considerably harder for me. Instead of moving slowly, with my line of sight broken by bushes, fallen trees, and other obstacles, I now had to rush from cover to cover. At the same time, the adventurers seemed a little less alert, either from fatigue or because there were fewer places for danger to hide. I kept my distance and chose my moments to move, and as far I could tell, they didn't spot me.

The shadows were long when the road ended at a gently sloping plateau, a few hundred meters out from a cliff face. Makanna stopped the group and took out a piece of folded paper. She consulted it for a while, pointed in a direction, and then they continued. I had been staying too far back to be able to hear what they said, but there was a spring in Makanna's step that suggested they had arrived at the end of a long day's travel. I was impressed, both with them and myself. I was also completely exhausted and had barely been able to keep up by the end. All three of the adventurers looked tired, but they also looked like they could have gone on for hours more if they had to. Even Herald, who was maybe sixteen years old.

I had been a climber. I could do that for a pretty long time when I wanted to. But I didn't really hike or run. Even if this body was better trained or whatever, I didn't have the mental capability to just keep going and going and going, and that seemed to be a big part of adventuring. I might have to get used to it. Of course, in the air, I could have covered the same distance much faster and with less effort, but since my objective was to stay hidden, that was not an option.

The adventurers' route was obvious. Old, deep ruts marked where heavy wagons had rolled, probably hundreds or thousands of them over the years. The tracks led to a group of buildings set toward the trees, and I could hear water rushing from not too far away, which was probably why the buildings were there instead of closer to the mine entrance. The group approached, and Makanna called out, but there was no reply except an echo off the mountainside. The group stopped and conferred silently, then came to a decision. Mak hefted her spear. Val had a shield strapped to his pack, which he took off and fastened to his arm, as well as a short sword with a wide blade. Herald had a short sword at her side too, plus a short bow. As Makanna and Val moved cautiously toward the buildings, Herald hung back, guarding their pack while still being in range to support them. There was no fuss and little talk. They looked experienced, competent, and deadly serious.

I stayed still in the shadow of a boulder. They were all on high alert now. I had no doubt that Herald would be able to spot me if I made a false move, and that was a distraction none of us needed right now.

Makanna and Val approached the first building, which I guessed to be the main administrative building by its nicer style and placement. Makanna posted up to the left of the large wooden front door, spear at the ready, while Val stood in front of it. Val held up his shield, reached out, and slowly opened the door, carefully covering them both with the shield while Makanna poked her spear past him. With the door fully open, they moved inside, and nothing happened for a while. Then they came out, shaking their heads to Herald, and moved on to the next building, which was the largest one. Probably a warehouse, workshop, or both. The same thing happened there, and at the next building, and the next. With all four buildings inspected and apparently found empty, they gathered in front of the office. The light was almost gone now, and I carefully crept closer to hear them.

"No, not a soul," Makanna was saying as I got close enough. "Not a single one in any of the buildings."

Herald looked around apprehensively. "What happened?"

"None can tell," Val said. "No battle was had, no room ransacked. All was in order, as much as can be expected for a labor camp. All have left. Though why, we do not know."

"Yeah," Makanna continued. "It's unsettling. Papers neatly stacked on the fore-man's desk, cooking pots scrubbed and put away. People's stuff is still there, which makes me worried."

"Why is that?" Herald asked.

"If they packed up and left for a good reason, they'd have, well, packed up, right? They wouldn't have left their belongings. This place looks like they tidied the place up, stepped out, and then never came back."

"So what do we do?"

Makanna shrugged. "We keep our wits about us, and we do the job. We go in, we kill or drive off the gremlins and destroy the nest so all the shafts can open again, and we make sure that we get paid for that. We'll keep our eyes open for any clues as to what happened here. Might get a bonus for reporting what we found, if we're lucky."

"But this is all wrong," Herald countered. "There were supposed to be dozens of people here, with most of the shafts still working. What if it is not just gremlins?"

There was a breeze coming off the mountain, and I was downwind. I could actually smell the fear coming from Herald. It was sour and unpleasant, but I knew what it was from my encounters with Guy and Lahnie. Still didn't care for it, though.

"Then we will deal with it," said Val. "There is no time for change, and an agreement was reached. We must do this job. We will be disgraced if we do not, and Tamor will be lost."

Even at my distance, I could read the three pretty well. Herald was afraid, and she was ashamed of her reluctance to go into the mine. Val was going to get paid and help Tamor, or he was going to die trying. There was some fear there, too, but he was hiding it well. Makanna was almost as determined as Val and didn't seem afraid for herself at all, but she was concerned for her friend, and more so for her sister. I suspected that she blamed herself for something, either for Tamor being in trouble or for Herald being with them, but that was speculation on my part.

And me, I was getting worried for them. They had known that this would be a difficult and dangerous job, but it had seemed straightforward. Now there was a weird twist to it that added uncertainty. The question for me was: Should I bail? Should I fly back to my cave and try again with a different group tomorrow? That would be the rational, smart thing to do. But over the course of the day, I had developed real sympathy for this group of strangers. I had heard their fears and their hopes for the immediate future. I knew that someone's future rested on the success of their mission, and I wanted them to succeed, to return to Karakan in triumph and bail out their missing member. Even if I never saw them again, I wanted to know that they had a chance, at least for the next few days. So I did the dumb, emotional thing, and I stayed. While they settled into the administrative building, which apparently doubled as the foreman or director or whatever's house, I found the largest, densest fir, or spruce or whatever, and climbed it. With some effort, I dug in my claws and wrapped my body and my tail around the trunk, getting as comfortable as I could and gambling on the tree hiding me. Then I went to sleep, hoping that I'd wake up if anything interesting happened.

CHAPTER EIGHT

Friends in Dark Places

I woke to the sound of scraping and hushed chattering. It was the middle of the night, but the moon and stars gave more than enough light for my sensitive eyes to see. Three small creatures had passed near my tree and were now heading to the building where the adventurers slept. The things walked on two long legs and had small bodies with long limbs and large heads with big ears like toothy leaves. They were completely naked except for simple belts that held many small bags and pouches. I couldn't see any color in the dim light, but the wind brought their scent to me and they smelled of stone and something wonderful. Not quite like gold, but something similar.

I was sure that the adventurers must have someone on guard at all times, but to be safe, I got down from my tree as silently as I could and followed the creatures. The things skulked around the building while I hid in the shadow of another. They were looking at windows, but all of the windows were shuttered. I still didn't hear any alarm from inside, but maybe the things wouldn't try anything.

I heard the door open, and the creatures froze.

"I will be right back. I just really need to step in the bushes." It was Herald's voice, soft and hushed. The door closed, and I heard slight steps. The things had pulled out short knives from their belts. I saw Herald come around the corner, the creatures looking ready to jump her, and I panicked.

I roared. The creatures froze, turning to search for the new threat. Herald whirled toward the sound and screamed, "Gremlins!" when she saw the creatures, jumping back and grabbing for the sword on her belt. Then things got chaotic.

The two gremlins closest to Herald leaped toward her, knives out, while she fought to draw her sword. The one at the rear instead ran around the back of the building, either to circle it or to flee. I heard the door slam open and Val and Makanna talking over each other. Figuring that I'd done all that I could to help Herald, and that the three would be distracted, I sprinted out of the shadow.

I ran parallel to the back wall of the office building, keeping the running creature in sight, and when it turned the corner instead of fleeing, I veered toward it. There was a short, decisive commotion from where I'd left the adventurers. The gremlin looked around the corner, seemed to think better of joining in the fight, and sprinted for the cliff face, presumably heading for the mine.

It didn't sound like the adventurers were pursuing it. I didn't even know if they knew about the last gremlin, but I did know that I didn't want it to reach the mine and possibly alert more of its kind. Hoping no one had moved to where they could see me, I used my wings to leap forward in a burst of speed, making for the cliff to put more distance between me and the humans before trying to cut the creature off.

"Shit!" I heard Herald shout. "One left!" She sounded rattled but not in any pain. Good.

"Herald, your bow!" That was Makanna.

"Not strung!"

"It flees in the dark," came Val's voice. "I cannot see it."

I hadn't reached the cliff, but the gremlin was far enough away from me now that I was worried I might not catch it. "Fuck it," I growled to myself. I turned and headed straight for where I thought the mine entrance was, again using my wings for a burst of speed. I heard an exclamation from Herald, and then I was on the creature. I twisted my head and snapped my jaws around its neck, knocking it over and dragging it. It was light for its size, and dragging it by my mouth was surprisingly easy. Not knowing what to do, I kept running, turning away from the cave and heading for the woods.

"What was that?" I heard Herald shouting from the camp. "Sorrows, what in all the hells was that?"

I didn't wait to hear the others. I was amazed that anyone could see me at all in the darkness. I dropped down a small slope and was gone from their sight. The gremlin in my jaws hung limp. I probably snapped its neck the moment I grabbed it. I dropped it on the ground, the taste of its blood metallic and vaguely pleasant in my mouth, and cautiously stuck my head up to spy toward the camp.

The adventurers were gone. Two small forms lay side by side in the dirt a distance from the building, and the door was closed. I hoped that meant that they had decided to get some more sleep, but I kept my ears sharp while I looked over the gremlin that I'd killed.

It was female, that was easy to see. In many ways it looked like a small, misshapen human, but the face was very different. Almost batlike, it had a flat, open nose, a wide mouth full of sharp teeth, and large eyes. I felt very little about killing it, and that disturbed me. Its companions had attacked someone I had stalked for a day. This one hadn't even done that. They were clearly intelligent on some level, using weapons and tools, and I'd just decided that its life meant less than . . . what, exactly? My convenience?

I knew I should feel bad, but I didn't. I felt less than when I'd killed the goat. In fact, the dragon in me was rather satisfied and wanted to eat the creature, which was a step too far for me. So I compromised by robbing it. Its belt was a simple piece of rope tied around its waist, and some of the pouches smelled very interesting. I couldn't undo the string holding them closed, so I resorted to carefully tearing one open with a claw. Some small, spiky, and angular pieces of metal fell out. I picked them up. They shone white in the moonlight, and when I smelled them, it was intoxicating. Not like my coins, not even close, but this would do as a second choice.

I realized that they must be bits of silver. I'd never seen native silver before, but what else could they be? They looked like silver, they smelled nearly as good as gold, and they had presumably come from that mine. Was it a silver mine, then, or had the gremlins had a lucky strike? Was that . . . ? I sniffed the silver, then the dead gremlin. Yes, that was the delicious smell I'd noticed coming off the gremlins. I wondered, did the other two gremlins also have bags of silver on them?

I got the belt off the gremlin by pulling it up over its torso. It was tough going, and I winced when I heard bone snap as I tried to narrow its shoulders. I really should have felt worse about what I was doing, but I didn't. Maybe the dragon was growing stronger when I dealt with nonhuman creatures.

Once I had the belt off, I hung it around my neck. It was far from perfect, and I'd have to be careful so it didn't slide off, but it worked.

I took a long, circuitous route back to the camp. When I got there, I cautiously snuck up to the two small bodies but froze when I heard voices.

". . . fine. I will be fine!" That was Herald.

Makanna answered, "Sure? I can go with you."

"I am not going out in the dark with that thing out there! I will hold it!"

I hoped that Herald would forgive me if she knew that I had probably saved her life.

I quietly checked the bodies, but their belts were gone. Maybe it was common knowledge that gremlins carried around bits of precious metal. It was too bad, but there was the mine, and that was supposed to be full of gremlins. And they must be getting their silver from somewhere.

With that in mind, I got back in my tree, settled in, and slept well.

"It's time."

I startled awake to my own voice in my ear, nearly losing my grip on the tree and catching myself from falling. Looking toward the camp, I could see the group outside the building getting their equipment in order. I left the tree and, keeping to the shadows, made my way closer.

"Final check," Makanna was saying. "Make sure that everything's in order. Buckles tight, swords and daggers secure. Herald, do you have the potion?"

The girl in question, who had been stringing and testing her bow, patted a thick pouch on her belt. "Here and safe."

"All right. The basic plan is simple. You remember the wolves, Herald?"

"I do."

"Same idea. You saw the gremlins last night. They're a little smarter than wolves, and they use tools, but the same tactics should work. Might even work better in the tunnels, where they can't circle us. Val holds the front, I poke past him. Herald, you take shots past us whenever you see an opening. Simple."

"It is a good thing that you are so short, dear sister," Herald replied with a grin that was only half-forced. Looking at them like this, I realized that Herald would probably indeed be able to easily shoot right over Makanna's head. She was even noticeably taller than Val.

"Funny," Makanna replied drily and pointed to Herald's hip. "That sword stays in its scabbard unless absolutely necessary, understood? If there's a group of them, I want you looking at the back and flanks, even if they press in."

"Understood."

"Good. Val, are you ready to go?"

"The sword is sharp, and the shield is buckled tight," he replied. "All is as ready as it can be."

"And I have the nest killer," Makanna said, grabbing a large package on her belt. "Last thing, then. Come here, both of you. I want to take care of the light before we go in."

Herald and Val both got close to Makanna, who put her hands on the exposed skin of their necks. She had an expression of intense concentration as they stood in respectful silence, and I thought that they might be praying. Then Makanna uttered a single word: "Sight."

I hadn't realized it until that moment, but a strange kind of light had been building in Makanna as they stood there. I could only describe it as a swirling ball inside her chest, near her heart, that I could see through her flesh. Now some of that light traveled up from her chest, through her arms, and into the other adventurers, who both took on some of the same glow. Herald gasped, and when they all opened their eyes, they had to squint against the light.

I sat there, stunned. Had I just witnessed magic? I had been open to the possibility ever since Guy healed himself, but there was something about seeing this that left me awestruck. I'd never even suspected that Makanna might be capable of something like that, whatever she had done. Magic had never once been mentioned in all the conversations I'd overheard. Why not? Was it illegal? Was it taboo to speak about it? What could you do with magic? Could anyone do it with training, or did you need to be special in some way? I had so many questions!

When I focused on the adventurers again, they were already on their way to the mine. That was fine. Except right by the cliff, there was nothing but open ground between here and the entrance, and I needed to keep my distance to stay hidden. I could tell that the three were all shading their eyes and guessed that Makanna had done something to help them see in the dark. Not needing to carry lamps or torches would probably be a huge advantage.

I waited until they had all disappeared inside the opening in the stone before I crossed the field to the cliff. There, I snuck in close, then stopped and used my ears and nose. As far as I could tell, they had moved in deeper, and so I carefully got right up to the entrance and looked inside. There was no one there. I followed them in.

As I moved in deeper, the light faded, but my eyes adapted quickly. I couldn't see perfectly by any means, but still well enough, and once there was no more natural light, the same bioluminescent lichen, or whatever it was, grew visible on the walls. A good distance inside, I found the group's packs resting neatly against the wall. That made sense. I wouldn't want to fight with a big, heavy backpack on either.

I could hear the sound of their footsteps ahead, and following them was easy. Soon the footsteps stopped, and I heard Makanna's hushed voice.

". . . should be here. Ten, eleven . . . twelve is there, thirteen over there. Ah, here! Fourteen. This is the one."

I had followed them to where the tunnel expanded into a large hall. It looked like a natural cave had been opened up and extended. It was messy, even for a cave. There were tables and benches standing in fair order, as well as bags, picks, and other equipment, but anything small, say, not too big for a gremlin to move, was dumped about the floor haphazardly. A number of tunnels left the hall, each with one or more symbols painted on the wall next to it, barely visible, even with the lichen and my excellent eyes. The adventurers were entering one of the tunnels, alert and in the formation Makanna had set out earlier.

I learned an interesting fact here. Knowing how to speak different languages did not allow me to read the symbols on the walls. There was a very real chance that I was illiterate in every language that mattered here, which didn't seem fair. But I also had no access to any text, so it was more of an annoyance than a problem.

While I was pondering the inherent unfairness of magically acquired language skills not being perfect, I heard the snap of a bowstring, followed in rapid succession by a squeal and a scream, a second snap, some truly vile cursing from Herald, a third snap, boots slapping on stone, and finally silence.

"Fine shooting," Val said quietly, and the sounds of their movements picked up again. I followed, as close as I dared and came upon two dead gremlins. One had an arrow in its neck, and the other lay a little farther down the tunnel with an arrow in its butt and its throat slit. Both had belts with pouches, which I quickly looted. Now wearing three loops of rope around my neck, festooned with small bags, I wondered if these three might be able to pull it off without me. The plan had been to wait until they were in trouble and then offer my help in exchange for a cut of the loot or money, but I wasn't going to reveal myself if there was a real chance of them turning me down. But I could always try again. Even if that did happen, though, I was already doing great. I didn't know how much silver I had in these little bags, but I hadn't had any silver at all before. Besides that, I had learned a lot from listening to the adventurers. For investing a single day, I was very satisfied.

As the minutes dragged on and nothing happened, I thought that I wouldn't feel too bad about bailing if I had to and decided to risk getting closer to the group. With my claws pulled in as far as they could go, I picked up some speed and closed in until I could hear the adventurers.

"Loose stone. Alcove here . . . clear." Makanna's voice was a terse whisper, barely audible even over the sounds of their steps. There was a lot of that. There were a myriad of little side shafts running off the main one, where I guessed that the miners had found something worth digging out, and they had to check every one to make sure there were no creatures in them.

I had no idea how long we had been going when I got my chance. I had a sense of great depth, which I chalked up to the dragon just being able to tell such things. I was wondering about how the air stayed fresh this far down and why it wasn't flooded. Sure, the walls were damp, which allowed the shiny lichen to grow, and the air wasn't great, but I felt like we should have suffocated or drowned by now. Magic, maybe? Simple machinery? I hadn't heard any pumps or anything, but, again, magic?

My musings were interrupted by Val's loud whisper.

"Two paths open. One more again on the right branch. Looks tight."

There was a rustle of paper, and Makanna spoke. "There's no second branch to the right on the map. That must be where the gremlins broke through."

"Should we go in?" That was Herald. She sounded excited, which was not at all what I would have expected, but I guessed that killing two gremlins had gotten her blood pumping.

There was a long silence. "Only two have been seen," Val said after some deliberation. This clearly carried a lot of context that I didn't understand.

"I agree," Makanna said. "If we're lucky, they're sleeping, and we can get the drop on them. Let's go. Herald, watch our backs and then follow. I think you'll need your sword in there."

They moved on, and I continued until I could see the fork in the tunnels they had talked about. There were two proper shafts leading away from each other at a sharp angle, and a ways down the right-hand one, there was a rough hole in the wall. Herald crouched outside that hole, facing down the mine shaft with her bow at the ready. The base of the hole was shoulder-high on her, crouched as she was, and not very wide.

I tensed when I heard a soft scrabbling from the left-hand shaft. Herald must not have heard it, because she didn't react. But then her posture changed. She froze completely, turning her head like she was listening to something, then straightened and fired her bow in one practiced motion.

"Oh, Sorrows! Mak, I need help!" Herald called out as she fired another arrow and backed up.

I could hear screeching and scratching from the right-hand shaft, but there was a group of gremlins coming from the left as well. Herald tried to jump into the hole in the wall but screamed and dropped back out, drawing her sword and backing up farther toward me. A gremlin was waving a short blade at her, and I could see a dark patch on her left thigh, below the skirt of her leather armor.

"Behind you! Mak, Val, behind you!" Herald called out while she fought. She cut down the gremlin in front of her, but I could hear more coming, and she was backing up right toward the four sneaking in from the left.

I could have fled there. I could have let them die, gone through their bags, and written the whole thing off as a partial success. Instead I roared, "Herald! Behind you!" and charged.

The gremlins heard me coming, but it was too late to change my mind now. I bowled into them, biting and slashing for all I was worth, while the ones in front of Herald slowly pressed her back toward me. I hurt two of the creatures in my group badly with my first charge, but the other two recovered and came in with their blades. I didn't know how to fight. I never learned how to in my old life, not really, but I didn't need to. I felt their blades hitting me, but they clattered off my scales without doing any real damage. I fought on instinct, almost an observer, while the dragon took over.

Herald was not doing well. She was calling out for help and in warning; the edge of fear in her voice getting steadily sharper as the gremlins pushed in. I risked a glance and saw her still falling back, fighting and losing, limping badly on her injured leg. If she fell, she wouldn't stand a chance, and there was no sign of Makanna or Val. I had to do something, so I risked everything.

I knocked one gremlin down by bashing it with my wing and threw myself at the gremlin separating me from Herald, bearing it to the ground with my greater weight. It stabbed me in the side, which felt like I'd been hit with a hammer, but I pinned it with my hands and raked it with one of my feet, and that was that. With a few loping strides, I was beside Herald and then between her and the gremlins, who fell back in fear and confusion, menacing me uncertainly with a collection of small knives, picks, and hammers.

"Behind you!" I shouted, turning my head to face Herald for a second while I raked my claws at the little bastards like a cornered cat. "There's still one behind you!"

She stared at me in dumb fear, but a sound behind her made her turn, and that was good enough for me.

There were more gremlins in front of me than I could count in the dim light. More than seven? I'd read somewhere that you could usually tell how many of something you had only up to seven. Regardless, male or female, big or small, all gremlins were armed and gathering their courage to close in on me, but none of them wanted to go first. There were too many of them. I—or rather we, since I hoped that Herald understood that I was on her side—needed an equalizer. We might have one, if I could only do this right. I thought that I had figured out the trick, but I hadn't practiced it. Worst case, at least I'd look scary.

I reared back, opened my wings as far as they would go in the cramped space, then threw my head forward and hissed while squeezing my venom glands as hard as I could. Noxious saliva sprayed out over the creatures, unfocused and ungraceful but instantly effective, hitting like tear gas in the narrow tunnel. The gremlins started screeching, coughing, and rubbing at their big eyes, and in their confusion, I threw myself at them, biting and clawing at anything in range. They tried to defend themselves blindly, but though I took some bumps and scratches, the fight was almost completely one-sided. The last few at the back tried to run, but by the time they broke away, it was too late, and I ran them down with sheer momentum. All I needed to do was barrel into them from behind and step on them, and they'd be out of the fight.

I left behind me a tunnel filled with bodies and blood. The few gremlins that were still alive were moaning and mewling on the ground, and I finished them off as efficiently as I could. Beyond the dead stood Herald, leaning against the side of the tunnel with her sword held in both hands and pointed at me. The dragon did not like that. My blood was running hot, and she was threatening me.

She dares? The thought came from somewhere deep inside me. This frightened, injured *child* would challenge me? Did she not know that she was prey? Had she not seen how easily I destroyed the creatures that were about to kill her?

I had to fight to control myself. It wasn't like when I was fighting, where my body seemed to move by reflex. Instead there was an endless spring of rage leaking into my mind. I wanted to hurt her. Maybe not kill her, but I wanted to show her who was the dominant one here, who ruled and who should serve.

"Put that away," I growled. "I'm friendly."

She didn't believe me. I could hardly blame her. I heard the menace and restrained violence in my voice, and I knew what I must've looked like. Herald did her best to move into more of a fighting stance and calm her ragged breathing, but her injured leg seemed to be hurting her more now that there was a break in battle. I consciously tried to calm myself, relaxing tensed muscles and taking a few deep breaths. I folded my wings tightly and sat back on my haunches, trying to look less threatening.

"Listen to me, kid," I said, voice a little more normal. "I know that you can understand me. Your friends are in trouble, right?"

Herald shifted on her feet, eyes flicking all over me. "You can talk," she said unhelpfully.

"Focus! Your friends?"

Her eyes went briefly to the tunnel opening. I could hear the sounds of fighting echoing from inside, and I was sure that Herald could as well.

"What are you?" she asked instead of sticking to the topic at hand.

"What does it look like?" I snapped. "I'm a fucking dragon. And I'm here to help, for a price. You've seen what I can do. Yes or no?"

There was another burst of noise from the side tunnel, and I heard a female voice scream in pain.

Herald's eyes went desperately toward the sound. "Yes! Anything, yes!" she said almost instantly, and I knew that I was in. I could almost see her mind racing, going through the horrible possibilities of what the beast in front of her might ask of her, and I knew that she'd meant what she said.

"Gold or silver," I told her simply. "We can decide on the amount once the job's done. I'll be fair, don't worry. Agreed?"

"Agreed!" she said quickly, relief plain on her face.

"Good. Can you move? Do you need to use a potion?" I very carefully asked this as if it were the most natural thing in the world, trying to sound like I was highly competent and experienced in these things.

Herald was already moving toward the hole in the wall. I couldn't help but notice that while her sword was down, it was still out and pointed in my general direction. "It hurts like a devil, but I can move. Potion will take too long to do any good anyway."

There was some awkward shuffling as we got closer to each other. She clearly didn't want to get too close to me. I was very aware of the fact that I was facing a scared teenage girl with a sword in her hands, which she was at the very least competent with. I wasn't keen on getting in range of that, and the dragon, still being furious, didn't help. Unfortunately for me, I knew that I would have to trust her to some degree for this to work.

"Can you shoot your bow inside that tunnel?" I asked her.

She looked dubiously at the hole, then at her bow where she had dropped it. Retrieving it meant that she would need to get closer to me. As she did so, she kept her eyes locked on me the whole time, flicking between my head and forelimbs, and then she scuttled back as fast as her injured leg would allow once she had her bow. I held my breath and stood my ground, trying to look like the one in control here.

"No," she said after holding the bow up to the hole. "Not well enough to be useful."

That was a big relief for me. "I'm going to go first," I told her. "I need you to call ahead and make sure that your friends don't try to kill me. Do it now. Hurry!"

She took another look at me, then stuck her head in the hole. "Mak! Val! Hold on, I am coming!"

"Hurry!" came Val's voice from the hole.

"I am bringing someone! She . . ." She paused and turned to me. "Are you male or female?" she whispered.

"Female. Appreciate it, but not the time," I hissed back.

"She is not human," Herald called down the tunnel. "Do not hurt her!"

I didn't wait to hear a reply and leaped up in the tunnel. As I passed her, I realized again how tall she was. I only came up to her hips when I stood on all fours, and the roof of the tunnel was low enough that I had to keep my wings tightly folded. Herald would probably have to crawl.

"Follow as fast as you can," I told Herald, and then I was off. I couldn't run, but I was sure that I could move faster than almost any adult human. I could hear Val shouting threateningly and the occasional slap of boots on stone, but there was no active fighting. There was no lichen in the tunnel, but the passage wasn't particularly long and was almost completely straight, so I could see the weak light of the exit. Near the end, I stumbled on a dead gremlin, then found two more right where the tunnel turned into a huge, high-ceilinged cavern.

Here, the lichen grew thick, making the cavern almost bright compared to the mine. It grew on the walls, on the ceiling, and on the multitude of stalactites, stalagmites, and pillars that spanned the vertical distance. Water dripped constantly, and I could see a large pool, almost an underground lake, that was lit up not only by the lichen but by a glow from below. Beyond the exit, I could see Val's back. He was surrounded by gremlins that circled him nervously, not attacking but unwilling to back off. The floor between them and Val was littered with their dead. I couldn't see or hear Makanna anywhere.

I wasn't sure how to proceed, but the situation seemed clear. Makanna was out of the fight, gone, dead or injured. The gremlins wouldn't let Val any deeper into the cavern, but they also weren't likely to let him leave, so he couldn't turn his back on them. Whichever way he faced, every so often one of the little creatures would try to sneak up on him, and he would whirl and lunge at it. It would back away, and then another one on the other side of the half circle would try the same thing. The many dead gremlins showed that they couldn't take Val straight on, but he was constantly in motion, and they were many. Soon he would get tired and slow, and then they could get him.

But now I was there. "Don't turn around," I called from the tunnel and instantly regretted it. That was possibly the dumbest, most obvious thing I could have said in this situation. "I'm here to help. Herald is behind me." I paused and decided to bring up the most pressing issue immediately. "I'm a dragon. Don't do anything stupid!"

I saw Val tense, but to his credit, his attention never left the gremlins, and he continued to keep them at bay. "What did she—?" Makanna's voice came weakly from beside the tunnel's exit, and I stuck my head out and looked around the corner. Makanna was sitting on the stone, her spear in one hand and supported under her armpit while the other covered a wound in her side. There was blood all the way down her side, pooling on the ground. It was a *lot* of blood. I couldn't see any color in the light of the lichen, but I was sure that her face would be ashen. Our eyes met.

Makanna swung her spear my way, and I wasn't quite fast enough. It caught me on the nose as I pulled my head in and drew back, and it was only thanks to the length of the shaft that I got a smack instead of a cut.

"Ow!" I exclaimed. "Oh, you absolute bitch! That hurt!" I forced myself to stop whining and turned my head back into the tunnel. "Hurry up!" I shouted. "Your sister's hurt pretty bad."

"What? Mak! Makanna! Oh, hells, oh, Mercies . . ." I could hear Herald groaning as she picked up speed, crawling as fast as she could.

"Tell her not to try to stab me again so I can get out of this hole!" I told her as she came into sight, and she quickly complied.

"Mak, let her out! She's friendly! I've got the potion, hang on, just . . . let her out!"

I turned back to the exit. "All right," Makanna said. Her voice was weak and tired. I saw the spear get pulled back and stuck my head out again. Makanna was looking straight at me, and we locked eyes for a moment. I couldn't help but notice that the spear point was aimed right in my direction.

"Introductions later," I told her before I jumped out.

I could have charged past Val, but the ceiling was high and I was in the mood to strike some awe into the creatures, human and gremlin, around me. Not waiting for Herald, I spread my wings and leaped up. Val stumbled forward half a step at the loud snap of my wings grasping the air, and the gremlins shrieked and scrambled away as I passed low above them. I climbed as high as I dared, circled a thick pillar, and came hurtling back toward the group. Some of the gremlins broke away and ran as I swooped toward them, trying to dodge me, but they weren't as agile as mountain goats.

I had always been an adrenaline junkie. Climbing and motorbikes fed into that. I'd gone bungee jumping plenty of times, done some skydiving and hang gliding, and tended to go way too fast for my skill level the few times I tried skiing. I had never been a stranger to taking risks, either to thrill myself or to impress others, so it seemed natural to me that I should come in as low and fast as I could, grab one of the gremlins, and then basically bomb it into the cave wall before turning away. The thing shrieked and howled as I snatched it, then went silent with a loud crack a fraction of a second after I released it. I felt nothing but a wild surge of joy.

As I turned back, the gremlins were in complete disarray, some fleeing, others trying to track me, and Val was among them, a whirling dervish cutting them down with every swing of his short blade, kicking and smashing with his shield when his rhythm didn't allow a cut.

Herald was with Makanna, probably giving her a healing potion. I saw a group of gremlins come together behind Val, preparing to rush the girls. I screeched, a sound I'd never made before, and dove. The cavern seemed to freeze at the sound for a second before I struck the group like a hawk, braking hard with my wings and pinning one of them with my feet. Two of the group fled, and the last one caught a slash of my claws to the throat. The one under my feet swiped at me with a small pick. The angle was awkward for both of us, so I took to the air, eliciting a gurgling shriek as I pushed off, and then simply dropped the unfortunate thing once I got high enough.

Then it was over. There were gremlins running in the distance, scrambling over stone formations and squeezing into crevices to get away, but the fight was done. Well over a dozen gremlins lay dead or dying. Val was kneeling by the girls, panting hard, and Herald was hugging her sister, who looked a little more lively.

I landed on a tall, broken stalagmite and let the dragon out. I spread my wings, raised my head, and roared. The sound filled the cavern, bouncing off the walls and echoing from every direction, and the humans stopped whatever they were doing and looked at me in fear and wonder.

Good, I thought, the human and the dragon for once in complete agreement. I looked down on them and smiled.

CHAPTER NINE

Establishing Dominance

Hey," I told the awestruck humans below me. "Some thanks would be nice."

That was my grand, formal introduction to Makanna and Val. Herald was probably already on board, and she was unlikely to change her mind about that after what had just happened. I heard Herald whisper a few short sentences to the others but couldn't make out the words, then Val stepped forward.

"Lady . . ." he began, licking his lips as his voice faltered. Feeding my ego was a good start! "Lady," he tried again, "we thank you for your help. Legends and stories are told, in hushed tones of wonder—"

"Shouldn't she be *bigger*?" Makanna mumbled, sounding half out of it.

Herald put her hand over Makanna's mouth as Val raised his voice and continued, "About your kind. Long has it been since you were seen in these lands. We are grateful for your benevolence."

Flatterer, I thought, enjoying every moment of it. The guy sounded properly scared, hesitating and shifting speeds with every other word. I'd never had someone be truly frightened of me before. I wondered if I'd overdone my entrance.

"I am Valmik of Karakan. My companions are the sisters Makanna and Herald," he continued, gesturing to each in turn, "also of Karakan. May we know your name?"

"I am Draka," I replied, trying to sound majestic. I'd decided that I liked the name Lahnie had given me. "Pleased to meet you all."

Val, or Valmik, as his full name was, hesitated for a moment. "An agreement has been made between my companion and yourself. It must be honored. The price was to be decided once my companion and I were safe—"

"I can wait until the job's done, but now works for me," I told him.

"Why's she talk like that?" Makanna half slurred before Herald quieted her again. Either the blood loss or the potion was really getting to her, but I recalled that Guy had been completely knocked out, so maybe that was normal?

"Ah, well." Valmik hesitated, clearly not wanting to say what he was about to and forcing out every phrase. "You understand . . . we are in great need . . . a companion is in dire trouble, and a large sum must be paid . . ."

He trailed off, and I couldn't help but notice that he was slowly placing himself directly in between myself and the women, his shield at the ready. I'd definitely overdone it.

I looked down at them, letting the silence settle. I'd thought about this. The fact that they'd risk so much for Tamor suggested that they were an honorable bunch, but I couldn't know if that extended beyond their friends and family. If I asked for cash, I might never see a single coin. Either way, I had never intended to ask for so much that they couldn't bail out Tamor and make a profit on this job.

"I may," I drawled magnanimously, "be satisfied with taking whatever loot we find as my price. The gremlins seem to love silver. So do I. We'll see." Worst case, I figured I could shake them down for whatever they had in their wallets—or money bags?—but I really didn't see myself doing that.

Valmik and Herald slumped a little with relief as I told them what I wanted.

"Will your aid be available until we've destroyed the nest, then, Lady Draka?" Valmik asked hopefully.

Lady Draka. Oh, I liked that.

"Sure, yeah. Of course. I'll make sure you get out of here. And"—here was the clincher—"perhaps we could help each other in the future."

"What kind of help might be in question?" Valmik asked cautiously.

"If you have a difficult job you might need help on," I suggested. "Or if I need something from the city. That kind of thing."

"You would not make us your servants?"

"Yes!" the dragon hissed in my ear.

"What? No!" I told them. "I'm looking for business partners. Quid pro quo, you know?"

"Those words are beyond my understanding, Lady Draka. Is it an ancient tongue?"

Oh, right. Latin. "Yes," I answered truthfully. "A favor for a favor."

Or something like that, anyway. I looked at the two sisters. "Makanna and Herald are both hurt. Will they be able to fight?"

"I will be healed enough in a few minutes," Herald answered. "Mak—"

"'m *fine!*" the woman drawled.

"Mak will need to stay in the back with me," Herald said firmly. "Mak, you swallowed most of that potion. You're a mess, and we will need you if one of us gets hurt."

Makanna grumbled nearly inaudibly but didn't argue.

"Okay, then," I said and jumped down from my perch. "I guess we have a deal."

Valmik drew back a little when I landed close to him but held his ground. "We'll wait and rest until Herald's leg is better," I said, "and then we'll move on. Is that good for you?"

I steeled myself, ready to bolt for the tunnel if they suddenly decided that they'd rather take their chances and fight me. Then I walked right past Valmik. When nothing bad happened, I sat just outside of stabbing range from Makanna and Herald, then curled up and relaxed as though the idea of them turning on me never even occurred to me. After a little while, Valmik came over and sat down against the wall, between me and the sisters, making himself a roadblock if I tried anything. Trust was in short supply. It would be nice if that changed, but I tried not to pin all my hopes on it. This was the first group I tried this with, after all, and it had been going unexpectedly well so far.

"So," I said from where I lay as the silence became uncomfortable, "do you know how to find the nest? And how do you plan to destroy it? Just kill everything?"

"Makanna will feel it when it is close," Valmik said. "And a device has been provided to kill it."

"Ah, good," I said, not understanding any better at all but trusting that he knew what he was talking about. "I wasn't sure."

"Issat way," Makanna added happily, gesturing with her spear past the shining pond. "Felt it for a while now. And the . . . the thing's right here. Nest killer." She patted the large package on her belt. "Should just go 'slurp' if we get it close enough to th' Heart. Don't worry!" Then she looked at me, leaned in, and asked, "Are you wearing gremlin belts assa necklace?"

I ignored her comments on my choice of accessories while Herald smothered a giggle. Makanna was slurring her words badly, and I was convinced that the healing potions were pretty much pure alcohol. Magic alcohol, sure, but it looked like it had hit her like one too many shots of tequila, and she wasn't a big girl either. I got to my feet and moved in closer to Valmik. I could see him tense, but he didn't flinch.

"We should get going," I whispered in his ear as he made a valiant effort to sit still. "I've seen this before. Pretty sure she won't be able to walk in a few more minutes."

Valmik, whose eyes hadn't left me since sitting down, now took a look at his leader. "Herald," he said. "Has your leg healed?"

Herald stood up slowly and shook her leg out. With great concentration, she did a few squats, then stretched her legs from side to side. "It aches a little, but otherwise I am fine," she concluded.

"Let's go, then," Valmik said, looking to me for confirmation. I nodded. "Makanna, if you would show us the way?" He stood and offered her his hand.

"I'm tired," she complained. "An' hungry."

"The time for food and rest will be later," Val told her. "The job must be finished."

"Yeah, yeah." Makanna took his hand, then swayed as she got to her feet. "Where's Tam?" she asked, looking around. "Tam!"

"Tam did not come on this job," Valmik answered her patiently. "He was imprisoned. His license was not paid. You remember. There was a fine, which we must pay."

"Oh! Right. Right. He's so lucky he found you, you know that, Val?"

Valmik blushed ever so slightly in the gloom as he turned to me. "Lady Draka, if you would accompany me at the front?"

"Let's go," I said, joining him, with Herald supporting her sister at the rear.

The pond was full of large crystals and something like the bioluminescent lichen. Or maybe the lichen was actually algae and it lived both on the rocks and in the water. Either way, the pond was the most brightly lit area of the entire underground world we had entered. There was nothing for us there, but the humans oohed and aahed appreciatively at the beauty of it. I did too, just not out loud. I loved caves and the stuff you could find in them, and the pond and cavern ranked way up there.

We went in the direction that some of the gremlins had fled, Makanna pointing the way. I didn't know how she knew where to go, but she said that she could feel it, which probably meant something magical. I had a feeling that I should be more impressed, but I had already seen two people saved from certain death by magic potions, and Makanna had somehow given her group the ability to see at least as well as I did in these caverns. Not to mention that I myself was a dragon who could speak all languages, which already strained belief to the point that magically sensing where some gremlins lived wasn't such a big deal.

I saw a few passages leading out of the giant space in various directions, but the one Makanna pointed us to led down deeper into the cave system.

"'S not far," she mumbled. She was not looking great. The potion was definitely mostly alcohol. She was right, though, because pretty soon, we came to another large cavern. Crude shelters had been carved into the stone, piled with stuff. In the more distant corners were piles of refuse. In the middle of the cavern was the most reality-defying thing I had ever seen.

"That is it," Val said, pointing. "The Nest Heart."

An oblong shape hung in the air, not touching the ground. It looked like it was made of shadow, but the shadow twisted and sent out thin tendrils that arched back on themselves. The whole thing seemed to distort the air around it, but right at the edge was a bright shimmer of the same light that had filled Makanna when she cast her magic on the surface. The thing was so obviously magical that I could only assume that this was what Makanna had been sensing.

The gremlins had gathered for a last-ditch defense. I wouldn't say that the place was teeming with them, but there were quite a few skulking about, many of them watching the only entrance and one of them so big that it was almost as tall as Makanna. This, I decided, was the leader. Killing it might make the others flee, or it might not, but it was definitely the biggest individual threat, and I wanted it dead.

It also had a belt full of big, heavy bags, which may have influenced me, and a loincloth, which was interesting. I hadn't seen that before.

Catching the gremlins by surprise had not ever been in the cards. They knew that we were coming. They had ambushed the adventurers, and then put up a defense in the large cavern with the pond. They had always known that the party was there. But they hadn't counted on me.

"How do you want to do this?" I asked Valmik and Herald. Makanna had been propped against a wall and was snoring softly.

"The nest must be destroyed. That is all," Valmik said.

"That's what Makanna said," Herald added. "If we get the device close enough to the Heart, the device should kill it pretty quickly, and that is it. The job is done."

"We don't need to wipe them out? And how quick?" I asked.

"Less than a minute," Herald replied. "I guess the company would appreciate us wiping them out, but they are not paying us for it."

"When the nest is dead, no more will come into the world," Val explained. "Some will survive. Some will stay, some will run. The company guards can deal with stragglers."

Did they mean that the magical thing in the center actually created the gremlins? Sure, why not? I could find out more once we were out. In the meantime, I didn't want to look ignorant. "Good," I told them. "That makes things easier."

"How do you mean?" Herald asked.

I gestured with my head. "Yeah, you've never heard of bombers. It's a wide cave with a high ceiling. I can fly in and drop the thing right in the middle. You just need to distract them so that no one picks it up or whatever while it does its thing."

Valmik and Herald looked at each other. "I can pick them off with my bow if you keep them off me," Herald suggested.

"They'd fear to go in the open," Valmik replied. "You shoot well."

"Great. No time like the present," I told them. "Give me the thing, and let's do it!"

Herald knelt down and opened the large bag Makanna had been carrying on her belt and took out a crystal about the size of my head and wrapped in cloth. I caught a whiff of something deeply unpleasant but forced myself to ignore it. It wasn't like the cave itself smelled great to begin with. Herald opened the cloth enough to remove a section at the top, which had seemingly been cut out for this reason. The crystal started shining with a weak, silvery light, and Herald wrapped it up again.

"There, it is active," she said. "Do not drop it, please. It should not shatter too easily, but if it does, it will not kill the Heart, so do not be too rough with it. Once the Heart is dead, take the crystal with you. We need to return it."

"No pay will be given if we cannot show that the task has been completed," Valmik agreed. "And the crystals are quite expensive."

"Right, small change of plans. Still easy enough," I told them. "Put the crystal by the black hole, wait until it eats it, and fight off anyone who steps up. Then bring it back. No problem. Ready?"

They both nodded, and Herald prepared an arrow.

"Pick one off, and I'll go."

Herald looked around the cavern, then drew back and released almost without aiming. The arrow arched high, crossing the entire space before it came down, taking a gremlin next to the boss in the gut. The gremlin screeched, the boss roared, and I took off with the package.

Gremlins were running to and fro, some going for cover, others running around for no reason I could see. The boss was waving a crude axe around, yelling at the others and trying to restore order. I didn't understand anything it said, so I had to guess that "tongues of men" really only meant human languages. I wondered briefly what I was missing out on and how many other species there might be with languages of their own, but then I was above the Heart—the magical rift in space?—and it was time for me to shine.

I landed as fast as I dared, but not too close to the Heart, just in case. That was probably a good thing, because I felt a strange pull from it, not on my body but, for lack of better words, on my soul. I unwrapped the crystal. The silvery white was darkening on the side facing the Heart. As arrows zipped down every few seconds, keeping the gremlins away from me, I put the crystal on the floor.

With a careful push, I rolled it toward the Heart. It wasn't a perfect roll. The sides of the crystal weren't parallel, and I didn't really know what I was doing, but it was good enough. Tendrils of shadow immediately started streaming into the crystal, which grew brighter while the color it gave off became steadily darker, starting as a silvery-pink hue and then shifting to a steadily darkening purple.

It was beautiful in a way. I stupidly stared at it for a second or two, then turned too late at a berserk howl. I saw a crude axe flashing at my head, and though I jerked away, it caught me a glancing blow that made my head ring. It hurt so bad that I couldn't see, and I scrambled back desperately, shaking my head to try to clear it. The gremlin boss was closing in for another blow, and I didn't know what to do. I wasn't a fighter. I hadn't been in a real fight since middle school, and that had been over a juice box!

So I let the dragon take over.

I hissed and sprayed venom, but the big gremlin closed its eyes and held its breath and avoided the worst of it. I lunged, snapping at the brute, but I had blood running into my left eye and couldn't judge depth very well. The gremlin danced back easily and swung its axe to fend me off. I heard small feet on the stone behind me, but I couldn't take my eyes off the big one, and then there was a weight on my tail and a sharp pain in my lower back, and I reflexively turned my head back to snap at whatever it was.

Stupid. So stupid! I saw in the corner of my eye how the boss came forward, axe raised in both hands, and the only thing I or the dragon could think of was to move forward as well. Instead of getting my head chopped off, I caught a double-fisted blow to the neck, which luckily didn't hurt too much, but then I felt another stabbing pain in my back, higher up this time, as the gremlin on me used its knife or pick or whatever it was as an anchor to climb toward my head. I had to get it off me! I had to . . .

Distracted again, I saw the boss step back and wind up its axe like a baseball bat. This was it. I'd fucked up, and now I was going to die. I wondered if I would wake up in a hospital bed or on the cave floor, or not at all.

An arrow sprouted from the big gremlin's armpit, and it stumbled in surprise. Not questioning my luck, I scuttled away, at the same time turning my head to stare right into the eyes of the gremlin on my back. It had a short, wide knife ready to stab me in the neck. I sprayed its face full of venom, every little bit I had left, and it screamed and fell off me, rolling on the stone floor. As its throat closed up and cut off its screeching, I saw two wounds on my back bleeding freely. I hoped it had only hit muscle and turned back to the boss.

To my astonishment, the boss had turned away from me and was fighting Valmik. Valmik was blocking its axe easily with his shield, but its long arms made it hard for him to get in with his short sword. But that didn't matter. The thing was distracted. It wasn't paying attention to me.

I lunged at it and dug my teeth into its throat, jerking back and tearing out a chunk of muscle, gristle, and blood. Before I really thought about it, I'd swallowed. Valmik stared at me with fair horror while the gremlin collapsed, twitching and gurgling, and then the crystal finished its work.

The Heart had been growing thinner and less substantial as layers of shadow vanished into the crystal. Now, without fanfare, the last shred disappeared, and the crystal turned completely black yet shone with a light that I thought of as the glow of magic. Then there was a wave of silence, an anti-sound that swallowed everything, even the rush of blood in my ears, and then the sound hurried back in and it was over. Gremlins still looked at us, screeching angrily from their hiding places, but the job was done.

"Take the crystal and let's go," I told Valmik tensely. Besides my head, my back was starting to throb, as did a point in my side. While Valmik did as I told him,

I grabbed the boss's belt, loincloth and all, and pulled it off. Male, I noticed. I threw the belt over my neck, and we made our way back up to the exit, Herald firing off an arrow every so often to keep the gremlins' heads down.

"Three left," Herald informed us when we got back to her. I wondered what she meant, then saw that her quiver was almost empty. She looked us over, and I saw her wince when she looked at me. I could guess what she saw. My head hurt like . . . well, like I'd been hit with an axe. I wasn't even trying to see out of my left eye anymore. I kept it shut and felt the blood flow over it and down my cheek.

"Scalp wounds, right?" I tried to sound nonchalant, but everything hurt so much that it came out as more of a groan.

"Yeah," Herald said uncertainly as we got going. "We . . . I think that Makanna can do something for it once we get her fed and sobered up a little."

"Much can be done for superficial wounds and worse with skills such as hers," Valmik agreed. He was supporting the woman in question, her arm around his waist and his under her armpit. She was very unhappy about being made to walk but in no state to resist.

"She's got some healing voodoo too?" I asked no one in particular.

"If that is a kind of magic, then yes, something similar," Herald said. "Except, well, I do not know if it will work on a . . . on you. As far as I know, she has only ever used it on people. On humans, I mean! Sorry. And she will not like that I told you."

"Nice save," I grumbled to myself, before looking up at her. "I'd love for her to give it a shot."

Herald took up the rear. A few gremlins were following us, she said, but they were keeping their distance. In the large cavern with the pond, I insisted that we collect all the gremlins' belts, and no one argued. The gremlins following us made angry noises, but I was in enough pain that I would be damned if I didn't get a worthwhile haul out of this. We did the same with the gremlins in a narrow tunnel and in the mine, with Herald taking time to collect her arrows while I looted and Valmik watched our backs. When we moved, we did so quickly and in silence.

Herald and Valmik were a little more relaxed around me than on before. Maybe it was that I'd put myself on the line for us. Or maybe I became less scary once they'd seen me bleed. Either way, they actually forgot themselves and turned their backs to me once or twice.

I had something like twenty little loops of rope around my neck when we stumbled into the light. The bags hung so thick and heavy that I could only hold my head up with effort, and they smelled like a blend of death and heaven. Each belt was a dead gremlin, and even then, we hadn't looted all of them. I thought a lot about that. About what we had done. Had we killed a village? A whole tribe or clan? There were a few survivors, sure, but could they rebuild? Did we want them to?

Why did I still not feel anything?

"Why were you sent to kill the gremlin nest?" I asked as we approached the cluster of buildings.

"Well, they are gremlins. The company needed them gone," Herald said, clearly surprised at my question.

"Li'l whoresons," Makanna slurred. "They closed down the shaft. Got into the rest. Killed some miners." She choked out a hiccup. This was the most she'd said in over an hour, by my estimate. "Ate 'em, I guess."

"This is the way of gremlins," Valmik agreed. "A nest appears. Tunnels are dug, mines or basements entered. They steal and prey on the lonely."

"Worse'n fuckin' goblins, I say," Makanna said. "Can talk to goblins, y'know? Bargain with 'em. Gremlins jus' kill an' die. An' prob'ly screw, there's so many of 'em."

A seed of anxious jealousy sprouted in my gut. "Can they appear anywhere?" I asked, trying to sound more interested than worried. "I'm not as familiar with gremlins as you may think."

"You have much to concern yourself with, I'm sure, Lady Draka," Valmik said. "Where there is an open space in the stone, and precious metals or gems nearby, they may appear. Be that native ore, coins, or other things made of such materials. They are a great nuisance."

"Right," I said. "Thank you, Valmik."

"Think nothing of it, Lady Draka."

Shit. Shitshitshit. I could have those little bastards tunnelling right into my cave and never know it until all my stuff was gone! What was I supposed to do about that? I wanted to ask, but the dragon insisted that the hoard must be kept secret, and I agreed. I had already risked a lot by showing myself, and I was sure that it was obvious that I had a home somewhere. Or a *lair*, if I was to embrace the whole dragon thing. Better not give any clues as to where, exactly, it might be, even if I did kind of like these people. But it was a serious problem to consider for the future.

CHAPTER TEN

Winding Down

We all blinked painfully as we emerged into the sunlight.

"Ah! No. No!" Makanna said, covering her eyes. "C'mere. I'll . . . you know. Here," she said as she waved the other two in.

The humans gathered. There was a pulse from Makanna, then she seemed to draw that golden glow out of them, and they all blinked a few times more and were fine in the light. She'd undone whatever spell she had cast when they went in.

It was around noon, judging by the sun. We had entered the mine in the morning, so the whole thing had taken at most four or five hours. It felt like it had been much longer, though, and everyone looked as tired as I felt. My injuries ached too, especially my head wound. At least the wooziness had passed quickly.

"The job is done, and well done at that," Valmik said a few minutes later. We were all inside the administrative building. I hadn't exactly been invited, but they hadn't said anything when I came inside.

"A far worse outcome was possible and almost came to pass," he continued. "You have our thanks, Lady Draka."

"Yeah, well, de nada," I said. "I mean you're welcome."

"Only, well," Herald cut in, "you were there last night too, right? That was you in the dark."

"Oh, yeah, it was," I replied. I had a feeling I knew what was coming.

"So, why? How did you know we needed help?"

There it was.

"Well," I started, then stopped. I was not going to tell them that I'd stalked them for a whole day. I was pretty embarrassed about that, to be honest. It had felt like a good idea, and obviously it had worked out pretty well, but now that I actually knew something about these people, I felt just plain bad about how I'd gotten here. Still, I figured that being selective with the truth was better than lying.

"I saw you on the road," I admitted, "and heard some of your conversation. It sounded like you were in over your heads. I thought you might need some help."

"Right," Herald said, "but—"

"*And*," I continued, "I thought you would be willing to make it worth my time." There. I'd read about con artists. I knew the drill. Kind of. Always give them a good, selfish motivation. Even better if it's true.

"Oh," Herald said. She seemed satisfied with that. No disappointment, no *I'd hoped you were better than that.* They were basically short-term contract mercenaries, and they understood taking a chance to make a buck.

"And fortune was with us that you did," Valmik said. "Death by ambush was certain otherwise. Instead we took only relatively light injuries, most of which are healed already."

"About that," I said and touched my head. I should not have done that. I hissed and pulled my hand away. "You said that Makanna could do something about this, maybe?"

"Perhaps. But rest is needed, and food. To put it simply, she is drunk and starved from the potion. She needs focus and energy to attempt a spell like that. You also will need to eat, to fuel the accelerated healing, should it work. We brought rations, but . . ." He trailed off, looking uncomfortable.

"But you didn't plan for a guest. I get it. Don't worry. I ate a lot a couple of days ago, and that should keep me going for another couple of days. I guess I'll get hungry earlier, that's all. But what I'm hearing is that it'll be a while."

Herald was forcing Makanna to drink from a waterskin. Makanna was protesting loudly between gulps, but she obediently drank everything Herald poured in her. It looked like this wasn't the first time Herald had taken care of her sister, and I wondered if it was always healing-potion-related or if young women here liked to party as much as my girlfriends and I did back home.

"Mak needs to eat," Herald said with authority, "and then sleep the potion off. It will be a few hours."

"'M tired," Makanna confirmed. It was the middle of the day, and she had one hell of a drunk going, but it looked like those potions really drained you. So Herald and Valmik forced a considerable amount of bread, cheese, and fruit into Makanna, and then Herald put her to bed in the foreman's bedroom.

I could hear snoring almost as soon as Herald exited the room. Herald and Valmik had some lunch while I relaxed on the floor, and then I asked Valmik to help me with the loot while Herald kept an eye on her sister.

I dumped all the belts on a table. Getting the very literal weight off my shoulders was a relief. "I could just tear all the bags open," I explained while showing off my claws, "but I'm going to need to be able to take the good stuff with me somehow."

"I understand," he said. "Bags must be opened, and contents sorted and repacked."

"Right. Except I can't really . . ." I tried to untie a bag and failed, my thick, clawed digits not nearly as clever as my old fingers. "You see the problem."

Valmik nodded and started untying bags from the belts. "Just get the bags loose before we take anything out," I told him. "I can smell that you won't like what's in some of them."

"In all honesty, Lady Draka, the smell is noticeable. I had not wanted to say anything."

When he'd gotten all the bags off the belts, I gathered the ones that smelled like death and dumped them outside a good distance from the building. Some of them opened up when I dropped them, and a rotten human hand missing two fingers fell out of one of them, an ear from another. That made me feel much better about not feeling bad for killing the gremlins.

Back inside, I put all the bags that smelled delicious in one pile and all the ones that didn't smell like anything in particular in another. Since we still had a long time before Makanna would be rested, I started with the less-interesting pile. Those bags mostly contained what could best be described as knickknacks and baubles. Pretty rocks of no value, pieces of metal like nails or a belt buckle, buttons, things like that. But there were also a few useful things, most interesting among them a tinderbox complete with a piece of fool's gold and flint. I wasn't sure if I could use them, but I could sure try. I kept that for myself and left the rest to the others.

Then came the good stuff. I emptied all the bags into a pile on the table and smiled at what I saw. The boss, of course, had the most and best pieces, but almost every gremlin had at least one and usually more pieces of silver. Jagged, square, thready, or lumpy, many of them were melded with pieces of stone or lumps or crystals of some other metal. I didn't care that they weren't pure, shiny silver; they looked and smelled wonderful. As I looked at them, handled them, and smelled them, my aches disappeared for a while. I tried to estimate how much there was, and taking the stones and other metals into consideration, I estimated that I had between three and four kilos of silver here. I was almost giddy with excitement and had to fight the impulse to take it all right now and fly back to my cave to add it to the box of gold coins. But I forced myself to be patient. I could hopefully get some medical attention here, and I wanted to talk some more to the adventurers.

Valmik helped me gather all the silver and the tinderbox in a few of the largest bags and then tied them to a double loop of rope that he sized to my neck. It was considerably lighter without all the junk, and I wore it from then on, even though a couple of kilos around your neck is not nothing.

I had gained treasure and experience here, but the third big gain was that I had actually gotten to spend a few hours with people, talking and doing stuff with them. After two weeks or longer with only one meeting that was lost in translation, and one with a rude child, spending a little time with Valmik and Herald had reminded me how much I missed having people around. Makanna didn't really count yet, since she'd been so blitzed for most of it that I wasn't sure if she'd even recognize me when she woke up. She had been pretty damn drunk.

It had been nice to see Herald taking care of her big sister. I wondered if anyone was taking care of me. Which of my friends and family would visit me at the hospital, if that was where I was? My roomie, Andrea, for sure, and my big brother, David, would probably show up once a week at least . . . I pushed those thoughts down. It hurt a lot, and I was not prepared to start crying in front of these people. The dragon does not blubber.

We rested. I had gone back to the tree I had spent the night in and enjoyed the gentle swaying as I napped. I guessed that Herald and Valmik ate and took care of their equipment and probably talked about me. It didn't seem arrogant to assume that. Hopefully they wouldn't try anything. Except for the silver, they didn't have much to gain from attacking me anyway. If they did . . . the smart thing to do would be to kill them, but there was no way I'd even try. I had my treasure on me. If I had to, I'd do the least harm I could and fly away. It wasn't like they could stop me. And, greed-induced paranoia aside, I couldn't see them doing that. They didn't seem like the kind of people to turn on someone who had bled with them.

I managed to sleep in fits, but my head was burning, flies were buzzing around, and I was getting worried. It was a huge relief when I heard Herald calling for me from the building.

Herald held the door open for me and I entered carefully. "Does she remember this morning?" I asked her. "She doesn't have her spear or anything near her, does she?"

"No worries," Herald said. "She knows that you are coming."

"She was supposed to know I was coming last time, and she nearly broke my nose," I reminded her.

"You do not have a nose."

"My snout, then. You know what I mean. It hurt. She got a good swing in!"

Herald actually rolled her eyes at me. "I will go in first," she said and walked into the bedroom. I followed, and when I saw Herald sitting on a bed between Makanna and myself, I entered.

Makanna was sitting up against the wall, a blanket over her legs. When she saw me come in, her eyes got a little bigger and her mouth a little tenser, but there was no other reaction.

"Hey," I said lamely. "How's your head? And your gut, I guess."

"Mercies bless the alchemists for healing potions, and the Sorrows take them for not dealing with hangovers. I think I have rocks grinding together in my brain.

At least the drunk passes quickly. But I'm alive and likely to stay that way, thank you." She paused for a moment. "I thought I dreamed you, you know? When Herald told me what to expect, I thought she was pulling my leg. But here you are. Draka, right?"

"Here I am," I agreed. "And yeah, Draka is right. And you're Makanna. Think you can do anything about this?" I turned my head to show her the wound and heard her hiss in sympathy. I'd not seen it myself, but from the humans' reactions, it was probably as bad as it felt.

"Let's go in the common room, shall we?" Makanna suggested, and I backed out through the door. The bedroom was small enough that there wasn't room for me to turn easily.

Makanna's loose trousers and shirt were stained and crusted with blood, and there was a cut a hand long in the fabric around her waist. Either they hadn't planned for a change or Herald hadn't wanted to go through with the ordeal of getting a drunk woman into a clean set of clothes. I guessed this was just a situation that came up sometimes, because no one seemed bothered.

"You should relax," Makanna told me. "Would you sit or lie down, please?"

I obediently lay down with my head resting on the floor.

"This is going to sting," Makanna warned, and then it hurt like hell when she started washing the blood off. I hissed and tensed my neck, forcing myself to keep my head in place. I had enough experience getting patched up by my parents, and later by my friends, that I was pretty good at suffering the consequences of my behavior with minimum fuss.

"I'm sorry," Makanna said. "I need to see the wound and get as near it as I can."

"No worries," I choked out. "At least you don't have any damn peroxide."

Makanna didn't answer but clearly took that as assent to keep going. An eternity of pain later, I felt a soft cloth drying my eye and the side of my head.

"Oh, hells, that's nasty," Makanna said under her breath.

"Not being very reassuring there, nurse," I said.

"I'm sorry," she said. "It's just . . . I'll see what I can do. I need you to keep still and relax now. I need to touch the wound, which will hurt, but otherwise it should be painless."

I did as she said. I looked up at her as she settled on her knees next to me. She gently put one hand on each side of my horn, then closed her eyes and relaxed, her breathing becoming deep and regular. Her lips moved, almost completely silently, and I could see the glow gathering in her chest. It was like a small ball of yarn, growing layer by layer as barely visible strands came in from every part of her, hovering right where her heart would be. I wondered if the magic traveled through the blood somehow. The strands looked like they might be following her veins, so if it was going to gather anywhere, the heart made sense.

Her lips stopped moving. Then she whispered, "Be whole!" and the ball swirled as several layers came off it, drifting out to and down her arms until I couldn't see it anymore. I felt a pressure, but for a moment nothing happened, and I saw Makanna screw her face up in concentration as she pushed more light into her hands. The pressure built gradually, and it felt like something popped. The effect was like getting a shot of anesthetic: first a sting, and then a slow, welcome numbness, a wonderful absence of pain. The difference was that here the numbness faded quickly, but the pain never returned.

It was pretty awesome!

"Wow," I breathed in wonder. "That was great."

Makanna sighing wearily, then chuckled. "Wasn't it? Stay there and I'll look at your side and back too."

She repeated the process for my other wounds, a deep puncture in my side and two long, shallower cuts in my back. When she was finished, she sat back against the wall panting, obviously exhausted.

"It's not instant," she warned me between breaths. "There should be no pain or fouling, but the wounds will need a few hours to heal properly. You might get pretty hungry and tired. The healing will eat your body if there is nothing else to draw on."

"Understood, Doc," I told her. "And thank you. That was amazing."

"Happy to help, especially after you helped us." She smiled but looked pretty wrung-out.

"Healing really takes it out of you, huh?"

"It really does. The healing itself comes from the patient, but it must be started by the one casting the spell. It's not perfect. It will leave scars and much more powerful forms than I know are needed for lost limbs or other parts. But it saves lives and relieves pain, so it's worth getting a little tired. I really had to push this time, though. You"—she pointed at me, her voice rising in mock accusation—"have some magic resistance."

That was news to me. Was that a good thing? I wanted to ask but just looked back at her enigmatically.

Herald and Valmik had been sitting in their chairs, watching silently. Now Herald got up and brought Makanna even more food. "Here," Herald said. "Eat up. Val and I can do half rations tonight. I'll get you some water, and then it's back to bed for you."

Makanna accepted the food without argument. "I don't know what I'd do without you, little sister," she said, clapping Herald on the calf.

Herald shrugged. "Most likely drown in a puddle of your own sick. Now, eat before you pass out!"

While Herald made sure that Makanna ate everything she'd been given, and Valmik went back to taking care of their gear, I excused myself and returned to the tree. The healing was already making me tired, and I needed a nap. And while they all had shown me nothing but respect, I still felt like I was intruding on them. Besides, the dragon didn't trust them to sleep where they could easily reach me or my treasure, and I felt it too. The dragon always leaked in when it felt something strongly enough. I wondered if it could ever trust someone else, especially when something shiny was involved.

If not, I'd just have to be stronger.

CHAPTER ELEVEN

Confidently Ignorant

I woke to my name being called. Well, I woke to "Draka," but that was probably me more than my old name now. My body was completely new, and my mind was . . . different. I pretty much had a second consciousness riding shotgun with me, one that belonged in this body much more than I did. I had wondered a few times if that was the mind that the body really belonged to and I had just crashed in and taken over. It definitely knew how to use this body better than I did. But it spoke to me in my own voice, in English, so who could tell?

It was almost dark, the sun barely touching the mountains. Herald was standing at the foot of the tree, outside the wide skirt of needle-covered branches.

"Draka!" she called again. "Hello? We were wondering if you wanted to come in and talk."

That caught me by surprise. I had thought they looked relieved when I left, and that they only didn't say anything out of gratitude or fear. Having them ask me to join them was . . . well, it felt nice. It really did.

"Uh, Herald," I said, blinking the sleep from my eyes. "Okay, yeah. I'll be right down."

I could hear the whole tree rustling as I pushed branches aside and almost dropped out of the tree. I must have been a little lonelier than I had thought. My head was itching like crazy, but the needles dragging against it felt good, and when I had gotten out of the tree and was facing Herald, I reached up and gave it a good scratch.

Something flaked off in my hand.

At first I wasn't sure what I was looking at. A flat, dry lump of small scales set around a piece of bone or something. Then I caught up, and I practically threw the thing, wanting it out of my hand. It went in Herald's general direction, and she snapped a hand out and caught it.

"Ugh, oh God!" I said. "Is that my *horn*?" I'd practically forgotten that I had the things! "Herald, how does my head look? Is it bad?"

Herald hesitated briefly before getting closer and taking a good look at the top of my head. "It looks like it is healing well," she said. "There are new scales growing there, though they are not as regular, and they are much paler. Gray. Can I . . . ?" She reached out tentatively, and when I didn't say anything, she touched them, then an uninjured part of my head. "They are a little softer too. Does the color come in as the scales mature?"

"Uh, I guess. Maybe?" I had no idea, and I was too shaken to cover for it. A piece of me had just fallen off!

"Draka . . . I do not know if the horn will grow back. It is all scales there. Maybe it will come later, through the scales?" she suggested.

"Yeah, maybe," I said and started walking toward the building. I didn't really care about the horn. I hadn't had horns for most of my life, and only having one of them now didn't affect me. It was still freaky to have a chunk of your head roughly the size and shape of a small phone fall off.

When Herald let me into the large common room of the building, I was greeted with a cautious smile from Makanna, who was sitting at the table sipping something steaming in a wooden mug.

"I'm glad you accepted our invitation, Draka," Makanna said. "How are your injuries?"

"A lot better, thanks," I replied. "Looks like my horn is gone, according to Herald. Could be worse. And, I mean, there's no pain. Couldn't have hoped for better. You? How's the hangover?"

"Eh," she said noncommittally, sipping her drink. "Better, I guess. I swear, only an alchemist can save your life and make you wish they hadn't. Sorry about the horn, for what it's worth. Regrowth's beyond me, I'm afraid."

"Not your fault. I'm grateful for what you could do, so don't worry about what you can't."

Valmik cleared his throat. "An early start is needed tomorrow," he began, "and we hoped to talk with you. About this job and other things."

"We usually talk it through after a job is done," Herald explained, leaning against the wall by the door. "To see what went well and what did not. The three of us already talked, but we hoped that you might have some insights to share with us."

I hadn't expected that. I wasn't sure what to say. If they wanted tactical input, I was the wrong person to ask, but they must have had an inflated opinion of me based on how much damage I had done.

"Well, uh," I said, trying to think fast, "there were pretty obvious signs of gremlins in the big central chamber, where all the shafts led off from. That didn't make you suspicious?"

"We also thought of that," Makanna said. "With the mine abandoned, the gremlins should have been more spread out."

"Yeah," I went on. "And they had two guards. I don't have much experience with gremlins, but they didn't feel like the type to set guards. Is that normal?"

"It has been known to happen," Valmik said. "If their leader is clever enough."

"Okay," I continued, "but if their leader is clever enough to set guards, then it might try other things. So that should have made you more careful, yeah? Especially after we killed three of them last night. I know I'd be nervous if three of my buddies were suddenly gone."

"That's a good point," Makanna conceded.

"What else . . . ? Herald, you didn't grab your arrows from the guards, and you almost ran out later. So grab your arrows whenever you have the time, I guess?" I was on a roll!

"I know," Herald said, looking away. "I forgot. I got excited, I guess."

"All right, but then one of your more experienced party members should have reminded you."

Valmik grunted in a way that I interpreted as agreement.

Then Makanna spoke up. "That's my mistake," she said. "I'm responsible for you being here, Herald. I should have supported you better."

Herald tried to argue, but I didn't want to lose my momentum. "Then we get to where everything went south," I said. The others looked at me. The expression clearly hadn't translated well. "The gremlin tunnel. I don't know what the plan was, exactly, but I think you two"—I looked at Makanna and Valmik in turn—"moved on too quickly. You were too far up the tunnel to help Herald when the gremlins sprung their ambush, and even if you'd been closer, you couldn't have turned around easily."

"We couldn't have known—" Makanna started defensively, her cheeks flushing.

"She would have died if I hadn't been there," I said loud enough to drown out her objection.

Makanna shut her mouth and looked at the floor, the wall, Valmik, anything except me and especially Herald. She knew very well what would have happened. I suspected that she'd been thinking about it a lot.

"It wouldn't have happened if Tam was there," Makanna grumbled.

"Then you're too reliant on him. Anyway, you should have moved slower in the tunnel," I went on, "or even just gotten in and waited a moment. It was a perfect place for an ambush. Even I could see that. A cramped tunnel where tall folk like humans could barely fight? Forcing the group to separate simply because you have to slowly get in, one by one, and get in each other's way? Two directions to attack from, and that's not counting the cramped tunnel where only the person in front could really fight, and badly." I waited for arguments, but none came. I must have been pretty convincing!

"And"—I turned to Herald—"you, Herald, were the wrong person to bring up the rear, yeah? Your shooting is fire, but as soon as more than one guy got in too close to use your bow, you were in trouble. They"—I nodded to Valmik and Makanna—"should have known that. But so should you. I know all about denying your weaknesses, but when I fuck up, I only get myself killed. If we hadn't held our end of the tunnel, those little shits would have swarmed through and taken Makanna and Valmik from behind."

Herald stared at her boots.

"A different choice of tactics, then," Valmik said from the table. "Lady Draka, what would you have done?"

God, I hoped that I was right about some things because I was just making this up as I went, trying to make a good impression. "Well," I said after thinking about it, "I would have probably put Valmik first in the tunnel, then Herald, leaving Makanna outside. You'd get a few yards in, wait for a little while, then Makanna would get in behind you. You'd all move in a group, and Makanna would move backward. Then, when you exited, Makanna is small enough that she can turn around if there is no one behind you. She'd have to use her sword until she was outside so she could turn her spear around, I guess."

Makanna and Valmik looked at each other as they considered and had a short conversation of facial expressions and small movements of the head. I guessed that the conclusion was *Maybe. Might have worked.* That was good enough for me and my ego.

"Other than that," I went on, wanting to conclude on a high note, "I didn't get to see Makanna fight, but your reflexes are great, and you whapped me really hard with one arm. Without your magic, you would have all needed torches or you'd have been blind down there, and I would probably have an infected head wound. Herald, you need practice with that sword, but your archery is great."

"You said my archery was *fire* before," Herald said.

"What? Oh, yeah," I replied. Had I really said that? I'd never said that anything was *fire* before in my life! And it seemed it hadn't come across either. "I meant it's good."

"I guessed," she said. "I just wondered. Is that a dragon thing? Is *fire* how you say *good* in the dragon tongue?"

I had absolutely no idea. "Where I'm from," I said carefully, "*fire* is one of many ways to say that something is good. There's also *dope, goat, Gucci, ace,* uh, *bonza . . .*"

I never used those either, but Herald's eyes shone with interest. "I would love to learn some of the dragon tongue."

I had a brief fantasy of teaching her English Gen Z slang. And why not? Could be funny. "Perhaps some other day," I said, then turned to Valmik. "Valmik, you're a goddamn monster, in the best way. I don't know how many you killed down there, but it was a lot. And if you hadn't moved in when you did in the nest, I would be dead, so thanks for that. I just need to know: How did Makanna get stabbed?"

"The fault was mine," Valmik said, looking at his hands. "Gremlins came up behind us, and she defended us. Others came from the cavern. I engaged, and some slipped by. One stabbed Makanna before we could kill it."

"You went in too far?" I guessed.

"Yes," he said simply. "Normally, Tamor would be right behind me to take care of anything that slipped by. In the excitement, I forgot that he was not."

"I'm guessing you usually go in hard. Your defense was great once you backed up to cover Makanna, though. And that's about all I have to say. I guess . . ." I kind of trailed off.

The others looked uncomfortable, which made sense. It's never fun to have an outsider come in and criticize you, especially when you know for a fact that they're right about at least some things.

"On the bright side," Herald said, "I am almost at a threshold!"

The others perked up. "Really?" Makanna asked. She smiled widely, all of her hurt pride apparently forgotten. "Congratulations! How close?"

"So close, I can almost taste it," Herald answered smugly. "I might get it tonight, and if not, it should not take much to push me through."

"There will be much to celebrate in the coming days," Valmik said with more warmth than I'd heard from him so far. As for me, I was confused. I had a vague idea of what was going on. A *threshold* was what the dragon had called it when I obtained my language comprehension. But I had gotten it from adding to, or rather starting, my hoard of treasure. How did Herald get closer, and how did she know? I had to ask. I didn't care if this put my ignorance on full display; I was too curious.

"That's great, Herald," I said, "I love that for you. One question to you all: How do thresholds work? For humans." I added the last part quickly.

"Well," she said, still basking in our congratulations, "I do not know if it is completely figured out, but it is connected to struggle and adversity."

"Going through something and coming out stronger," Makanna agreed.

"Right," Herald continued. "Fighting and almost dying like we did is an obvious way to get closer, but people have reached thresholds in lots of ways. Facing fear and overcoming it, getting through a long period of mourning or depression or sickness, even learning a skill to the point where you feel like you truly understand it. And then you get an advancement," she concluded happily.

"And the advancements, do you get to pick *anything*, or . . . ?" I asked.

"I think different people can experience it in different ways, but we've all had the same experience, right?" Makanna asked the room. "It's like you can feel a couple different paths, usually two, and you know pretty much where each one leads, and you have to pick one."

"Immediately," Herald cut in with emphasis. "I tried to hold off so I could think it through on my first one and got so sick, I threw up. It got worse from there until I picked one."

"And what did you pick?" I asked.

"Oh, I have two already," Herald said proudly. "Hand-eye coordination and improved sight."

"Herald!" Makanna exclaimed.

"What?" Herald shot back. "She helped us. She very literally saved my life, twice, and yours too, probably. If I can tell anyone outside the family, it is her!"

Makanna looked at me out of the corner of her eye, then back at Herald. "Yes, sure, but still—"

"Ugh, I know," Herald said, crossing her arms. "I should not tell people. Everyone knows that!" She leaned into the wall and lapsed into a sullen silence.

There was an awkward pause. Valmik broke it, saying, "Apologies, Lady Draka. Makanna is only thinking of her sister."

"Yeah, no dramas. I get it," I said. And I did. "If no one knows how far along you are or what you have, they can't be sure how strong you are, yeah? That's important, especially for a young woman like Herald or Makanna. So it's all right. We don't know each other like that. I won't ask either of you if you don't ask me."

It would have been interesting to know, but I had a pretty good idea about Makanna's and Valmik's skills anyway. Makanna had some magic, and Valmik was honestly terrifying with that short sword of his, so he probably had some strength or speed or something else to make him better at fighting. Since I didn't plan on ever fighting either of them, it didn't matter.

"So," I said, wanting to get back on topic. "Where do the paths come from? Like, why do you get certain choices?"

"That situation is similar to thresholds," Valmik said. "It is not known for certain. Deep desires or needs appear to be key. Many attempts have been made to influence which options are available, through meditation or magic, but I know of no repeatable successes."

"Huh. Interesting," I said. "I'll try to think of that next time I reach a threshold. Thanks for the information." So, at least for humans, the subconscious was involved. But what about me? I was still mentally human, but what about the dragon? There had been several choices when I reached that threshold, but did I or the dragon influence the choices more?

While I thought about that, I saw Makanna and Valmik share some looks again. They seemed to reach a conclusion, and Makanna glanced at Herald, who shrugged and looked away. Makanna sighed softly and spoke up.

"Draka," she said, "if you don't mind, there is something else we wanted to talk about. Herald and Valmik say that you mentioned . . . helping each other in the future?"

I perked up at that. "Oh, yeah," I said, trying not to look too eager. "I think that would be good for all of us."

"What did you have in mind?" she asked.

"Well," I said. I'd been thinking about this a lot recently. "I can't enter the city. I mean, I can, but that would be a hell of a situation, yeah? But there's stuff I want from there. So I need people I can trust to help me out." And I wanted some actual friends to talk to, but I didn't want to sound that sad just yet.

"And you offered to help us in exchange?" Makanna continued carefully.

"Sure. You've seen me," I said with some pride. "I can fly and I can fight. And, not to be cute about it, I want gold. Or silver. Maybe precious stones and other things like that. I'll know when I see it."

"So you would essentially—and I'm not trying to insult you," she added hastily, "be available to us as a mercenary?"

"That sounds about right, yeah," I said. "I'd prefer *adventurer*, or maybe *consultant*, I guess. But that's pretty much what I had in mind."

There was another silent conversation. Herald was back in and very clearly in favor of this arrangement, smiling and nodding. Valmik was unreadably thoughtful, and Makanna looked uncertain.

"You understand," Makanna said slowly, "if we were known to be working with, or for, a . . ." She faltered.

"A dragon," I supplied.

"Yes," she said. "A dragon. If we were associated with a dragon, especially us, there would be consequences. We had not heard even a rumor that there was a dragon here. There was talk of a wyvern, but . . . there are legends. I'm sure you know. Dragon worshipers who create secret cults to provide their masters with gold and magic items and . . ." She paused for a moment and glanced at Herald.

Oh God, I thought. *She's going to say* maidens. *She's going to say* maidens, *isn't she?*

"And young women," she concluded.

Ugh. The worst part was that I had no idea how valid this was. Maybe dragons created cults of servants all the time. And I could definitely see the appeal of having a bunch of goons constantly bringing you treasure. But why maidens, specifically? Was there any truth to that at all? Did they mean specifically young, virgin women or just young women? Or any women who were virgins? Why women at all? Did they taste better, or was it a power play based on objectification, telling the men of the city or village that *Ha ha, I can take your stuff*?

I was getting pretty damn mad thinking about it, and I must have showed it on my face because Makanna was sitting back stiffly, her eyes slightly wide and laser-focused as she tried to get as far back from me as she could without actually moving or leaving her chair.

"But we could give it a try!" she said quickly, holding her hands up toward me. "No one has noticed you yet, and we never knew you were here until you showed yourself! I'm sure it'll be fine!"

Was I that scary? I knew that I looked dangerous, but I'd hoped that talking to them might win them over. I wanted these people to like or at least respect me, not fear me.

I looked around. Valmik was like a spring waiting to uncoil, but if he had wanted to make a move, he could have. I'd had my back to him for a while, and his sword was right there, so he clearly didn't want or expect the situation to escalate.

Herald . . . Well, Herald looked excited. Perhaps a little smug at her sister's reaction. It was hard to tell. Either way, I was pretty sure that Herald, at least, wanted to work with me more. I didn't know if it was for money or curiosity about me as a dragon, or because she liked me as a person. Whatever the reason, I liked it.

I tried to relax as completely as I could. Tail curled, claws in, head back. "Listen," I told them. "I don't want to pressure you. I would like to work with you, but I get it if you need to think about it. No hard feelings if you decide not to for whatever reason. Just don't tell anyone about me, yeah? Only a handful of people have seen me, and if you haven't heard any rumors, that means they're keeping quiet." I put a little edge in my voice. I didn't like to, but it felt necessary. "I'd *appreciate it* if you did the same."

"By what way would we contact you, Lady Draka?" Valmik asked after a tense silence.

I'd thought about that and come up with what I thought was a pretty good solution. Very cloak-and-dagger. "A few hours, two or three, I guess, north of the city, there's a side path that leads east to a lake with a campsite. There was a small battle there about not too long ago. Do you know what I'm talking about?"

I saw recognition in Makanna's and Herald's eyes, and Valmik spoke up. "We know of this. A camp of the Gray Wolves company was attacked there by bandits. Only one man from the company survived."

Nothing about a dragon. That was good.

"That's the one," I said. "I visit it every couple days. There is an old tree there, a big, knobby one, that sits alone between the campground and the lake. Hide a piece of silver or gold by the tree. It shouldn't matter if it's a coin or a ring or whatever. I should be able to find it, and I'll know that you're looking for me. Go back there the next day, maybe, and the one after that."

"Oooh," Herald cooed. "Like spies or thieves arranging a secret meeting?"

"Kind of like that," I agreed. I liked Herald. She got me. "Now," I said, getting up, "I'm going back to my tree to sleep. Get the door for me, Herald, would you?"

"Sure," she said, opening it.

I started to go but remembered something. "By the way," I said, turning my head around to look at the two at the table, "did you find any clues as to what happened with the miners?"

"No, not really," Makanna said with a frown. "Valmik had a more thorough look at the buildings while I slept. All the carts and wagons are gone, and the warehouse is empty of ore."

"A mystery for now," Valmik added.

"Creepy," I said. "Well, g'night. Wake me up before you go, will you?"

"Sure," Herald said. As I walked away, it took a few seconds before I heard the door close.

I was pretty sure that I had a fan.

Makanna had been dead-on about the healing. I was getting hungry, but I could handle it. Instead of searching for food, I made my way down to the stream and filled up on water. If I felt like it, I could go hunting the next day.

I got back in my tree. I listened to the rushing water in the distance and the wind off the mountains whispering through the brush. It was so peaceful. My situation was messed up, but it had gotten a tiny bit better, and I started to feel some real hope. Perhaps I could do more than just survive. I could be satisfied, maybe even happy.

As I drifted off, rocked to sleep by the gentle swaying of the tree, I wondered for a moment what had happened to the miners. *Not my problem*, I decided, and then I was asleep.

CHAPTER TWELVE

Anticipation

Draka! Hello? Madam Dragon? Wake up!"

I woke up groggy but thankful. Herald's voice, insistent and unfairly chipper, had rescued me from a terrible dream. I had been back home, with my friends and my mom and dad and my brothers, but everyone was terrified of me. When I tried to talk to them, they'd scream and run or try to hide, and I didn't understand why until I remembered that *Oh, right, I'm a monster now.* And anger kept building in me at the unfairness of it all. I didn't ask for this. This wasn't my fault. I was still the same person; I just looked different. Why couldn't they see that? The anger grew hotter and hotter, until it blossomed into a roaring rage, and I lashed out . . .

I shook the last of the nightmare from my head and climbed down unsteadily.

"Morning, Herald," I told her as I emerged from the tree. "You guys ready to go?"

"We are fed, packed, and ready," she confirmed. "If we get started soon, we should be back in Karakan by sundown before the guild hall closes. If we are lucky."

"Is that who handles the jobs?" I asked as we started back to the building, assuming that she was talking about some kind of mercenaries' or adventurers' guild.

"That is right," Herald answered. "If we are really lucky, we may even be able to get Tam out tonight, though that seems less likely. Still, it would be good to have the coins in hand."

"How much are you getting paid?"

"Two hundred silver eagles," she said a little breathlessly.

"How much is that? How much silver, I mean?"

"It is two hundred . . ." she started with some confusion, before her eyes brightened with comprehension. "Oh, I see. Well, the Karakani eagle is supposed to be one-fortieth of a pound of pure silver, so five pounds, I guess. But you never know. People clip the edges or the mint facility mixes in lead to stretch the silver, and it can be hard to tell unless you know what to look for. Still, an eagle is always an eagle, right? That is the whole point."

I wondered how much she knew about inflation but decided not to sour the mood.

"What about the gold coins?" I asked instead. By then, we had reached the building and were waiting for Makanna and Valmik to come out.

"Dragons? People rarely use those. They are too valuable. A dragon is an eight-ieth of a pound of pure gold and buys a pound of silver, so it's forty eagles to a dragon."

"But two hundred eagles is a lot of money, right?"

"It is," Herald said, nodding. "A laborer might only make an eagle every week, or less if they are unfortunate. Though they would probably rarely see an eagle. They would be paid a few peacocks at the end of each day instead. Those are brass or bronze, depending on the year they were minted. They might even get paid in bits. Those are quarter-peacocks."

"Right," I said, trying to work things out in my head. If I had three and a half kilos of silver in my bags, and the pound here was close to the pound back home, that would be more than they were getting paid! Several years' wages for a simple laborer. I had a fortune around my neck! And if I had nine dragons already, and one dragon was a pound of silver, then I'd nearly double my hoard! I was almost giddy with excitement.

The dragon leaked through more at certain times than others. When treasure was involved it was particularly strong, and I refused to feel bad about it.

"Draka?" Herald said with some concern. "Are you all right? You are rumbling."

"Am I?" I asked. I hadn't noticed anything. Was that a thing I could do? "I was just thinking of something nice."

"Oh," she said. There was a short silence, then she reached out and touched the scales on my healed wound. I was a little surprised, but I didn't make a fuss.

"Your new scales are completely black now," she said. "And very hard." Without warning, she tapped one with a nail. It made a *tik-tik* sound.

"Hey!" I said, pulling my head away and looking at her. She had the good taste to look embarrassed, at least.

"Sorry," she said, glancing away. "I do not know what came over me. I am just . . . happy! We can help Tam, and . . ." She looked at the closed door, then leaned in conspiratorially. "I passed the threshold while I slept." She almost squealed with delight before going on. "I guess processing yesterday was enough to push me through. That happens sometimes," she added, remembering my questions the night before.

"That's great!" I told her. Her joy was infectious, and this was clearly very important to her. "I guess I shouldn't ask—"

"Reflexes!" She answered like she'd been dying for someone to ask. "It is so good," she continued, her excitement taking over and her voice getting faster and higher as she spoke. "And I have never met anyone my age with all three minor advancements. At this rate, in a year I should get my next one, and that will be a *major!*"

She squeaked the last word, and I grinned at her, hoping that I looked suitably happy for her instead of terrifying. She took it in stride.

"Tell me all about it when you do, yeah?" I told her. Then the door opened, and Herald pulled herself together as Makanna and Valmik brought out their packs.

"Morning," I told them.

"Good morning to you, uh, madam," Makanna said.

Ugh, why the sudden formality? I wondered.

"Are you here to see us off?"

"Yeah, if you think you'll be all right on the road," I told them. "I could always follow you among the trees, just in case."

"Our thanks, Lady Draka," Valmik said, and he sounded like he meant it. "But there is no need for you to trouble yourself."

"Sure? You'd never know I was there," I added. I'm not sure why I decided to be so creepy about it. Maybe just to see Makanna's reaction?

She blanched. "There really is no need, madam," Makanna said. "Thank you for the offer."

I must have really scared her the night before. Oh well. It would have been nice to talk to them some more, but I couldn't exactly walk with them openly.

"Well, then I guess I'll be going," I told them. "Good luck with Tamor. Really. And think about my offer, all right?"

"That is assured, Lady Draka," Valmik said and inclined his head.

"Right. See y'all later."

With that, I turned around, took a few running steps, and launched myself into the air. I climbed sharply to above treetops, taking in the fresh air and the delicious smell of pine. My necklace threw my balance off a little, so I felt it out, figuring out how to compensate before turning in a big circle and heading back over the mining camp northward, toward my cave.

"Goodbye, Draka!" I heard Herald's voice, faint in the distance, and I smiled. I wasn't sure about the others, but I had a feeling I'd be seeing her again. I hoped that I would, anyway. The tall, dark-skinned girl didn't remind me of myself at her age at all, but she had a good vibe and I liked her.

Unfortunately, Makanna clearly didn't want anything to do with me. I wasn't sure why. She'd been friendly enough when she fixed my wounds, but as soon as

I'd started talking about teaming up in the future, she'd gone cold. Fair enough, but I wished I knew why.

I didn't want to give them directions to my cave, Makanna especially, so I initially headed away at an angle from the mountains, staying low over the treetops. The mine lay in a high, U-shaped valley that cut west through the mountains, and once I was out over the forest proper, I took a turn to look back. That valley, I realized, was one of the landmarks I'd been using to navigate, perhaps half an hour from home on the wing. *I should go back sometime soon*, I decided. There was sure to be more silver. After all, we had never looked in the gremlins' shelters, and there were always what the gremlins had on themselves. If they didn't run away into the mountains, of course.

I messed with some birds on the way just for the hell of it. Maybe it was mean, but I didn't actually hurt any of them. I wasn't sure that I could, what with the way they dodged, but it was fun to see their flocks break apart when I dove through them and to hear the indignant quacks and squawks of ducks and geese as I overtook them in the air. But soon I saw the crack high on the side of a mountain, the ledge with its scraggly grass and malnourished little tree, and behind it the entrance to my cave. It was strange. I hadn't picked the place. I hadn't done anything with it to spruce it up. But landing there felt like coming home just the same. I felt that something terrible, or possibly wonderful, had happened to me there. I wasn't sure which. For that matter, I still wasn't sure if this was real at all. But either way, I felt safe there—completely. I could relax and not worry about anything . . . except possibly little bat-faced monsters tunneling in and trying to steal my stuff. But even that felt like a very distant possibility, and I knew in my bones that if my hoard was threatened, I would know.

So I didn't worry. I went inside, left the bag with the tinderbox near my sleeping spot, and made my way down, beyond the daylight and into the depths where the only light came from the slime on the walls. I squeezed through the crevice. In the dark, I found the box with the gold coins—dragons, I reminded myself and smiled—right where I had left it. I ran my hand over them and heard them tinkle softly in the darkness. Then I took off my necklace, and, one by one, I used a claw to cut the strings that fixed the bags to the rope and emptied them all around the wooden box.

The pile it made was small, but the contentment I felt was enormous.

CHAPTER THIRTEEN

New Toys

Y*our hoard has grown!"* my own, human voice purred in my ear as I lay down, resting my head on my treasures. I smiled. I had thought that this might happen. *"A second minor threshold has been reached. How will you increase your power?"*

This was different from what the humans had described. They got only vague sensations. I got a voice spelling things out for me.

"Strength, to overwhelm your enemies. Fortitude, to shrug off harm. Physical greatness, to increase the power of your body in all ways—at a cost. Stealth, to strike unseen. Cunning, to plot and see through the schemes of others. Choose!"

Huh. Same choices as last time, except tongues had been replaced with a new one. Knowing that it would only be moments before the pain came, I went with my gut. I had almost died against the gremlin chief, so: "Fortitude!" I whispered into the darkness. The dragon inside me rumbled with contentment, and as it did, I felt a crawling sensation over every part of my body, not only my skin but my eyes and even the inside of my mouth. It lingered, then passed. I guessed my skin must have changed in some way, but I couldn't tell in the darkness.

"Good," the dragon whispered with obvious pleasure. *"A third minor threshold has been reached. How will you increase your power?"*

This was *not* something I had expected. I must have been very close to the second threshold and barely made it over the third one. That was great!

"Strength, to overwhelm your enemies. Greater fortitude, to weather all but the mightiest blows. Physical greatness, to increase the power of your body in all ways—at a cost. Stealth, to strike unseen. Cunning, to plot and see through the schemes of others. Choose!"

Okay, think fast, I told myself. I'd just picked fortitude. Strength and physical greatness? Nice, sure, but not what I needed. Cunning? Plotting and scheming? Not my thing. No, I needed to stay hidden and be able to evade detection if anyone came for me.

"Stealth," I said, and I felt another tingle across my body, not as unpleasant as the first one but still weird. I could feel my wings change a little, and the pads of my hands and feet became more sensitive. Where before I had only felt cold stone, now I felt dampness in some places, grit and dust in others. To help choose my footing when moving stealthily, I assumed.

I stayed there for a while longer, luxuriating in the presence of my treasures, but my curiosity grew too strong and I soon returned to the light. With my increased sensitivity, my footing was surer than it had ever been on the damp stone, and when I looked at the backs of my hands in the dim light, I could tell that they were not simply pits of blackness like they had been before. Instead, the edges looked a little fuzzy, the color more like a deep shadow against the background than a black object. I could easily see how that would help, and I couldn't wait to try it out.

It just so happened that I was hungry. I had always imagined dragons hunting with fire from the air. Well, I didn't have any fire, but I did have venom that could choke many creatures to death, or at least blind and confuse them. Now that I knew how to use it reliably, I had thought of two ways to use it. The first was like I'd imagined: fly in and, instead of fire, spray venom. That seemed tricky. The problem was that in order for the venom to actually take anything out, I needed to be pretty accurate, and doing that while flying, against a target that might have seen me coming and was trying to avoid me, would probably require a lot of practice. Like, *a lot* a lot.

The other strategy was perhaps how I was *supposed* to hunt. I was a different kind of dragon than the *Lord of the Rings*–style ones I was used to. I was pretty small, I could hide well, I had a great sense of smell, and I had venom. I was pretty much a mix between a snake and a large cat. That meant that I should stalk and ambush prey, and that was what I was going to try to do.

I had tried before, during my days of starvation, but had failed miserably. I just didn't have the speed and agility that a cat had to pounce on prey in hiding. At least, I didn't back then. But I shouldn't need them. I had my venom spray, and with one good hit from that, it was game over. All I needed to do was to find a likely prey animal and wait. When it got close enough, it would be *Hiss, spray,* and dinner was served.

At least, that was the plan, anyway. In practice, it took ages. I flew around some and found a likely place to the north. The forest was less dense there, with many meadows and mostly smaller trees surrounded by thick undergrowth. Landing in the tall grass, I listened carefully and breathed deeply, trying to find any sign of a deer or a pig or even a rabbit. When I didn't find anything, I started prowling around, sniffing, until finally I smelled something . . . stinky, to be honest. Whatever it was, it smelled very much like a dirty animal, and that was all I could say about it.

The smell came on the breeze, so I moved upwind, tracking it as silently as I could. The stealth advancement made itself useful here. My newly sensitive hands and feet helped greatly, allowing me to feel sticks and the like before I put my weight on down and risked snapping them. I had also noticed, while flying, that the beat of my wings made noticeably less noise. When I glided, I was almost completely silent. Hell, maybe I *could* have hunted from the air after all. I'd have to try those damn smug mountain goats in the high passes again sometime.

For now, though, I was focused on the pig or deer or whatever it was I'd smelled. I kept creeping closer until I heard a snuffling and bushes or some other plant being broken. Whatever this was, it sounded pretty big, and I doubted that it was something I wanted to take on. I wasn't *that* hungry. But I had gone this far, and I was curious.

The smell was strong now, and the sounds loud. I crept into the shadow of a large tree, noting with satisfaction how well I blended in. To anything looking at me, I would just be a deeper patch of shadow as long as I stood still. Sure, they'd see my outline if they looked too carefully, but this newfound camouflage should hide me from anything that wasn't intently searching for me.

Keeping low to the ground, I snaked my head around the trunk of the tree and froze. There, in a glade, was a bear. She was bigger than any grizzly, or at least I thought as much. I had never actually seen a grizzly, or any bear at all, but she was, to put it in simple terms, fucking huge. She was calmly tearing into what looked like a blackberry bramble, munching up juicy berries and thorny stems, leaves and all. I wanted nothing to do with her and would have made myself scarce immediately, but she had cubs! Two adorably fat, fuzzy cubs that were bigger than I was, playing clumsily, occasionally taking a chomp of the bramble before getting distracted by a passing butterfly or each other. They were so cute! I risked life and limb hiding in the shadow the best I could while suppressing my giggles just to watch them bumble around.

The dragon wanted to try to eat one. The dragon was a heartless idiot, because even if I did lose enough of my soul to hurt one of the fluff balls, the mama bear looked like she could tear my neck from my body with barely any effort, fortitude or no. And I was pretty sure that I'd once heard David Attenborough say that bears can run as fast as a horse. Now, maybe that was someone else, or maybe I'd read it somewhere. But the point stood: don't fuck with bears unless you're completely sure that you'll win.

After some time, I reluctantly had to admit that I'd indulged myself for long enough, and I snuck off. I went so far as to fly to another meadow some kilometers away, on the assumption that anything with half a brain would put a lot of distance between themselves and Mount Teddy. The second meadow was a bust. In the third, I found a boar, but it noticed me and fucked right off. In the fourth, though, I caught a new scent, and I followed it back to a lone, small-antlered deer.

It was nibbling grass and leaves off little trees and bushes, and I had a good feeling about it. I mean, I felt bad too, but I suppressed that. I was hungry, and I have always liked venison.

I slid into the shadow of a thick bush full of young leaves and waited. It took a while, but sure enough, the deer slowly made its way around the small open space to the bush. It was less than a meter from me, and I could see it clearly through the stems, when it stopped and sniffed the air. It didn't seem immediately concerned but leaned in closer, sniffing carefully in my direction.

I gave it a face full of venom. Even through the bush, I hit it almost full-on, and it reared back with a weird barking noise, then turned and ran blindly. I exploded after it. It was faster than me, but that didn't matter. It kept hitting things, tripping, then getting up, and it hadn't made a sound since that first bark. It couldn't have taken more than twenty seconds before I saw it stumble and fall far ahead of me. As I closed in, it tried to stand but couldn't. It had used up all its oxygen, and when I reached it, its mouth was frothing, the tongue sticking out almost obscenely. Except for an occasional twitch, it lay still.

First, I tore its throat out with my teeth, hoping that I got both veins and arteries. The poor thing was dead in seconds, or at least completely unconscious. Then I dug in—no hesitation. I was still planning to try cooking meat over a fire, but I had learned that, with a dragon's tongue and nose, hot, raw meat was delicious. I had the tinderbox. I'd bring some wood home with me and experiment. But not until I had eaten my own weight in fresh deer meat.

When I had eaten so much that my jaw and throat were exhausted and I was feeling suitably sick and bloated, I decided that returning to the cave was not going to happen. It was only barely the afternoon, but I was not flying anywhere today in my state. Drawing on my pleasant experience at the mine, I found a huge old broad-leaved tree of some kind and climbed it. High in the branches, I settled in to a spot where I could securely lay with all four limbs hanging free and no fear of falling. I wrapped my tail around a smaller branch, laid my head on my back, and covered myself with my wings. Moments later, I was out.

CHAPTER FOURTEEN

Disappointment

I spent the rest of that day and all of the next one drifting in and out of sleep. It rained heavily during the first night. I woke briefly, enjoying the smell of my first rain here, but between the twin canopies of the tree and my wings, I stayed comfortably dry and soon dozed off again. I dreamed, some good, some bad, but nothing that stayed with me. Birds and other scavengers came and picked the deer carcass clean, and I magnanimously let them. I was full beyond what should be possible, and what was left was more trouble than it was worth. It made several decent meals for the crows and foxes, though.

At one point, a large boar passed right under the tree. If I hadn't been exhausted from digesting my meal, I could have just dropped on it from my perch. Easy-peasy piggy-squeezy. I made a note to try to remember that for next time.

The boar made me think of Lahnie. I thought again how she was doing and decided that I should go check on Pine Hill in the next few days. I wondered if saving someone always made you feel responsible for them. The dragon disagreed, but since it had wanted to eat Lahnie, it didn't get a vote.

Sometime before noon on the third day, my stomach had settled enough that I figured I could make it back to the cave. I felt considerably less bloated and heavy, though it would probably be another day or two before I was fit to really do any-thing again. I still had no idea where all the food actually went, but that was not really a concern at the time. What I did know was that I had eaten most of two medium-size animals in the last two weeks or so, which added up to several kilos of meat per day on average. I really hoped that was not representative of how much I was supposed to be choking down.

Getting airborne was hard. Not just harder than usual, but properly difficult. I needed some initial height to be able to flap my wings to full effect, and I was too damn fat and heavy to jump the way I had gotten used to doing. After a few failed attempts, I resorted to wandering around, looking for something to jump off. It took half an hour or so, but I found a large rock next to a gully that looked promising. It was significantly harder to climb the rock than the tree I had slept in since I couldn't sink my claws in, but I made it. I got up, walked to the edge, and leaped.

Of course I miscalculated and had to spread my wings wide to slow myself before I hit the ground. *Right.* After another arduous climb, I stood at the top again, and this time I started beating my wings as hard as I could the instant I leaped. I was well and truly cranky at this point, but finally I was airborne.

This, I decided, was a mistake. Getting home was possibly the most exhausting thing I had ever done, in this body or my previous one, and I hated every second of it. I hated flying. That's how damn bloated I was.

When at long last I landed on the ledge in front of my lair, I kind of skidded to a halt and lay there for a while. I wasn't hurt or anything, just utterly exhausted. The sun and the mountain air felt nice. Very nice. In fact, it felt so nice that instead of dragging my gluttonous butt into the cave, I turned around and dragged it to the edge. There, I curled up, looking out over the forest, and went to sleep.

It rained again that night. I didn't even wake up. I only knew because when I woke up in the morning, I had my wings up over me, and I could smell the hot, wet stone around me. I stretched languidly. How many days had I slept away? Two and most of a third? I felt pretty good, though still very full. Three or four days seemed to be how long it took me to completely deal with a large meal. There was still the question of where it all went, but magic was probably involved, considering I could fly the way I did with wings that were way too small, pronounce everything in any language properly with a snout full of sharp teeth, and learn things and improve my body by collecting loot. That, or I had a black hole or a portal to another dimension in my gut.

No. If that were the case, I wouldn't have to deal with half-hour visits to the little dragon's room. Or the bushes, as the case might be. If only.

I didn't want to sleep another day away, though I easily could have. After a visit to the hoard, I was again in the air, my destination Pine Hill. I had no idea if I'd be able to find Lahnie, but even if I could, I didn't intend to talk to her. I just wanted to check on the place and make sure that everything looked okay.

I started at the lake, landing a little ways off just in case but finding no one there when I approached the campsite. I checked the tree where I'd found Guy but didn't smell anything interesting. *Oh well.* It had only been a few days since I left the adventurers, so even if they were interested it was no surprise that they hadn't left me any signs yet. I'd check again later.

I didn't remember exactly where the village was, but that was fine. I still knew how to find it. I found the stream I had been following when I first heard Lahnie and took a moment to wash myself, getting rid of the accumulated dust and crusty deer blood that still lingered on my head and neck. I followed the burbling water upstream, staying in the shadows and sniffing the air for the scent of boar, which I thought I could recognize. After a while, I could hear axes echoing in the distance, and I soon reached the road and the stone bridge that led to the village.

Pine Hill was a small place by my standards, though I had no idea of how it measured up to other villages in the forest. I walked in a large circle to get a sense of it. Two dozen or so houses crowded around the road and the smaller side paths that led off in different directions, with a few more cottages placed farther away. I guessed that maybe thirty or forty families lived there, working the forest and the small fields and pastures that had been cleared around the village. The pastures held a few shaggy cows, but mostly birds that looked like big turkeys. The birds sometimes hopped onto the fence surrounding their pasture but did not seem at all interested in fleeing into the forest, and I figured the fences were there to keep other things out.

A handful of the homes in the village doubled as workshops, and the preferred style seemed to be to have one wall that could be opened completely, with another wall and a door separating it from the rest of the house. I saw a few people moving around, but all of the workshops were busy with one or two people in each making wooden crafts. Curious, I crept closer, daring to go so far as to sit in some tall grass in the shadow of one of the houses. I saw stacks of wooden trays, plates and cups, little figurines that might have been religious, decorative, or toys, for all I knew, and in one of the workshops, I saw Lahnie. She was sitting patiently on a small wooden stool, her hands gripping the edges, rocking back as she watched an old man with rapt attention. The old man was carving a round piece of wood the size of a dinner plate. A section of a younger tree, perhaps. Using various tools, sometimes helped by a small hammer, he cut away small curls of wood while he talked in a low, cheerful voice. I couldn't make out any words, but Lahnie would sometimes answer with am *Mm-hmm* or *Uh-huh*, completely fascinated by the process.

I wondered if he was a granddad or just a kindly old man who'd offered to keep an eye on the girl. Maybe she'd be his apprentice? She seemed to be interested in what he was doing, but she was also a little kid, so who knew how long that would last?

Whatever the case may be, I was satisfied. The mood in the village was peaceful, Lahnie looked healthy and happy, and I didn't smell the monster pig anywhere. I'd come back some other day when I had nothing to do. For now, I had fire to make!

After hours of trying, I came to the depressing conclusion that making fire was not going to happen. At least not with the shitty little pieces of rock I had available in the tinder box that I'd taken off the gremlins.

I had dragged a considerable amount of wood with me up the mountain. That hadn't been so bad. Finding mostly dry wood had been easy, and I had picked two large pieces that I could grip with my hands and feet. Flying with them had been a little awkward but not a huge deal. I knew that I needed various sizes of wood besides the tinder in the box to start a fire, so I'd used my claws to shave off the wet outer part of the dead branches and laid them to dry in the sun while I broke up the rest. That was a frustrating fucking job with no tools, but I managed. Then, working off some half-remembered descriptions and my memories of, like, two YouTube videos, I got to work.

The only stumbling block that mattered was my hands. I had set everything up right, as far as I could tell, but I couldn't hold the two pieces the way I needed to. The problem was my claws. Not directly. They weren't in the way, and my stealth advancement even let me pull them in completely. The issue was that I had retractable claws at all, and that apparently made my fingers too damn clumsy to do anything with the aforementioned shitty little pieces of rock. I was basically all thumbs, with the last knuckle of each finger controlling the claw. I couldn't hold the things in a way that allowed me to strike a spark. I had tried. I honestly didn't know. I had experimented with different ways of holding each piece and looked at them from every angle, I just couldn't do it.

I really wanted this even though I didn't *need* fire. I wasn't cold, and I could see well in the dark. I didn't even mind eating my food raw anymore. I honestly didn't know why this was so important to me.

"C'mon," I muttered as I tried for about the millionth time to strike the things together. I accidentally smacked the flint into my finger, but I didn't care at that point. It didn't do any damage anyway.

"Come. On!" I was growling as I tried again and again. "Stupid fucking . . ." I was pretty much smashing my fists together now. "Spark, you little shits! Make a goddamn spark!" I felt my eyes burning, I was so frustrated. "Why won't you make a fucking—AH!"

With a scream, I turned and hurled the things at a nearby wall. As they hit, the piece of fool's gold sparked, and that really set me off.

"You think that's funny?" I roared at the little piece of stone. I scrambled over to where it lay glinting in the sun and scooped it up.

"You think you're fucking clever, you little shit?" I screamed at my own hand. On it, I could see saliva speckling the dust. "Fuck! You!"

I hurled the fool's gold off the ledge, then found the flint and threw that into the void too. I kicked the little pile of tinder and splintered wood a few times for good measure, scattering it across the ledge. Sobbing with rage, I ranted incoherently.

When I finally calmed down, just a little bit, I fled into the cave, finding my way down to my hoard on autopilot. There, with my head resting on the most important thing in the world, I cried myself to sleep and prayed—actually, literally prayed—that I would wake up in a hospital bed.

I felt a little better when I woke up later. At least, I didn't feel so damn sorry for myself anymore. But I still wanted, so bad, to feel human. I wanted to go drink stupid sugary coffee with my friends and post climbing reels on Instagram just to show off and teach some newbies how to grip and balance properly. I wanted to cuddle under a blanket with Andrea while bingeing Netflix, and I wanted to go to a club and get drunk and dance and maybe meet some cute guy and have meaningless, stupid sex just because it felt good.

I wanted to be able to just start talking to some stranger and at worst get a brush-off and a dirty look.

But I couldn't because I was a monster, and the only way I could have a conversation was if the other person was too scared to tell me to fuck off.

When I got back to the ledge, it was morning. Again. Another day to fill, to try to keep my mind off how much of a mess everything was, but with nothing to do.

"*Hunt!*" the dragon suggested. *Shut up*, I thought back. *I just ate a whole Bambi.*

"*Then lay waste this pathetic Pine Hill and take their treasures for your own!*" the dragon insisted.

"No!" I said, out loud this time. "We're not doing that!"

Oh shit, was I having a conversation with myself? Or with my other half or whatever? Was I that desperate for company? Literally talking to myself?

"*Then at least fly for the joy of it!*" the dragon grumbled. "*This wallowing is a disgrace to what we are.*"

Great. I was listening to myself telling myself how pathetic I was. "You know what? Fine!"

I took a few running strides and leaped off the ledge as far out as I could and allowed myself to plummet. I had a brief moment of stupidity and considered just letting myself fall, but then I came back to my senses, opening my wings with a snap and turning my suicide dive into a soaring rise.

Stupid dragon. The damn thing had no right to be so right; I felt better already. All the things I missed were still there in the back of my mind, but as long as I focused on the rushing air and stunning views, I could keep a smile on my face. I might not be able to snap my fingers anymore, but at least I had this.

I decided to take a trip over to the mine. Unfortunately, it looked as if someone had reoccupied the place while I spent several days digesting a year's worth of meat. As I sat among the rocks overlooking the mining camp, I could see horses posted and a handful of people walking between the buildings and the mine entrance. They all looked armed and armored, so my guess was that mercenaries had been sent to secure the mine now that the tricky job of killing the nest was taken care of.

That was annoying. But I still wanted to get in there before anyone else got to the nest and the silver that might be there, so I'd have to try finding another entrance. There had been tunnels leading up from the chamber with the pond, I recalled. Unfortunately, that left me with approximately the whole local mountain range to search.

Since I had nothing to do and didn't want to have too much time on my hands to think, I gave it a shot and flew around looking for caves. I found a few shallow openings in the rock, but nothing deep. Every so often, I'd land and take a sniff, hoping to pick up the scent of either silver or a gremlin, but all I detected were goats and a bear or two. That was, until I smelled death.

The smell of death is unmistakable. It's comprised of two chemicals, cadaverine and putrescine—I learned that because I thought the words were funny. To a human, they're absolutely vomit-inducing, but to me as I was now, they were simply interesting. I followed the scent, thinking I'd find another goat that had taken a spill or something like that. What I found instead was the bloated corpse of a man.

The poor bastard lay in the middle of a shallow rising valley leading farther into the mountains. I had no idea how long he'd been lying there, but there were way more maggots than even the dragon wanted to deal with. I let him be, not even wanting to check if he had anything valuable on him. When I looked around the area, though, I found unmistakable wheel tracks, and around them were lots of hoof and boot prints. A whole bunch of people must have come through here.

I looked down the valley, then I took off to confirm my suspicions. I was right: You could definitely get here from the mine without much effort. I turned back and followed the tracks in the other direction. The valley narrowed to a point, but before that, the tracks turned off toward the mountainside. There, hidden behind what looked like a rockslide, I found something: A rectangular trough, a couple meters long on one side, had been cut into the stone. It looked a bit like a small quarry, with straight sides and tool marks like you'd expect. Nothing remarkable, but in the back, there was a gate.

The rock wall was straight and slightly rough. To anyone else, it would have looked like nothing more than a place where people had cut stone blocks; there wasn't even so much as a crack in the rock. But I could see bright lines of magical light running straight and at right angles across the face of the stone. There was no decoration, nothing fancy. No riddle in flowing elvish script. Just lines marking a huge rectangle split vertically in the middle. It was definitely a gate. I had no doubt, especially since the dust was disturbed in two sweeping arcs from the center out to the edges of the trough and the tracks ended at the stone face.

Unfortunately, I couldn't see or think of any way of opening the thing. I ran a claw across the stone at the center, and it skittered right over the glowing line. I didn't feel anything, and nothing happened. Getting in on my own was not happening. But this . . . this was something interesting. Something to keep my mind busy.

I remembered how surprised Makanna and the others had been that the mining camp was deserted, and how it looked like everyone had just walked out. Missing miners. Tracks that lead here. To a massive stone gate. This all must mean something.

I needed Herald and the others.

CHAPTER FIFTEEN

Hurry Up and Wait

For the next six days, I fell into a routine. I'd check the lake, then I'd check on Pine Hill. Sometimes I'd hang out by the road and people watch or go creep on a different village. Sometimes I'd head back to the mysterious gate in the mountain. Nothing ever happened, but the people of the forest became anxious as the days passed, turning to the mountains with worried expressions as they spoke in hushed tones among themselves.

I saw Lahnie a few times, sitting with the old wood carver or helping adults with various tasks. Once I saw her just stand and look out into the forest, and I wondered if she was thinking about me. I couldn't help it. I made sure that no one else could see me, then uncurled from where I was hiding and waved to her.

Her giant grin and happy wave back warmed my heart. They really did.

While people watching, I could clearly see the signs of advancements now that I knew about them. They'd been there before, I guess, but I'd probably dismissed them as one-offs. But now things made sense. People living in small villages in the forest probably went through all kinds of crap. I saw a wrinkly, crooked old lady easily splitting wood for what felt like an hour, stack most of it, then load up a sack as big as she was. She threw it on her back without the slightest sign of effort and brought it inside her home. Nothing off about that. She had a strength advancement, or maybe two. And some endurance, probably. Being strong must be very useful when you're a peasant, or whatever these people would call themselves.

Two men carrying a giant tree through the village by themselves? Same thing. A woman hemming a dress with the speed and precision of a sewing machine? A speed advancement, perhaps dexterity.

I didn't see any little kids doing anything extraordinary, but Herald had been incredibly smug about having three advancements at her age, so I guessed most people didn't get any at all until they grew up a bit. Maybe there was a level of maturity needed first. I saw a boy who looked maybe ten years old turning a grindstone without complaint while his dad, or maybe his uncle, sharpened axes and knives and shovels and stuff like that, so he must have had an advancement for endurance. Or maybe patience.

What would that do to a society and an economy? What about technology? Why would you bother developing something like a sawmill when two specialized men could work a saw all day, cutting trees just as quickly and cleanly as any machine? People still used wagons, but who would ever bother building an engine when someone with the right advancements could pull a heavy wagon while jogging? They may not get the same effect, and it may not benefit as many people, but would anyone bother trying to solve a problem that didn't even exist in their eyes? Sure, carts drawn by animals were way more common than hand carts, but that was because people didn't want to pull their own wagons, not because they couldn't.

With everything I saw, I was surprised that in all those days I didn't see anyone using magic, or at least none that I could recognize. I thought I should be able to see the glow, but I hadn't. Either there was magic that I couldn't see or it was rarer than Makanna had made me believe.

This was going to be hard to get used to.

Despite all that, the most interesting thing that happened was that I saw Guy again. He and his girlfriend were riding with some others who I assumed were mercenaries from their company, and I followed along. They looked tense, so I figured something must be wrong. They set their eyes sharply on the forest surrounding them and kept talking to a minimum. Every so often, Guy's girlfriend would signal one of the other riders, and they would go into the forest for a short while before returning. But nothing happened, and when they reached a village on the road, they stopped and rested. Then they headed back toward Karakan, and I went back to the gate. I wanted to talk to Guy, but I was not crazy enough to do it when he was surrounded by armed, nervous people.

On the seventh day, as I made my daily visit to the lake, I found a small silver earring pinned to a crevice on a tree. I dug it out and, lacking pockets, put it in my mouth. I washed myself and filled up on water, as I usually did, and then took off to go to the stone doors again. I had a good feeling about that day, sure that something would happen.

That feeling lasted until I rose above the trees and saw smoke. A tall, dark cloud rose from the forest in a long, low valley far west of Pine Hill. Always too curious for my own good, I headed straight for it.

From the air, I saw a village in flames. It wasn't one I had visited before, but it was heartbreaking all the same. Landing nearby and quickly sneaking up to where the forest ended and a clearing began, I could see some people desperately trying to salvage houses that were beyond saving. Others stood around, watching in shock as their homes burned.

In the village square, in front of the largest home, a woman screamed out her grief. There were two bodies on the square in front of her. She hugged a third to her chest, a small form that hung limply in her arms. A few people clustered around her in silent support, but what could they do? Their village was gone. The woman's family, presumably, was dead. I wondered what could have possibly caused this, and then I started to see the signs. It had been so foreign to me that it hadn't even registered it.

Some people were hurt, but not because of the fire. They'd been beaten. All their homes were burning at once. That didn't just happen by accident. And then I saw the blood. I hadn't smelled it because of the smoke, but it was there, around the dead bodies in the square and on the grieving woman and the child she held. Her torn dress was soaked in it. There was so much blood. Her family hadn't died from the fire. They'd been killed.

Someone had attacked this village and torched it. They had killed three people. One of the victims was a child. My mind went numb at the realization. I felt like I should be sick, but my body didn't react at all. The dragon didn't care. It just watched.

I understood what people had been so nervous about all these days and why the mercenaries on the road had been so tense. I knew what this was. I'd heard about it. There were bandits in the forest. They robbed travelers and extorted villages. That's why the mercenaries were here. Bandits had even attacked Guy and his people when they were camped by the lake.

And now they had burned down a village. I thought of Pine Hill and Lahnie, and my gut clenched.

I was angry. No, I was properly pissed off. I had been furious before, but that had mostly been the dragon. This time, it was a completely human fury, a moral outrage at the injustice and stupid cruelty of what I saw, and at how impotent I was to do fuck all to help.

But maybe I could do *something*.

This must have happened very recently. There hadn't been any smoke when I flew out to the lake this morning, and I hadn't taken that long checking on Pine Hill.

There was a small road leading from the burning village. I could see fresh hoofprints in the dirt. Not caring if I was spotted, I took to the air. I followed the small road north to a larger east-west one that would eventually join the main road to Karakan. Horse tracks led toward the mountains, so that was where I went, flying low and fast and watching the road for any sign of riders.

I found none. Landing, I confirmed there were still fresh tracks on the road. I continued in short bursts of flight, where I alternated searching from the sky, then checking the road. On one landing, there were no tracks.

Right.

I backtracked until I found tracks again, then went forward until they disappeared. In one place, there was a confusion of tracks, as though the horses had milled around for a while. I looked around but didn't see any signs of where they might have gone. So I used my nose. There was a strong animal scent here, hopefully the horses'. I sniffed around the edges of the road.

Jackpot! The scent led to a narrow path that went into, the forest. It was hidden by thick overhanging bushes and led northwest toward the mountains. I had accepted that I wasn't going to catch the bastards, so I stayed low and slow, stalking through the forest as I followed both the trail and my nose. I followed that damn track for ages. I couldn't go both fast and sneakily, so I chose sneakily. I got into the foothills proper, and they were more densely forested than farther south, so staying hidden was easy. I lost the smell of horse after a while and had to rely on the visible tracks, but then the scent picked up again, this time with new smells: unwashed humans and smoke.

The bandits had good taste in dwellings, at least. The hills were terraced, consisting of diagonal bands of naked rock bearing small trees and scrubby brush, and at their base, the bandits had turned a natural cave with a large overhang into an improvised fort, with a wall of wooden stakes surrounding it. Naked rock walls extended on each side for as far as I could see, making it tricky to circle the place, and they had cleared away the trees for about fifty meters around the wall. As far as I could tell, it was a solid hideout, well hidden and defensible. The only way in without going through the gate was if you could come down from the overhang somehow, or if you could fly.

I could smell cooking fires roasting meat, as well as unwashed people and sweaty horses. There were voices, lots of them, both men and women, many of them laughing cheerfully together. It all felt very wrong after what they'd done. The atmosphere should have been oppressive, the laughter hard and cruel. They had destroyed a village and abused its people, killing at least three of them. Why were they happy? How dare they after what they had done? It just didn't fit into my understanding of the world.

But the dragon understood them. I was sure of that, but it stayed quiet.

I wanted to get closer so I could get a head count and listen in on them, but the risk was too great. My fury was long gone, I was sure that they'd have guards, and there was no way I could take them all on. I wasn't even sure if I could bring myself to kill a human if it came to it. But I had to do something. I'd make sure they didn't hurt anyone else ever again. There would be, if not justice, then retribution.

Wiping these bastards out was the mercs' job. So I needed to let the mercs know where they were, and that again brought me back to Herald and the gang. Luckily, they already wanted to see me. I would just have to hope that the villains would be satisfied for a few days and didn't torch any more villages before I could do anything.

Before I left for the lake, I got some distance away and leaped back in the air. I did my best to remain unseen and memorized all the nearby landmarks I could. Then I made my way back to the road where the path branched off and did the same, and again where that road joined the main road to Karakan. Like hell I was going to forget how to find the hideout, and with any luck, I'd even be able to describe how to get there. I tried as hard as I could until I was sure that I couldn't get it down any better, and only then did I head out to wait for my meeting with the adventurers.

CHAPTER SIXTEEN

Cloak-and-Dagger

It was well into the afternoon when I reached the lake. I approached from the forest, but the campsite was empty like it always was. In fact, I had not seen a single person there since meeting Guy. That was . . . three weeks ago, maybe? Keeping track of time with no calendar or schedule was hard.

For most of the shoreline, the forest grew right up to the edge, with the cleared part near the camp being the exception. A lone tree where I'd met Guy was large enough that it had been spared—out of respect or because it was too much of a hassle to cut it down, who could tell? There was no one there, anyway, so I settled in among the trees, in the ferns and other undergrowth that grew thick near the water. There I curled up and dozed off.

I could only hope that they'd show up and that I hadn't missed them. We hadn't said anything about what time to meet, after all, but Herald and I seemed to have the same idea about this cloak-and-dagger stuff, and I thought that we'd understood each other. When else could we meet but at night? Where was the drama in meeting while the sun was still up?

I woke to moonlight and the sound of horse's hooves. In the dark, I could see a single rider approaching, tall and wearing a hood that hid their face in deep shadow. They rode up to the tree and dismounted, then uncovered a lantern and started inspecting the bark right where the earring had been. As she turned, I could see her face clearly. It was Herald. Of course it was, I thought. I wasn't sure why she had come alone, or if I approved of the risk, but if only one of those three was going to come, it would be her.

After finding the earring gone, Herald let the horse wander while she sat down against the trunk of the tree, looking out across the lake. I considered messing with her but decided that was a bad idea. She looked nervous enough as it was, and I was determined not to screw this up.

So instead, I rose from the ferns with a rustle. Herald's head snapped around, and she half rose into something like a sprinter's stance, her hand on the handle of her short sword.

"Hello, Herald," I said, stepping out of the darkness.

Herald visibly relaxed. "Oh, good," she said with a relieved sigh. "Hello, Draka."

"I was starting to wonder, you know," I said. "Where are the others?"

Herald looked back the way she had come, her face scrunching a little, as though she was worried about getting caught doing something she wasn't supposed to. "They do not know that I am here," she said.

"Makanna?" I asked.

"And Tamor," she confirmed.

"How is he?" I asked, more to be polite than because I actually cared.

"All went as well as we could have hoped," she said, her worry shifting into a smile. "We could not get him out the same night, but first thing in the morning, we paid his fine and the fee for his license. He is unharmed but thin, of course. They do not feed you well in the cells."

"A happy reunion, huh?"

"Yes, especially him and Val. They were . . . I am happy Mak and I have a room across the hall and not wall-to-wall with theirs," she said, and I could see her darken in a blush even in the lantern light.

"So," I continued quickly, throwing her a lifeline, "what are you doing here if the others were against it?" I knew the general answer, which was that she was like sixteen or seventeen years old and her older siblings had told her no, but I wanted to hear what she'd say.

Herald was silent for a moment and then blurted, "You are completely wrong!"

I blinked. I wasn't sure what to say about that.

"You are too intelligent, and you do not behave the way you should," she continued quickly, and I could see she was about to ramble.

"Wait, wait, stop!" I broke in. "What are you on about?" I wasn't even offended, just very confused.

"Dragons!" she exclaimed, throwing her hands out. "You are not at all like how the books say you should be!"

Okay. That was interesting. "Let's get back to that later," I tried. "Where are—"

"Nobody ever mentioned a dragon with black scales, do you know that?" she went on, not even listening to me. "Red or brown or green or even pale blue, but never black. Why do you have black scales, Draka?"

"What?" I said, completely thrown. "What does that have to do with anything? Why do *you* have black hair?"

"*And* you are too small!" she accused. "Makanna was right; you should be bigger! You should still be lying in a nest somewhere, begging your mother to feed you."

"I can feed myself perfectly fine, thank you very much!" I was on the defensive. Somehow she had completely taken control of this conversation, and I didn't like it.

"You look different than before," she said, suddenly changing topics and ruining my attempt to regain my balance.

"Oh, yeah. I got a, you know. Threshold." It felt bizarre to say out loud.

"You have grown. Not much, but you have." She closed in, squatted in front of me, and touched one of the scales on my shoulder. I let her. She was in control, and I was just along for the ride. "Your scales have little ridges on them that were not there before. It is subtle, but I can see them. And they are less black somehow? But still completely black. It throws the eye a little."

I was bigger, and my scales were different. That made sense. But it wasn't important at that moment. What was important was that Herald had paused to look closer at my scales, giving me an opening.

"Herald!" I said in my most authoritative voice, which I had reserved for misbehaving newbies at the gym and, very rarely, my ex. "Hi! It's nice to see you. Why are you here alone?"

Herald looked at me, face turning sullen. "They do not know," she said. I waited. "They went on a job without me," she continued after a long silence.

Ah. There it was. They'd ditched her. I didn't say anything, waiting for her to get it all out.

"Makanna got scared because I got hurt on the gremlin job," she said after a while, standing up and beginning to pace. When she stood, I noticed that, when sitting, my head actually reached her breast bone now. I really must have grown!

"I have never been wounded before," she went on. "A few cuts and scrapes, but nothing like that. And now she thinks I should not do anything remotely dangerous, and Tam listens to Mak because she is the head, the older, responsible one, and Val listens to Tam because Val is a brilliant fighter, but he becomes a lost puppy around my brother. And I think that we should work with you, because I think that it is stupid to waste an opportunity like this. You. Are. A. Dragon! A dragon who is friendly and wants to cooperate with humans! How can they not see . . . Augh!" Herald screamed with frustration and drifted into a tense silence.

In the distance, her horse whinnied.

"Do you feel like they don't respect you?" I asked carefully.

"They respect me," she said heavily. There was much less confidence in her voice than she probably intended. "But they do not think that I can take care of myself. They think that I am a child and that anything that happens to me is their responsibility."

"You're their baby sister," I pointed out. This was a mistake.

"I am not a baby!" Herald snapped. "I am seventeen years old and then some. I am an adult and have been for over a year. I can drink at a tavern or get married without anyone's permission or join the army if I so choose. I can make my own mistakes and get hurt for them, and it will be my own damn responsibility."

I raised a clawed hand placatingly. "I know. I know all about being babied and needing to show that you're your own woman." That got me a strange look, but Herald let it go. "But . . . okay, let me ask you this: Makanna, she is quite a bit older than you, isn't she?"

"She is twenty-five," Herald admitted.

"And Tamor?"

"Two years younger than Mak," she said. "Though his birthday is a little earlier in the year. He is twenty-four."

"Right. So there's the problem. Herald, they have loved you as a baby. That is not going to go away. I had the same problem with my oldest brother. God, the dumb shit I did just to show him . . ."

Herald was quiet for a time after I trailed off. "So I should do some 'dumb shit.' Is that what you are saying?"

"Officially, no," I told her with a smile, "but I had some bloody fun doing it. And, you know, a teenage girl riding through a bandit-infested forest at night to meet up with a dragon, well . . . I'd say that qualifies as some dumb shit."

"Makanna is going to be furious," Herald said with a little laugh, and I laughed with her. "You have brothers?" she asked after we wound down.

"Two of them," I told her honestly. "One much older, one a bit younger."

"I thought dragons were hatched several at a time," she said.

"I don't know what to tell you. I have two brothers, and that's it," I said. And that was the truth. I had no idea about how many eggs a dragon laid at a time, and I had no plan or desire to find out. I just prayed that I wasn't like a chicken, laying eggs whether I wanted to or not.

"Does that mean that there are more dragons here?" Herald said, sitting forward with growing excitement.

"Sorry," I told her sadly. "They're . . . I dunno. Somewhere else. Far away, I guess."

"Then why is it that you are here?" she asked.

I didn't see any harm in telling her some of the truth. "I wish I knew," I said. "I woke up here a few weeks ago. One moment I was somewhere else, the next I was here."

"Oh," she said, her expression turning soft with sympathy. "That must have been very confusing."

"Yeah, you have no idea," I told her. I had a sudden impulse to tell her the whole truth, about being a human trapped . . . No, that didn't feel right . . .

Merged with? Yeah, merged with a dragon. But that would be a step too far, at least until I was totally sure that I could trust her.

"So you just wanted to talk?" I asked. "Show that you can do what you want and not always listen to your sister and brother?"

"I guess so," Herald said, rubbing the back of her neck. "It sounds childish like that. I wanted you to know that at least one of us is interested in working with you."

"Well, I appreciate it," I told her.

"Is there anything you need?"

"Well . . ." I said, and told her about my trouble with the tinderbox. I left out my tantrum.

"Oh, that is easy," Herald said. "Instead of the improvised garbage you had, you need a proper fire striker. I could get you one of those, and you can get a bigger piece of flint or chert from any stream around Karakan."

"Seriously? That would be great," I told her. "Honestly, there's a bunch of other stuff I want, but I think that can wait. Pillows and rugs and stuff are nice, but I don't know how I'd take them home, anyway."

"Well," Herald said, "if transporting things is a problem for you, there are a few bag-makers in the city. They make custom pieces all the time. I might be able to ask around a little. Something like a backpack or, uh . . . saddlebags?"

I couldn't imagine how I'd strap a backpack to myself, but it would be useful. "You know," I said, "if you don't mind and have the time, that'd be great."

"I do not know what it might cost, though," she said carefully. *Right. Money. Paying for things. Handing money over.* "A few eagles at least."

The idea of parting with silver made me feel sick to my stomach. I fought it down.

"Let's deal with that once you have a quote, all right?" I told her, suddenly a little short of breath.

"Yes," she said, with an odd look. "That is reasonable."

"Speaking of money," I went on, forcing some cheer into my voice, "I bet there's a bounty on those bandits, yeah?"

"There is . . ." Herald answered, inviting me to go on.

"Well," I said, "I happen to know where a bunch of the murdering bastards are hiding out."

"Really?" she said, her eyebrows shooting up. "The Gray Wolves or the Herons would pay well for that information if it is right! Gray Wolves would be easier since we're friends with some of them. How did you find these bandits?"

"They torched a village today," I said, repressing the anger that flared up at the memory. I'd make them pay one way or another. "Killed some people. Hurt a lot more. I saw the smoke and went to check it out. One of the dead was a little kid." I paused as Herald's face went from somber to sad.

"Yeah," I continued with a sigh. "Like . . . a toddler. So I tracked them and found their camp. It's hidden pretty well but easy to get to if you know how."

"Where is it?" Herald asked. There was anger in her voice but also a growing excitement that was way too familiar.

"Okay, so from the main road . . . Wait, I should get a stick or something . . ." I said and started looking for a tool to scratch in the dirt.

"No, show me!" she insisted. "I will need to be able to lead the soldiers there or they will never trust the information. Or pay us."

"Are you sure that's safe?" I asked. But on her face, I could see the moment when she decided to do some dumb shit. Slowly, she grinned, and I grinned back.

We agreed to go at sunrise. I worried about the horse, but Melon, as the mare was called, was surprisingly chill about the whole thing. I sat down in the open by a lantern while Herald slowly brought her closer, and while Melon was obviously nervous and doubtful about the whole situation, Herald finally coaxed her close enough that she could have touched me with her nose if she wanted. She didn't, but she also didn't run off when I stood and took a few steps in front of her. I could only assume that I had been classified as some kind of strange but tame dog: big, with claws and teeth, but unlikely to do anything.

Herald tied Melon to what was effectively a tent peg. When I expressed my doubt about how well that would hold Melon if she decided to take off, Herald agreed it wouldn't. But Melon knew that the peg meant that she wasn't allowed to wander off, and that was apparently good enough. Herald wrapped her cloak tightly around herself and sat down, leaning against a tree, while I curled up among the ferns, where I could keep an eye on her.

"Hey, Draka," Herald whispered as I was drifting off.

"Yeah?" I answered sleepily.

"Do you have my earring?" she asked.

I thought about it, then got up and walked over to her. After some lingual gymnastics, I presented the little piece of worked silver to her on the tip of my tongue, where it gleamed softly in the moonlight.

Herald leaned forward and looked at the earring, then at me.

"You keep it," she said finally and settled back.

We headed out early. Herald had been prepared to wait all night, and she ate a light breakfast on Melon's back while we moved. I stuck to the edge of the trees, and she was on the edge of the road, so we could talk as we went. Not that I added much to the conversation. I wanted to trust her, but there were things I wasn't ready to tell anyone, and that limited the topics I could bring up.

To my relief, I discovered that my increased fortitude apparently extended to plain endurance as well. I had no problem keeping up with Melon's pretty energetic pace, and we made good time.

"So, magic," I said after we had walked in silence for maybe twenty minutes. Or five. Keeping track of time with no phone is hard. "It's rarer here than I thought."

"Really?" Herald asked. "Is it more common where you came from?"

"No, I guess not. It's just that you were all so casual when Makanna used it."

"Well, not everyone gets magic, that is true," Herald began thoughtfully. "Mak did, of course, and so did Tam, though his is different. The limiting factor is that not everyone can learn it. As far as I have heard, magical talent can only come at a major threshold. And most people never reach their second major. Some unfortunate people—or very fortunate, depending on how you look at it—never reach their first one, even if they live a long time."

"Because their lives are too easy?" I asked.

"That, or because they never learn anything from their struggles, I suppose. Not everyone does."

"So not everyone gets a major advancement, and of those who do, not everyone gets magic. That would cut down the numbers, sure," I said. "It still feels like I should've seen more."

"Oh, not everyone who gets the option chooses it," Herald said casually.

"What? Why?" I was completely thrown by this revelation. Utterly flabbergasted. "Why would anyone not choose magic?"

"Fear, mostly, I think," Herald said. "It can put a lot of pressure on you, and using magic can be painful and exhausting. We are very careful about letting anyone know that Makanna can heal, for example. Can you imagine the stress she would be under if everyone with an injury came to her? You saw how much it took out of her to heal your fairly minor wounds."

"And the worse the injuries, the more exhausting it is to heal?"

"Just so. Now, the money can be good, and I think she might have tried that if we had not found the gremlin job. She has her license, just in case. But right now, it is not worth it."

"It still seems like something that would be better to have than not."

"But you also have to consider the options! Imagine that a terribly sick man reaches his major threshold. He has two paths before him. On one, he can heal others, or fuse stone, or empower himself with magic to fight better. On the other, he would live in perfect health to a ripe old age. He would choose health, would he not?"

"I guess," I agreed.

"You rarely meet someone who would tell you what their choices were. Neither Makanna nor Tamor have told me, for example. But I believe that the choices, however many you get, are usually equally valuable, in different ways. And so, we end up with few magic users in the world."

"Would you pass, if you got the chance?" I asked.

Herald smiled. "I will have to see the options first, will I not?"

CHAPTER SEVENTEEN

Trauma Bonding

The rest of the way, I tried to learn more about Herald and her siblings, and she told me a little about Karakan as a place to live. I asked about her childhood and gathered that her siblings hadn't been born there, but she had. There was a lot of pain there, though. She either evaded or simply didn't answer most of my questions, so I let it go.

The little family, Valmik included, didn't have a permanent home in the city, which surprised me. They carried most of their stuff with them, staying a few days or weeks at an inn and then moving to another when they wanted some change. Adventuring paid well enough, and inns could be cheap enough, that this hadn't been a problem for years. Until Tamor got locked up, that was. Apparently, another reason to avoid becoming a magic user was that you needed a license to use magic inside the city, which Tamor had neglected to pay. He'd excused himself by saying that he would simply not use any magic in the city, but then Makanna had gotten drunk, and some merc had gotten handsy, and Tamor saw that and . . .

"My sister can take care of herself!" Herald insisted on that. "Her judgment is usually sound, and you have not seen her fight. She is good. But sometimes she has a bad night, and she tries to drink it away. Alone. And there are many men, and some women, who would take advantage."

Assholes with no conscience were a universal constant.

Tamor hadn't been locked up for getting in a fight. The guards had been pretty sympathetic on that point, since he had a good reputation and the merc did not. But unlicensed magic was apparently serious shit, and he'd been slapped with a one-hundred-eagle fine on top of the twenty eagles for the license. When he couldn't pay, they'd thrown him in a cell, and he was looking at several years of what was essentially slave labor overseas until everything was paid off.

Without Tamor, Makanna and Valmik were very limited in the jobs they could do without seriously risking their lives, and money started running out. Their friends had lent them some, but there was a limit to what they could afford. And when the money was almost gone, and the deadline before Tam got shipped off was only days away, Makanna had accepted the job in the mine. It was dangerous, they knew that, but it was their last chance. Makanna and Valmik had planned to go alone, and when Herald found out, she was furious. The older adventurers had taken Herald along on a few simple jobs before, so after a lot of wearing-down, Herald had convinced them to take her along.

"I know that I am not Tamor," she said bitterly from on top of Melon. "I cannot fight like him, and I cannot spot danger like him. But I am good at what I do. I can shoot fast and accurately at fifty paces, a hundred or more if I take a second to aim properly. And I can spot things that those two would have never seen. I know that we would have all been dead without you, but I think that they would have been dead without me no matter if you were there or not. And then I would have been alone!" I could hear the threat of tears in her voice. "Tam would get shipped off, and they would just never come back. And I would be left with no one and no money. What were they thinking? I would rather be dead with them than left behind!"

I believed her. I could have said something about Tam being the last one left if Herald had died with the others, but right now she felt every word she said. I understood Makanna and Valmik not wanting to risk her life along with their own, but of course Herald was angry! In their eyes, she was still a kid. A kid who they had all helped raise, if I had it right. But she was seventeen, which was a whole thing in itself, and beyond that, she was literally more advanced than others her age. Of course she wanted to be treated as an equal! And of course she didn't want to be left suddenly all alone at a really confusing time in her life. It was a damn mess, and I hoped that they all would work things out before shit blew up.

At that point, it had been a while since we'd left the main road, and it wouldn't be much longer before we reached the bandits' hidden path. Neither of us had said a thing since Herald's short rant, but we weren't as on-guard as we should have been either.

"Hello, miss," came a cheerful voice from the trees. There was a rustle of disturbed foliage from the opposite side of the road, and two men on horseback appeared, cutting Herald off in both directions. They wore shabby leather armor and carried swords, with bows on their saddles, and couldn't have looked more like outlaws if they'd tried. Herald had her bow with her, of course, but it was unstrung. Not that it would have mattered at that distance.

I froze among the bushes. *Fuck! Fuck-fuck-fucking . . .* Why had I been so careless? I should have smelled them if nothing else. Of course they would have people watching the road. They were bandits! Robbing people on the road was half of what they did!

Herald, to her credit, didn't freak out. As soon as the men came out of the trees, she was turning Melon to face them so that she had them on her right and left instead of in front and behind.

"Where might a pretty girl like you be going this fine morning?" the man to her left continued. He had a long face, his hair cropped short, and I hated his smile.

"My, she's a tall one, isn't she, Paak?" commented the other with a serious look on his round, bearded face.

I couldn't see Herald's expression, but her voice was a little unsteady when she answered.

"I am on my way to visit some family." She was slowly sidestepping Melon, putting her closer to the man on her right but also getting out of my way. Smart.

"Isn't that nice, Tor?" the man called Paak said to the other one as both began to close in. "But you must know that these roads are dangerous, miss. Why don't you come with us, and we'll keep you safe?

"I have some money—" Herald began, opening her cloak on one side to show her money pouch.

"I'm sure that you do," the man called Tor said jovially. "But there is no need for that. Your company and cooperation will be reward enough, won't they, Paak?"

"Indeed! Now, why don't you get off that fine horse," Paak said, loosening his sword in its scabbard, "and we'll all go and get to know each other?"

Oh. Hell. No. That was far enough. Paak was almost right in front of me, thanks to Herald's maneuvering, and Herald's sword was still hidden under her cloak. With any luck, they'd focus on me.

A switch flipped, and I stopped thinking. I just acted. I didn't say anything. I didn't roar or hiss or spit venom. I simply crashed out of the bushes and launched myself at Paak. Of course, since I couldn't use my wings among the trees, I couldn't leap and bowl him out of the saddle the way I'd wanted to, but I got high enough.

Paak reacted almost instantly, and the man was fast and strong. I went straight for his throat, but he batted my head away with his right arm while he drew his sword with his left. My head ringing, I dug my claws into the armor around his waist and dragged him from the saddle. As he fell, he tried to stab me, and I felt a blow high on my chest, but the point of the sword skidded off my scales and rattled down my side. Thank you, fortitude!

The bandit fell on top of me, screaming as he tried to maneuver his sword to cut or stab me again while his other hand closed around my neck, just under my jaw. Unfortunately for him I had four clawed limbs. Clamping my talons around his armpits, I pulled my legs up and kicked at anything I could reach. I didn't know what killed him or when it happened; I just kicked over and over until he went limp.

Rolling the dead man off me, I looked up and saw Herald sitting on Melon, who was stomping and snorting unhappily. The bandits' horses were gone, and beyond Melon's legs, I could see Tor lying still in the dust, blood pooling around him.

"Herald!" I called up. She didn't answer or even move. I walked around Melon, leaving bloody prints behind me, and looked at her.

Herald was staring at the dead man. Her sword was in her hand, the tip of it red with blood, and she held it out, pointing at him.

"Herald?" I said again, more gently as my bloodlust slowly cooled. "Are you hurt, Herald?"

She turned her head slowly to look at me. "No," she said distantly. "He never got his sword out."

"Oh, okay," I said lamely. "That's good."

"Yeah," she said and returned to staring at Tor's body. "They were going to . . ."

"Yeah," I said softly. "I think so."

"Men look at me. They always look at me. Some words here and there. But no one ever . . ." She waved her sword slowly at the corpse.

"They'll regret it if they do," I said, trying to sound reassuring. "You're like a fucking snake with that sword."

"I just reacted faster than him," she said, then turned to look at me. "I never killed someone before."

Oh boy. The trauma kept piling up, didn't it? And then I realized that *I* had just killed someone. A piece of shit who deserved it, sure, but I had killed a human being. I was covered in his blood from thighs to tail, and I could smell his innards cooling on the ground.

"Yeah," I said. "Me neither." I felt sick. My human side wanted to throw up, but the dragon saved me from that. Something must have come across to Herald, though, because her face changed. She looked less dazed and more concerned.

"Are *you* okay, Draka?" she said.

"I don't know," I said honestly. How could either of us be okay? "I think I will be."

"Do you need a hug?" Herald asked, as though it was the most natural question in the world.

Did I need a hug? What kind of question was that? The dragon was outraged at the mere suggestion that I, the mighty Draka, the terror of the forest, would accept pity from this soft creature. It was insulting. It was unforgivable!

Herald slid heavily out of Melon's saddle and crouched in front of me. "Can I give you a hug?" she said, and I could see tears in her eyes.

"Yeah," I said. "Sure."

So she threw her arms around my neck, and with my head resting gently on her shoulders, she cried softly into my scales.

"We should get off the road," Herald said a few minutes later, releasing me and sitting back. She sniffled and wiped her eyes, then moved over to Tor's body. She looked at him, then steeled herself. She bent down and rolled him over, and then started undoing his belt.

"Uh, what're you doing?" I asked.

"They have swords and money pouches," she said flatly. "No sense in leaving them here."

"Right," I said, turning to look at the other dead man. His face was oddly peaceful, considering he was a ruined mess of blood and shredded meat below the waist. I had torn the belt while I kicked him, but the scabbard and money bag looked whole, if badly stained with blood, so after some hesitation, I took them. I pried the sword out of his hand and slid it into the scabbard with some difficulty. I handed them to her.

"You, uh, probably shouldn't look at the other guy. It's pretty nasty."

"All right." She strapped the two swords to Melon's saddle and put Tor's money pouch on her own belt. "Here." She put the strap of Paak's bloodied money pouch over my head. "I will sell the swords in the city and bring you your share when I can."

"Yeah, great," I told her. "Hey, Melon's pretty calm, isn't she?"

"She is," Herald said. She rubbed the mare's flank, then plucked a small yellow fruit from her saddle bag and offered it to her. Melon grabbed it with her lips and crunched placidly. "She is not a trained warhorse, but I borrowed her from a mercenary I know. She has seen worse."

"Should we get them off the road?" I asked.

Herald shook her head. "There is so much blood on the road that it will be obvious what happened here. The bodies may as well be found. Besides, the horses will likely find their way back home, and these two will be missed anyway."

"I could . . ." I trailed off, swiping my claws through the air with no enthusiasm. "Make it look like a monster attack?"

"That . . . Yeah. Good idea," Herald said, looking slightly sick about it. Placing her foot in a stirrup, she leaped smoothly into the saddle. "I will go on ahead. Then let us continue," she said, putting some courage into her voice. "I want to be back in the city before nightfall, and I need something to show the Wolves."

I needed to work up some nerve, but I savaged Tor pretty convincingly. It felt wrong. He was already dead, and he'd been a piece of shit when he was alive, but desecrating a corpse like that still felt wrong.

At my insistence we stayed off the road after that, with me moving far enough ahead of Herald for her to be able to bolt if I found anything else. But no one else was watching the road, at least not here, and I showed her the secret path and where it joined the road. After pointing out the track and how easy it was to follow, I took Herald the long way around so that we approached the bandit camp from the south, along the hills, instead of from the forest. I showed her the path that led into the hills and above the camp and pointed out the place with its wall and gate under the overhang. There was very little activity that I could see; either they were out or the bandits were late risers.

After that, we turned back. I followed her all the way to where the forest ended and the fields began, the stone walls and a few towers of the city visible in the distance. We talked little over the hours and only stopped to rest and water Melon. I kept wanting to apologize to Herald for putting her in danger the way I had. If there had been one or two more bandits on the road, the outcome might have been very different. I should have known better. But every time, I stopped myself. More than anything, Herald wanted to feel free and capable. She wanted to show that she could handle herself, and she had. Besides, I felt that Herald would not be happy about an apology. Today had been hard on her, but she had a look of quiet satisfaction on her face that I didn't want to disturb.

I wasn't going to stop her from taking risks if that's what she felt that she needed to do. Even if I wanted to, it would be laughably hypocritical for me of all people to lecture her. I was only there because I decided to go spelunking alone, and then I made that worse by checking out a new opening. Crevices do not just appear in caves. If they do, something very bad has happened. And I, in my wisdom, had gone *Hey, cool!* and jumped right in. So if Herald wanted to take some risks, I was right there behind her. Right now that meant making sure that she didn't get killed leading these mercs to the bandits.

Among the rage, greed, and jealousy that kept coming through, the dragon had one virtue. Dragons were patient. At least, I was. So I found a tree, close enough by the road that I could keep an eye on it but far enough away and with leaves thick and shady enough that I was virtually invisible. There I climbed up, wrapped my tail around a branch, and settled in to wait.

CHAPTER EIGHTEEN

Cleaning Up

Staying so close to the city might have been a mistake. I learned very early on that people hunted here, since the fields attracted boar, deer, and hares, who all used the forest as a base for their raids on crops. The very first morning here, a gray, balding man with a bow snuck by almost right below me. The dragon woke me as soon as we could hear the soft crunch of his steps on the dry leaves, but there was no danger. He passed, as did everyone else who came near that day or the next. In the dense, shady crown of the tree, I may as well have been invisible.

There was a wide stream nearby that I visited to drink, but other than that, I spent two days and three nights in that tree. While I slept, the dragon watched and, I assume, vice versa. It should have been boring. But the dragon was patient and, somehow, so was I. I'd sleep, then wake and watch the road a little. I'd sniff the air, look at the birds and other animals that passed by, and then I'd sleep again. The traffic on the road was the same as ever: lone travelers, a few groups of adventurers, merchants, villagers, and patrols of guards or mercenaries. It was mostly sunny, but on the second day, it rained for an hour. It was all very peaceful.

On the morning of the third day since I led Herald to the bandit camp, I woke to a voice in my ear. *"The humans march,"* the dragon said, and I was instantly alert. It was nearly dark, shortly after dawn, with a heavy rain falling straight down. On the road, a long column of mounted people in heavy cloaks trotted along. The mercenaries were on the move, and they were out for blood.

They were moving fast enough that it would be hard for me to keep up on foot, so I just took a look at the column. The mercs were out in force, and I counted about thirty of them. Between the rain and the cloaks, it was hard to be sure, but I thought I saw Herald, tall and lithe, toward the middle of the pack. That made sense. She had been pretty sure that she wouldn't get paid if she didn't actually show the way herself, and I think that she wouldn't have been left behind if she could help it anyway. The fact that the figure in question scanned not just the forest but the sky and the treetops every now and then only made me more certain. We hadn't discussed me coming along, but she was smart. She knew I'd want to see what happened.

Once the column had passed, I waited a minute, then found a clearing and took to the sky. Since I knew where they were going and by which route they were likely to go, I went ahead, posted up in a tree, and waited some more. Sure enough after a good while they passed, first two of them who I barely noticed in the trees, then the main column, and then while I waited for them to gain some distance, two more, again in the trees. There was probably a great reason the main group of people were sneaking ahead and behind them like that. I had never been interested in military strategy or tactics, but my guess was that they were scouts or something.

Once everyone went well past me, I repeated the process of moving ahead, waiting, and so on.

Soon after the mercs left the main road, the rain petered out. It was close to noon, judging by the sun, and the mercenaries took their cloaks off with obvious relief. Once they were exposed, I recognized two people. The first, obviously, was Herald. She had her hair tied back and was wiping down her bow. The other was Guy's girlfriend.

I didn't know why that surprised me, but it did. She and Herald seemed friendly, smiling and laughing as they talked together in low voices. I immediately felt a spike of jealousy, almost anger. This woman had been one of the people who ran me off when I met Guy, and here she was again to wreck the day!

I tried to fight the feeling and was at least partially successful. I knew that I couldn't blame her for how she'd reacted. She had probably just been relieved to find her man alive, and there I was, all teeth and claws. If my boyfriend had gone missing in the mountains and I found him sitting next to a cougar, I would've freaked out too.

I still didn't like her. It was hard to get over someone waving a sword at you.

As they got within a kilometer or two of the hidden path, a change came over the mercs. They slowed down and started adjusting their armor and readying their weapons. Those who had bows stopped a moment to string them if they hadn't already. At that point, they were going slow enough for me to keep up, and I shadowed them from deep inside the trees. The two who had been riding ahead rejoined the column and talked to the older, bearded man at the front, who nodded and gave some signals with his hand. In a quick and orderly fashion, the whole column turned and rode in among the trees. I knew things were about to get interesting.

A small group of mercenaries had gotten off their horses and went ahead on foot, running almost silently through the leaves and the undergrowth. I was curious about their purpose, but I needed to stay close to Herald. Trying to get past the line of mercs would have been risky anyway. However, I didn't need to wonder for long.

I had seen Valmik fighting in the mines. He was a fighter, and a good one, as far as I could tell. These five—four men and one woman—were killers. When they left, they disappeared into the bushes and shadows, and that was the last I saw of them. Every so often, I would hear an animal call, a bird or frog or something else that suited the environment, and the line would move forward.

Bodies were on the ground. Bandit sentries, I guessed. I hadn't heard a single scream, cry, or even rustle. The five mercs moved forward, and bandits died. It was hard to look at the bodies. A couple of the dead sentries were no older than Herald. I could only assume that those five mercs were being paid well and on time, because I would not want to be the person trying to screw them out of a paycheck.

Before the main force got in sight of the camp, the leader gave a signal, and most of the mercs dismounted. They tied their horses to branches or to tent pegs, like Herald had done at the lake. Only a few, including Herald and Guy's girl-friend, stayed in the saddle. Some of them strapped shields to their arms. All of them readied weapons. Then, once given a signal, they advanced.

I felt responsible for what was about to go down. People were going to die on both sides. Lots of people. The bandits had brought this on themselves, and the mercs accepted the risk together with their pay, but if not for me, this battle would not be happening.

All I needed to do was to make sure that Herald was safe. When I felt reason-ably sure that no one would be able to see me, I quickly and silently scaled the back of a tall pine a few dozen meters behind her. Between the trees, I had a decent view of the clearing and the wall, but most importantly, I could keep an eye on the young woman.

The soldiers on foot reached the line where the trees ended. Everyone without a bow broke into a voiceless jog while archers stayed at the tree line and readied their arrows.

The mercs approaching the makeshift fort had crossed half of the fifty or so meters that they had to go when a head popped up over the wall. They had crossed half the remaining distance when an alarm had been raised and the observant bandit died with an arrow to his neck. Seconds later, the mercs reached the gate. One of them had carried an oversize sledgehammer, like a keg on a wooden post. He'd been half dragging it, and I had no idea how he expected to fight with the thing. Then I understood that he didn't.

The man was a living siege weapon. As the soldiers reached the gate, the man stopped and concentrated, and a bright glow came alive in him. It traveled from his heart down his arms and to the sledge, and with a yell and one swing, he made the gate buckle. Another yell and swing and the gate shattered and swung inward. He slumped to the ground, exhausted.

About twenty seconds after the soldiers left the trees, they began to pour through the gate. I could see now that they moved in pairs, one soldier with a shield and some weapon together with one wielding a large, two-handed sword, axe, or other heavy weapon. Now the archers started moving up, keeping their eyes on the palisade, as Herald had taught me the wooden wall was called.

Twenty-five seconds after it all began, the screaming grew unbearable.

Forty seconds and a section of the palisade by the rock wall fell outward, and almost a dozen bandits on horses came charging out. I noted their armor and weapons. The dragon, however, noted the lumpy bags strapped to their saddles.

They headed for the trees at a full gallop, straight toward Herald and the others still on horseback. Herald had already loosed her first arrow when I understood what was happening. Archers in the clearing were turning in surprise, but the riders weren't paying any attention to them. The bandits were fleeing, and seemed determined to go through Herald and the handful of mercs with her as a last attempt at a *fuck you* to the mercenaries.

"Brace! Brace!" Guy's girlfriend's voice came clear over the distant sounds of fighting and the roar of hooves, but I still barely heard it. I was flying, hurtling through the air toward a point somewhere between Herald and the charging horses. Two riders on the edge of the pack jerked as arrows from the clearing hit them, but their horses came on. I didn't remember leaping. I may have been cut out of the decision entirely, and above all the noise of the battle and the screamed commands of the woman next to Herald, the one thing I heard loud and clear was the voice of the dragon roaring in my ears:

"Mine!"

That was probably a bad sign, but I had no time to analyze it. The bandit riders were about to hit the few mounted mercenaries, swords and spears poised to kill, when I passed over Herald's head. I caught a glimpse of the leader's eyes going wide just as I sprayed the whole group with a furious hiss of venom and smacked into him like a cannonball. The man basically stopped in midair as his horse continued without him, and then the horse behind him slammed into us and everything went to hell.

There was a moment of silence and white blindness as my brain tried to catch up with what was happening. Then light and sound and everything else came back all at once, and I was fighting. Humans and horses were screaming around me, and I was slashing, kicking, and biting wildly with only one thought guiding me: *Protect Herald. They don't get to hurt her. They don't get to damage what is mine.*

Yeah. Thinking about Herald like that was probably a bad sign.

I had a flash of wide-eyed recognition from Guy's girlfriend, but she was fighting a bandit with a long, curved sword, and the distraction almost cost her a hand. A man stumbled to his feet and tried to simultaneously grab the reins from

Herald's hand and stab up at her, and I struck like a snake, my sharp teeth closing over his forearm. He looked at me with more surprise than pain and bashed me in the face with his free hand once, then twice. It hurt like hell, but it didn't feel like anything broke. Then his eyes went wide as a bar of shining steel appeared in front of my eyes, lancing down from above into the bandit's chest through the hollow of his throat.

The bandit fell with a bubbling whisper as Herald drew her sword back out, and I slowly realized that the fighting around us had ended. The bandits were dying on the ground or fleeing with the surviving mounted mercenaries in pursuit. Herald looked down at me from her horse, her bloody sword in her hand and a wild elation in her eyes.

"Draka! I knew it! I fucking knew it!"

I was about to reply when there was suddenly a mass of sweaty horse between us, carrying a blood-spattered woman wildly swinging a sword at me. The damn thing caught me on the neck as I jumped back. It didn't go through my scales, but it still hurt!

"Back!" the wild-eyed woman screamed at me. Again with this fucking bitch! "Herald, stay behind me and get your bow!"

"Try me, skank!" I screamed back at her and prepared to fucking *end* her at the same time that Herald dropped her own weapon and took a two-handed grip on the woman's sword arm.

"Lalia, stop!" Herald shouted in the woman's ear. "Stop! Stop! This is my informant! My friend! Stop!"

Then, when the woman almost pulled Herald out of the saddle in trying to swing at me again, Herald hauled off and punched her.

I didn't know which of us was more surprised. The bitch, *Lalia*, turned her head and just stared at Herald. Herald sat back, her mouth locked in a silent *Oh*, hand still clutching the other woman's wrist.

Lalia. The name sounded familiar somehow. Where had I heard it before?

"Now! While her back is turned!" the dragon screamed at me, and it was hard to resist. My claws dug into the dirt as I prepared to pounce, but then I looked at Herald and came to my senses. Whoever Lalia was, and whatever I felt about her, she was Herald's friend, and Herald was my friend, and friends didn't kill each other's friends in front of one another—a lesson Lalia needed to learn, but that was beside the point.

In the distance, I saw riders returning. Mercs, not bandits. "Herald," I said, and then again, louder, when she didn't react the first time. Herald and Laila broke their shocked stares and looked at me.

"Herald, are you safe with this woman?" I asked.

"It talks!" Lalia said, almost dreamily. I ignored it.

"Herald! Will you be safe?" I asked, louder this time.

"Is it wearing a damn *necklace?*" Lalia said. I was still wearing the money pouch Herald and I had taken from the would-be rapist a few days earlier.

"Yes!" Herald said, breaking out of her stupor. "Yes, I am. I will be! I am fine!"

I believed her. Punch or no, they had looked friendly enough on the way here. And so I took that as my cue to leave. I did not want to be there when the others returned and Lalia got over her shock. The dragon was annoyed that we wouldn't be killing and preferably eating the woman, but it could be pragmatic when it needed to. And it always kept track of the important things.

"*The bags,*" it hissed in my ear. "*Take the bags!*"

The bandits' fallen horses were right there. Some of them had gotten back up and scattered, but some were clearly injured beyond help. The leading man's horse had broken its neck charging into a tree, and that's the one I went for.

The lumpy bag had been held to the saddle with only a simple rope and had rolled off when the horse fell. I simply ran past and grabbed it in my teeth, nearly breaking my neck at the weight of it.

"Wait!" I heard Lalia shouting behind me as I angled for the clearing, but I was *not* slowing down for *her.* The heavy bag in my teeth and the many, many deep aches and pains from the short but furious fight tried to keep me down, but I was not sticking around to see what happened when the mercs got back together and found me. Some fast and powerful flaps of my wings powered by dragon adrenaline got me into the air, and then . . .

Then everyone knew I was there as I passed right above the bandit base. The fighting was over, and everyone, surviving mercenary or captured bandit, looked up to see me fly by. Even if Guy, Lalia, and the other mercs who had seen me at the lakeside camp hadn't told anyone, well, I was pretty sure that the cat was well and truly out of the bag.

CHAPTER NINETEEN

In the Shadows

Knowing that I had revealed myself to a bunch of people made me more than a little paranoid. Though I knew that they couldn't actually track me, I still took a long route back to my cave, first heading north and then turning west to fly among the mountains and valleys as I eventually made my way south. Out of caution, I settled down by the spring near my cave to wait for full darkness before I actually returned home.

I'd transferred the bag to my hands shortly after getting airborne. It was lumpy and jangly and wonderfully heavy. However, flying with it had been torture. Not because of the weight, but because I could smell silver and gold, and I longed to open it, but I didn't dare to, not yet, in case I couldn't get it closed again. As I curled up around it, waiting for the sun to set, I inhaled the wonderful scent, and I felt a rumble roll from my chest and through my body. I was full-on purring with pleasure, and if anyone had been there to hear, I might have died of embarrassment.

When the sun set on my resting place, I didn't waste any time. I flew through the darkness, landing hard with only my legs to deflect the shock, but it didn't matter; my body still ached terribly from crashing into a man at highway speeds and the following fight. I was sure that my chest and neck would be a mess of bruises if I didn't have scales covering them. That damn woman—Lalia—was *strong*. But I didn't care. Nothing was broken, and nothing was preventing me from picking the bag up in my mouth and rushing down into the depths of my cave. I was going to my hoard, and it was going to grow *substantially*.

Getting through the crevice this time was a squeeze. I had always needed to sidle, but now I was actually having to work for it, sucking in my gut and spreading my wings to the sides to get through. It took a while. I thought back to what Herald had said, that I was bigger. Was I getting *fat*? I didn't know how to feel about that. I had never cared about my figure, but then, I had never really needed to. I'd always been active as a kid, and after I took up climbing as a personality, the problem was getting enough calories rather than cutting back. But I had also eaten, like, seventy or eighty kilos of meat in the last few weeks. That was probably more calories than I needed, and they had to go somewhere.

When I finally plopped out on the other side, I briefly considered moving my hoard, but this was the safest place I could think of, so that idea was out. I'd just have to watch my weight. It was a weird and disturbing idea, but at least I had a good reason for it. And that reason was about to get even better.

Finally, after so many hours of delayed gratification, I began to open the bag. I could barely see, but I didn't need to. Smell and touch sufficed. The top of the bag was tied closed with a simple thick string, and I cut it easily with my claws. Then I opened the top and started taking things out.

One by one, I removed items from the bag, touching them, smelling them, looking at their contours and their barely there gleams in the light of the lichen. There were silver candlesticks, plates, and cutlery and gold and silver rings, earrings, and necklaces, plain or set with precious stones. I could tell a precious stone from a semiprecious one by smell and taste alone, so I licked the loot. It wasn't the first time or nor would it be last. Hell, I'd been carrying a silver earring in my mouth for the last few days. It had been comforting to do so, but I dropped the earring on the pile as well.

I did feel a little bad about keeping things that were clearly precious valuables looted from people's homes, but I deserved a reward, right? Of course I did. Anyway, they were in my hoard now, and they weren't going anywhere.

Then there were the coins. In adding Paak's pouch, there were dozens of them, mostly silver but a few gold, and hundreds of lesser ones that did nothing for me. I guessed those must've been peacocks. It seemed like a waste to have dragged them here, but then I had a thought. Spending my gold and silver coins was unthinkable. It was not going to happen. If someone had kidnapped my best friend and roomie, Andrea, and demanded a single silver eagle as ransom, I would have thanked Andrea for her years of friendship and hoped to meet her in the next life. But peacocks? I could spend those! As long as Herald—

Shit. I hoped that Herald wasn't in trouble because of me. She had sounded convinced that she was safe, but I hoped that she would get in touch very soon. I'd have to check the tree. Otherwise I might have to go into the city, and I was not looking forward to that. Anyway, her little family would be back by now, and they'd look after her. Makanna would be unhappy, of course. I wondered what Herald had told them. Had she said anything about me?

Then it happened. I'd been expecting it, but it still brought a shiver of pleasure up my spine. The first time had hurt, but the two times after that had been wonderful.

"Our hoard has grown!" the voice purred. It was in a tone that had just never been in my repertoire, and hearing my own voice like that, well, to call it embarrassing wouldn't begin to cover it. If I could have blushed, I would have done so furiously.

Wait. "Our" hoard?

"By gathering a hoard worthy of a young dragon, a major threshold has been reached," the voice continued, heavy with contentment. *"We will embrace the shadow!"*

That surprised me. What, I didn't get a choice? Had the dragon chosen for me, or was this just how it was for dragons?

"The dark will hold no fear for us, for we are what others fear in the dark! The shadows will be our allies, and they will do as we command! We are a dragon of shadow. We are the darkness! We are the night!"

Oh, great. The dragon was some kind of scaly goth girl.

Then the dragon began to purr in a long, luxuriating rumble, and I felt a change wash over me and through me, mind and body. It was not only instinct, but the barest understanding of what the dragon's words meant. My vision blurred, which didn't make sense, since I could barely see anyway, but when everything came back into focus, *everything came back into focus*! As if the brightness had been inverted, what had been nearly pitch-black now shone in bright tones of gray. Edges were the clearest, and though there was no color, I could see every single individual item in the cave and even some details on them. I could see every coin, every chunk of silver, and every string and stone. When I turned around, I could see the bottom of the pit I had fallen into all those weeks ago, and for the first time, I could actually make out what was down there.

For a moment, I hoped that I might find some of my gear, but no. No flashlight or smartphone for me. The flashlight wasn't any use to me anymore, but it would have been nice to listen to some music on my phone. I'd been on a major Sia trip before my fall, and I hadn't been close to wearing her hits out yet.

What I did see, though, was not anything I'd expected. The pit was roughly circular. I'd known that already. And there was an opening that slanted slightly down, deeper into the mountain. What I hadn't expected was that the opening was an archway of cut stone, or that the pit was lined with regularly placed bricks, about the size and shape of milk cartons. There were twelve of the things, spaced about a meter apart. It looked like there might be some kind of carvings on them, and I wondered what the point of them was. Still, I didn't feel like going down there to explore right then. I was going to, at some point. That was a forgone conclusion. But I'd had some bad times after going down there before. The thought of going down now felt plain bad, and I needed to build up some nerve first.

The dragon was still purring lazily, but I was getting a little hungry. I tried to count backward and realized it had been well over a week since I ate anything. There had been the deer, and then I'd had my little tantrum about the fire, and I'd found the magical gate in the mountains—which I had completely forgotten to tell Herald about—and then there were the bandits and all that. I hadn't thought about food in all that time. It was incredible how easy it was to break the habit of eating three square meals a day plus snacks when you didn't get hungry every day.

I knew that I should eat before I got too hungry, but I also didn't have time to go into a meat coma for two or three days. I was pretty sure that, no matter what I killed, once I started eating, I would just keep going, so I'd have to go for something small, like a rabbit. Or hare. There was some kind of animal here that looked like a large version of one or the other, though I didn't know which and couldn't have told them apart back home anyway. I wasn't sure how to catch the things, but I'd figure it out. I'd start by hanging out in a tree by a meadow and take it from there.

After giving my hoard a loving cuddle, I got up on two legs, sucked in my gut, and flattened my wings to the sides. I started sidling through the crevice and got perhaps a few meters before, to my great surprise, I got stuck. That couldn't happen. Or rather, the fact that it had happened made me very upset. I had gotten in here less than an hour ago, and while I'd had to squeeze a little to get in, it hadn't been a real problem.

Grumbling a little, I wriggled and pushed, the rock pressing my scales into my bruised flesh painfully. I tried to change the angle. No dice. I tried changing the height, first getting up on my tiptoes, which was horrible with these feet, and then bending my legs a little. Nothing worked. I could go back, carefully, but I could not go forward. I pushed harder, my frustration growing, and felt some pain as my leading wing pressed into the rock and my skin threatened to tear.

I had a very real problem. I had never suffered from claustrophobia, but I also hadn't ever truly felt physically trapped anywhere. I pushed harder with my feet until the pain in my wing and chest got so bad that I had to stop. *Shit.* I had to go back. I'd try the passage down. Maybe it led to another exit. Maybe—

This time when I tried to move back, nothing happened. I couldn't go back. I'd wedged myself stuck in a way where I couldn't push myself back with my legs. I started to breathe fast and hard, and every breath was agony.

"No," I whispered in disbelief into the silence of the cave. "No, no, no, no! C'mon!"

I scrabbled at the stone with my feet but got nowhere. This couldn't be happening! This wasn't right! I couldn't die here! After surviving for about a goddamn month as a dragon, I was not going to die wedged in a rock because my ass decided to inexplicably become fatter in half an hour! I tried to help myself along with my hands, but nothing. I tried using my claws, hoping they'd catch on something and give me some extra leverage, but they only skittered across the stone. *No, no, no, no, NO!*

The dragon stirred. *"Fool,"* it muttered contemptuously. *"Just go!"*

"I can't!" I cried, arms and legs working uselessly. "I'm stuck!"

"Just go!" it said again, annoyed now. *"We are darkness! Know where we need to be and go!"*

"I just want to get out!" I shouted. I could see the end of the crevice, limned in silver, and beyond it, the shining beacon of freedom that was the lichen, black stars in my new mode of seeing. I could imagine standing there, taking deep breaths and flexing all my limbs, free to move around as I wanted, to go anywhere.

And then I *melted*.

I don't know exactly how to describe the sensation. It took a few seconds, and then it was like my body wasn't fully solid anymore, like when you let ice cream get too warm. It wasn't just that I was no longer painfully wedged in, unable to move. And my skin didn't slide over the rock as I moved. It was more like my skin didn't touch the rock at all, like I was there but I wasn't, the way you can walk through mist and see it and feel it but it's like you're not really touching it; it just moves around you.

I was the mist.

I moved through the crevice. All my senses were distorted, as though they weren't coming to me through my eyes and ears and nose and skin anymore. I didn't walk or sidle or fly. I flowed or poured or drifted past and over the stone with no effort, and then I was out in the open air of the cave tunnel. There was a momentary sense of wrongness, of being thin and spread out in a horribly inappropriate way, and then I—I don't know—condensed, I guess. I felt myself gather in one place and become solid, and the first thing I did was drop to all fours and throw up whatever water had remained in my stomach.

"What the hell?" I groaned. "What was that?"

"We are darkness," the dragon said with unconcealed scorn. *"We are shadow."*

"That doesn't make any fucking sense!" I complained.

"Yet here we stand," the dragon said with finality.

There we stood. I looked at the crevice where I'd been stuck only moments before. I steeled myself and tried to go back through. I got barely a meter before I felt myself getting stuck again and backpedaled as fast as I could. I had just come through there, even though it was too narrow, or I was too wide. I had . . . what? Teleported? No. I had drifted. I had become a mist, or a cloud. Or shadow.

That made absolutely no sense, but there I was. And this was a world of dragons and magic. My other half had called us a shadow dragon and claimed the shadows would be our allies. I was beginning—just barely—to understand what that meant.

CHAPTER TWENTY

Shadow Play

barely got any sleep that night. I kept waking from nightmares, one after the other, of being trapped in that garbage compactor from *Star Wars*, or of melting and never being able to touch or feel anything again, seeping into the cracks in the stone and spreading out until I practically stopped existing. *127 Hours* featured heavily too. Finally, when it felt like dawn should be getting close, I gave up on sleep and left the cave. Every joint and muscle protested loudly, and my neck ached like an absolute bastard, reminding me that I was very much not invincible. It was a good thing that I was so skilled at napping. I was going to need all the rest I could get.

My first destination was a nearby spring. Some mountain goats scattered when I approached, but I wanted to try for a bunny or two, just to take the edge off. I filled up on water, then flew north for a few minutes before turning toward the forest and the lake.

I landed far from the lake this time. I didn't *think* the mercs would try to ambush me, even if Herald had told them about our system, but I also wasn't trusting my freedom and my life to hope and goodwill. That woman, Lalia, had been there again, after all.

I settled down by the stream that led to Pine Hill and followed it toward the lake, trying to balance stealth with speed as well as my aches would allow, trusting my nose more than my eyes or ears. I didn't see or hear anyone, but the mercs who had taken care of the bandit sentries had been almost invisible when they moved.

I couldn't smell any people, though, as I got close to the lake, I started picking up the faint scent of horses growing stronger the nearer I got. They had been here, a bunch of them, and not that long ago. I scaled a tree from which I could barely see the campground and the one lone tree and waited patiently. I didn't see any people. I didn't hear them, and I didn't smell them. Even when the wind shifted, there was no sign of humans.

Dropping from my tree, I approached. I had my wings half-open, prepared to take off at the slightest surprise, but none came. The trees cast long shadows in the morning sun, and I kept to them the best I could before rushing across the open space to the lone tree.

There was a silver coin wedged into the bark, along with a pinned note. I popped the coin in my mouth after a cursory sniff, then looked at the note. Three vertical lines each connected a number of symbols. It meant nothing at all to me. I knew every language spoken by humans in this world but I didn't know how to read. *Bullshit.*

With an annoyed shrug, I folded the note and stuck it under one of the large scales covering my chest. If it fell, it fell. For now, it was rabbit season.

I went back up the stream toward Pine Hill. About halfway out, there was a meadow where I had seen some of the little fur balls before, but I hadn't even bothered trying to catch them back then. This time, when I got there, I climbed up a gumlike tree and waited. And waited. And waited. When no tasty bunnies showed themselves, I settled in for some much-needed naptime. The dragon would let me know if anything happened, and if I didn't eat that day, there was always the next. I could afford to be patient.

When the dragon woke me, the sun had moved quite a bit. I guessed it'd been two hours or so. "*Food . . .*" it whispered hungrily, and after some searching, I saw two fat little bunnies, floppy ears and all, munching on something in the tall grass. Their brown fur stood out against the green, but they were still hard to spot, and if I hadn't been high up, I would have never stood a chance.

Unfortunately, they were nowhere near the tree, and since the ground under the tree's canopy was covered in nothing but dead leaves and acorns, they were unlikely to come any closer. I couldn't drop on them, and I couldn't spit either. I considered trying to sneak up on them, but they looked way too wary for that to work, considering how open the ground was. Instead, I went for broke. I wasn't too bothered about success, which was a relief. If it didn't work, I'd just try again.

My genius plan was to launch myself through the air and strike from above. This, surprisingly, did not work. As I approached soundlessly, the rabbits, which had probably spent millions of years evolving to avoid being eaten by flying things with claws, spotted me and took off through the trees. I crashed down where they had been, with only some swaying grass to tell me where they'd gone.

But, hell, I decided, why not try something? Rabbits lived in holes in the ground, right? That's where I'd run off to if I were a delicious bunny trying to hide from a scary flying thing.

I sniffed the ground where the bunnies had sat. There was a distinct smell there, for sure, a little musty and grassy, and to be completely honest, it smelled a little like pee too. I sniffed the way they'd gone, and sure enough, the smell was there. Faint but there.

With my nose to the ground, I made my way into the grass. Between the faint scent and a scattering of crushed plants, I made my way to a hole dug steeply into the dirt, and the scent of bunny was strong. *Bingo!* I tried to stick my head in, which worked for all of a second before I saw a flash of furry lump rush up, turn around, and *whamp!*

I saw stars. I jerked my head out, my remaining horn pulling painfully as it caught on dirt and grass roots, and tried to blink the pain away. The damn thing had kicked me right in the nose, and Jesus Hopscotching Christ, did it kick hard!

To hell with subtlety! I got my claws out and started digging. It was slow going, and I had to tear roots and shovel dirt until my arms and chest ached, but I got steadily deeper. Finally, I breached some kind of chamber, and the moment I'd made a sizable hole, a furious fuzzy little warrior launched itself at me. I don't know if it was trying to fight or flee, but I saw it coming and snatched it out of the air with my jaws. Pretty proud of myself for that one!

The little thing screamed piteously, and before I had time to feel bad about it, I bit down even harder until I felt something crunch. Then I tried to shake my head like a dog for good measure, which didn't work at all with my long neck. The poor thing was limp and silent, though. I'd broken its spine.

I didn't even need to think about how to eat the poor little creature. With very minimal input from me, the dragon simply had us tear off its legs and swallow them whole, one by one, skin and all. Then we just took the whole body and choked it down. Apparently we could swallow anything that made it past our jaws, which was extremely disturbing, both to consider and to feel. As it slid down my throat, I kept thinking that I should be choking, but somehow I was fine.

I wasn't eager to repeat the experience, though. One bunny would have to do for now. My snack took the edge off pretty well. I should be good for another day, I hoped, and then I could have a proper three-day-coma meal.

I quickly checked on Pine Hill, but it was peaceful. There were some horses I didn't recognize outside Lahnie's house. They had Gray Wolves colors on their saddles, so I didn't worry, but I didn't stick around either. I had to prepare.

I assumed that Herald would be meeting me that night. At least, I hoped that she would. There had been a lot of people around when that silver coin was left on the tree, and there was no way that Herald would be alone, if she was the one to show up at all. Neither my own nor the dragon's pride would let us hide from this challenge, but I wasn't going to just walk into a potential trap.

The tools I had at my disposal were: good eyesight and a great sense of smell. I would be very likely to know that they were coming and if there were a few or lots of them.

I also had claws for climbing trees and wings for mobility. These were very important.

Additionally, I had stealth, both natural and from my advancement, which allowed me to move quietly and remain almost invisible as long as I was still in a dark place. I'd be leaning heavily on this.

I had skin like a suit of medieval armor, but hopefully that wouldn't come into play. Same for my claws, teeth, and venom. These were the absolute last, last, last resorts.

Finally . . . I had the shadows. I didn't understand it, but I had gotten some kind of affinity for shadows as a major advancement, as the adventurers had called it, and these were supposed to be major, life-changing things. I'd already turned into dragon vapor to move through a crevice I couldn't fit through, but I wasn't entirely sure how. Thus, I needed to use the rest of my time to figure it out.

Doing so would require shadows, and it was sometime after noon and the sun was high, so they were short but in good supply. I was in a forest, after all. I picked a tall, leafy tree with a wide, dense crown and sat down under it. *Now what?*

In the cave, I'd focused on where I wanted to go. I'd kind of visualized what it would be like to be there. But when I tried that now, nothing happened. I focused on a spot a few meters away, really tried to picture in my mind what I would see and feel when I was there, and for a moment, it felt almost like my body was trying to go. Or I was imagining it, because nothing happened. I tried again, for longer and with more focus, and I felt that melty feeling, but again, nothing. What was I missing?

I kept trying for at least an hour, and I must have been doing something right, because I felt something every time. But over and over again, I got right to where I got that tingly, melting sensation, and then it just drew back. It was horrible!

The dragon must have had enough, because it grumbled, *"Not deep enough"* in my ear. *"The shadow must be deeper!"*

Great—direct and useful info! Just one problem: This was as deep and dark a shadow as I was going to find before nightfall without going underground.

"Deepen it!" the dragon commanded dismissively. *"We* are *shadow. Impose our will upon it!"*

"Fuckin' . . . how?" I asked the wind, but there was no response from the dragon. In a way, I was relieved. I had yet to have a proper dialogue with it, and I wasn't sure that I was ready to have a conversation with what was, in a sense, myself.

Deepen the shadow. Right. Just . . . make it darker. A shadow is not even an object; it's a patch where the sunlight doesn't hit the ground directly, but sure. I'll make it do things. *Come on, shadow! Be darker!*

To my complete lack of surprise, my snark did not work.

I considered simply having a sook, but that wouldn't help. And the dragon hadn't steered me wrong yet. It had made some unhelpful and completely amoral suggestions that I had ignored, but it had never lied to me. It had told me that I could move through the darkness, and I had. If it told me that I couldn't move through this shadow because it wasn't dark enough, but that I could fix it, then I believed it. The idea was insane, but I believed it. I just needed to figure out how.

Will sounded like the key. The dragon wanted me to impose my will on the shadow. In the crevice, I wanted to move. I had imagined what everything would be like if I moved, and I had willed myself to do so. Visualization. Willpower. Imagine what reality should be like, and make it so. *Right.*

I looked at the canopy of the tree, its trunk, and the wide patch of shade under it. I looked at the edge of its shadow. There was no sharp line there. Instead, the shade got progressively lighter as fewer and fewer leaves blocked the light, until only direct sunlight remained. No, not lighter. Shallower, or thinner. That felt right. The shadow *was* an object; that's how I needed to think of it. The light was a lack of shadow, not the other way around. And just like how the light could get brighter with more sun, the dark could get darker with more shadow.

I focused on that edge again, the gradual border between light and dark. I imagined it becoming sharper, really visualizing a sharp edge between shadow and light as though an opaque disc had been put in front of the sun. I saw it, and I wanted it. I demanded it. I focused, forgetting about smells and sounds and all sight outside of the little patch of shadow that should—that *would*—become darker.

I felt something happening inside me. It was weak at first, like a kind of heat that warmed a part of me that had never felt warm before, and then it became stronger, hotter, as it swirled throughout my body, gathering in my chest—gathering, I knew, in my heart. I wanted to look down, but even that want was a threat to my focus, so I pushed the urge aside. Then, all at once, it left me in a pulse of swirling darkness that condensed into tendrils of shadow limned with the glow of magic. It reminded me of the substance of the Heart of the gremlin nest. The tendrils quested outward, and the tree's shadow responded to them, becoming deeper and darker. The magical glow didn't actually cast any light. It wasn't a glow, as such, but something else, like it was painted onto reality. The edge of the shadow became a sharp line of darkness against light, and then it pulsed and pushed, and the border between sun and shadow was pushed outward by just a few centimeters. In the near pitch-black around me, my eyes adjusted quickly, but it wasn't enough. My other sight kicked in, and everything within the shade of the tree became gray on black, the world simply ending at the border. Nothing in or past the light was visible.

I willed myself forward, imagined myself right at that border, and I melted, evaporated, turned to black dust on the wind, and then I drifted right up to the border. I tried to push against it, but I might as well have tried to walk through a lead wall, and when I became solid, I fell back on my tail.

I just sat on the ground for a while. Despite all my aches, I couldn't stop grinning. I'd done it. I had told physics to take a hike. I had made the shadow deeper, and I had moved through that shadow at will. I was tired, but I had done it!

I had done magic. I had done goddamn *magic*! Intentionally! Magic was real, and I could *do it*! I was a witch! No, wait, I was a shadow dragon sorceress!

"Wooo!" I howled, and birds scattered in panic as I exulted in my own magnificence. "I am the shadow! I am the night! Batman, eat your heart out!"

CHAPTER TWENTY-ONE

Old Friends

I spent the rest of the afternoon practicing my shadow ability. It made me hungry again, and it was exhausting, both physically and mentally. Together with the pain I still felt in most of my bruised body, I was not in a good mood, but I did learn some basic rules.

First, as long as a shadow was dark enough, I could move through it. Exactly where that line was wasn't obvious to me yet, but it didn't need to be pitch-black.

Second, I could move between shadows. That should have perhaps been obvious since the shadow of the tree was actually thousands and thousands of shadows from individual leaves and branches, but it was still a nice surprise. As long as two shadows flowed together and were each dark enough, I could just keep going.

Third, at a certain level of brightness, it was like hitting a wall. If a shadow was barely dark enough, I could move through it with effort, but as the shadow got weaker, it became harder and harder until I couldn't move any farther.

Fourth, and this was important, as long as I was shadowed, I could only use the shadowsight, as I was calling it, that I'd gotten with my advancement. And with that shadowsight, I couldn't see anything that was too bright. It was effectively the opposite of how I'd always known vision to work: The darker things were, the easier they were to see. The shadows of the forest became a patchwork of clearly visible areas mixed with dim, blurred, or completely invisible ones. And I couldn't see past where the light fell. It was like the landscape was full of pillars of smoky glass, blocking my sight. My hearing got distorted too, and I couldn't smell anything at all, which was a lot more annoying than I would have imagined a month or so before.

So, I concluded, using this ability in a dangerous situation would take some brain power. It took a few seconds to melt and another few seconds to become solid again. I needed to make sure that I could move from where I was to where

I needed to be. Torches or other sources of light that could move around could become a huge problem. I couldn't test it, but I assumed that not only could they stop me dead in my tracks, but I wouldn't be able to see anything around them while I moved.

Basically, I would need to be careful. This ability to move and move in the shadows didn't make me invincible any more than my scales did. If someone stabbed me from the wrong direction, my scales would do jack shit. Similarly, if someone lit a torch while I was moving in a shadow, especially if I was in a small space, what would happen? Probably nothing good.

Be smart, girl, I told myself. *Be careful.*

Having carefully checked that no one was at the lake yet, I set myself up to rest and wait. I did what I usually did and found a suitable tree—the denser, gumlike ones were my favorites—near the campsite, where I could see the path from the road, then settled in.

It never ceased to amaze me how good I was at waiting. A month ago, I would have been bouncing around, bored out of my mind after only an hour, but now I could relax and enjoy the sensations of the forest. If I wanted to think, I did. If I didn't want to, I didn't. I almost never had any intrusive thoughts. The dragon grumbled sometimes, but that was different. I'd never heard an actual voice in my head before I came here. I wished I could know for sure if it was because I had a different brain or because I had changed from my experiences here. Was there a disconnect between the mind, or soul, and the body? Did the body always have a will of its own, and was the id, ego, superego thing more true than I'd ever thought?

Ugh. This train of thought was tiring, and I needed to watch the road. I stopped thinking.

The sun was long gone, and the crescent moon was high when I saw three riders coming down the path. The moonlight was bright enough that I could recognize them with my excellent night vision. The first was Herald, easy to spot, thanks to her height. The second, and the only one wearing visible armor, was my least favorite person so far, Lalia. Where Herald was relaxed and had her hair loose, Lalia had hers in a long braid like she'd had for the attack on the bandit camp. No points for guessing if she was still feeling hostile.

The third, riding Melon, was Guy.

He was a far more pleasant surprise than perhaps he should have been. But it wasn't just the fact that he was a very pretty fella that made me want to meet him again. He was the first person I had met here, and he had accepted me. Sure, I had to save him from certain death first, but that, together with not eating him, had been enough for him to not treat me like I was a dangerous animal. Even Valmik had taken much longer to come around.

I wanted to . . . I didn't even know. Thank him? Talk to him? It felt important.

I could hear them talking to each other, but they were too far away for me to make out any words. The forest was dense enough that only a few patches of moonlight were scattered on the trunks of the trees and the ground between them, and with my regular dark vision, I could easily see a path to them through the shadows. I considered breaking out my new trick, but I was pretty tired and didn't see any point in it. Instead, I waited until they'd passed and then crept down from my tree and made my way toward the road, making sure there was no one following them or waiting for a signal or something dumb like that. Satisfied that I couldn't see anyone, even with my shadowsight, or smell them, I spread my wings and took off.

I was going to make an entrance.

I rose high toward the mountains, then turned and dove to build speed. As I approached the lake again, I could see the pinprick lights of the humans' lanterns, and I went into a nearly silent glide, sure that I would be almost invisible against the night sky. As I passed above them, I beat my wings once, just for the sound of it, and I heard one of the horses wandering the campground whinny behind me.

Flying out over the lake, I circled around in a long turn, trying to pass in front of the moon. I came back to settle down not more than a dozen meters in front of them, wings stretched out wide to brake. I flapped once more to come to a stop, and dust and debris whirled toward and around them. I'd made a good landing!

I shook my wings and folded them partially, then looked at my audience. Herald was grinning like an idiot, though there was something sad around her eyes. Lalia was cursing up a storm, her sword ready and pointed at me in a two-handed grip. Guy was staring at me with a look of almost-childish wonder, eyes wide and a small smile raising the corners of his open mouth.

Entrance well and truly made.

"You wanted to see me," I said grandly. "Here I am. Hi, Herald. How's the family?" I turned to the other two. "Guy I saved. Bitch." I smiled at Lalia, which Herald had informed me only meant that I showed most of my teeth. She scowled back.

"Hello, Draka. The others are not back yet," Herald said. She looked tired and worried. "I am glad you came. I was not sure that you would. And please do not be so unkind to Lalia. She is a good woman. Truly."

"I'll believe that when I've seen it," I grumbled.

"I am sure that you will," Herald said. "Did you read my note?"

I checked my scales. The note was gone. *Oh well.*

"I *found* it . . ." I said slowly. "But I couldn't read it."

Herald blinked slowly. "You cannot read?"

"Hey, I can read *and* write just fine, yeah? Just not in any language you know."

"Forget about reading!" Guy exclaimed, and I could hear traces of an accent. "You talk!" He turned to Lalia and put his hand on her shoulder. "I told you all that she talked to me!"

"I did!" I confirmed cheerfully. "Hadn't learned the local lingo yet, though. Maybe your psycho girlfriend would have been nicer if I had."

"Draka . . ." Herald said, her tone pleading.

"Yeah, fine." Lalia still had her sword pointed at me, and I was getting fed up. "Make her put her little knife away, and we can all play nice, yeah?"

"Lalia," Guy said softly, then stepped in between us, carefully pushing her sword to the side. "I told you that she's harmless. She saved me. Herald has told you the same thing. The commander wants us to talk to her. I know what your uncle and grandparents told you about creatures in the forest, but please, can't you give her a chance? Can't you?"

"You wouldn't call her harmless if you'd seen her yesterday," Lalia replied hotly. "You haven't seen what she can do!"

"I saw her tear a lake lizard to shreds, if that counts," he answered with a little chuckle. "But who has she hurt, my love? Only those who deserved it. Can you claim anything else?"

"No, but—"

"Then, please, Lalia. My dearest star, my beating heart. For my sake, and for Herald's, can you put down your sword?"

She looked from me to Guy and back. The way she looked at him was uncertain and almost disgustingly sweet. Her sword wavered, and then she stepped away from Guy with a deep frown and sheathed it with a fluid motion.

"Fine!" she hissed and looked at me. "But one false move—"

I cut her off. "Won't happen, don't wanna, not gonna," I said. "Thanks. Now, can we all talk?"

"Thank you," Guy said softly to Lalia, squeezing both of her arms gently before turning to me. "I tried to introduce myself last time we met, but, like you said, we didn't understand each other. I am Garal of Barlea. You already know Herald, of course. And this protective beauty is . . ." He turned and gestured to Lalia.

"Lalia of Karakan," the woman finished unhappily.

"Now that we have introduced ourselves," Guy—or Garal, rather—said as he turned back to me. "May I have the pleasure of knowing the name of the one who saved my life?"

"I'm Draka," I said. "Of nowhere, I guess. Or maybe Earth. Nice to meet you again."

"Then, Draka, allow me to thank you. I was a stranger to you, defenseless and dying. You brought me healing and food and drink and tended to me when there was nothing I could offer you. I am alive today because of your kindness. You have my deep and abiding gratitude." He put both hands over his heart and bowed almost double.

"Ah," I said, looking away in embarrassment. "I couldn't, you know . . . I'm glad you're okay. You're welcome."

He really was very pretty.

"You never told me that you were the one who saved Garal," Herald accused, interrupting the moment.

"Hmm?" I answered eloquently.

"I only found out from him today, and even then, it was only because he was part of the debriefing! They had questions. About you," she said, looking like she regretted her outburst.

"Yeah, I thought they might," I said. "Come on, Herald, what do they know? Better to just tell me. I won't be mad or anything."

"If I may?" Garal said, looking from Herald to me and back. Herald looked at me.

"Sure." I sighed. "Herald, tell me if something he says isn't right, yeah?"

"Let me start from the beginning. Miss Herald came to Lalia and myself a few nights ago. She told us that she could show us where to find a group of bandits who have preyed on the people of this forest for some time. Now, we've known Herald and her family for a long while and know them to be trustworthy, so we believed her. But when we asked how she'd found these bandits, she told us that she had an informant, but she couldn't tell us who. She said they would be in danger if it came out."

"I was not lying," Herald cut in defensively.

"No one said that you were," Garal reassured her. "In any case, Herald described the location and roughly pointed it out on a map. It fit well as a staging point for known bandit attacks in that area. We decided to take her case to our commander, Rallon of Tavvanar, who took Lalia's squad and his own to find and hopefully destroy this bandit lair. I was left behind to train my new squad, so you all know what happened next better than I."

"Yeah, those bastards got what they deserved," I said. I knew a lot of people had died, but damn if it didn't feel good to know that the bandits had been wiped out.

"They did! And I'm told that you fouled a charge by the leader and his riders, quite possibly saving the lives of Herald and maybe even the fullness of my soul here—"

Lalia scoffed behind him, though I saw her blushing, and he went on with a somewhat desperate smile. "So thank you again for that. Of course, a lot of people, both Wolves and bandit prisoners, saw you. And Herald clearly declared you as her informant and her friend, although only Lalia heard that, so just a few of us know that part. Lalia told me, of course, when they returned to

Karakan. And several of her squad recognized you from, well, here. You're hard to mistake."

"Then it kind of flowed from there," Herald took over. "Commander Rallon does not miss much, and Lalia told him everything immediately, of course."

Lalia began to protest, but Herald raised her voice and spoke over her. "Lalia, I do not blame you at all. Of course you told him. I know that you would never keep anything important from him. Anyway, Draka, they all wanted to know how I knew you. And I told them that if they wanted to know, they could ask you, and you would answer or you would not. But then of course the commander wanted to talk to you, and they just kept asking, and I . . . I let it slip, I suppose, that I could arrange a meeting with you. So we left the coin and the note on the way back to the city. Then today, when we were ready to come here, suddenly Garal was coming instead of the commander."

"Like I was going to let him . . ." Lalia grumbled, staring daggers at me.

"All right," I said. "So I get why Herald is here. I like her, and she's the one who can get in touch with me. And I get why Guy—sorry, Garal—is here. We've met, I hope that I'll like you, and I'm arrogant enough to think that you might want to meet me. Which you did. What I don't get is why she's here." I lifted one hand and pointed a claw at Lalia.

"Ah. Well," Garal said, looking more than a little uncomfortable, "she's here to represent the commander."

CHAPTER TWENTY-TWO

Understanding

Excuse me?" I said incredulously.

"What?!" Herald said at the same time.

"To be clear," Garal continued, "both she and I are here in the commander's stead. After talking to Lalia, he felt that it would be good to get a sense of your motives before he met with you himself."

"So he sent the bitch who tried to kill me?" I asked flatly. "Is he trying to piss me off? Is that what this is?"

Garal frowned. "Please," he said. "I know that she has been . . . protective of the ones around her when you've met, but—"

"She chopped me in the neck with a sword!"

Garal stopped midsentence and turned to Lalia. "Did you . . . ?" he asked in a low voice.

"I might have," she hissed back. "I don't know. I don't think so. Things usually die when I score a strike!"

"Right here!" I said, pointing to my neck. It still ached like hell. "Herald, bring that lantern over here and take a look!"

Herald hesitated briefly, then stepped up and looked closely. "Oh," she said. "It looks like the scales are chipped here." She drew her finger in a line across my neck.

"Fuckin' hurts too. Bet my whole neck would be purple if I didn't have scales."

"Bet you would be dead," Herald corrected in a whisper. "She must have gotten a good strike in."

"Listen," I said to the two lovers, who were quarrelling in low voices. "Listen! Right now I don't care about your commander—Rallon, right? I'm guessing that's the old guy with the beard?—or what he wants. If he wants to talk to me, and if she"—I pointed to Lalia again—"wants to talk to me about anything, on behalf of him or her or anyone else, I want a damn apology!"

I saw Lalia bristle behind Garal. "I don't—" she started, but I cut her off.

"Every single time you've seen me, you've pointed a sword at me," I shouted. "Yesterday you tried to cut my head off! I don't care if you think you had a good reason! An apology! I want it! Why do you have to be such a massive bitch to me, anyway?"

"What?" Lalia sputtered. "You're a dragon! A. Drag. On! You're not supposed to exist, not here, not anymore! Your kind enslaves towns and destroys provinces and small kingdoms! You expect me to believe that you can be trusted?!"

I was . . . a little taken aback by that. She was just about spitting at the end, working herself up into some kind of righteous fury. "So that's it?" I flung back, all my pain and fatigue from the day suddenly crashing down on me in the face of this fanatical bullshit. "I am what I am, so I'm a dangerous monster, no matter what? It doesn't matter what I do? I save your lover, I show you where to find those shitheads who'd been burning villages, and it doesn't matter? I throw myself in the way of the fucking cavalry, and I deserve a sword to the neck for my trouble?"

"Demons or dragons," Lalia spat back. It sounded like she was quoting someone. "They will tell the sweetest lies, in word and in deed, and it will be your ruin."

"Again with the fucking demons!" I exclaimed. I was so tired. I wished I still had my hair so I could run my hands through it in frustration. "Who told you that, your uncle?"

"Yes," Lalia shot back, "as a matter of fact, he did!"

"Well, I already told you my name, and I know yours, so either you're already fucked or I'm not a demon. *Jesus Christ*, I thought it would be enough to go through this once with Lahnie, but *no*—"

I had to choke off my sentence and jump back as Lalia bodily shoved Garal to the side and went for her sword. "Which Lahnie?" she roared at me as Garal twisted and grabbed her from behind in a full-body hug, barely hanging on, and Herald leaped in between us. "Let go of me, Garal! Which Lahnie are you talking about, you scaly bitch?"

"A little girl I found in a tree and saved from getting eaten!" I shouted back, and I could taste the bitter venom leaking from my glands. "That Lahnie! Another one of my unforgivable crimes!"

The dragon was awake, and it was furious. I just wanted her gone, but it wanted blood and meat. It wanted to damn well *eat* her, the ultimate way to dominate those who would challenge you. My wings were out wide, my fully extended claws digging into the dirt, and it was only a supreme act of willpower that kept me from leaping at her, Herald and Garal be damned if they didn't get out of my way.

I couldn't tell if it was what I said or fear or Garal's soothing words in her ear that did it, but some of the fight went out of Lalia. She still looked angry but not bloodthirsty.

"Say that again," she said, and it actually sounded like she was asking, not telling.

"I found a girl who'd been chased up a tree by a giant damn boar," I spat at her. "Three or four weeks ago. I scared it off and got her home. You have a problem with that?"

Lalia was silent for a moment and stopped struggling against Garal's grip. "You're the lady in the forest," she stated, her voice flat. "You."

"What the hell are you talking about?"

"Last time I went home, my parents told me that my sister had gotten lost in the woods. She came back fine. When I asked her about it, she said that she'd been chased by a big pig, but a scary lady had chased it off, and she wouldn't tell us any more about this lady. We thought she'd made it up!" Lalia's face had twisted into something I would almost call despair. "Gods above, you're the scary lady, aren't you?"

"Wait—*Lalia*!" I exclaimed as it finally clicked. "You're the sister who went off to be a soldier! Who doesn't think much of men!"

"She told you that?"

"Yeah. Sweet kid. Kind of rude. I've been keeping an eye on her."

Lalia's anger flared in her eyes. "I was worried about the monster pig!" I elaborated, annoyed. "What the hell is wrong with you, really?" I snorted. "You know what? I'm done. Garal, it was nice to see you again. Herald, I'll see you later, right? Bye."

I turned to take off, when there came an angry, choking sound behind me.

"Wait!" Lalia called. *"Please."*

I turned my head to look at her. She still didn't appear friendly, exactly.

"I'm . . . sorry," she said. It looked like it took a lot out of her. "I will not apologize for how I reacted the first time I saw you, but I'm sorry for striking you. Can we talk?"

"Can you listen?" I asked back.

"I can try," she said, and she sounded like she meant it. "I will not promise to trust you, but I can promise to try."

I turned back, folding my wings. The dragon still seethed inside me, but I pushed it down. "All right, I can work with that," I said and sat down. "So, what did your commander want us to talk about?"

"Commander Rallon wants to know if you're a danger to Karakan and its territory," Garal said, releasing Lalia and stepping to her side. "As a sign of his goodwill, he has kept your existence an internal secret of the company ever since our first meeting. He's even gone so far as to encourage rumors about wyverns in the area to cast doubt on any sightings of you."

"He's wanted to talk to you for weeks," Lalia added, "ever since Garal convinced him that you could speak. I was against it."

"No shit," I muttered.

"He also seemed pretty impressed that you found this bandit camp," Garal continued. "He didn't say so outright, but I'd guess that he might be interested in working with you in the future if the two of you can get along. A chance to hire a flying scout is something he wouldn't pass up, if you're willing."

"Well . . . maybe?" I replied.

"That's for the commander to speak about, though, if you were to meet with him," Garal continued. "Would you?"

"I mean . . . I would have talked to him tonight if he'd been here," I said and looked at Garal's girlfriend. "And Lalia did make an effort. Kind of a shitty apology, but I'll take it, I guess."

"That's good to hear," Garal said with a smile. "Lalia," he continued, turning to her, "are you convinced? Will you recommend the commander meet with our new . . . acquaintance?"

"If he has a proper guard, perhaps," Lalia agreed reluctantly.

"Thank you," he said to her warmly, squeezing her shoulder. "Then . . . I suppose that we are done here for tonight. I have many things I would love to ask you, Draka, but I'm sure that we are all tired, and it's a fairly long ride back to the city."

"Wait!" Herald spoke up. "Draka, I want to speak with you." She turned to the others. "Privately, if you do not mind."

"Herald . . ." Lalia said immediately, looking apprehensive, but Garal threw his arm over her shoulders. "Come, my love," he said, leading her away. "Let's gather the horses."

"But—" I heard her say.

"She needs this," Garal said softly, and then they were too far for their voices to carry.

When we were alone, Herald approached, pulling out a small pouch. "I . . . Here. This is your half of the reward," she said. "Fifteen eagles each, plus an eagle and thirty peacocks from the swords we took," she said. She'd even put a long loop on the pouch. At my request, she opened it, and I dropped the coin in my mouth into it. That got me a raised eyebrow, but she closed the bag up and hung it around my neck. The bag was fairly heavy, which I loved, considering what was in it.

I could see on Herald's face that this was not all she wanted to talk about, though. Her whole demeanor was different than usual, tired and worried.

"So . . ." I said, prompting her.

"The others still have not come back!" she said, her voice cracking a little, the words coming out in an uncharacteristic rush. "It's been over a week, and they should've been back days ago! I looked at one of the Wolves' maps. The village that they were going to is only two days from the city on foot. Something's gone wrong, and they *left me*!"

Herald's voice broke, and I could see tears streaking her cheeks in the lantern light.

"Oh, darling!" I said, moving in closer. "I'm sure they're fine. Something just came up."

"No," she said. She was sniffling but leveled her voice back under control. "I helped them pack. They had supplies for a week, and none of them can hunt worth shit. They should have been back yesterday at the latest. Two days there, three days at most to investigate the place, though that seems excessive, and two days back."

"What was the job?" I asked.

"Village gone missing," she said ominously. "A few of the villagers had been to the city for market day, and when they returned, everyone was gone, both people and animals. Houses were in order and everything, just like the mining camp. Apparently it is neither the first nor the second time this has happened, but it has been many years since the last. The council put out a job, and the guild offered it to us first since we had been at the mine. It's not even a fucking combat job, and they still left me!"

Herald crouched in front of me, and I saw fiery determination in her shining eyes. "I am going after them," she said, and there was no room to argue with her. "I have talked to Lalia and Garal. They cannot come, and they do not want me to go. But they will not try to stop me."

"So when are we going?" I asked. No hesitation. This was Herald. If I had one friend here, it was her. Like hell was I going to let her go alone.

"Thank you," Herald said thickly, a tension leaving her as she blinked away a few more tears. "Thank you. Blessed Mercies, I was hoping that you would say that."

"Yeah," I said. "Of course! Look, get back to the city. Get some sleep, pack whatever you need. I'll be waiting for you at the edge of the forest. I'll be there all day if I have to be, so take your time. All right?"

She looked at me, her eyes still sad but her mouth twisting into a smile that looked more like her. "All right," she said and leaned in to give me a quick hug. "I will see you in the morning."

Then she was off to rejoin the others. I watched her mount up and expected them to go but got a surprise when Lalia trotted over, her sword still, thankfully, in its sheath.

"She asked you?" Lalia said.

"Yeah," I answered.

"And you're going with her?"

"Yeah."

Lalia frowned, then relaxed a little. "Good," she said. "But if anything happens to her, know that I will hunt you."

"You can try," I replied.

Lalia looked back toward Herald, who was talking softly to Garal.

"She is not as strong as she pretends. Not as . . . calloused."

"I think she's stronger than she looks," I answered. The fucking nerve of this woman.

"You think. You have not spent the last few nights at her inn, sleeping in her sister's bed because she cannot bear to be alone at night," the woman said, turning to give me a withering look. "She wakes up crying in the night. And I know why, because when she can't, or won't, talk to her sister, she talks to me. I know what she's been through. In a few days, she has been threatened with rape, killed her first men, and maybe lost her family. The wounds are still fresh, and some of them are partially your fault. I expect you to take care of her, and I will hold you responsible if you don't. Do we understand each other?"

Fuck, she could be intense!

"Yeah," I said. "We're clear. Though I'd hope that yesterday should have shown you that I won't let anything happen to her if I can help it."

She looked at me, frowning again, and it was like I could actually see her swallow her pride. "That was the leader you killed. Melkason, a cruel and dangerous man. Well done."

Then she turned and rode back to the others. Herald waved once, and they left me there, thinking about what Lalia had said. Herald wanted so much to be recognized as an adult, which she was by the local standard, apparently. She tried to be mature and well spoken and to take responsibility for herself and her actions. But I had seen her kill several gremlins and two men, which was, when I thought about it, heartbreaking. Back home, she'd be just another kid starting her last or second to last year of high school and stressing out about her grades and which universities she should apply to, maybe playing basketball or volleyball or something, considering how tall and active she was. Here she was, a killer facing a real possibility that her family had left her and wasn't coming back.

I tried not to think about that. I liked Valmik, and I really had nothing against Makanna. She didn't trust me, probably because she was overly, or maybe appropriately, protective of Herald. That was fine. I could respect that. As for Tamor, I didn't know him at all. But they were all important to Herald, and I'd be damned if I didn't do my best to help her find them.

CHAPTER TWENTY-THREE

Suspicions

By morning, I was in a tree near where the road entered the forest. I'd slept by the lake, and then around dawn I got the drop—literally—on an unfortunate rabbit that stopped for too long under my tree. Since I was already awake by then, I headed over to where I should be meeting Herald and climbed another tree for one of my vigilant naps.

Herald wasn't the first person on the road. Instead, I found Big Beardy, Short-and-Wide, Awesome Curls, and Baran, one of the first groups of adventurers I'd seen here. Curls and Baran must have hit a rough patch in their relationship, since they walked at the back and front of the group respectively and weren't talking. I hoped that whatever it was, they'd work it out.

Still, Herald was earlier than I'd expected, though I figured I shouldn't be surprised. She'd probably gotten as little rest as she thought she could get away with and then headed out as early as she could. She was riding Melon again, scanning the trees attentively. She looked well prepared, with her armor, sword, and bow, as well as various small bags on her belt and a large pack strapped behind her.

Uncurling from my perch, I climbed the first few meters and then dropped. When I reached the road Herald was waiting, looking in my direction as I emerged.

"Good morning," I said. "Good eyes."

"Morning," she replied roughly. She looked like hell, honestly, pale with dark rings around her eyes. I didn't doubt what Lalia had said about Herald not sleeping well. "Let us get going, huh? The village is in the mountains southwest of Karakan, so we will need to circle around. I think heading for the foothills first will be best."

"Yeah, sure," I said. *South?* I'd never been farther south than this. This could be exciting! Herald was a mess, and her family might be in danger or worse, so I shouldn't think of it as a fun trip, but still!

We traveled west along the edge of the fields, following them into the hills as they curved southwest toward the mountains. Herald kept her bow strung and her eyes open, and her obvious tiredness hadn't stopped her from shooting two rabbits by the time we stopped to rest Melon.

"I want to stretch the dry stuff as far as I can, in case the others are hungry," Herald explained as she dressed the rabbits and made a fire. She lit it using a piece of flint, which she struck with a piece of steel that looked a bit like a knuckle-duster. "This is your firesteel," she said, showing me how she used it. "See, I had the smith make it oversize so you should be able to hold it."

"You remembered!" I said, honestly touched.

"Of course I remembered!" Herald scoffed. Once she had the fire going, I took the firesteel and tried hitting the large piece of flint with it. It worked! I actually made sparks! Nothing like what Herald had managed, but I was sure that was a matter of practice.

I handed the two pieces back to her, asking her to hold on to them for now.

"Can you keep an eye on these?" Herald asked me as she skewered the rabbit carcasses and set them to cook on a stand she'd made from a few lengths of wood. "Do you know what to . . . ?"

"I know how to barbecue!" I said, slightly offended. Herald gave me one of her odd looks. She did that sometimes, and I still hadn't figured out what she meant by them.

"Good," she said and stood. "I will try to find some vegetables."

"Yeah, shout if you need anything," I said as she left.

Keeping an eye on the rabbits was easy. Turning them was harder, but I managed. The smell of roasting meat was indescribable. I had always liked any-thing on the barbie, but with my draconic sense of smell, this was something else entirely. If I hadn't just eaten two whole rabbits in two days, I might have gobbled them up, which would have been a seriously assholish thing to do. The fact that this was the first cooked food I'd really smelled in a month didn't make resisting any easier.

I'm not sure how long Herald was gone, but the rabbits were pretty much done when she returned with a handful of what looked like wild onions and garlic. She set the meat to cool, then unrolled a piece of oiled or waxed leather on the ground. After rinsing the onions and slicing them up on a small wooden cutting board, she quickly took the rabbits apart. She set one aside, then took out a small box of salt, which she sprinkled on the meat.

"You're good at this," I told her. "The wilderness stuff."

"I had a good teacher. Lalia. She grew up in the forest. You have seen her with a sword . . ."

"More than seen her," I added under my breath.

Herald smiled. "I suppose. But she is very good with a bow as well. I do not think her advancements complement archery, but she is still almost as good as me, and I am specialized."

"I'd rather not find out," I commented drily.

"We both talked to her, Garal and I. I think she will warm up to you if you give her time. Now, dig in," she said and picked up a leg.

"Oh," I said. "I—"

Herald just looked at me and bit a piece of onion, then nodded invitingly to the meat.

"You know what? Yeah. Cheers," I said and grabbed a piece with my teeth. Oh God, it was so good! I'd been eating raw meat, which had been fine, even tasty, though I had known that I missed cooked food. But tasting it . . . This was a whole other thing. I did my best to chew and savor the meat, which was tricky to do with the bones and a mouthful of fangs, and it was the best thing I'd eaten for weeks. I think I might have cried if I hadn't had company.

"Oh, man, I've missed that," I said after swallowing, bones and all.

"What?" Herald said with a speculative look. "Rabbit?"

"Nah," I said. "Barbecue!"

"It is odd," she said thoughtfully between bites. "I have read about dragons that breathe fire. Those are the ones in all the stories. And I have read about those that do not. But there is no record of dragons, fire-breathing or not, that use fire as a tool. The book I read said that fire dragons would kill their prey with fire and then eat them whole, charred or raw. I would not imagine that fireless dragons would care much about cooking their meat."

"Yeah, so?" I asked, not sure where this was going, nor that I liked it.

"In fact," she continued, her eyes narrowing slightly, "I still have not seen any description of a dragon like you, with black scales and an intelligence like yours. Dragons are supposed to be cunning, capable of speech, certainly, but never more intelligent than a small, vicious child."

"Uh-huh," I said. The dragon was aggressive and all, but I never thought of it as dumb or childish. "So you're saying I'm a genius for my species. Thanks, I guess?"

"Perhaps," she said, and I could see in her eyes that she was going in for the kill. "But you say such odd things. Like 'species.' And it is not just your choice of words and idioms, but things like how you know what it is like to be a young *woman*. How you miss your friends, which is very strange for a solitary creature, which dragons are, supposedly. When I told you how I missed my dog, you told me that you also had a dog when you were growing up. Is that not odd for a predator like you? And," she said, raising a finger as though she were presenting the most damning evidence in her case, "you know how to grill meat on a skewer."

Shit. I'd been careless. I had said too much, and Herald was too attentive and too smart. But maybe she hadn't figured it out, not really. Maybe—

"Draka," she said, putting down her food and looking me intently in the eyes. "Are you an enchanted princess?"

What do you say to something like that? Me, I laughed and I laughed, and I laughed some more. I laughed until I was lying with my neck flat on the forest floor and my wings were jerking weakly above me. It was just, the whole . . . Herald was smart. I knew that. And she was probably well read. She laid it on a little thick sometimes with the diction, but she was seventeen and trying to be her own woman, so there was no harm there. To hear her say some ridiculous fairy-tale crap like that, her face totally straight, completely serious . . . I couldn't help myself.

When I finally got myself under control and looked at Herald, she seemed much less offended than she deserved to be.

"I'm . . ." I started, biting down another chuckle. "I'm no princess. Whatever my dad told me."

"There it is again," Herald said seriously. "And I note that you are not disputing the 'enchanted' part."

Well, shit. She wasn't letting this go. How was I going to get her off the trail? Should I try to get her off the trail?

I was tired of not having someone I could talk openly with. I thought of Herald as a friend—my only friend here. And she had called me a friend and treated me like one. Didn't she deserve my honesty? Who was I ever going to confide in if not her?

I studied her. She was still completely serious. She didn't look offended either, just tired and like she was waiting for something.

"Will you keep anything I tell you to yourself?" I asked her.

"I already consider everything you tell me to be in confidence," she said solemnly.

"From everyone? Even your family?"

She only hesitated for a moment. "Yes."

"All right," I said and thought about it. "Tell you what." I got to my feet. "I'll tell you all about it once we're moving again. Are we ready to pack up here?"

"We are." All the remaining food was simply wrapped up in the leather mat, which she tied together with some string. Utensils were packed away, and I put some dirt on the fire. We left the circle of stones and the cooking stand in case someone else passed by and wanted to use them.

Melon whickered in protest as Herald led her away from the tall grass she'd been munching on, but she was as obedient as ever when Herald mounted up.

It was well into the afternoon when I started talking. We had kept up a decent speed and made it to the hills west of Karakan, where we could cut south along the mountains without worrying about meeting anyone. Even if we did, there were plenty of places for me to hide out until they passed. The constant movement was doing me good. My bruises didn't ache so much as long as I kept moving, and while flying would always be the superior choice for travel, there would be times when flying would either give me away or was simply not possible, like in the mines. For the first time in a long time, I was enjoying some cardio.

It didn't hurt that the view was amazing. I had seen the farmlands and the city in the distance, from my cave's ledge and from the air, but with the way the forest rolled and sloped, there was rarely a clear view. From here, I could appreciate the fields, green or yellow with ripening grain that waved in the wind. A wide river flowed from the mountains in the south, joined by smaller ones and winding lazily northeast through the farmland until it reached the city, and I could see boats floating on it. Past the fields, far in the distance, I could see the city. Its sandstone walls, its tiled or thatched roofs, and its towers were barely visible, but the mass of it sprawled. It must have been miles wide, and I wondered if the figures I'd heard were right: I could easily imagine three or four hundred thousand people living there, large as it was. And beyond that was the coastline, passing the city and then sweeping back in to form a narrow, rocky peninsula and a natural harbor for the city. I imagined the harbor full of ships, but really, I couldn't see anything at that distance. It made me long to fly over the city and see it for real.

We had traveled in relative silence, only pointing out interesting things to each other. I hadn't been sure where to start or how much to tell Herald, and she hadn't pushed me, her only sign of impatience being an occasional sideways glance.

"You're right," I started. "I am enchanted, or cursed, or something. There's some kind of magical bullshit going on, anyway. I'm not a dragon. I mean, I wasn't born like this. Or hatched, I guess. I've only been like this for . . . a month, I guess."

"But you were born? Human, I mean," Herald asked.

"Yeah."

"What happened?"

"Couldn't tell you," I said with a sigh, which came out more like a huff. "Basically, I fell. I like to climb rocks. Probably sounds strange to you, doing something like that for fun, but I love it. I'm damn good at it too. Good enough to get paid teaching others how to do it, arrange trips to good walls, stuff like that. And I like to take risks. I like the danger. The thrill."

I could see by the curving of her lips that she knew exactly what I was talking about.

"So", I continued, "I went climbing alone, in a cave, of all places, and I had a bad fall. Really bad. At first, when I woke up here, I thought that I'd died or gone into a coma or something and this was all a dream. But now . . . it's been a while, you know? And everything feels real. Completely real! And I sleep and dream here, and I wake up and everything is the same. So now I don't know what to think."

"That sounds terrible," Herald said quietly. There was no judgment there, no scolding me for my carelessness. Just sympathy.

"You don't know the half of it. I don't even know if this is my own body that was changed or if I took over someone else's. There's . . ." I almost told her about the dragon inside me, but decided not to. Too soon. I didn't want to freak her out more than necessary.

"It doesn't feel like my body," I said instead. "I can feel every part of it, and I can move like I've always had it, but it still feels wrong. Like, you're right, you and Makanna: I feel too small! And sometimes when I wake up, I stand up and try to walk on two legs, which works for a while, but I get tired real fast. Or I try to use my hands for something that they can't do, or I forget that I can, you know, fly?" I gave a small flap of my wings to make my point.

"You must miss your home," Herald said carefully.

"Hell yeah, I do! I miss my people, you know? My friends and my family. I miss my *phone* and my music and eating ice cream on the couch with Andrea. I miss climbing, but at least I can fly now, so that's something. And I miss just hanging out or going out to get drunk and dance with my friends. I even miss my ex-boyfriend. My last weekend before this happened, I was going to call him to come over for . . . you know. But Andrea talked me out of it. I wish she hadn't. God, I miss getting *laid!*" I said with a groan. "I mean, it had been *a while*, sure, but at least I always had the option to go out and find someone if I wanted to. Now . . . It's not like I've been in the mood, but I don't know if I could even, y'know, take care of myself like this."

I looked at Herald. She did indeed know, judging by how stiffly she sat in the saddle, how dark her face had become, and how she wouldn't meet my eyes.

"Ah, shit, I'm sorry!" I couldn't help but laugh. "I didn't mean to embarrass you!"

"I am not embarrassed," Herald lied into Melon's mane. "I am not some blushing maiden. I have . . . done things!"

"You're still blushing, though," I teased. "I'm not judging! What you do is your business—and that of whatever consenting adult you may involve."

Herald went even darker. I could almost see the heat coming off her face.

"Sorry, sorry," I said, laughing harder now. "I get it—change the subject! You know, it's not all bad. This body, yeah? I miss a lot of things, but there are good sides too. When I forget about what I've lost, I feel free in a way I think I've been looking for my entire life. Sure, I've got to survive on my own, but I think I've got that down now. Food and shelter and all that. And I can *fly*. That almost makes up for all the downsides. It's like . . . There was this poem my granddad loved. 'I have slipped the surly bonds of Earth and danced the skies . . .'" I paused. "Something about silver wings, I think?"

Herald looked at me blankly.

"I don't remember the rest. It sounds better in English, anyway, and I'm not enough of a poet to describe what flying is like. The rush of the air, the way the world looks from up there . . . Sometimes I go up and just fly for hours for the joy of it. I hope that tells you something."

Of course, I didn't tell her about the really dark moments during those first few days. Moments when I'd been high in the air, looking at the ground, so far below me, and the hunger and confusion and loneliness made me think about just folding my wings and hoping that I would wake up somewhere better. I wasn't ready to admit that out loud, and I'd left those thoughts behind me pretty quickly.

Herald was looking at me again, a little dreamily, her mouth curled into a small smile as I talked.

"Oh!" I said, interrupting my own train of thought as something occurred to me. "And you know what? It's been a month and I haven't had a period yet, so I might be rid of that!"

"Gods!" Herald covered her mouth as she giggled. "I had not thought of that! I think that makes me more jealous than the flying! Rich women here use healing potions to get it over with in a night, but even a cheap one will cost you ten eagles, and anyway, you can only use it once the bleeding starts. You are so lucky!"

"Yeah," I preened. "It's pretty great. Fingers crossed, though I'd better give it a year, I guess. Hope I don't go into heat or some bullshit like that. Do reptiles go into heat?"

Honestly, I was glad that Herald had figured me out. Or been suspicious enough to get me talking, at least. It was so nice, just speaking openly about what had happened. I still wasn't comfortable telling her about the dragon in me. It would have to remain a secret for the meantime. But being open felt good. And if Herald had been honest with me about her advancements, which were apparently the most important secrets you could have, shouldn't I do the same? We'd hopefully be working and fighting together, right?

"You know what?" I told her. "I can do other stuff, besides flying and fighting, that would be just impossible where I'm from. Remind me to show you when it gets darker."

CHAPTER TWENTY-FOUR

Agony Aunt

I spent the rest of the afternoon telling Herald about my old life. I tried to avoid technology as much as possible, both because I barely knew how any of it worked and because I didn't want to derail too much, but I had to explain smartphones and motorbikes. They'd both been important to me.

In both cases, she was amazed, not at what they could do but at how widely available they were. Apparently it was totally doable to enchant something to move on its own or to send and receive sound or pictures. It was just extremely expensive, with the cost increasing with the complexity of the enchantment. Herald thought the city council might have one single artifact that allowed them to basically video call the rulers of other cities, but that was it.

You could also enchant other things, but again, it was expensive, and for one simple reason. It took two major advancements to make an enchanter: one to be able to use magic at all, and one to bind it into an object, however that worked. Considering how rare it was to reach your second major, that meant that even those who gained the power usually didn't live for more than another decade or two, maybe three at the very best. Something fairly simple, like a box that always stayed cold on the inside or a plate that heated up, could be afforded by an affluent home or a reputable inn. But things escalated quickly when it came to weapons. Something like a knife or sword that would never get dull, one of the simplest weapon enchantments, would cost many gold dragons. That was years of earnings for most people, even if they never spent a brass bit.

"If I had a hundred dragons," Herald said, "I would get a bow that would never break and that could withstand any weather so I would never need to worry about having it strung in the rain and a matching quiver of arrows." She looked ahead wistfully for a while, then sighed. "No, I lie. If I ever have a hundred dragons, I will retire with the others. For that money, I could buy a cheap inn with plenty to spare to pay people to run it for me. I'm sure Mak would like that. It would be a big step up for us as a family. We might even be a House, in time."

She didn't sound all too excited, and I got it. As short a time as I had known her, I couldn't see her giving up on adventuring to run a bar/bed-and-breakfast.

"But if I did not," she said, getting that faraway look again, "I would get that bow."

"Is the weather thing such a big deal?"

"It can be. The string goes bad if it stays wet, and the staff does too. But besides being impervious to the weather, such a bow would be one of the finest money could buy, to start with. No one would bother to enchant a weapon that was not already a masterpiece." She sighed. "Perhaps if I work hard and save, I can at least get the bow itself one day, or a few enchanted arrows."

"Oh, that makes sense, I guess," I agreed. If an enchantment is going to cost a lifetime's earnings for a normal person, who'd worry about the few years' earnings that a basic item would be worth?

"I . . . I have been reading a lot about enchanting," Herald confessed. "I think it is fascinating. And I was hoping . . . You know that Mak has magic, and remember I told you that Tam does too? Well, so did our mother. There is no conclusive evidence that magic runs in families, not really, but I was hoping, you know. And you need magic to become an enchanter, and as fast as I am gaining advancements . . ."

"That sounds like an amazing goal," I told her.

"Yeah," she said, almost shyly, like she was confessing a great secret. "I am hoping that if I learn enough about it, I might get the chance. Understand, I will never consider it wasted time. It is fascinating on its own. But if I could become an enchantress . . ."

"You would never need to worry about money again," I finished for her.

She looked at me for a moment. "Oh, right," she said. "Of course. I was thinking we could have any enchanted equipment we wanted, me and the others. But the money would be nice too."

"You, ah, you mentioned you used to have a lover," Herald said thoughtfully after another long silence. "What happened?"

Ugh. That brought my mood down a bit. Not because of any old anger or anything. It was just so . . . banal.

"Alex and me," I said, "we just weren't good, yeah? He was in university and I'd barely graduated. He never tried to make me feel stupid or anything, but he had this way of assuming that people knew and understood shit, so he'd be talking about something, and then he'd have to dumb it down until we were both embarrassed. He played chess and Go and stuff like that, and I couldn't care less. And he always fussed about me getting hurt, both with climbing and the motorbike, and some other stuff I did, and I just wanted him to join in the fun."

I sighed and thought about it for a while, wondering how we even stayed together as long as we did. "Basically, I kept trying to get him to push his limits, and he kept trying to slow me down. In the end, all we had was sex and comfort. It was nice, but that was all it was. We didn't do anything together, and we didn't love each other. So we talked, and I moved in with Andrea, and that was that. No big breakup, no drama. We still send each other funny shit on TikTok sometimes. I mean, we did," I finished sadly.

I looked up at Herald, high above me on Melon's back, and she was lost in thought. "So," I said carefully. "What about you?"

From the way she started talking almost instantly, it was obvious that she'd been waiting for the question. "There is a boy I know. Maglan. A man. A soldier." She paused.

Ah, that couldn't be good. Wasn't there a war brewing somewhere?

"I have known him since I was small," she continued, her voice laced with worry, "though we were not really friends until a few years ago. He joined one of the regiments as an archer about two years back, as soon as he became an adult. And it was good! He got training and regular pay, and we could still see each other when he was off duty and I was in the city. We had fun, he taught me how to shoot, things like that. And then one day we kissed. And then a few months ago, the regiments got sent off to the south, because there is some disagreement with Happar, and there might be fighting. And I like him, and we were both so worried, and I wanted to make our last night before they marched special, and . . ." She trailed off.

Ah, right. "So you . . . ?" I asked.

"Yes," she said, blushing again.

"Was it good?" I went on teasingly.

"I . . ." She looked at me, shocked at the question.

"Was it?"

"It . . . Yes! It hurt a little. At first. But then it was . . . nice," she said, continuing to blush furiously.

"And you were careful?" I pushed.

"Yes," she said again, her pitch rising. She was clearly regretting bringing the subject of boys up at all. "I asked Lalia. She got me tea. To make sure."

"Okay, good. That's good. You couldn't ask your sister?"

Herald's voice was a pained squeak. "No! She has opinions! Strong opinions!"

"Really?" I asked, honestly a little surprised. I didn't know her that well, but she didn't strike me as stuck-up or anything like that. I certainly never thought that she might be a prude.

"She does not want me to 'repeat her mistakes,'" Herald said, imitating Makanna's somewhat-nasal soprano. "She was very clear when she gave me the girls-and-boys talk and every time the subject came up after that. Besides, she never particularly liked Maglan."

"She probably just doesn't want you to get hurt." I was trying to be charitable. Prudishness didn't sound like Makanna, though I couldn't pretend to know her. Being overly protective, though, well . . .

Herald scoffed. "Sometimes I think that she would lock me in a tower if she could."

Right. Change of subject.

"So, this Maglan. Did you hear from him? You know, after?" I dreaded the answer, but I had to know.

"Yes," Herald said with a small smile, much to my relief. "We kissed as they marched off. His friends made fun of him because, you know, I am a bit taller than him. And he smacked them and told them that they would be lucky to have a girl like me even look at them."

"Cute. And after that?"

Her face slowly fell. "I got some letters a few weeks apart. Mag never learned to write, so he must have had someone write them for him. Then, in the last one from six weeks ago, he said that they were moving, and no one would be allowed to send any more letters. And that was that." She sighed, then lapsed into a sad silence.

All in all, much less bad than I had feared. Still, I was not the person I myself would have gone to for advice about guys, especially in a situation like this. I tried my best to channel every romantic movie I'd ever seen and every piece of relationship advice I'd ever read.

"You miss him, right?" I asked carefully.

"Yes."

"Do you regret sleeping with him?"

"No." Her voice was very soft, very quiet. "I am glad that I did. That he was my first."

That answered two questions. "Are you in love with him?"

Herald paused. "I lay with him," she said uncertainly.

"Wanting to feel good together with someone doesn't have to mean that you're in love."

She didn't answer.

"*How* do you miss him?" I tried instead, after a pause.

"What do you mean?"

"Do you miss him like your heart hurts because he's away, or like you're worried for your friend and you hope he'll be okay?"

She was quiet. I couldn't tell if she wasn't sure or if she didn't like the answer. Either way, she'd tell me if and when she was ready.

We made camp while there was still a little light. Herald picked a spot where an overhang and a large boulder created a natural shelter from the wind, and a clear stream ran only a few dozen meters away. When I asked about a fire, Herald was dead against it, not wanting to draw any attention.

"You were going to show me something when it got darker." Herald was sitting on her bedroll after a dinner of leftover rabbit and onions. I had declined dinner, not wanting to be a burden on her food stores. "It is darker now."

And it was. With the sun behind the mountains, it was not completely dark yet, but it should be enough for showing off and doing some testing.

"Yeah," I said, feeling that excitement that comes when you expect to impress someone. "Let's do it! Can you see all right?"

"I can see well even in moonlight, and decently by starlight. This is fine. My advancement gives me better night vision than most, though I still need a light or Makanna's spell when it gets properly dark."

"Great," I said, preparing to move to a point about ten meters in front of me. "Keep your eyes on me. I don't know what this is going to look like, but it might be weird, so don't freak out on me, all right?"

"I am sure it cannot be that strange—" she said, and I *flowed*.

Herald shrieked and jumped back. It was a tinny, muffled sound while I was shadowed. She did it again when I became solid, though this time it was muffled by her hands clamped tightly over her mouth.

"Ta-da?" I suggested.

"What did you do?!" Her eyes were huge as she rushed over to me. She reached out and touched me, as if to make sure that I was real. "How? How did you do that?"

"Advancement," I said smugly. "Just got it. What did it look like?"

"This is amazing! It must have been a major! Did you not get a minor just . . . ? No, do not tell me. I cannot handle more envy right now. You were there"—she pointed—"and you just . . . melted like honey in warm water! It was like I was not looking at *you* anymore, but a deeper patch of shadow stretching off toward the horizon. And then it moved, like a torch was moving behind whatever is casting a shadow. I have never seen, never heard of anything similar!"

I basked in her adulation. I *was* pretty awesome.

Then I had a sudden, horrible realization. There was a scent that was missing.

"My bag," I exclaimed. "Where's my bag?"

Herald glanced at my neck, then looked around. So did I, frantically. My bag had not come with me! That bag had seventeen silver eagles in it! Where was my bag? Where was my silver?

Quicker than me, Herald took a few long steps to where I had been and returned with my bag, slipping it back over my neck, and all was right again. When she had picked it up, I had a sudden fear that the dragon would do something terrible. If I felt the loss of my silver like this, what must it be like for the dragon? What would it do if someone tried to take it from us?

"Not her," the dragon purred in my ear, calming me. *"There is nothing to fear from this one. She adores us. She would never steal what is ours. As is only right for one who belongs to us herself."*

That last part. That was not good.

There is an old joke: *The real treasure was the friends we made along the way.* The dragon took this concept very seriously.

"Thanks," I said, trying my best to hide my inner turmoil.

"Of course," she replied slowly, giving me a searching look. "I know what it is like to realize your money pouch is missing."

Yeah. I don't know what I looked like when I realized the bag was missing, but my reaction had freaked her out way more than the melting-into-shadow thing.

"You know," I said, trying to distract her with something fun and shiny, "when I move like that, I can change size. I think. I can move through holes that my body could never fit through. Wanna see?"

"Oh, yes! Absolutely!" Herald said, brightening.

"All right, let's see . . ." I murmured, looking around. "There!"

There was a kind of tree that grew here, in the rockier parts of the hills where the vegetation was sparse. It looked like an olive tree, except with thin, dropping needles as long as my arm that grew in dense bunches. I'd spotted one with a root coming up off the ground and back down again, forming a hoop roughly the size of a basketball.

"I haven't tried something this small," I hedged to Herald as I led her over to the tree. "But I'm gonna. Take my bag, yeah?"

"Sure," she said, lifting the loop of thick twine over my head. I waited for a reaction from the dragon, but it didn't mind. Then I positioned myself on one side of the hoop and focused.

I could maneuver a little once I'd melted, but to be sure, I willed myself to go straight through that hoop. After a few seconds, I felt the now-familiar melting sensation. I flowed toward the hoop, flattening to the ground. When I reached the rounded root, my head and neck went through without any problem, but my shoulders felt a resistance that I hadn't noticed before. There was a strange but not-exactly-unpleasant stretching feeling, and my body began to pass under the root, each part of me, from my shoulders to my chest and belly and hips, stretching and then relaxing once making it through to the other side. Lastly, my tail went through without any strangeness.

"That was disturbing," Herald said as I came back together, but despite her choice of words, she spoke with the excitement of someone discovering something new and interesting. "There was the same appearance of shadow stretching into the distance, and then it . . . I am not sure how to describe it—you folded around the inside of the root? It seems to have worked, though! How far can you go like that?"

That was a good question. One that I myself hadn't asked yet. "I don't know," I admitted. "I haven't tried to go very far, only a few dozen meters."

Herald looked at me blankly. "How much is a *me-ter*?" she asked.

Dammit. No one here had ever heard of the metric system. From what Herald told me, the local units were close enough to Imperial inches, feet, and yards, but I was no good with those. I'd learned them in school, but I used metric all the way. And it wasn't like knowing the language let me do conversions any more easily. I was going to have to relearn my whole system of reference.

"Uh . . . about a yard, I think?" I said. "Like . . ." I sat back and gestured with my hands to indicate how far. I hoped it was accurate.

"And you can only do it in the dark?" she asked.

"Or in deep shadow," I said. "There's a pretty tight limit for what is dark enough."

"What happens if it's too bright somewhere?"

"It's like hitting a wall," I said, then reconsidered. "A padded wall, I guess. It doesn't hurt or anything, but I just stop."

"It is still amazing," Herald said with appropriate wonder.

"I know, right?" I said happily. God, it was nice to be appreciated! "Oh, and that reminds me! One more thing."

"There is more?" Herald said with mock outrage.

"Yeah! Can you see the shadow of this tree?"

Herald looked closely. To be fair, with only the moonlight to illuminate the tree, the shadow was not easy to see. I think I had an advantage in distinguishing what part of the darkness belonged to what, thanks to my whole shadowsight deal.

"I think so," she said finally. "Right by the base, at least."

"All right," I said. "Focus on that and where the rest of the shadow should be."

I padded up into the barely there shadow of the tree. I might have been able to do this without standing in the actual shadow, but I didn't want to mess up with an audience watching me. Focusing on the shadow, I willed it to darken. Well, more like I begged it to; I really needed this to work.

Tendrils flowed from me, and gradually the edge of the shadow grew sharper. It was only very slight at first, but I heard a sharp intake of breath from Herald as it became deep and distinct against the lesser darkness around it. I pushed until it stood out as clearly, as if it were lit by the midday sun, then glanced at Herald. She stood, staring at me with her mouth slightly open.

With a surge of pride, I pushed. I hadn't been sure about this, but Herald already seemed pretty impressed, and if nothing actually happened, she'd never know. But now, using all my will, I made the shadow move. It bent slowly toward Herald, and her eyes widened until the tip of a shadowy branch barely touched her foot. She snapped out of her stupor and looked at me with a small smile, and I dropped my focus, the shadow changing back to normal as though nothing had happened.

"That is amazing," she said, almost reverently.

"It is, isn't it?" I said in the same tone.

As fun as it would have been to keep experimenting, it was late, and we needed to get moving as soon as possible. It was a cloudy night, the moon only partially lighting up some of the cover and a single star shining through a break every so often. Herald trusted Melon to wander freely and graze however she wanted, the reliable mare returning to us to sleep. I had expected Melon to sleep standing up, but she picked a patch of scrubby grass and lay down in it, and was asleep before either of us.

As we bedded down, Herald on her sleeping roll in the shelter and me curled up between her and the opening, I had an urge to reassure her that we would find her family tomorrow. But she had avoided the subject all day, and I would rather not make her worry right before she went to sleep.

"Draka," Herald said softly in the darkness, "I am glad that you are here."

"Me too. And I'm not going anywhere. Don't worry," I said, making it a promise.

"Thank you. Good night, Draka."

"Good night, Herald."

I woke up some time later. Herald was jerking in her bedroll, hugging her knees as she whimpered wordlessly.

"It's all right, kid," I whispered to her, padding over and lying down beside her. "I'm here. You're not alone. Don't worry. Someone's here."

She looked so scared and vulnerable that my heart hurt. I remembered what Lalia had told me about staying with Herald so that she wouldn't be alone, comforting her when she'd wake up crying in the night. Perhaps she deserved better than I'd given her.

I curled around the tall girl best I could, covering her with a wing as I kept muttering soothing words to her until she quieted down. After a little while, her shaking stopped, and I went back to sleep.

CHAPTER TWENTY-FIVE

Bandit Killers Anonymous

The next morning, we woke to a light, unexpected rain, which a persistent wind brought with it into our simple shelter. Herald had shifted in her sleep so that she was snuggled against my side, most of her curled up and dry under my wing.

"Ugh, should have put up the tent," was the first thing I heard that morning as Herald pulled her knees up to her chest so that she was completely covered by my wing.

I snorted with amusement. "And a good morning to you!"

She grunted at me, then ran the back of her hand against the leather of my wing. "Better than it might have been. Thank you."

We stayed like that for a little while as Herald fought to wake up properly. "You grow fast, do you know that?" she mumbled. "You are bigger again. Not much, but you are."

"Yeah, that makes sense," I said, thinking about how I'd gotten stuck in that crevice.

Once Herald actually forced herself to get up, she was ready quickly. I made us a canopy with both my wings while she packed her bedroll and finished the cold rabbit for breakfast.

"You have all sorts of uses," she said lightheartedly as she put on her rainproof cloak and made sure that her pack and bags were closed up tight against the weather. Since she had some shelter from the rain, she took out a simple map and showed me roughly where we were, southwest of the city, and where the village should be. The village was high in the hills, even higher up than we were. Makanna, Valmik, and Tamor would have gone there by road through the farmlands, but our route shouldn't take any longer, especially with Herald riding Melon.

The biggest obstacles would be two small roads and a river that we had to cross, the same river that flowed into the sea through Karakan. We had crossed some smaller streams already, fording them easily, but this one was large and fast enough that Herald and Melon would have to use a bridge. The roads led to other small communities in the hills and mountains, but according to Herald those were barely a concern, unlikely to see much traffic. For the bridge, I would have to cross upstream on my own to make sure we weren't seen together.

Poor Melon would have to bear the weather, though she seemed to take it with the same calm she displayed for almost everything so far. Her biggest complaint had been when Herald saddled her and dragged her away from eating her bedding, though she was rewarded for her patience with one of the small yellow fruits she loved.

Herald and I talked little that morning, and as we traveled on, Herald's mood slowly turned darker. Maybe the rain and the lack of sun did it, or maybe she was thinking of whatever nightmare she'd had that night. Or maybe this was normal for her, and I hadn't spent enough time with her to know that yet.

"Draka," she said as we descended one of the many hills we'd cross that day, "do you think about the men you killed?"

"Sometimes."

"Me too. I remember their eyes when they understood that they would die. Their spirits haunt me, I think. I dream about them. I cut and stab, and they take forever to die." Her voice became quiet, so quiet I could barely hear her over the rain. "Sometimes they do not die at all. Despite their wounds they just do not stop. Sometimes I cannot hit them, or my sword cannot pierce their skin, or I cannot even lift my sword against them. I hesitate. I am too slow or too unskilled or too unobservant, and they kill and kill and kill. They kill me. Everyone with me. Everyone I love."

"I was there, Herald. You didn't hesitate." In fact, I remembered the wildness, the almost-joy in her eyes as the bandits charged her. I doubted she would ever hesitate.

"No, I did not. I killed them. And sometimes I think I hate myself for it."

"Do you think you could have done anything differently? Without you or the people around you getting hurt?"

"I could have not been there. I could have done nothing, stayed at my inn, and those men might still be alive."

"And how many others would they have hurt? How many innocent people have you helped by killing them?"

Herald stayed silent for a long time before answering. "Perhaps dozens. Perhaps none."

I wasn't sure what to say to that. It had been barely a week since we came across those two bandits on the road and only a few days since the attack on the hideout, and I hadn't thought much about how Herald would be affected. Maybe I'd been too caught up in my own lack of a reaction.

We rode on in silence for a few minutes before I spoke again.

"I think," I said, trying to pick my words carefully, "that it is a good thing that you feel bad." At the pained look she shot me, I quickly continued. "I don't mean that I like to see you hurting. I hate it. But you killed two men. I think that's supposed to hurt, even if they were completely rotten. One of those men you killed was going to rape you, Herald, and then who knows what they'd do? The other one sure as shit wanted to kill you. If you feel bad about killing *them*, then I think you can feel safe that you'll never kill anyone just because you're angry or because they're inconvenient. It shows that you're much better than those two."

Herald didn't say anything, but she looked thoughtful.

"I wish I felt bad," I said without thinking about it. If we were going to be open with each other, she might as well know how I felt too.

"I feel worse about the animals I eat than the two men I killed. Do you remember the gremlin I ran down outside the mine on the night before we met?"

"I do."

"That gremlin was the first thing I ever killed that wasn't an animal, and I just . . . I felt nothing. I told myself that, hey, its buddies had tried to hurt you guys, right? And it was probably going to bring more buddies to finish the job. So I had to. I was justified. Same thing once we were down there. They were going to hurt you guys, so they needed to go. Never mind that I didn't even really know you. The strongest feeling I had about killing them was feeling bad *because I wasn't feeling bad*. You understand?"

"I think so."

"And then on the road I killed that guy, Pike? Paak? By then, I knew that I liked you. I thought of you as a friend, and he and his partner were going to hurt you, and they were part of a group that hurt a lot of other people, so they needed to go, yeah? He was the first human I ever hurt worse than a slap, and I didn't even hesitate. I killed him and I felt nothing but anger. No regret, no remorse. I looked at him afterward, and I was annoyed that there was blood on his money pouch."

I had felt hungry too, but that was more than I was willing to let on.

I sighed and decided to tell her something that had been gnawing at me for nearly a week now. I needed someone to hear it. "Do you know what the worst thing is?"

"No," she said, her voice low and tremulous.

"I don't know if it's me or this new body," I confessed. "I want to think that it's being a dragon that changes how I feel, but what if it's not? I want to tell myself that, yeah, I'm a dragon now. My brain works differently. That would be such a nice, convenient explanation. But what if that's not true? What if I was always some sort of sociopath who could hurt and kill people and not feel anything about it? Sure, I've felt bad about hurting people before. You know, emotionally. But was that because there were consequences?" I looked at Herald, hoping for an answer that didn't come. "How can I know?"

"I cannot tell you. But I think that you are far too worried about being a bad person to truly be one, if that is any comfort."

Crossing the river was uneventful. I wanted to be sure that I wouldn't be spotted, so I left Herald on the road and made my way far upstream, flew across, then returned to the road. Staying among the trees I set up in a spot we'd picked so that Herald knew to look for me and signaled for her to go ahead. A few miserable travelers used the bridge in that time, but no one stopped in the rain to question a young woman riding alone. About an hour after that, we reached the road that would lead us west into the mountains and to the abandoned village. On the way, we didn't see another living soul for a while, probably thanks to the increasingly heavy rain, but decided to stay off the road, just in case someone came by.

"Unimpressive" was the kindest way I could think of to describe this tiny village. Fewer than twenty houses crowded together near the bottom of a grassy valley, surrounded by open pasture and a few fenced-off fields. The stream that ran down the channel of the valley might have been calm and clear on any other day, but with the rain, it was a torrent, running fast and hard.

It might have once been rustic or quaint, even idyllic, but now, instead of boasting the charm of villages I'd seen in videos from Switzerland or Austria, this place just felt sad. Perhaps it was the rain influencing me, but the place had an aura of poverty and desperate survival.

And then something moved.

"Down!" Herald hissed, quickly dismounting and leading Melon behind the knoll we'd been looking from.

"Goblins," she said as we crept back up to peek into the abandoned settlement. "Dammit! I wanted to look through the village for signs of where the others might be."

At first, I didn't see anything, but now and then small shapes would dart from one house to another, sometimes holding something over their heads to keep the rain off. I couldn't tell anything about what they looked like, though, being too far away and hidden by the rain.

"Are goblins a big problem?" I asked.

"They can be. These ones are either living in or plundering the village, which means that my family may have avoided this place or the goblins have ruined their tracks."

"Makanna said that you can negotiate with goblins. Couldn't she and the others have talked to them?"

"Perhaps. The ones on Mallin prefer not to fight. They have a culture of making deals. They may not always make them fairly, but they will honor them."

"Wait. Mallin?"

"Yes?"

"Where's Mallin?"

She looked at me like she didn't understand the question, then smiled slightly. "I am sorry. I keep forgetting. Mallin is the island that we are on."

"We're on an island?"

"Yes? A large one, in the Sea of Sareya. Please, can this wait?"

I shut up.

She thought for a moment, then came to a decision. "Stay here. I am going to talk with them."

"What do you mean 'stay here'? If you're going, I'm coming with you."

Herald shook her head inside her hood. "Goblins talk to each other, and they talk to humans. If they see you I doubt they will keep it to themselves. Better to keep you hidden as long as possible. It is better if I go alone."

"Are you sure? Is that safe?"

She thought for a few seconds. "I will take Melon. If anything happens, I can ride away, and we will have to think of something else."

"All right," I said. I didn't like this, but I needed to trust Herald. "Don't hesitate to get out of there. And I won't hesitate to go in if I need to."

"I am counting on it," she said, reaching out and patting me just above one wing.

I stayed in place on the knoll while Herald hopped back on Melon. She headed down to the road and approached the village, riding in the open and giving the goblins plenty of time to see her coming.

A small figure ran into the open from the largest, most central house. It spotted Herald, stopped, then ran back into the house. Herald continued to the center of the village, then stopped. She didn't have to wait long. Soon a group of goblins emerged from the house, a few of them running to other houses and bringing out more of their kind. Of the main group, one was obviously the leader, singled out by the fact that a few of its companions were holding a table over its head as a cover from the rain.

Herald held her hands out to the sides. I assumed that she was talking, but it was impossible to hear anything over the rain. Most of the goblins had a weapon of some sort, though they didn't hold them threateningly. It was more like they were just showing that they had them.

God, I wished that I could hear something. I could see both Herald and the goblin leader gesticulating, but I couldn't interpret the mood of the conversation at all.

Then things began to go wrong. A smaller group of goblins snuck around the edge of the village, where Herald couldn't see them. They began to surround her, and the leader was gesticulating more and more. Herald had to put her hands on her reins to control Melon, who was prancing and pawing, and she was turning to flee when the surrounding goblins closed in on her. Still, they were not openly threatening, but clearly showing that Herald wasn't going anywhere.

That shit did not fly with me. I moved, but unlike last time, at the bandit camp, I was in full control. Two bounds and a leap and I was in the air. A few flaps of my wings and seconds later I landed heavily in front of the leader, spreading my wings and roaring in its face at the top of my lungs. I really only needed to make an opening for Herald to get out, but I chose to shock and awe the goblins.

They panicked. If they had stood and fought, they might have had a chance given their numbers, but they didn't. Most of them, including two of the four holding the table over their leader, simply ran. The remaining two under the table were both on the same side, so the heavy piece of furniture dropped onto the wide-eyed leader and knocked it on its ass. A quick look over my shoulder showed Herald with her sword out, menacing the surrounding goblins while spewing curses foul enough to make a biker blush.

When I looked back at the goblin leader, I saw it trying to crawl out from under the table, away from me. I took a flapping leap and twisted in the air, landing sideways in front of it. The leader yelped and started scrabbling backward. I could have killed it right there. It would have been so damn *easy*. But these little bastards might know something that could help Herald, so I held myself back.

"Stop!" I ordered. "Give up!"

The goblin's eyes went somehow wider still. "You talk!" it squealed.

"Do I need to repeat myself?" I growled as I stalked forward. "Give! Up!"

"Yes! Yes!" the goblin exclaimed, followed by a rapid mass of words in a language that I didn't understand and had no chance of following. "Tongues of men," was apparently specific to human languages, which made sense in hindsight, but it was frustrating to discover like this. The other goblins, those that had not run away yet, backed off with obvious relief and dropped their weapons. Oddly, they seemed suddenly almost comfortable with the situation, relaxing visibly and beginning to talk with each other in that fast language the leader had used.

"We negotiate, yes?" the leader said to me hopefully.

I looked at it and decided that it was probably a female. It was wearing a simple full-length dress that I assumed must have been meant for a child, but it was completely soaked through with rain and the chest bulged more than I'd expect from a male. She, if that was right, was maybe 120 centimeters tall and seemed of average size compared to the others, with arms and legs that would have looked proportional on a human child but with slightly larger hands and feet. She had a wide mouth set in a wider face, smiling nervously and showing teeth that were surprisingly like a human's, though she had a lot more of them than I'd ever had. She and the other goblins had pale brown skin, wide eyes, and small yet bulbous noses with large nostrils, as well as big, pointy ears. All in all, the goblins looked far more human than the gremlins had.

"Sure," I told the goblin. "I offer to let you live. What can you give me for that?"

"If I can make a suggestion?" Herald spoke up before the goblin had a chance to reply. "As I was saying before, we are looking for three humans, two dark like me, one paler. We also want to know what happened to this village. Before, you wanted my horse and weapons. Now the situation has changed. Draka, if they answer all of our questions truthfully, will we be satisfied?"

I made a show of thinking about it, trying to look unhappy as I said, "I suppose so."

"Then, Nallekka of the Slanted Hills tribe, we offer this: You will answer all of our questions. You will tell the truth, and you will not hold anything back that might be of use to us. You will not try to harm us or my horse. And you will certainly not tell anyone, human, goblin, or otherwise, anything about my companion! In exchange, neither she nor I will kill any of you, and we will all leave each other in peace. Are these terms acceptable?"

Nallekka, still smiling nervously, looked from Herald to myself, then back to Herald.

"Yes!" she said, nodding vigorously, her ears flapping. "Good terms. No one loses. I accept for Slanted Hills tribe." She gestured to the house she had come from. "We talk inside?"

"After you," Herald said and dismounted. She led Melon under the extended roof of the house where she would be out of the rain, and then we followed Nallekka inside.

CHAPTER TWENTY-SIX

To the Gate

So, that went pretty well," I said to Herald as we stepped inside the rough wooden house. Then I stopped and looked around.

"Is something wrong?" Herald regarded me with concern.

Nothing was. Not really. The house, being the biggest one in the village, probably belonged to the chief or mayor or headman or whatever they had here. It wasn't actually that big, but it was big enough. The goblins had cleared out the main room to make space for their loot, but there was a fire burning in the fireplace and it was pleasantly warm. Being inside and cozy like this, smelling the smoke from the fire, it was almost enough to make me feel human again.

"Are you all right?"

"I'm fine," I told Herald, not sure how I really felt. "Let's ask our questions and find your family."

There were a handful of goblins inside, and Nallekka, their leader, fired off a few quick sentences that led to three of them appearing with chairs from another room. The one that approached me looked at me uncertainly, then seemed to decide that this was beyond his pay grade. He went around me and put his chair down. Job done, he backed away, and I sat on the floor while Herald and Nallekka sat on their chairs.

It all felt very civilized, really. The effect of the chairs, the fire, and the two clearly separated parties was spoiled a little by the pile on the floor made up of clothes, rugs, cutlery, candlesticks, tools, and everything else the goblins had gotten their hands on, but you can't have everything.

"Please," Nallekka said, "ask questions. Speak easy, please. Not so good with trade tongue."

"What're you doing here?" I blurted.

Nallekka frowned. "Village break deal. Do not pay tribute at agreed time. We take ourselves."

"You had a deal with the village?"

"Yes. We leave them alone, watch for monsters, warn them. They pay tribute. Every moon, one goat, one roll cloth. Good deal! Half moon ago, they all leave. We wonder, but we do not care. They can go. But they do not come back, do not pay tribute at agreed time!"

"Where did they go?" Herald asked.

Nallekka shrugged. It didn't look natural, and I wondered if she'd learned it like it was a part of this language. "Do not know. Go up valley along stream, toward mountain. We do not follow after they go in territory of Wandering Goat tribe."

"Did you see any other humans come here after they left?" Herald continued.

"Yes! Scouts watch village after humans leave. First three humans of village come. They leave again. Some days ago, three other humans come. Not of village. They look much. Spot scouts, try talk. We not interested. Too much bother. They stay two days, then leave."

"In the same direction as the villagers?" Herald asked, leaning forward.

"Yes!" Nallekka confirmed. "Humans of village leave tracks. New humans follow, I think. We watch them until they go in territory of Wandering Goat tribe. Then do not know."

"Just to be sure," I said, wanting to head off any disappointment. "The three humans who were not from the village, they were a woman and two men? The woman was short?"

"Small female, two male, yes."

"Two of them dark, like my friend?"

"Like you say, yes."

"Sounds like them, all right," I said to Herald.

"Let's go, then!" Herald said, standing up. She was almost vibrating with excitement.

"You don't want to wait out the rain?" I asked. I was getting comfortable here. A dry, warmish floor, a crackling fire. It even smelled kind of nice. Besides the woodsmoke, I'd noticed a vaguely pleasant earthy scent coming off the goblins. They still smelled wet and dirty, but just the same.

"How can you suggest that? Every minute might count!" Herald said, interrupting my musings. The look of betrayal in her eyes was too much for me to bear, and I folded without a fight.

"Yeah, nah, you're right," I said, feeling a little ashamed under her gaze. "Let's go. Nallekka, you, uh . . . thanks. Enjoy the village, I guess. Peace?"

"Peace, yes!" the goblin said happily with a wide, wide grin.

"You trust them?" I asked Herald outside as she mounted poor Melon.

"I do," she said. "Makanna and Lalia both agree that the goblins do not break deals unless in truly desperate straits, or if they feel that the other party has already violated the terms. As long as we do no harm to them, they should leave us alone."

"All right. In that case, will you be okay to ride alone for a while? I want to stretch my wings and scout ahead."

"Can you fly in this rain? I do not mean to doubt you, but . . ."

"No, fair, fair. I honestly don't know. Just now was fine, but that was only a few seconds. Good time to find out, though." Meaning it was better than trying from my cave, which was over a couple hundred meters' drop.

So Herald started riding up the valley along the stream. Any tracks were long gone, but there was a trail of mud in the grass that might have been where they were before the rain came. As for me, I flew.

It was a truly miserable experience. The rain made my wings heavy, and even with my extra eyelids, I still had to blink constantly to be able to see. And when I craned my neck forward, the water got under my scales, which . . . blech. Not a nice feeling. Like wearing a damp shirt. But it got me up the valley fast enough. Soon, there wasn't even the mud tracks to follow, but I knew roughly what I was looking for, and as awful as flying was right then, it got me around *fast*. It must have taken an hour, but I found what I suspected I would.

Many smaller valleys cut into and joined the larger one we were following, and in one of them, I found a straight-sided cutout much like the one I'd seen near the gremlin mine. I landed nearby to check it out, and sure enough I saw the lines, the magical glow that marked a gate in the stone. This gate was much more worn than the one I'd found before near the mine, but it was impossible to mistake. Satisfied, I returned to Herald.

"I found it!" I told her as soon as I landed, skidding in the mud. I had to shout to be heard over the combined noise of the rain and the stream.

"Found what?" she shouted back.

"A gate, like . . . Ah, shit! I'm so sorry. I never told you! I got so caught up in the bandits, and then there was the whole thing with Lalia, and this . . ." I would have smacked myself if I still had a proper forehead.

"I found a gate. Magical," I tried to explain, getting closer so I wouldn't have to shout. "Near the mine. I followed some tracks from the mine into the mountains, and I found this gate. And there's one here too! Bet you anything that's where everybody went!"

Herald matched my excitement, smiling despite the rain running down her face. "A secret gate? Lead on! Why do you say it's magical?"

"It just looks like it," I said. "It's got this glow, yeah? Like when Makanna uses magic. You know?"

Herald looked at me with wonder. "I have no idea. You can see magic?"

"Yeah?"

"That . . . is not a thing that I have ever heard of before."

"Oh."

I'd say it took an hour and a half to reach the gate by foot. It made me appreciate the speed I could fly at and the strength and endurance of my flight muscles, my "extra pecs," all over again. That and the magic that must be involved. I was no biologist, but I knew something about how much wing you needed to lift something. Birds had hollow, fragile bones. I definitely did not, considering the abuse I'd survived. And my wings, while big, were not *that* big.

Herald and I didn't talk that whole time. We were good at comfortable silences. Herald was a thoughtful young woman, and I had a newfound ability to not think and just be, thanks to the dragon. She did keep looking at me as though she was going to say something, but she kept her thoughts to herself, which was fine with me. When she had something to say, she would.

"Is that it?" Herald asked when the cut stone surrounding the gate came into view in the distance.

"That's it," I confirmed, and she urged Melon on, pulling far ahead of me, eager to get there.

I plodded along at the same pace I'd kept up the whole way here. When I arrived, Herald had dismounted and was searching the area around a trough, and as I got close, she held up something small and green.

"A garron stone!" she shouted in triumph. "Tam loves them! They must have been here!"

When I got closer, she came up to me, and I saw that the thing was, in fact, not a *stone* stone but a fruit stone, like from a fist-size plum.

"Come on!" she said. "Show me this gate!"

"It's right here," I said, leading her up to the smooth stone surface at the end of the trough. It was set about half a meter into the stone, about two and a half meters tall and three wide.

"This is just a wall," Herald said skeptically, some of her excitement fading. "Cut stone, yes, but . . ." Then she looked closely and approached the wall. "Wait," she said. "Here! Look! And there, where the big chunk is missing! That is not just a pit; it is a hole!"

She'd been running her finger along the center line of the gate, right where I saw a magical line. Unlike the gate near the mine, this one was chipped and pitted, and if you looked closely, you could see the individual doors outlined by damage. And she was completely correct in that at the top, one whole corner of the left door had been broken off, leaving a hole bigger than my head into the pitch-dark beyond.

"Mak, Tam, and Val must have come here and gotten inside somehow!" Herald said, still inspecting the doors. "It is the only explanation! Why else would they not have come back?"

I could think of some reasons, but they were not anything I wanted to share with Herald. She would have thought of the same things, and what she needed was hope.

"Yeah, probably," I agreed. "Now, how do we get this thing open? I don't see any handles or levers. Not even a keyhole."

Herald looked at me, bit her top lip, then looked at the damaged corner of the door.

"Draka," she said thoughtfully, "how small do you think you can get?"

It was still early in the afternoon, and despite the heavy clouds, it was far too bright for me to try melting into the shadows. Herald had jumped up, gripped the sides of the hole, and pulled herself up to look inside, declaring angrily that it was "too godsdamn dark to see a godsdamn thing." We huddled up, Melon included, in the shallow alcove in front of the gate. Thankfully, the rain was falling from the closed side, and we could stay out of the rain while we waited.

As we waited for the light to fade, we spent the hours mostly talking. I told Herald about growing up with two parents in academia who turned me off the idea of education from their very existence. It was not because of any crushing expectations. There was no nagging or disapproval when I did badly in school, just offers to help me study and a *You'll do better next time.* But I was a contrarian little shit, and by the time I accepted that, it was way too late for me to want to change. I told her about doing stupid shit with my friends for fun, losing my virginity before I was at all ready because I wanted to be cool, and getting into climbing, which became my life for the next several years.

Herald was amazed at the fact that I had twelve years of schooling and that both my parents and my brothers were "scholars," as she called them. This apparently put me on the same level as children of the upper crust, something that Herald and her siblings would never even think to dream of.

When she told me about her own childhood, I felt honestly ashamed of how I'd pissed away all my advantages. She remembered very little about her parents. She knew that they had come to Karakan from overseas, a place called Tekeretek, fleeing with Makanna and Tamor to avoid slavery. Her parents had both died when she was very small, her mother in an accident and her father a few years later from some disease. After that, Makanna and Tamor, both just kids, did what they could to keep themselves and Herald fed and a shitty roof over their heads. At first they'd made sure that one of them was always at home with Herald, but as the money their father had left ran out and Herald got a little older, they'd all been forced to leave their home while Makanna and Tamor both worked.

"Tam got work as a runner. Packages and messages, you know? He got a lot of tips, probably because he has always been polite and charming. Oh, that is how he met Val, by the way, years later. Making a delivery from a blacksmith to Val's inn, I think."

"Ha, cute," I said, trying to smile with as few teeth showing as I could. Herald had been helping me practice nonthreatening facial expressions. "What about Makanna?"

"Well, she got work in the kitchen at a tavern where Father had known the owner," she said. "Then, when she got older, she started serving, and when she got to be an adult, she became an . . . entertainer."

I could see Herald closing herself off. I didn't want to push, but curiosity made me open my mouth anyway.

"What kind of entertainer?" I asked.

"Oh, singing and dancing," Herald answered in a rush. I could see her blushing. "She never . . . She told me she never did anything more, and I believe her."

"Is it common for singers and dancers to . . . do more here?"

"Usually only pretty girls get work as entertainers," Herald said in a small voice. "And boys, I suppose, sometimes. And usually they do not have much money." She left the rest unsaid.

I hadn't heard her sing, but I could see Makanna as a dancer. She was pretty, and I imagined her darker complexion and long, straight hair would make her stand out. Besides that, she had a curvy build, and she moved gracefully. I hoped that she'd told the truth about not offering anything extra. I wouldn't judge her for it, it was just . . . I didn't like her much, but I also didn't want to think that she'd felt the need to sell herself because she needed the money to feed her little sister.

God, I'd been so spoiled.

"So how'd you all end up adventuring?" I asked, desperately wanting to change the topic.

"Oh!" Herald said, brightening again. "So, Tam met Val, and it was just, blech, disgusting how in love they fell. Val was already a fighter doing odd jobs with teams the Guild put together, and he started pushing Tam to learn to fight too. And then Mak met Lalia, and met Garal through her, and Lalia taught Mak a little about how to defend herself. And me too," she said proudly. "She, um . . . I think she saw some patrons mistreat Mak, and she disapproved. I am not sure, and they have not wanted to tell me, really."

"Uh-huh. So . . ."

"Yes, so Val and Garal helped Tam learn to fight," she said, and the rest came in a torrent. "Garal wanted Tam to join the Wolves, of course, but Val convinced him that they could do some easy jobs together instead. Better money, more freedom, and all that. And then by the time Mak got her magic, Lalia taught her to use a dagger or a sword pretty well, so Val and Tam asked if she wanted to join them so they could do more dangerous jobs that paid better. That is when Mak started to learn to use a spear. And, you know, Maglan had been teaching me archery, and Lalia had been taking me into the forest when she could, when the others were away, and she taught me to hunt and use a sword and ride and all kinds of other useful things. So when I became an adult, they started taking me along on the safer jobs."

She smiled ruefully. "It took some work to convince them, though. I had to sneak after them the first two times before they would let me come along. Then they took me, but I had to promise not to sneak after them on the dangerous jobs, so I never went on a hard one. Until the mine, that is."

She frowned and became silent for a moment. "And now we are back to me not going with them at all, apparently."

"Don't worry. We'll find them, or get them out or whatever, and then they won't be able to pretend that you can't handle yourself."

"Do you think so?" Her voice was so small, and her eyes filled with such desperate hope that it made my heart ache.

"Yeah. They're idiots otherwise, and I don't think that they are." The sun was getting low, nearly touching the mountains. "Look, it's almost dark enough. We'll get this thing open, and then you'll show them."

CHAPTER TWENTY-SEVEN

Into the Dark

As the afternoon turned into evening, the light began to fail, and the heavy clouds were a great help. Finally, I decided that with some effort, I should be able to make it dark enough, at least right in front of the gate, to try to make it through that hole. That, and Herald's mood was falling while I was getting bored and impatient. And, truthfully, I wanted to show off. I've never been perfect.

"Are you sure?" Herald asked doubtfully. "It was much darker than this last night."

"Yeah, this should be fine. You might want to step into the rain, though, so you can get a good look."

She glanced at the sky with a small frown, then at me. "Okay. But this had better work."

"Bet," I told her and gave her an all-teeth grin.

I shook myself, getting the stiffness out from sitting for so long. It probably didn't make any difference, but it made me feel better. More focused. Then I blinked myself over to using my shadowsight, and everything briefly became a barely distinct blur before clearing up. It was still hard to see anything. It was a little too bright. But this way, I'd be able to tell much more easily when it was dark enough to go shadow mode, and I didn't really need to see anything except the hole in the gate where a corner of one door was missing.

Clearing my mind, I tried to focus on the shadow around the gate. There was no single, defined shadow, of course, but if there had been, it would have been the shadow of the stone above the recessed gate, and with effort, I could almost distinguish it. Once I had a good idea of what I was working with, I put my will to it. It needed to be darker. I wanted it to be darker. I demanded that it should be darker, and I was a shadow dragon, dammit. I was shadow, I was darkness, and it would do what I told it to do. It would become as deep as it needed to be for me to change, because that was the only thing that could possibly happen. I commanded, and it obeyed. That was just how it was.

I commanded, and it obeyed.

Even over the sound of the rain, I heard Herald gasp. Dark tendrils flowed from me, grasping and merging with shadow, and the shadow around the gate became deeper and darker until it was clearly outlined against the stone and the alcove was plunged into almost-complete darkness. Even I was somewhat surprised. It had taken a lot out of me, and I actually felt a little winded. I might have overdone it, but hey, I had wanted to show off, and Herald sounded and looked appropriately impressed. She was actually bouncing excitedly on her toes. I assumed that she was also grinning like an idiot, but she stood in the light and with how my shadowsight inverted things, making the darkness bright and the light dark, it was hard to see that kind of detail.

"All right," I said, breathing heavily but happily as I maintained the darkness. "Here I go!"

With that, I focused on the small opening and reached for it as I dissolved into shadow. At first, I thought that I wouldn't be able to reach it, which would have been very embarrassing, but with the dragon in my ear urging me to *simply go*," I discovered that not being solid meant that I could control the shape of my body to some degree. Which is to say that, when I stretched desperately for the opening, because I didn't want to look like an idiot in front of my friend, my body responded by elongating like taffy until I reached it.

My head was the first part of me to make it to the opening, and it fit through easily. On the other side was a smooth stone tunnel. It was straight, sloping down into the distance, and looked like it was exactly the same height and width as the gate. With my head inside, I willed the rest of myself to move through, and I was met with the same resistance as last night as my body forced itself through like an octopus squeezing itself inside a bottle. On the other side of the gate, I poured onto the ground and solidified with a sense of triumph.

I looked around. There was the gate, still outlined in magical light on this side. There was the tunnel, which I couldn't see the end of. It must have been pitch-black, because I could see very well.

Herald was still outside the gate. Now what?

I'd passed through the hole quickly, so the doors couldn't be very thick. Could I push them open? I put my shoulder to one side of the center line and heaved. Nothing happened. I tried again, harder and for longer, and still nothing happened. I stopped as I heard a scrabbling above me.

"Draka!" Herald's voice came in a loud whisper. "What is in there, Draka?"

"A tunnel into the mountain," I whispered back.

"What?"

"A tunnel into the mountain!" I repeated, louder this time.

"Oh!" she replied. "That makes sense, I suppose. Can you get the gate open?"

"I'm trying, but either it's too heavy or something . . ." I heaved. "Is holding . . ." I heaved harder. "It shut!" I heaved again with all my might, my claws scraping on the stone floor, and a whole lot of nothing happened.

"Draka, it is all right if you cannot get it open," Herald said, but I could hear the disappointment in her voice. "I will just stay here with Melon, and . . . and you can go ahead and let me know what you—"

"Fuck that!" I said angrily and heaved as hard as I could on the stone. "Come on, you fucking . . ."

I was a dragon, dammit! I could fly and get chopped in the neck with swords. I could defy physics. I was going to get this thing open. I wanted it open. I demanded that it open!

"Open!" I roared, and I felt something leave me. The lines around the gate flared briefly, and the gate slowly ground open, Herald dropping lightly to the ground in front of me and getting Melon out of the way.

"Is foul language the secret, then?" she asked jokingly as she peered into the dark.

"It usually helps, yeah. But it felt like I did something. Like I pushed magic into it, and then it just opened."

"Perhaps that is how the others got in. It would be just like Tam to stumble onto something like that."

"Yeah? Is he smart?"

Herald laughed. "Draka, I love my brother, and he is not dumb. But no, he is far more lucky than smart. Extraordinarily lucky. Come on now, let's go."

I hoped that she was right about that, and that his luck had held. Wherever he was.

Herald took her bow and her bags but left Melon loose outside. "Is that safe?" I asked.

"Oh, yes," Herald answered. "She'll wander a little for food and water, but she'll stay in the area. If we do not come back in a long while, she might find her way home, but I am willing to risk that. She's a clever old girl."

And so the two of us entered the tunnel. The darkness and silence quickly swallowed us, and Herald treaded carefully, holding on to my wing for guidance. There was no dripping, no scratching. No distant echoes. Only our footsteps. The tunnel curved subtly in a downward spiral as it went along, and once the gate was out of sight, it was almost like being in a small, separate world. There were barely even any scents in the weirdly dry air. All I smelled was stone, dust, and Herald.

"Can you see at all?" I whispered to Herald after a minute, when there was no longer any light visible from the open gate. It was so quiet in there that even saying that felt loud, and I was starting to wonder about who or what else might be in here.

"No, nothing," Herald whispered back. "I have a lantern, but I did not want to light it in case there is something unfriendly in here. But if all those people came here, there must be light coming up sooner or later, right?"

"Right," I said, but it was hard to believe it in this bubble of darkness. "Where's that shiny stuff on the walls when you need it?"

"It is too dry," Herald said, reaching out to touch the wall. "Glow slime needs enough water that it trickles down the walls."

As we descended, I kept thinking that there were things we should have asked ourselves before we went in here. Like, why would a whole village just up and leave for a hole in the mountains? Why hadn't they left any sign or message for the villagers who'd gone to Karakan, and returned to find them gone? And why would a whole mining camp do the same? The goblins hadn't said anything about anyone *taking* them. Just that they'd walked off into the mountains together.

What the hell might we find down here?

I had no idea how long we walked through that tunnel. It might have been ten minutes or two hours. The tunnel wasn't smooth, but it was still completely featureless. Just one long, curving rectangular tube, going on and on and on, with no light and no sound. No luminescent algae. No dripping water. No small critters scuttling in the dark. Nothing but our footsteps and our breathing, our heartbeats and the rustle of Herald's clothing.

I could have cried with relief when I actually heard a sound in the distance that wasn't us. I stopped, and Herald took another step and then stopped as well.

"What is it?" Herald whispered tensely, bending toward me and keeping her voice as low as she could.

"Do you hear that?"

She was silent for perhaps a minute. "Yes. A . . . creaking, grinding sound. Rhythmic."

"Yeah. That's the one. Can't be far."

"Gods, I hope that you are right."

"Let's go. Slowly and quietly."

As we went on, the sound got louder and was then joined by other sounds, scratches and taps and thuds, and a rushing in the background that might've been water. Soon there was a faint light at the far side of the bend, and we crept forward ever more cautiously until, without warning, the tunnel ended.

It opened into a large space, a natural cavern that had clearly been expanded in places. It was lit with a pale blue light, and I could see large stalactites hanging from the ceiling. From where we were, we could see across the space, and it looked like there was a walkway cut around the side of it that led to other openings in the wall much like the one we entered through. Whatever lay deeper was hidden by a wide rock ledge and the first step of what must've been a staircase.

At this distance, we could hear sporadic voices, mutterings and sometimes harsh laughter, though most of it was drowned out by creaking. We got low, me flattening myself to the floor and Herald on her hands and knees, and crept forward toward the ledge. Herald reached it before I did, and her breath caught with an almost-silent "Oh!" as she looked down.

I wasn't completely sure what I was seeing. Rows of people sat along the walls of the lower level. Some of them looked like they were making simple crafts or mending clothes. Others turned a large horizontal wheel, which creaked loudly with every push. I couldn't see that the thing was attached to anything, so I guessed there must be more to it under the floor. The people were men, women, and children of all ages, dressed in simple homemade clothes, and the cavern smelled of unwashed bodies. No humans spoke. No children cried. Their faces, from what I could see at my distance, looked completely blank, as though they were sleepwalking.

I was pretty sure we had found our missing villagers.

Besides the smell of the villagers, there was something else there. Something I couldn't separate from the other scents, few as they were, but it was definitely there, like a backdrop. The dragon stirred, and though it didn't say anything, I felt anxiety and confusion from it, emotions that it rarely expressed.

I was sure the smell wasn't coming from the other group of beings in the cavern. Watching over the humans were a few tall, thin creatures. In the blue light, I could only tell that their skin was paler than the humans', and they were hairless, with large eyes but no noses or ears, just slits and openings. They all held spears, but their posture and the way they paid more attention to each other than the humans suggested boredom more than anything else.

I watched one of them walk up to a woman who was sewing something. It knocked the piece out of her hands with the butt of its spear. The woman calmly picked up her work and continued. But the guard knocked it out of her hands again. She picked it up again. He kicked her lightly in the side with his boot, and she didn't react at all. Finally, the creature seemed to slump a little, finding no entertainment there and walking up to one of its fellows, which spoke to it in a language full of hisses and guttural consonants and laughed. At it or the woman or at the whole situation, who could tell?

Every now and then, the guards would take one of the people pushing the wheel and sit them down by the wall. Then they would get someone who had been sitting and put them at the wheel. The prisoners just did as directed with no sign of fatigue or emotion.

The source of the pale blue light was four small orbs set like torches on the walls. They shone with different levels of brightness, and as one of the guards passed a particularly dim one, it stopped and looked at the orb, then reached out and touched it. Even at a distance, I saw a little bit of magic gather in the guard and then flow into the orb, which immediately became much brighter. *Magical torches? Neat.* I wanted one.

"These must be the villagers," Herald whispered. "Do you see their eyes? It is like there is nothing there."

"Fucking creepy, yeah. What are those creatures guarding them?"

"I have no idea. They do not resemble anything I have ever seen or heard or read about."

"They're valkin," a male voice whispered behind us, and I only barely swallowed a shriek.

CHAPTER TWENTY-EIGHT

Reunion

Herald gave off a strangled "Eeep!" as she simultaneously tried to draw her sword and turn to face whoever was behind us. Unfortunately, she still had her pack on, which both threw her off balance and got in the way as she turned. Unable to get her sword free, she instead kicked out with one long, booted leg, and I heard a pained "Oof!"

I got my head around in time to see whoever it was hit the floor with a soft thump. My first instinct was to pounce while he was down, but I didn't want him to scream. I'd have to go for the throat.

I turned, preparing to leap.

"Ouch. Sorry," the man groaned softly. He held out one hand in surrender as he pushed himself up to a sitting position. "Mercies, kitten, did Lalia teach you to kick like that?"

"Tam!" Herald exclaimed in a whisper that expressed all her relief and pent-up fears.

I felt much better about not clawing or biting him. Or choking him to death with venom, which I had also considered. That would have been very awkward.

"And hello, uh, miss?" Tamor said, turning to me with a guilty smile. He was the first person I'd met who didn't seem the least bit nervous. I liked him immediately.

"Madam? Lady? Draka, I am Tamor of Karakan, as you may have guessed. Now, come on! Those bastards don't hear well, but let's get safe, yeah?"

He turned and began half crawling away from the ledge, then got up and continued in a crouch. Herald followed her brother, and a tug on my wing from her got me moving as well. There was no alarm from below, nor any other sign that we'd been heard, but Tamor was right. For all we knew, the guards might patrol up here now and then, and even though they looked like we could take them, I'd rather avoid anything that might be a fair fight.

"Here, this should be far enough," Tamor said, straightening after leading us into a tunnel that opened a couple dozen meters farther along the wall.

Herald stood and threw her arms around her brother without a word. In both height and appearance, Tamor was much more like his older sister, sharing Makanna's rounded face and slightly stockier build. He was also just barely tall enough to avoid embarrassment when Herald hugged him.

After a long, silent embrace, Herald released her brother, then smacked him repeatedly on the arm.

"Ow!" Tamor protested with a laugh as Herald smacked him.

"You idiots," she hissed, though there was no real heat to it. "I cannot believe you! Do you have any idea . . . Gods, I am so glad that you are all right." Her eyes became worried. "What about the others?"

Tamor became serious and gently placed his hands on her arms. "They're fine, kitten! We have a safe little hidey-hole. I was on guard; they're resting. We've been short on rations for a few days, so we try not to move too much, especially Mak."

Still holding his sister, Tamor turned to me. "Thank you, madam, truly," he said, settling on a title for me. "My family told me how you helped them get the money to free me, and here you are, coming to our rescue again. I can only guess that you've been sent by the Mercies themselves."

"'Madam' makes me feel old. Just call me Draka. Or Lady, I suppose. I like Lady. And you're welcome. Happy to help."

His mouth twitched. "Glad to hear it, Lady. So, let's get to the others, yeah? They'll be overjoyed to see the two of you."

Tamor led us up the tunnel. He really looked very much like a male version of Makanna. If you knew one and met the other, you would almost certainly know, in your gut, that they were siblings. Tamor's hair was shorter and slightly wavy, and he had a few days' stubble on his face, but it was still very easy to see the resemblance.

He also stank, which I had to forgive since he probably hadn't had a chance to wash himself for several days. I was pretty disappointed in myself that I hadn't smelled him when he crept up on us, though, honestly, Herald didn't smell a whole lot better.

In behavior, though, he had a completely different vibe than either of his sisters. He was open and friendly where Makanna was reserved, and he seemed relaxed and spontaneous compared to Herald, who was thoughtful and still had that teenage sense of *me against the world*.

I was not at all surprised that he'd been locked up for not getting his magicking-in-the-city license.

Tam talked as he led us. "We've been here for . . . a few days, I'd guess? Can't tell time worth shit down here. My gut says three or four days. We tried to get out after we found the villagers back there, but when we got back up the tunnel, it was closed off. Probably should have seen that coming," he said with a self-deprecating laugh. "That's supposed to be my thing, right, kitten? To see problems coming? But we can't be perfect."

The tunnel that we followed was not a long, curving affair like the one Herald and I had come through. This one was rougher, rounder, and seemed to wind almost naturally through the stone. I had to lead Herald, since again there was no light, but Tamor seemed able to see well enough. Thanks to Makanna, probably. Now that I was focusing on thinking with my nose, I knew we were getting close to the group's hideout long before I saw it. It smelled extremely lived-in.

The hideaway was a small, rough room that opened off the side of the tunnel. I could see Valmik stick his head out as we approached, his face splitting almost in two as he saw Herald and I following Tamor.

"Hello, my dears!" Tamor announced as he reached the opening. "I've brought guests!" With a quick peck on Valmik's bald head, he ushered us inside.

The place was set up like a camp, with the exception of there not being a fire. They had bedrolls on the ground, and their most commonly used equipment was out, but otherwise everything was ready to move quickly, and their weapons were close at hand.

Makanna had been sleeping but stirred as we arrived. There was another round of hugs and kisses between Herald, Makanna, and Valmik. Then, with a whisper, Makanna cast a spell on Herald to let her see in the dark. Herald had some choice words for them about leaving her alone and then disappearing, and they looked too tired to argue when she was obviously in the right. Then Herald announced the good news.

"I have plenty of food for you idiots," she said as she began unpacking bread, hard cheese, dried meats, fruit, and spare waterskins. "And we can get you out."

"Well, that's a relief," Makanna said while giving me a side-eye. "Madam Draka. I see my sister reached out to you for help."

Valmik sighed. "Mak . . ."

"Yeah, she did," I replied before Herald had a chance to say anything. "Your friends in the Gray Wolves couldn't go with her. Not like I could live with myself if I let her go alone."

"What has she promised—" Makanna started, but Herald cut her off.

"Oh, shut up, Mak," she said, sounding more tired than upset. "I told her that I was worried, she offered to come with me, I accepted. I have not promised her anything, and she has not asked. And you are lucky that she came, because I could not have gotten in here without her. How much food and water did you have left, Mak?"

Mak scowled silently. "Food remains for two days at quarter rations," an embarrassed Valmik supplied when no one else looked likely to say anything.

"Drinkable water can be brought from a cistern, but carefully so we are not spotted."

"So you are already starving. And here I am, with food to spare for all of us for days. Thanks to Draka. And do you know what? This is not the first time I have been out with her either."

"Is that so?" Makanna asked, looking at me.

"Yeah," Herald shot back. I considered stopping her, but I honestly didn't care about Makanna's opinion, and Herald clearly needed to get this off her chest.

"I went to see her a few days after you left. You all left me! What did you expect, that I would sit at the inn all week until you came back? I was dying of boredom!"

"Did you at least take Garal or Lalia with you?" Makanna asked.

"No, of course I did not!" Herald said with frustration. "I was not going to tell anyone about Draka, because we promised not to! I went alone! And I was fine! We met, and we had a good talk, right, Draka?"

"Uh, yeah," I said, surprised to be drawn into the conversation.

"And then in the morning, she showed me a bandit camp, and we were attacked on the road by two utter bastards—"

"*What—?*" Makanna exclaimed, but Herald rolled on.

"And we dealt with them! And then we brought the Wolves there, and we wiped the rest of the fuckers out!" Herald said with a gleam in her eyes that was visible even to my shadowsight. "I have killed two men," she said tensely, wielding her pain as a weapon.

"Oh, kitten," Tamor said sadly.

Herald kept talking, ignoring the interruption, her words tumbling out faster and louder as her eyes stayed locked on Makanna. "I killed two of the murdering bastards, and I feel like shit about it sometimes, but you know what? I am glad for it. It was exciting, and I did the world some good, and it was thanks to Draka. And here we are now, pulling your asses out of a hole you dug yourselves into, and *you* owe *that* to Draka."

She took a breath. "I love you, Mak. You are my dear sister, the head of our family, and I will always be thankful for all you have done to give me the best life you could. But right now, respectfully, take your suspicion and your awful attitude toward my *friend* and shove it up your *ass!*"

At Herald's final word, the room fell silent, and Herald, looking spent, almost faint, sat back against the wall, knees pulled up. She was breathing heavily, and with my shadowsight, I could see sweat on her forehead, dark gray against the bright background of her face.

"I am sorry," Herald said softly into the silence. "I have not slept well the last few nights."

Makanna sat on her bedroll, looking stunned. I waited, not wanting to stick my nose in this but worried that she would explode at any moment. Instead, her face went from shock to . . . not quite sadness. Regret, perhaps? She hesitated, then moved a little closer to Herald.

"Herald?" Her voice quavered a little. When Herald looked away, Makanna moved even closer, slowly reaching out to touch Herald's shoulder. I looked at the two men. Valmik was stunned, while Tamor's eyes flicked rapidly between his sisters, as if not sure what to do.

"I'm sorry, Herald," Makanna said softly, her hand firmly on Herald's shoulder. When Herald still didn't react, Makanna closed the rest of the distance and gathered her much bigger sister into her arms.

"Oh, Herald," she murmured into her sister's hair. "Sweet little sister. I'm sorry. I'm so sorry. We shouldn't have left you. Of course we shouldn't have."

At first, Herald did nothing. She just sat there for a long moment, her arms around her knees, before she finally returned the hug.

"I am not a fucking baby," she complained into her sister's chest.

"I know," Makanna agreed.

Herald sniffled. "I'm not."

"I know," Makanna said, gently stroking her sister's hair.

I saw Herald shake silently. "Why don't you idiots see that?" she choked out.

"I know. I know," Makanna repeated, still holding her, still stroking her hair. "I'm sorry."

Tamor approached me silently and gestured toward the tunnel, then did the same to Valmik. We followed him out.

"I thought Herald might bolt there," Tamor said after we had put some distance between us and his sisters. "They'll need some time. Makanna is embarrassed to cry in front of anyone, and there's usually a lot of crying after those two fight. Or when I fight with either of them, really." He shrugged. "We're an emotional family."

"'Truth can only pass with pain,'" Valmik quoted sagely.

"You just made that up," Tamor accused.

"And if I did?" Valmik returned.

"I'd probably love you even more, my beautiful warrior poet," Tamor said, bumping his lover with his shoulder.

I didn't really want to interrupt them. They were pretty cute together. But we needed to talk.

"So, about what Herald just told you . . ."

"I assume that it's true," Tamor said. "Herald very rarely lies. She's so bad at it."

"There is much sweat, and her eyes look everywhere except the person she is talking to," Valmik agreed. "It is quite obvious."

"Yeah," Tamor said. "But we should have brought her with us. It's lucky that we didn't, but we should have. I knew that, but I didn't know she would take it so hard." He paused. "So. Two men?"

"Like she said," I told them, "the first one was a bandit we met on the road. It was quick and clean, I think. Not like what I did to his partner. The other one was at the bandits' camp. He went for her. I held him in place, and Herald saw an opening and finished him off."

"How is she handling it?" Valmik asked, his voice full of concern.

"Not well. Or I don't know. I don't know anything about shit like this. She has nightmares. Sometimes she gets really dark when she thinks about it. Is that normal?"

"The first man I killed, he haunted me for months," Valmik said. "I think I will always remember. It's . . ." He thought for a second. "It's a little like the loss of a loved one. You carry it with you. But it gets easier."

"Well, I'm not sorry for taking her out, but I am sorry for putting her in danger. Or letting her put herself in danger, I guess. But I think she'll be all right. She's got dark moments, but she's confident otherwise. And I was never going to let her get hurt. Not on my life."

"Thank you," Tamor said. "For the apology and for looking after her. But if you're going to apologize to anyone, it should probably be Herald, but I don't think she'll want to hear it. She sounds satisfied with how things turned out." He sighed. "It's a lot to take in, though. My little kitten's a killer."

He fell silent for a while, staring at the wall. "I, uh . . ." he started, then faltered before rallying. "Oh hells, I suppose it's nothing to be ashamed of. I have no idea what she's feeling. I've never killed anyone. Not a person, that is. I don't think that Makanna has, either. At least not that she ever told me. Val's probably the best person here to talk to her."

Valmik nodded solemnly.

"Oh," I said. I had kind of assumed that both Makanna and Tamor would have killed people, as if doing so went with the adventuring lifestyle. "Well, I know that she's been talking to Lalia about it. Maybe Garal too."

"That's good," Tamor said. "Have you met them?"

"Yeah, I have. Believe it or not, but they were actually the first two people I met here. And the first person I ever really talked to was Lalia's sister, which is just weird, now that I know."

"A great coincidence," Valmik said with raised eyebrows. I saw him glance at Tamor. "What happened?"

"I saved Garal's life, and Lalia tried to kill me. Couldn't talk to them yet, so that didn't help."

"What do you mean?" Tamor asked. "You met them, what, ten days before Mak, Val, and Herald?" He turned to Valmik. "Is that right?"

"It was ten days after Garal and his team were attacked that we entered the mines, yes," Valmik confirmed.

Tamor turned back to me. "So you learned to speak in ten days? Or less, since you spoke to Lalia's sister before then?"

"Lahnie," Valmik supplied.

"Right. Lahnie. You spoke to her less than ten days after you *couldn't* speak to Garal and Lalia?"

"Well, yeah. Advancements, you know? I got one to let me speak to humans."

"Oh! All right, then." Tamor and Valmik both seemed to accept that without further objection.

"Yeah, so after meeting Garal and Lalia and almost getting skewered, I saved Lahnie from a monster pig. Anyway, I think Lalia hates me. Garal seems like a good guy, though."

"Oh, he is," Tamor said fondly. Valmik gave him a theatrically dirty look. "Oh, lose it!" Tamor said to Valmik and threw his arm around him. "He is! And you know that you have nothing to worry about, my sweet. That man is *far* too concerned with his appearance to interest me." Tamor smiled and primped his hair. "If anything, maybe *I* should be worried, hm? You always liked the pretty ones."

Valmik made a show of considering this. "Well," he said after some time. "He is very easy on the eyes."

"Traitor," Tamor said happily and hugged Valmik tighter, then turned to me. "So, what's this about you saving Garal's life? I know he was injured when his camp was attacked, but no one would talk about it."

I told them. I cleaned up the details so I didn't have to admit my near panic and complete ignorance, but they got the broad strokes as accurately as I remembered them.

"To be fair to Lalia, it wasn't her who tried to kill me that time. It was some guy on a horse."

"That time?" Valmik asked.

"She did try to kill me a couple days ago, at the bandit camp. But she apologized. Kind of."

Tamor scoffed. "Lady, I can believe that I'm sitting here, deep underground, having a conversation with a dragon. And I'll believe what my sisters and my love have told me about your short adventure together in the mines. But Lalia apologizing?" He pointed a finger accusingly. "That's too far!"

"Be nice," Valmik told him, elbowing him in the side lightly but smiling as he did so. "Apologies are rare from her, but they happen."

"When she's well and truly piss drunk, perhaps. Were you in or around any taverns at all?"

"No," I said drily.

"Well, in that case, I can't imagine what made her stow away her pride. Regardless, don't take it too hard. Lalia doesn't trust easily. She's a lot like Mak in that way."

"You do, though. You've known me for all of five minutes and you're talking to me like an old friend. You didn't even blink at what I am when you ambushed us in that cavern."

"I'm usually lucky with people," he said happily. Then something odd happened. I saw Valmik nudge Tamor's foot with his own and give him a very pointed look, but he barely moved his head to do so. I thought he might be trying to be stealthy, but he wasn't very good at it.

"You're a lucky guy in general, aren't you?" I asked, trying to lead him, but he didn't take the bait.

"I've been luckier than most in some things, less so in others." Valmik nudged Tamor again. I couldn't tell if Tamor even noticed, but he shrugged and continued. "In any case, I like to give people a chance. According to Herald and this fine man here"—he indicated to Valmik—"you are not just a person, but a good one. And Mak . . . Well, like I said, she doesn't trust easily. For good reason, unfortunately. So I try to consider that when I get her opinion on someone. If it helps, I did take a minute to work up my courage before approaching you two."

"A minute?" I said in mock horror. "I can't believe I didn't smell you! I don't know if my pride will ever recover."

Tamor smiled indulgently. "As for *what* you are, I admit that your kind are always villains in our stories and our history. But here's the thing: Dragons are said to have a lot of treasure, and when the hero inevitably slays the dragon, he usually ends up with enough gold and jewels to buy a city. I don't like to think of myself as a devious person—"

Valmik scoffed.

"Thank you, my love," Tamor said without missing a beat. "But if I were to murder someone and take their stuff, I imagine I might try to make sure everyone thought the dead guy was a much bigger bastard than I was, and good riddance. So I figure I should judge you as a person and my darling sister's friend first."

I definitely liked this guy. "Thank you," I said after a long pause. "That means a lot."

"Don't mention it." After a moment's hesitation, he reached across the tunnel and clapped me on the shoulder. "Shall we get back?"

CHAPTER TWENTY-NINE

Bad Business

When we returned to the small room where Herald's family had set up camp, Makanna was sitting on her bedroll, sniffling occasionally while stroking Herald's hair. Herald was lying with her head in Makanna's lap, her eyes closed. She was relaxed with a small smile on her face.

"Did you have a good talk, girls?" Tamor asked as we settled in.

"Tell them," Herald said without opening her eyes.

Makanna sighed. "We've come to an agreement," she said, her tone making it clear that she was reluctantly reciting a prepared statement. "Herald will be coming with us on jobs as a regular member of the group."

"And . . ." Herald said.

"And," Makanna said, looking at me. "If you're willing, Madam Draka, we will sometimes ask for your help, if the job seems harder than we can handle safely. Herald, for her part, will stop taking unnecessary risks without discussing with us first."

Meaning Herald got everything she wanted while giving nothing up. I didn't know if Herald was a good negotiator, or if she'd browbeaten Makanna into giving her what she wanted. Probably the latter, honestly. Either way, it was clear that the balance of their relationship had changed.

"Lovely!" Tamor said. Valmik, who'd been watching Tamor, nodded. "Now, how about we eat something?"

Herald may have gotten what she wanted, but other than that, the hierarchy she'd described to me that first night by the lake was still easy to see. Makanna made a decision. Tamor went with whatever she had decided, and Valmik followed Tamor. Which was good at the moment, but I'd have to keep an eye on Makanna. Or, I scolded myself, I could try to show her that she could trust me.

We talked while the others ate. Herald's three half-starved family members showed some respectable restraint, eating slowly instead of shoveling down food the way I'd expected them to. I declined, since I wasn't that hungry, and most of what they had was bread and fruit anyway.

What the goblins had told Herald and me was pretty much spot-on. The group had arrived at the village a few days ago. It had been empty, of course, and they'd searched it. Just like the mining camp, it looked like people had put their things in order and left all at once. They had tried to speak with some goblins they saw watching the place, but with no success. Luckily, Tamor had found some clear tracks leading from the village and up the valley, and they followed those all the way to the gate. Of course, when they got there, the gate was open, and the doors were so flush with the walls that they didn't even see them. As far as they could tell, there was just an open tunnel leading into the mountain.

They set up an ambush, hoping to catch someone coming in or out, but after waiting a full day, they decided to go in. Thanks to Makanna, they could see fine in the dark, similar to my shadowsight. They followed the tunnel all the way to the large chamber, saw the villagers and the valkin, decided that they were in over their heads, and tried to leave. Unfortunately for them, in the hours it had taken to go down and back again, the gates had closed. They had no way to break through, nor did they want to be trapped if the valkin came. That left only one option.

First they considered looking for another way out. They'd explored one other tunnel before this one, but it had been a dead end, though now Tamor wondered if it was a gate like the one at the entrance. When, hungry and exhausted, they found the small side room in this tunnel, they'd decided to set up camp and wait for an opportunity.

"You don't want to go farther in this tunnel, though, unless you need to take care of business," Tamor told me. "There's another, smaller room a minute away that we've been using for, you know. Natural needs."

"Warning duly noted," I told him, suddenly glad that the smell of the camp was strong enough to mask anything that might come wafting down the tunnel.

Their new plan had been to keep an eye on the valkin and hopefully follow them out, if and when they left. Unfortunately, no one seemed to use the tunnel to the surface, and when we found them, they were planning to do something desperate. They were almost out of food. If they ran out of food, Makanna would no longer be able to let them see in the darkness, and they would be at a terrible disadvantage, unable to move around without torches, possibly giving themselves away. But the villagers were being fed something somewhere. So they were going to have to fight while they still could.

They would kill the guards and take what food they could. Then they would look around for heavy tools to break through the gate or, if that failed, try to find a different way out. They were extremely pessimistic about their chances, but it was fight or starve in the darkness.

"So, you've been here a while. What've you found?" I asked as they were finishing up.

"Some scouting has been possible," Valmik said, "but the passages down are in sight of the guards. There is at least one more chamber below the workshop where the villagers go, to sleep and eat, we assume. More likely, there are many other chambers for the valkin. Tunnels must also exist, we think, since the valkin come up from the chamber."

"Any idea how many of these valkin there are?"

"Nah," Tamor said. "They're hard to tell apart, and we only see a few at a time. There's one that we've seen a few times that might be a leader, though. Easy to recognize 'cause he's got a scar on his face. He carries a staff, looks like it's made of some kind of bone, with a big fang on the end."

"He comes up from the lower chambers sometimes," Makanna added, "and looks over the villagers. Might have something to do with keeping them obedient, or asleep, or whatever is going on with them."

"What about the big wheel? Any idea what that's about?" I asked.

"Not really," Tamor answered. "My best guess is that it's for exercise, but as to why they're keeping these people at all . . . we have some unpleasant guesses, and we hope that we're wrong. On the bright side, none of the villagers have disappeared as long as we've been here, so I don't think that the valkin are eating them, at least."

"So, what are you going to do?" I asked, making sure to look directly at Makanna when I did.

"I don't know." She sighed. "The job was to find out what happened to the villagers. Now we know. We could return home and report what we've found, but then we'd need to prove it. I doubt that anyone will believe us."

"Yeah," Tamor agreed. "A magical door with a tunnel into the depths of the mountains sounds a little far-fetched. At the very least, we would have to return here with an official to verify our report."

"Like Tamor says," Makanna said with a frown. "Still, the smart thing to do is return now that you've opened the way for us. I don't like the idea of leaving the villagers here, but I'm not sure what else we could do."

"The number of foes, and their individual strength, is unknown," Valmik said. "I recognize them from an illustration, but I know nothing of their capabilities."

"We think there can't be that many of them, though," Tamor added. "They don't guard the surface entrance. It makes no sense to leave it unguarded unless they can't spare anyone."

"I saw one of them recharging a light-ball," I said. "At least some of them must have some kind of magic—if that wasn't obvious already with the sleepwalking villagers back there."

"Which is why we won't be changing our original plan. We're returning to Karakan as soon as we've eaten and rested," Makanna said bitterly. "This is far beyond us, and as much as I dislike it, I'm not willing to risk any of us getting seriously hurt to get these people out. We'll report what we've seen and return with an official, or a raiding party, or not at all."

"You know," I told them, "there's another one of these gates in the mountains not that far from the mine we went to. Seems likely that's where our missing miners are."

Makanna almost smiled at me when I said that. "That's excellent news! Both the mining company and the city council are offering rewards for any clues to where they went, especially since these villagers disappeared. If we could show them two of these places—"

"Yeah, one problem, though," I said, interrupting her. "We need to see if you can open the gates without me, because I'd rather not be there if you're bringing the authorities around."

"That is a problem," Tamor said thoughtfully.

"Did you try to open the gate here? When you tried to leave," I asked.

"Of course we tried," Makanna said. "Nothing would budge. There was a hole, but it was too small for any of us to fit through."

"All right, so when we get up there, we'll have to see if you can open the gate, because I don't know if that was a magic thing or a dragon thing."

I left the others there to rest, offering to take guard duty until they were ready to go. Makanna looked ready to argue, but a pointed expression from Herald made her thank me for the offer instead. The tunnel back to the large chamber wasn't straight, but there were no side tunnels, so there was no risk of getting lost.

The chamber was silent. I used my shadowsight to find the darkest shadow I could that had a good view of the bottom as well as the stairway leading up to my level, but all of the humans were gone. Eating or resting, I guessed, which made me wonder what time it was. It had been evening when we went down, and several hours had passed since then. It must be the middle of the night.

The humans were gone, but there was still one guard, looking as bored as any security guard I had ever seen. With nothing else to do, I observed the lone valkin. I had no way of telling if it was male or female. For that matter, I had no way of knowing if they even had two genders or if there were any obvious differences between them. I settled on thinking of the valkin as an it.

It walked around a bit, stood still a bit, then sat for a bit. It walked over to each of the shining orbs and chose not to charge any of them. It looked up the stairs. It looked back toward an opening in the wall on the lower level. Then it repeated these things in various combinations for what felt like hours.

At one point, it collected some pebbles and amused itself by throwing them at one of the orbs. When it hit it, though, the orb flickered, and the guard quickly scattered the pebbles and looked around nervously.

I was so very, very bored. It got so bad that I considered taking a nap and relying on the dragon to wake me if anything happened. The dragon was useful that way. But in this case, I was so bored that I worried that even the dragon might pass out from the sheer monotony. It seemed unusually subdued. It usually spoke up if something interested or annoyed it, and I'd thought that it would at least comment on the valkin or their magical lights, but I got nothing from it but a sense of vague anxiety.

I was saved by the arrival of a second guard. It spoke to the first quickly, and both hurried through the doorway behind them, leaving the chamber unguarded.

That sure woke me up. This was a golden opportunity! I could sneak down there and follow the guards, see what was through that hole in the wall. Knowing what lay below this chamber, and how many of the valkin there were, would be valuable information if and when we returned. I couldn't pass on a chance like this, could I? And the fact that I was bored out of my mind and burning with curiosity definitely had nothing to do with anything.

So I went for it. I found a spot where all four light-balls were blocked and the shadow was nice and dark. I flowed down to the floor of the lower level, then snuck across to the door as carefully as I could. Beyond was a steep, curving staircase, lit dimly by light leaking in from the top and bottom. From beyond the bottom exit of the staircase, I could hear angry voices. They were speaking in the local language, and one of those voices sounded distinctly human.

I would have made a terrible soldier. Guard duty had been awful. But maybe I would have made a good spy, because this part was exciting. Sneaking into an enemy stronghold, listening in on their dirty dealings? Knowing that I might have to run to avoid discovery, or fight my way out? I felt a thrill that went all the way to my bones, and it had nothing to do with the dragon.

Following the voices, I crept down the stairs and peeked out the door. There was a corridor there, not just a tunnel but a straight, finished corridor of stone, with a closed door at the far end. Halfway down the tunnel, in the right-hand wall, was an open door from which the same pale blue light as upstairs spilled, broken by faint shadows. The voices I'd heard came from there.

". . . grandfathers and hags!" the human voice said. It was a high, male voice, tight with restrained anger. "We will not pay for what we did not order!"

"Yooou will paaay," replied a breathy voice flatly. It sounded like the vowels were giving it trouble. "Assss agreeed, yoooou will paaay, or nooo mooore busssinesss!"

"We'll pay, all right. As agreed. Children, young women, strong men. That was the agreement. I don't care if you procured the wrong merchandise. We will take the kids, the three men there, her, him, him, those two. The three girls there . . . and her. The rest are worthless to us. Push me on this and we'll call the whole thing off."

"Yooou wooould nooot—"

"Try me! My boss would rather see me wash my hands of a bad deal than buy bad merchandise, and I know that you need our goods much more than we need yours. Look into my eyes and tell me I'm lying!"

There was a short silence.

"Whaaat aaare weee tooo dooo with—"

"Does it look like I give a fuck?" the human voice shouted. "Keep them, get rid of them, I don't care! As long as they don't bother my boss, I do not care! They're your mistake and your fucking problem!"

There was a knot of cold anger in my belly. It was obvious what I was hearing. They were trading in people. Human trafficking. Slavers. Someone was here to buy people from the valkin, and they'd had an agreement ahead of time. These villagers had been kidnapped on order.

I'd been expecting villagers to be used for labor. There were only so many uses for a large group of prisoners, after all. This disgusted me, but it didn't surprise me. But when the situation changed from monsters capturing people to humans paying monsters to deliver people to them, I wanted to attack. I wanted to kill every bastard in there and see them suffer for what they'd done. It was the cold-hearted, organized nature of it. I knew that the same thing happened back home, but to actually see it . . .

I held myself back. It was hard, but I did it. This was no time for hot fury. I crept toward the door. An angry burst of magic sent the shadows of the corridor spilling forward, swallowing the light in the corridor, and I flowed in front of the door.

The room was large, and it was full. It looked like some kind of meeting hall, with benches and light-balls along the walls. Facing me at one end was a group of half a dozen humans, one obvious leader and five others backing him up. Unfortunately, as long as I was in shadow form, everything looked odd, my vision too distorted to make out any detail. On top of that, the room was too bright for my shadowsight to be much good. On the other side of the room, the human captives stood lined up together with a dozen or more valkin. At the head was a particularly tall one, holding the staff topped with a large fang that had been described to me. The valkin outnumbered the human slavers, but from their postures and voices, it was clear how the balance of power lay.

I had to see their faces. I had to know who they were. I backed up and made myself solid again, keeping the shadows nice and dark around me. I slowly stuck my head forward . . .

A scent struck me. Even with everything else, and through my anger, it stood out clearly. The room was full of the smell of unwashed humans, a dry, metallic scent that was probably the valkin, but above everything, there was that same strange background scent from the chamber. I had no idea what it was, but the dragon . . .

When I saw the staff, together with that scent, the dragon went wild inside me. Not with rage, or greed, but with fear. The anxiety that I had felt from it in the upstairs chamber was multiplied ten- or a hundred-fold, washing over me and filling me with a sudden urge—no, a desperate need—to flee. The scent was one of pain and fear and confusion, of not knowing what was happening but knowing that terror and death waited for me if I could not get away.

The voices of the two leaders went on, but I didn't hear them. I turned, shifted, and fled, flowing up the stairs in my shadow form and surging into the chamber until I hit the barrier of the pale blue light. I came back together and leaped onto the high ledge with two powerful beats of my wings, then ran full tilt into the tunnel toward the camp. I needed help. I needed my allies. They would protect me. They could hide me! They . . .

As I left the chamber behind me, the panicked need to flee slowly faded, but I kept running.

"Jesus Christ," I panted. "What was that? What was that?"

"*Death!*" the dragon whined in my head. *"Dragon bone!"*

CHAPTER THIRTY

Parting

When I arrived at the camp, I was met by Makanna and her spear. Thankfully, she swung the point to the side and moved to try to see past me.

"What's wrong?" she said urgently. "Are you being chased?"

"No," I said, panting to catch my breath. "Bastards! Slaving bastards!"

"Calm down!" Herald demanded as the others stirred. "What are you talking about?"

"Human slavers!" I said, taking a moment to collect myself. "There are humans back there, right now, talking to the valkin about buying people!"

"Damn," Makanna hissed and turned back to the others. "Come on, it's time. Pack up quickly. We should be there if there's an opportunity."

I'd hoped to rest before we left. I was tired and hungry, but the situation had changed. Five minutes later, we were moving, and I explained how I'd snuck down to the lower level and down the stairs.

"There were about twenty of them in total. Six humans," I told them. "There's no way we can take them head-on."

"I know," Makanna said. "You say you can open the gate at the surface?"

"I did before."

"Then we'll get out, set up an ambush outside, and hope they come out that way," she said. "If the group that comes out is small, just the humans, we take them, maybe follow them. At the first sign that we've been spotted, or if we can't win the fight in the first seconds, we get out. Is that clear, everyone?"

"Got it, Mak," Tamor said. Valmik gave an "Mmm" of agreement.

"That means you too, Herald," Makanna said, looking back.

"I understand," Herald said. I could *hear* the eye roll behind her words.

Makanna frowned at that and looked at me. "And you?"

"Don't worry about me. If you need to pull out, I'll try to hold them off. Don't forget what I am. I can take a hit."

I saw her eyes flick to my missing horn, where she'd healed my pretty nasty head wound three weeks earlier.

"Lalia chopped me in the neck with her sword, and I'm still standing," I told her, not mentioning that I still felt the bruise a little. That earned me a surprised look.

"Well. In that case, I won't tell you what risks not to take."

When we got close to the chamber, I went ahead. The guard was still missing, and I quickly returned to the group to hurry them along. Then came a long, monotonous climb through the featureless tunnel, made even more boring by the silence that Makanna strictly enforced. When I couldn't take it anymore, I offered to scout ahead, increasing my speed until I was out of sight and then switching to my shadow form. I could move at least as quickly as I walked, with the added benefit of being completely silent. It drained me faster, but we'd be out soon, so I didn't worry about it.

That was my longest jaunt in shadow form so far. I went all the way to the exit but found it still closed. There was no sound from the outside, but soft light spilled in through the hole, so I couldn't check without opening the gate, and I wanted the others there when I did. So instead, I walked back, passing the time by trying to talk to the dragon, which was a sure sign that the boredom was getting to me. The dragon didn't respond, but it rarely did. This time, though, I had a feeling that it was hiding. *Dragon bone.* That was what it had called the valkin leader's staff, and it was still badly shaken.

I felt kind of bad for it.

I met the others after ten, maybe fifteen minutes, and told them that the tunnel was clear and that it was daylight outside. That gave them a boost, and they picked up the pace.

"So," Makanna said pointedly as we reached the gate, "are you going to let us out?"

"I want you to do it," I replied after some hesitation.

"You told us—" Makanna said, her eyes narrowing.

"I know, and I'm almost completely sure that I can open the thing. But I want to see if *you* can."

I'd considered saying *you or Tamor*, but there was pretty much only one way I could know about Tamor having magic, and I didn't want to upset the balance between the two sisters.

"Listen, Makanna," I said as she looked about to argue, "if it doesn't work, I'll do it. Just put your hand on the stone and will it to open. Push some magic into it. I don't know how you do it with healing or the sight thing, but try that, maybe?"

Makanna looked at me doubtfully, then pressed the palm of her hand against the flat stone of the gate. "Open," she said. Nothing happened, but then, I didn't expect anything to. I hadn't even seen any gathering of magic in her.

"C'mon," I said, trying to sound encouraging. "You need to believe it. Try again. Really focus. You have to want it to open, the way you want a wound to heal. Like . . . make yourself know that there is no other way for this to go than for the door to open. All right?"

Makanna looked at me with a small frown, clearly not enjoying being lectured, then turned back to the gate. I tried not to hold it against her. She'd had a rough couple of days.

She pushed her hand more firmly against the stone and closed her eyes. I saw her relax gradually, from her face to her shoulders and out into her arms, and she started whispering to herself under her breath, too low for me to hear. Whatever she was doing, it seemed to be working. A small ball of magic gathered in her chest, and she opened her eyes and whispered, "Open!"

The lines around the door flared, and the gates swung outward. Makanna stared at me, eyes wide and mouth slightly open, before Tamor grabbed her in a fierce hug from behind.

"Great work, sister!" he said with a big smile and stepped out into the morning sun.

The rain was long gone. Puddles decorated the ground in places, and small, fluffy clouds drifted in an otherwise-blue sky. Everything smelled of wet stone, fresh and clean, and in a patch of scrubby grass not far from the gate, Melon raised her head and whickered a greeting.

I wasn't sure how much of that the others saw right away. Almost as one, they squeezed their eyes shut, shading them with their hands as Makanna called out, "Right, dammit. Every damn time. Here. Come here." They huddled up, she undid her spell, and they all could finally look around.

Herald smiled and walked over to Melon, while Makanna and Valmik began to look around the tunnel entrance and talk in low voices. Tamor stood smiling in the sunlight, the long sword strapped across the small of his back rattling as he stretched and breathed deep in the fresh mountain air. I walked back to the gate and put my hand against the stone.

It took a few tries, during which I became more and more conscious of the others glancing at me. Finally, I got myself worked up to the point that, with a muttered *"Come on, you fucking wanker!"* in good old English, the gate slowly swung shut. The shadow magic came pretty naturally to me, but I could apparently only manage opening and closing the gate when I was acutely embarrassed. I was going to need to work on that.

"Gather around," Makanna ordered after a short while, and we did. "We'll take places here, here, here, there, and over there," she said, pointing to five spots above and then to the sides of the gate. "Herald, I want you over there, where you can hide Melon and use your bow to good effect. I'll be here. Tamor and Valmik, I want you above the gate. Madam Draka, if you don't mind, I'd like you to stay by the door and listen for anyone coming. I think that with your wings, you'll be the fastest at getting out of the way."

"Yeah, sounds good," I said. It wasn't like I had any better ideas. I'd much rather leave the planning to the pros than try to meddle.

"Thank you. Once you hear something, take a position there," she said, indicating a place to the side of the gate across from where she would be. "When I give the signal, I want you to smash into them and confuse them, then get out immediately before the rest of us strike. If you can take out the leader, that would be best. Together with Herald, your primary job after that is to catch anyone who runs. Otherwise use your judgment."

"Yes, boss!" I said, half joking. I tried to give a salute but forgot about my long neck, so I probably just looked like an idiot.

"As for the rest of us, this is the plan: Once Draka is out, we hit them with all we can, quick and dirty. Strike to disable and disarm first, then clean up. All right?"

"Understood," Valmik said, and Herald and Tamor both confirmed as well.

As we prepared to take our places, Makanna got close to Tamor and said something I couldn't hear, glancing at me. Tamor nodded and clapped her on the shoulder, then went to his assigned place. My guess was that it was something about his abilities, and Makanna didn't want to share. That was all right. She'd use me, but trust could only grow so fast in a day.

We took our places, and we waited, making small talk and joking in low voices to take the edge off. There was even some soft singing, and Makanna impressed me by singing a ballad in a surprisingly rich soprano. Still, the air was thick with anxiety and tension. I thought about what Tamor had told me, how neither him nor Makanna had ever killed a human. Now they might be about to, and who knew how they'd handle it? And though we'd try our best to avoid it, some of us may soon be injured or dead, and we all knew it.

The others impressed me. Despite the risk we were taking, no one had argued against it. No one had even hesitated when Makanna said that we would be ambushing the slavers. We wouldn't hang around if the fight looked like it might go bad, but we were sure as hell going to try to free those people. At least the ones the slavers had wanted. As for the rest . . . we would just have to hope that they were still here when we could return with reinforcements.

After some time, definitely more than an hour, I heard the sounds of distant footsteps coming from the tunnel. I spread my wings to catch the others' attention. Tamor was already alert and looking my way. I shouldn't have been surprised. They had told me that he was supposed to be good at sensing danger.

"They're coming," I hissed and moved quickly to my assigned position to the side of and a short distance from the gate.

Everyone else immediately quieted down. They checked their straps and readied their weapons, then hunkered down to where I could barely see them. I waited in silence, too far from the gate to hear any sounds escaping from inside. Then the gate slowly opened to the sound of stone grinding on stone.

First came a small group of prisoners, blinking in the sunlight but otherwise not reacting to what must have been their first trip outside in days. They walked forward, their faces as blank as they had been inside the mountain.

The first thing that made me realize something was off was seeing the couple at the front. Probably in their sixties or older, they were followed by a matronly woman, then an older man missing a hand. All in all, nearly twenty people left the tunnel, not a child, a young adult, or an able-bodied man among them. These were not the prisoners the humans had agreed to take. These were the others, the ones they had told the valkin to deal with.

As if to confirm my thoughts, four valkin guards carrying spears and looking as bored as I'd ever seen them stepped out into the light behind the prisoners, their skin a pale blue-tinted gray in the sunlight. They were blinking and shielding their eyes, briefly blinded. Makanna and I shared a look, and she nodded.

I took two loping strides, beat my wings hard, and launched myself forward. One of the four blinked in my direction, its eyes opening wide in surprise. It opened its mouth, to speak or scream, and then I slammed into them.

They were too close to the prisoners for me to want to risk using my venom, so I settled for landing on the one that had spotted me, knocking it back at least two meters as I hit. I snapped at its throat, but even stunned, it twisted away just in time, and my mouth closed over its shoulder, drawing out a hissing scream that became choked and shrill as I bore it down, dug in my claws, and used it as a springboard to continue in the direction I'd been going. I heard gasps and angry shouts from the others, and as I landed a few meters away, I turned in time to see Valmik and Tamor drop behind them as Makanna came in from one side.

The three standing valkin were all facing me, meaning they saw Makanna but not the two men behind them. The creatures clearly had some experience, recovering quickly from their shock and turning to attack Makanna. The one closest to her thrust its spear at her chest, but she dodged easily, almost flowing to the side as she responded with a thrust of her own. The valkin parried quickly with the butt of its spear, but Makanna used the momentum of the parry and let it carry her point down and forward into the creature's back leg. It let out a scream, which was cut off suddenly as one of Herald's arrows took it in the hollow of its throat. As it gurgled, Makanna grabbed its spear and swept its legs out from under it.

The whole exchange had taken perhaps three seconds.

The two guards that were left had been slightly farther from Makanna. When Makanna's spear lodged in their companion's leg, they tried to use the opening, but one was forced to throw itself backward and face the two men as Tamor lunged, driving his long sword through the chest of the other. I saw an orb of magic swirling in Tamor's chest, and when he struck, some of it flowed from him and into his blade, which cut through the valkin like the creature were made of tofu. Between Tamor and the remaining guard stood Valmik, his shield up and his short sword ready above it.

The valkin looked around itself with wild eyes. Its spear pointed at Valmik, but it was backing up, clearly more concerned with keeping the three humans it could see at a distance than with trying to attack. Then it saw me and stared.

I don't know what it had thought it was that attacked its companion. A pitch-black mountain lion, maybe. If they had mountain lions here, that was. Whatever it had thought, it was not ready for the reality. *"Hassaaak!"* it hissed almost under its breath, eyes wide as they flicked between Valmik and me. *"Hassaaak! Hassaaak!"* It kept repeating the word, its voice growing louder and louder until it suddenly stumbled forward with an arrow in its side.

Valmik used the advantage. He easily battered its spear to the side with his shield, closed in, and opened its throat with a swift slash of his sword.

It was staring at me as its blood spilled, and it crumpled to the ground.

To my surprise, both the valkin that I had pounced on and the one that Herald had shot were still alive, though barely. Any thought I might have had about trying to interrogate them was cut short as Makanna drew her knife and grimly slit their throats.

I didn't feel bad, of course. This time, I wouldn't have had any concerns about killing anyway. With the gremlins, we had gone into their home. They'd been eating miners, but I didn't know that at the time. The bandits had been murdering, raping bastards, but they'd also been human, which should count for something. Nonhuman slavers? I looked at the dead valkin and felt nothing but anger, pride, and satisfaction.

I did hate that we only had some of the prisoners, and a small part of me insisted that we had the wrong ones. The less valuable ones. *That,* I felt bad about, and it fed my anger. And on top of that, I was still tired and growing hungrier. The hunger meant that the dragon was getting cranky, and that leaked in and made everything worse.

"Is everyone all right?" Makanna asked as she rose to her feet. Tamor and Valmik both confirmed that they were, and when she looked at me, I dipped my head in a nod. Herald waved and grinned, never having been in harm's way. Makanna looked satisfied with that.

"Well done, everybody," she said with obvious relief. "I don't think that could have gone better."

"What about the prisoners?" Tamor said as he approached the group of humans. They hadn't reacted at all to the violence, only having stopped when there was no one urging them on. Now they stood, as if waiting to be told what to do.

"I don't know," Makanna said. She walked up to them. "Grandmother," she said, standing in front of an old woman. "Can you hear me? Do you understand me?"

The lady didn't answer. She stared blankly ahead, her lips moving now and then as she sucked her teeth, and that was it. Makanna and Tamor both tried to speak to several of the prisoners with the same lack of effect.

"Okay . . ." Makanna said. "Sit down?"

The humans all sat. They didn't just drop to the ground, but sat down carefully as if it was their own idea. One or two even brushed away some pebbles before settling in.

"Stand up," Makanna said. They did so. One old man had trouble getting up, and a one-armed man helped him with a firm grip.

"So they're not completely thoughtless," Makanna mused. "Follow me!" she ordered and walked ahead of the group. The villagers followed.

"Stop!"

They did.

"All right, so we can move them. That's good."

"But many are missing," Valmik stated.

"Yeah," I said, my throat tight with anger. "The leader of the slavers said that they wanted the kids, the young women, and the strong men. Easy to guess why."

Valmik's face twisted with disgust. "They were separated. So where are the others?"

"Still inside?" Tamor suggested. "Or another exit?"

"I cannot imagine the slave traders wanting to remain in the tunnels for longer than necessary," Herald said as she joined us with Melon. "I was only there for a couple of hours, and I am glad to be out. There must be a different exit. Farther down in the hills, perhaps? Closer to the city?"

"The city would be avoided, would it not?" Valmik said. "The risk of discovery would be great. Perhaps they have a ship on the coast?"

"Slavery's illegal, I hope," I said.

"Enslaving innocent people? Here, yes," Valmik said. "Punishable by death."

I looked at the people we had freed, then at my companions. My friends, perhaps. "Do you think you can handle these people?" I asked tersely.

"We'll take them to their village," Makanna said. "If they haven't recovered by then . . . I guess we'll have to try to get them to Karakan."

"Not like we can leave them to fend for themselves," Tamor agreed.

"There may not be much for them in the village, in any case," Herald said, her voice creaking with guilt. "I believe that goblins have taken everything of value."

"Little bastards," Makanna grumbled.

"There was an agreement, and it was broken," Herald said with a sigh. "It was not the villagers' fault, but you know goblins better than I do."

"I still don't like it," her sister replied.

What the hell were they doing babbling about damn goblins? There were still people in the hands of those fucking slavers!

"Anyway!" I cut in loudly, silencing them. "I'm gonna fly off and see if I can find a bunch of slavers and their victims."

Herald stared at me. "I forgot that you could do that."

"Yeah, no worries," I snapped. "I'll come back if I find anything that I can't deal with. Otherwise . . . see you at the lake in three or four days."

Herald looked at me, her face hard to read. She turned her head to look at the villagers, then back at me. "Better make it four," she said softly, then looked at Makanna, who nodded reluctantly.

"All right, good." I turned to go but hesitated and turned back. That had been bad. I was angry, but not at them.

"Herald, it was good traveling with you. Really. The rest of you, I'm glad you're all right." I said. "I'm . . . You all are great. You could have gone home as soon as you got out, and I wouldn't have blamed you, but you risked a lot for these people. That's . . . I respect that, yeah?"

With that, and still angry but also more than a little awkward and embarrassed, I took off.

CHAPTER THIRTY-ONE

Party of One

After leaving Herald and her family in the mountains with the villagers we had rescued, I spent the rest of that day flying back and forth across the hills and lower mountains of eastern Mallin. I never saw the slavers or their prisoners. I went up and down valleys and along mountain roads, from the forest in the north to south of the road Herald, and I had taken to the abandoned village. I found nothing worth noting. I saw some small groups, of twos and threes, mostly, traveling on the roads. I may have been spotted. I didn't care, trusting the rumors about a wyvern to cover for me. I didn't even know what a wyvern was, exactly. A flying lizard of some kind, I guessed. I wasn't really concerned about it. I had a righteous anger burning inside me and no way to quench it, and it was killing me.

Late in the day, I saw my perhaps-friends on their way to the main road, which would lead them north to the city. They seemed to have given up on the idea of leaving the rescued people at their village. I silently wished them well, but I was too embarrassed about how I had left them to want to talk. So instead, I continued my fruitless search. I barely even knew what I was looking for beyond "a largish group of people."

By the time the sun went down behind the mountains, a combination of hunger and exhaustion forced me to give up for the day, and I settled in a tall tree a little ways in from the edge of the northern forest. I hadn't had a proper meal for days, and between the walking, the magic, and the flying, I was feeling my hunger worse than I had for weeks. This time I wasn't worried about whether I'd be able to feed myself, but hunger was still a powerful, motivating force and a constant distraction, and I caught myself time and again looking for prey rather than the people I was searching for. Still, I wanted to force myself to put it off for one more day. It would take the slavers at least another full day to reach the city, and a little less, I guessed, if they were trying to get to the coast. But crossing the farmlands would be hard without looking suspicious. It didn't make sense to me that they'd risk going to the city if slavery carried the death penalty. My guess was that Valmik was right, and they'd have a ship on the coast. If I were them, I'd go through the forest, where they could cross to the coast under cover. I'd never find them if they were among the trees, but if they had a ship . . .

I had to go to the coast. It was my best idea that didn't involve scouring thousands of square kilometers of forest and farmland, and I couldn't do it during the day. Flying along the coast in daylight meant I would be almost guaranteed to be spotted, especially since I'd need to pass the city just in case the slavers had a way to cross the farmland. I estimated that it would take me under an hour to cross to the coast, so I had some time to rest before continuing. I didn't dare to sleep, though. I doubted that the dragon cared enough to wake me before I'd had a full night's sleep, and if I let the slavers slip away because I was sleeping, I'd never forgive myself.

I gave myself about two hours to rest. I didn't think much, but when I did, I tried to determine what I was looking for. If Valmik was right and there was a ship, it would have to be fairly big. And I imagined that it would have to be somewhat hidden so that other passing ships wouldn't get suspicious. There would probably need to be some kind of boats to take people to and from land. In pirate movies, they always had big rowboats, but I had no idea what kinds of ships they had here.

Honestly, I had no idea what I was doing.

After I'd given myself a minimal amount of rest, I crossed the forest to the coast. It was a cloudy night, but my shadowsight let me see just fine. I flew low and silent over the trees, and it was an exercise in willpower to keep myself from looking for birds' nests to raid in the treetops.

The forest continued all the way to the coast. As low as I'd been flying, I hadn't seen where the land gave way to the sea, and I suddenly found myself over open water. Surprised, I wheeled around and landed on the coast. It consisted mostly of undulating, forested sandstone cliffs, dropping roughly for dozens of meters to a narrow line of rocky shore. I took to the air again and flew a short distance. I could see places where the cliffs sloped to the shore. In those places were small fishing villages, their docks and jetties easy to see against the water.

The cool sea air tickled my nose, and even through the hunger, fatigue, and lingering anger, it was vaguely pleasant. I'd never cared much about beaches or the seaside, but there was something here that calmed me a little. I guessed the feelings came from the dragon, but whether they were its or my own, I still enjoyed them. I'd have to come back here in better times.

For now, though, I had a job to do. I didn't expect the slavers to want to go particularly far north, but since I could move much, much faster than them, I decided to start my search several kilometers north of where the forest gave way to farmland. Or pasture, rather, with piles of sleeping sheep and other livestock dotting the landscape.

I didn't see anything that matched what I was looking for, though there were some small boats. Fishermen, I assumed, catching fish that came up closer to the surface during the night. Farther out, I could see larger ships, but they all seemed to be moving, heading toward or away from the city.

I didn't know much about sailing ships, but the ones I saw definitely didn't look like the ones in *Pirates of the Caribbean*. They were smaller, for one thing. Only one ship I saw had two masts, most of them with only one, and all of them had at least some oars. They were like Viking ships, or the ones I thought they used to have in the Mediterranean.

I searched all damn night. I searched around the stony shore. I searched small coves and inlets. I passed by the city, feeling amazed at the size of the harbor there and all the ships that were docked. And I searched sandy beaches and rocky beaches and every other kind of shore that there was for all the many kilometers of coast that the slavers could possibly reach in a reasonable time. I found no ship that seemed like a likely candidate, only fishermen, merchant vessels trying to reach the city or get an early start on their journey, and what were clearly military ships with weapons at the front and back, looking like they were on patrol. The cliffs were lined with birds' nests, and I even saw some seal colonies, which I'd have to remember for the future. It would probably be a bad idea to eat a seal and fall asleep next to the water since that would leave me exposed and easy to spot, but it might be good to have the option.

I didn't find what I was searching for. What I did find on my first pass south, which was very interesting, was a large cave in the cliffs near the city of Karakan.

Karakan was built around a river, which flowed out into a natural harbor protected by a long, rocky spit of land. The landscape rose steeply around the river, and much of the city was set on the cliffs that rose high above the water. No more than a hundred meters north of the city's northern walls, there was a large sea cave in the cliffside, wide enough for me to fly inside. On the off chance that someone might be hiding there, I decided to have a look. That, or it was a convenient excuse for my curiosity. Or it was the dragon hoping to eat a bat or five. Either way, I flew inside.

The stench that hit me before I even got close to the entrance was almost a solid thing. It was, quite simply, a sewer. Deep inside the cave and close to the waterline was a large opening, nearly two meters wide and lined with stone bricks. There were thick, horizontal metal bars set into the stone, close together enough to prevent a person from going through—if they were insane enough to brave the sludge and stench. Because that hole was, apparently, the final destination of much of the city's waste.

For all its disgusting horror, it was also an opportunity. Not one that I intended to act on now, but one which might be invaluable in the future. The cave was pitch-black. So was the sewer tunnel.

I had a sneaky way into and out of the city, and I wasn't going to be able to stay away from Karakan forever. I was pretty sure that I could get across the walls at night undetected if I had to, but however disgusting the idea was, the sewers should remain dark enough for me to use even in the middle of the day. Maybe the sun would get in here a few days a year at sunrise, but that should be it. And I didn't really touch anything when I was in shadow form. And my sense of smell was gone too, so that should be fine. I hoped.

It would be fine.

I continued searching the coast until the sky began to lighten, and the horizon took on the faint greens and yellows of predawn. I was out of time. It was a bitter feeling, but all I'd had was hope, righteous anger, and no real expectation of success. I could come back again the next night, maybe, but if I didn't eat very soon, I would probably do something stupid, like steal one of the large birds that many of the forest villages raised. And even if a couple rabbits could take the edge off the hunger without putting me in a stupor, I had also missed two nights of sleep. First under the mountains, and then again tonight, and I was feeling it. My mind kept either drifting or going blank, my eyes were drooping, and I had a tingly, floaty feeling in my whole body telling me that if I relaxed for even a single moment, it would be lights out.

Besides that, I hadn't seen my hoard for days. That was like an itch with only one way to scratch it. I didn't even have the pouch that Herald had given me since I'd left that with her in case I needed to shift.

I had to eat, and I had to sleep. I had to face the fact that I had failed. I wouldn't be able to search anymore because I was hungry and tired, and I was afraid of what would happen if I couldn't continue to resist the dragon. It wasn't that it ever tried to take over, as such, but it pushed me to do things. It gave me impulses. It made suggestions. For example, my friends had a big, juicy horse with them, one that didn't even mind my presence. Why not eat Melon? The others might protest, but if we killed Makanna, they'd probably be too afraid to do anything. Or, as another option, some of the villagers were old and weak. No one would miss the old lady, right?

It made suggestions like that.

I didn't want to find myself dozing off and then wake up on my way to get an equine snack, so I had to deal with it on my own terms. I needed to have a proper meal, and proper rest, or I might do something terrible. I wanted to help the rest of the captured villagers, but I could choose between accepting my failure or failing worse. I hated it, but that was the reality I had to face.

I flew low and close to the cliffs as I headed north toward the edge of the forest, low enough to feel the spray of waves breaking on the rocks. It was refreshing and helped keep me alert. I could barely keep my eyes open, and every time a spray of water hit me, I tried to really feel it. I anticipated each time, watching the waves ahead of me, trying to hear the surge as they hit the rocks and—

The world spun. No, I was spinning. I didn't have time to be surprised before I plunged into the cold water, my nose and mouth filling immediately as I gasped reflexively. The wave of adrenaline that hit me cleared my mind a little, and I remembered the last time I'd been underwater, my first day at the lake, sinking and only barely able to make it to shore. In a way, I was luckier this time. With my wings still out, the next surge of water picked me up and threw me against the rocks. It hurt like hell when I hit them, but I rolled over them, and as the water flowed back to the sea, I was left in a cleft, able to cough up the water and take a breath.

I started to feel a dull ache in my right wing, just above the middle joint.

What the hell had happened? I'd just been flying along, trying to stay awake, and—

The next wave crashed over me, and I choked and sputtered on salt water. *Right.* I had to get up, or at least closer to the cliff. I lifted my head, looking around to find which way was sea and which was land. With claws out, I fought for any kind of purchase and slowly made my way across the wet, slimy rocks. Another wave knocked me down, but it knocked me in the right direction. After a few more waves, I was curled up by the cliff face, only occasionally hit by the spray of the waves. My heart was still pounding in my chest, but even through the rush of adrenaline still surging through me, I could feel my battered body, and especially my wing, ache.

Nothing felt broken. I hoped to God that nothing was.

I looked around, trying to clear my mind and piece together what had happened. I'd been flying. The cliff had been on my right, and something must have hit me, or—

I looked back the way I had come. There was a break in the cliff creating a small inlet, free of stones. In that inlet was a boat. I could see now what had happened. Behind the boat were some tall rocks, so I wouldn't have seen it even if I'd been paying attention, especially at the speed I was going. It had a mast with a rolled up sail—that must have been what I had hit—and on the boat were four people, three men of various ages and a middle-aged woman. And they were all staring at me.

CHAPTER THIRTY-TWO

A Full Dragon

Some days the bullshit just keeps piling up. I was hungry. I was tired, both from flying all day and night and from not sleeping for far too long. And now I was in pain. My whole body ached, especially my right wing and my left side. This was the second time in one week that I had slammed into something at high speed, and this time I hadn't seen it coming. My wing was bleeding too. I hoped it was only split skin. Then I'd fallen into the sea, been half-drowned and slammed onto the rocks, and now all I wanted was to get back to my hoard and rest.

But no. There were humans staring at me, no more than ten meters away, and I had to deal with them one way or another. I was still curled up on a large, flat rock by the cliffs that rose above the shore, and I was staring back at the four people, willing them to just go away.

No such luck. Without taking his eyes off me, the oldest-looking of the three men leaned toward the two younger ones. In a different language than the one I'd gotten used to, one full of complicated vowels and repetitions, he told them, "Get the harpoons."

I hated the sound of that, but I'd give them a chance. Interestingly, they were not from the ethnic group that I had identified as the majority here, which Lalia and most of the villagers belonged to. These people all had a vaguely Middle Eastern look about them that reminded me of Garal. I was going to hope that they thought I was that wyvern people had been talking about and that they'd either leave or at least leave me alone. I was too tired, too goddamn fed up with everything, to escalate the situation, but I did not have much energy for patience. I understood that they might be scared. If they wanted those harpoons in case I attacked, everything would be fine. But if they tried to start anything, there would be consequences. The dragon was already roused and ready, and it was not happy at all. It already wanted to kill them for owning the boat that *we* had flown into.

Taking responsibility was not in its nature, and holding back was a lot harder than usual considering all the aforementioned bullshit.

The two younger men—boys, really. The older of them couldn't be sixteen yet—had grabbed two harpoons from some other part of the small boat. The youngest gave his to the older man, who gripped it. He looked nervous, but he also looked like he knew how to use the thing.

"If this is what I think it is, if it is," he said, keeping his voice low and steady, "there is a full dragon bounty on it. A full dragon. What do you think?"

Well, shit.

"I don't know, Uncle," said the older of the two boys, who was holding the other harpoon. "What if we only hurt it? What if?"

"And what if you strike true, boy?" said the woman, who had picked up a long oar. "A full dragon, think about that—think about it! We could pay our debts, patch up the roof, get you boys some new clothes, and have eagles to spare. To spare! And what do you think that Lina girl would think about the young man who brought home a wyvern?"

So they thought that I was a wyvern. And there was a huge bounty on said wyvern, for whatever reason. *Great.* There went that cover.

"No sudden movements. Don't rile it up, do not. Aim for the chest or the belly," the older man said, readying his harpoon. "Just like a seal, just like that. On three, now. One—"

"Don't even try it. Don't try," I growled in their language. The man aborted his count, his mouth hanging open. "If you throw those fucking things, I will make you regret it, I will."

No point in pretending to be a dumb animal if they were going to do something stupid anyway.

"What is it?" the youngest man said with wonder.

"*It* can hear you," I said, putting my feet under myself painfully. "And *it* wants to be left alone. So put those harpoons away, put them away, before I do something we all will regret!"

The dragon was furious. It had wanted to kill them *before* they threatened us, and now I wasn't sure if I'd be able to hold back. They were close. I might even be able to reach them with my venom. I could almost taste them, and I was so hungry.

I spread my wings threateningly. Maybe that was a mistake. I hissed with pain as I flexed the right one. It was probably not broken, but I couldn't rule out a sprain or something like that. The middle joint felt like it was on fire, the pain shooting all the way to my shoulder when I moved it. Flying was clearly out of the question, for the near future, at least.

That might have been a good thing, though. It meant I couldn't just leap across the few meters separating us when the older boy threw his harpoon and my self-control slipped. I couldn't tell if I didn't get through to him, or if I scared him, or what. As I was trying to work some of the ache out of my wing, he suddenly threw it, and he threw it hard. I didn't see it coming. I felt a blow, off-center on my chest, followed by a sharp sting, and I lost it.

Before I knew it, I was scrambling and slipping across the slick stones, hissing furiously, trying to get into the air but only managing abortive jerks. Something terrible was going to happen, and I felt powerless to stop it. Part of my mind was screaming for me to turn and run in the other direction, but the rest of me was no less murderous than the dragon. If I could have flown at that moment, the poor bastards would already be screaming. The last two days had been a mess of anger, disappointment, hunger, exhaustion, and pain, and they were going to pay for it, whether they deserved to or not.

The older man recovered from his surprise and drew back to throw his harpoon as well, but I sprayed, wild and wide across the group, and as the venom hit his eyes, his weapon went wide. I still felt it hit my back and rattle along my scales, but that was their last chance. The humans fell back into their boat, coughing and screaming as they rubbed their eyes, and I clumsily made my way up a taller rock near the boat and stretched across to grab the edge—the gunwale?—my claws sinking deep into the wood.

The boat was a simple thing, seven or eight meters from end to end with no shelter and spaces for two oars on each side. It had a couple of benches, and the mast, of course, and the sail hanging slack against it might have been the only reason my wing wasn't properly broken. It also had a simple wooden grille as a floor, and the space under that was full of fish of various sizes.

The inside of the boat was a mess. Nets and other equipment were strewn everywhere. I must have rocked the boat pretty bad when I hit it. The mess was made worse by the four mostly blinded humans rolling around, wailing and coughing and, in one case, puking into the boat. The only one who wasn't completely incapacitated was the younger of the boys, who was still blinking rapidly and coughing while trying to pour water in the older boy's eyes.

When he saw me heaving myself over the edge of the boat, teeth bared and growling, he became very still. Well, except for the coughing. He looked at me with utter terror, and the first thing I thought was how easy it would be to pull him out of the boat. He was a scrawny thing, maybe eleven or twelve years old, and pretty short for his age too. He couldn't weigh that much.

Luckily for both of us, my slow, clumsy scramble across the rocks had given me time to get myself under control, if only barely. Maybe the fact that he was a kid helped too. I didn't give him a face full of venom or bite his throat out. I didn't finish off the bastards who had tried to goddamn *harpoon* me. Instead, I squeezed the edge of the boat until my hands hurt, the wood crackling as my claws dug in deeper, trying to channel my rage somewhere.

"I told you," I growled slowly, "not to try anything. I told you."

"I . . . I . . ." the boy stuttered as the others moaned.

"I told you that I wanted to be left alone."

Under my weight and strength, the boat had drifted toward me, and I could hear it bumping against the stones. I leaned my head in as far as I could without tipping the boat, less than a meter from the boy's terrified face. His eyes were as green as Garal's.

"I . . . I . . ." he stuttered again, quivering as he pressed himself into the back of the boat. I was a little impressed that he hadn't just leaped into the water, leaving the others to their fate.

I could tell who these people were. It was easy enough, based on what they'd said and what they had. They were some poor fisherfolk, probably from some poor fishing village, and a gold dragon would likely change their lives. I could understand that, somewhere in the back of my mind. And if it were up to me, the rational part of me, then I might be satisfied that I'd taught them their lesson. But the dragon still raged inside me. It was not going to be satisfied with just hurting and terrifying these people. They had threatened us. They had hurt us. The harpoon hadn't stuck, but they had made us *bleed*. And they had intended to kill us and sell our carcass like we were a goddamn animal. No, the dragon needed something, and a pound of flesh was not going to cut it.

I took a deep breath. I smelled blood and puke and piss and fear and, above everything else, fish. I looked down and found myself an out, a way to avoid doing something justified, perhaps, but something I might not be able to live with.

"Boy." I fought to control my voice. "Do you want to live? Do you want to?"

He only coughed and stuttered wordlessly.

"I said, do you want to live?" I growled again, pushing myself that last bit closer, the boat listing as I put my full weight onto my arms.

"Yes!" he exclaimed. "Yes! Please!"

"Do you want these people to live? Your family?"

"Yes!"

"Then take those two fish," I told him carefully. "The big ones. Take them."

He looked down, seeing what I meant.

My claws gouged the wood as I fought for control. "Lift them out of the boat. Wash them, and bring them to where I was lying. Then help your family, and get the hell out of here. If you do not do exactly what I have told you, I will kill you. I will. Do you understand me?"

"I . . ."

"Do you understand me?" I repeated, my voice now ice-cold and calm.

"Yes!" he squeaked and rushed to do as I had instructed. The fish were each big enough that the scrawny kid could only carry one at a time, but he managed. He hesitated when he had to climb out of the boat past me, but a hard look and an encouraging growl got him moving. He washed the first fish in the waves spraying over the rocks and put it where I had told him to, then returned and did the same with the other.

By the time he had finished, the others had mostly stopped coughing. When the woman looked at me, blinking, I snarled at her, and she sat back in the front of the boat, pulling the older boy close and away from me.

With the second fish cleaned and delivered, the boy got back in the boat, scrambling past me as fast as he could. "Good," I told him. "Well done. If you tell anyone about this, I will find you. I will. Now *fuck off!*"

The gouged wood splintered in my hands as I shoved the boat away and carefully clambered across the rocks to my prizes. I had no way or intention of making good on my threat, of course, whatever they told anyone. But it was worth a shot. When I looked back, the boy had grabbed an oar and was pushing the boat away from the rocks, not making much headway against the waves but clearly determined to put as much distance between me and them as he possibly could.

The dragon was still literally spitting mad. I'd had the bitter taste of venom in my mouth ever since I first saw the boat. But when I tore into the sweet, fatty fish, it was at least a little mollified. It still wanted to kill the fisherfolk, but at least they had paid us some tribute, so not all was wrong in the world anymore.

I finished off the first large fish quickly, guts and all. The dragon wanted me to eat the second fish immediately, and my body screamed for me to sleep. But this was not a good spot to pass out, even if it was warm and fairly dry. I couldn't go south, where the boat had been, because of the inlet. I had no desire to go back in the water. Instead I headed north, picking my way carefully across the stones with the second fish gripped securely in my jaws. Having a mouthful of backward-curving fangs really helped there.

After a fairly long walk, I found a spot that would have to do. It looked like a large section of the cliffside had broken off in the distant past and tumbled into the sea, and now a tall, weathered rock stood between the water and the cliff, creating a natural shelter from both the waves and searching eyes. There I settled in and tore into the second fish, relishing the sweetness of the fatty flesh. I would have liked to drink something as well, but I had no idea if my kidneys could handle seawater and decided against it. Instead I curled up against the stone, hoped that no one would see me from the cliff and drop a rock on me, and settled in for sleep to the sound of waves crashing against the shore.

My last day and a half had been absolutely vile. I felt deep guilt about not being able to help the rest of the captured villagers, and I was in a lot of pain. Hell, my neck still ached a little where Lalia had hacked me if I moved it the wrong way. But I hadn't killed any poor people just trying to survive, and I hadn't eaten any kids, and at least now, with a belly full of fish and the sound of the sea in my ears, I could sleep.

CHAPTER THIRTY-THREE

Walkabout

I woke when I breathed in water.

I had never lived near the coast. I was generally aware of the concept of high tide as a thing that existed, but that did not, unfortunately, mean it was something that I'd thought about when I picked a place to sleep. I was not sure what time of day it was, since I was only half-awake and what little focus I had was spent on not drowning. Coughing and sputtering I made my way to the base of the cliff and settled down again. The wound on my chest stung like hell from the salt water, and it took a while for that to mellow out, but I had barely gone back to sleep before I felt the water lapping at me and the wound started burning again. Around that point, I was awake enough to realize what was happening and that I had no idea how high the water was going to rise.

Still groggy, I looked around but didn't see anywhere higher up that I could easily get to. Grumbling, cursing fishermen, the sea, and myself, I continued north, feeling heavy, sluggish, and more bloated than I'd ever been in my life. The water came up to my belly by the time I found a small ledge with some rocks stacked beneath it where a whole column of the banded tan-and-pink rock must have cracked and tumbled into the sea. With a titanic effort I managed to drag myself up and then collapse in a panting heap.

By then, I was at least a meter above the water, and I could only hope that would be enough. I was also completely exposed, but there was nothing I could do about it. I couldn't fly, I couldn't swim, and I couldn't climb, not these cliffs and not as full of fish as I was. So I curled up and covered myself with my left wing, hoping that I'd look like a weird black rock. I napped there for a few hours. When I woke, I saw the water was receding.

With another round of grumbling, I made my way back to the comparative safety of the large rock, where I wouldn't be so visible, and settled in. I figured I could sleep there for the rest of the day and wake up to move in the morning before the tide came in again.

That was how I learned that there were two high tides every day.

This time, I woke at night, sputtering, cursing, and hating the world and everything in it. The sky was dark and heavy with clouds, and even with my night vision, I could only barely see where the moon was behind the clouds. Behind me, the cliff was a black blur. However, with my shadowsight, I could see nearly perfectly as I angrily trudged back toward the ledge I'd napped on earlier.

Being repeatedly woken up had me well and truly cranky, and I couldn't stand the idea of being half-drowned in my sleep again. I needed to get up the cliff somehow, but my wing still hurt like a bitch, and I was definitely too heavy to climb. Maybe, *maybe* I could have done it in my old body if I'd found the right line, but unfortunately my skills didn't translate as well as I wished, especially with forty or fifty kilos of fish in me. If only my wing—

I caught myself. *Stupid.* I could be so goddamn *stupid* sometimes. When I wasn't thinking like a human, I was thinking like a dragon. But what I needed to think like was a *dragon with magic.*

I looked at the wall of stone in front of me. It was definitely tall. From the ledge I'd napped on, it must be ten or fifteen meters high, and even that was one of the lower points on the cliffs. But why should I let that hinder me? I had to try, right? When I'd gone through the magic gate, the hole I needed to get through had been too high, and I'd still managed it. It hadn't been too high by much, but still.

I splashed my way to the ledge and climbed the rocks up to it. Then I looked at the distant edge of the cliff and shifted.

Then I stretched. I stretched like I'd never stretched before. I could *feel* myself getting longer and thinner, but it wasn't enough. I'd gotten impressively high, though, and I quested along the rock face until I found a nice, big jug hold. I flowed over it and willed myself to anchor onto it—and it worked! I relaxed upward from the ground, pulling myself together, then stretched again until I found an edge, then a couple crimps, and a few meters at a time, I made my way up and over the top of the cliff.

I felt extremely pleased with myself as I shifted back, becoming solid again on the wide, grassy field between the forest and the sea. I was good at climbing, and I could do magic. I was, in a word, awesome. I shouldn't let myself forget that.

Smug about my accomplishment, I proceeded to climb a tall tree. It was laborious, and climbing hurt, like everything else, but this was a place where I was guaranteed not to drown in my sleep, and I finally got to rest undisturbed.

The next time I woke it was to a cloudless sky, with the sun hanging low in the east. I felt much better. Or at least I felt well fed and rested and not as bloated anymore. I was pretty sure that I was supposed to meet Herald and the others that day, but I didn't see that happening. I couldn't fly, and I wasn't sure I could find the lake if I wasn't in the air. Even if I knew which direction it was in, I doubted I could cover the distance on foot in a day. It was disappointing, but it was just one more thing that I'd have to accept.

So instead, I tried to go as straight inland from the coast as I could. That would take me to the main north-south road through the forest, and then to the mountains. By my reckoning I couldn't be more than a few kilometers north of the forest's edge, which would put me far to the southeast of my cave. I could have stayed where I was until my wing felt better, but I didn't feel like it. I wanted to get home to my hoard. My meal and my triumph over the tides and the cliff had left me full of restless energy, and if I couldn't fly, then I would damn well run. If I only reached the mountains I could follow them north to where my cave was. I'd deal with getting up when I got there.

Since my whole left side was probably one big bruise under my scales from being smashed on the rocks by a jealous sea, I soon slowed to a walk, letting myself breathe at a rate and depth that didn't cause constant agony.

The forest was dotted with small villages, so I knew that I had to be alert for the sound and smell of people, especially now that there was a bounty out on me. Other than that, it was just a walk in the forest. I'd gotten pretty used to the huge, rolling forest that covered everything I could see from Karakan in the south to the northern horizon and from the sea in the east to the mountains in the west. This part of the land had more conifers than leafy trees, but other than that, it was pretty much more of the same. I amused myself by gently flexing my wing and trying to remember curses in the local language before inventing my own as pain shot all the way to my back.

I didn't see any villages, but I crossed smaller roads, a few of which were barely larger than footpaths, so I knew I must be near some. I smelled plenty of boar, deer, rabbits, and other scents I couldn't identify, but since I had just eaten, I didn't pay them much attention. I did smell a bear at one point and kept my senses peeled for that. I had no desire to run across something like the giant bear from all those days ago. Though, to be fair, I had no idea if the deer and boar I smelled were also giant monsters, so I might be chased up a tree again anyway.

I did have to dodge the occasional hunter and even a small group of adventurers, but that was easy enough to do. If I'd been in a better mood, it might have even been fun.

My enhanced endurance let me walk almost all day, but I rested when I needed to, drank when I found flowing water, and slept in a tree when it got dark.

The next day, I reached the main road. I didn't know if there were fewer bandits on the road since the raid—I sure hoped so—but it felt like there were more people than there had been. Without any other destination in mind, I followed the road north, heading for the lake. For once, I actually had to be a little careful when crossing side roads, checking both directions before scurrying across.

It took a while, but I got to the lake in the afternoon. People had been using the campsite again. Recently too. I could see where the grass had been flattened, and there were fresh, if cold, ashes in the firepit. There was no piece of precious metal on the tree, but I decided that I'd gone far enough for the day and settled myself up a tree that overlooked the camp. There, I dozed away the afternoon, and the evening, and, when no one came, the night as well.

I woke very late the next morning—closer to noon—disappointed. It wasn't fair to feel this way, I knew that. I was the one who'd missed the agreed-upon meeting, even if it wasn't entirely my fault. But I'd hoped that Herald, at least, would've stuck around in case I showed. And I'd wanted my money bag and the firesteel she'd gotten me. But it was probably for the best that I didn't have them. I wouldn't be able to carry them if I needed to go shadow again. Besides, Herald had a life to live, just like the others did, and they probably had a lot of questions to answer after bringing the blank-faced population of half a village into the city.

I hoped that those people had recovered and it wasn't something permanent. Sleepwalking for the rest of your life didn't sound very pleasant to me.

I stuck around into the evening, hoping to see someone I knew, but instead a completely unfamiliar group of people arrived to set up camp. It looked like a trader and some guards, but I didn't stay for a closer look. There was no point. I didn't want to share the campground, so I left my tree and continued west.

This far from the coast, the mountains were visible every time there was a break in the trees, which let me see some of the landmarks I'd used to navigate. The peaks, gullies, and valleys didn't look that different from how they did from the air, and I was pretty sure that I could find my cave. It would take another day at least to walk to the foot of the mountain. After that, I had no idea what I'd do.

I considered trying to hunt before I went home. I decided I probably should have rather than struggling to get up to the cave only to immediately leave it to find food. But if I was going to hunt now, I should do it closer to home so I could sleep it off in the cave afterward. And maybe my wing would be all right soon and it wouldn't be a problem. I realized I was trying to make excuses to get right back to my cave and, more importantly, my hoard. Counting back, I had been away for over a week, and I felt a need, an almost-physical pull, drawing me to it.

I wanted to see it, to feel it and smell it, to make sure that it was safe. Over the last few days, I had become more and more conscious of what Valmik had told me, how gremlin nests could seemingly appear anywhere there was a decently large cave. I felt myself getting anxious. When I thought about it, though, all I got from the dragon was a kind of dismissive disgust about it. It had clearly not been impressed last time we faced the things.

I walked throughout the night. I had never been a night owl in my old life, but now it felt surprisingly natural for me. The darkness and cool air relaxed me, soothing my nerves and my sore flesh, and when dawn came, I climbed a tree and slept the day away, continuing into the high hills in the evening.

I had a lot of time to think while walking back to the mountains. I tried not to, for the most part, because I might have gone out of my mind with boredom, but when I did, my thoughts were about who I was. What I was and where I was. I wasn't sure how long it had been now since I woke up in the cave. More than a month, I was sure of that much. Every time I slept, I woke up exactly where I'd gone to sleep, and at some point the fact that I didn't wake up in some hospital bed had stopped surprising or disappointing me. I dreamed about my old life often enough, but I couldn't remember having a dream that might have been a moment of waking up in the "real" world. And while there was a lot of strange stuff going on here, none of it ever had a dreamlike quality to it.

I was becoming more and more accepting of the idea that, whatever had happened to me, this was real. It might have been a different reality, a parallel dimension, a different time, or a different planet. It didn't really matter because it was as real as my old life now, and I shouldn't expect things to ever change back to the way they had been.

Once I got on that train of thought, I usually didn't want to think anymore, but as I walked into the hills that night, I forced myself to press on anyway.

If I accepted this, that this was the world and the body that I was going to live out the rest of my life in, I had to learn to actually live in it. My experience on the coast had made me realize that I was still thinking like a human. This was good sometimes, but it limited me. I had been relying on the dragon's instincts, and while those had helped me survive, it wasn't enough.

Other than the times when I got to feed my addiction to all things shiny, the happiest I had been here was when I got to spend time with Herald. Maybe she was special, or maybe it was because she'd accepted me so fast, but what it showed me for sure was that I needed companionship. I had always been a social person. I did stuff alone sometimes—that was how I'd ended up here, after all—but I loved hanging out and talking to my friends or meeting new people. I needed it, and that hadn't changed. Hell, I'd been stalking people on the roads and in their villages just to . . . what? Feel like I was part of their lives? Feel like a person? But how was I going to feel like a person if I spent all my time alone in a literal cave, hundreds of meters up a mountainside, or sneaking around the forest?

I didn't have any answers, but I knew one thing. All the people I liked, except for one little girl, were in the city. I could get in and out easily enough. I was sure of that. It was getting around and staying hidden that might be a problem. So I needed to learn and adapt.

I could do magic. I could move around soundlessly, and I could make myself almost invisible. I could even mess with shadows, making them darker and pushing them around. But I had a nagging suspicion that I'd only scratched the surface of what I could do. It hadn't even occurred to me that I might be able to climb a near-vertical cliff until I absolutely had to.

However, magic wasn't natural to me, and so it didn't come naturally. When I needed to solve a problem I had to actively remind myself that *Hey, this is something you can do.* What I needed was to make it second nature. Like, for example, climbing a damn tree hurt right now. It hurt a lot. Why didn't I simply shift and flow up? It would probably be much easier than climbing a cliff, what with all the branches for support. And what else could I do? How long and thin could I get? What was the smallest hole I could get through? I really had to get serious about exploring these things, because not using my magic—actual, real-life magic—to its fullest was a ridiculous waste. It was like not flying when you had wings.

Assuming you hadn't sprained one of them by blindly flying into a boat at fifty-plus kilometers per hour, that was. I finally understood why tall chimneys had those little lights on them.

And the body I was in—that was a whole other thing. I had gotten used to it and how to move in it. It felt completely natural to me, as natural as my human body had ever been, but I couldn't help but wonder how much of that was thanks to the dragon I shared it with. And that was something I hadn't gotten any closer to figuring out. She—I didn't feel comfortable thinking of someone who spoke with my own voice as "it" anymore—didn't seem particularly bothered to be sharing a body with me, even with me in the driver's seat. But judging by her reactions, everything that was strange to me, the magic of this world, was natural to her, and because of that, I couldn't help but feel that I was the plus-one in this shared body. That I was somehow possessing her, like a confused ghost, or an incompetent demon or something. No matter how okay she seemed to be with the situation, it made me uncomfortable. It was a little like if I had taken over someone's house one day, and all they did about it was to hang around and make helpful suggestions.

Until someone tried to break in. Then the claws came out, and I stayed behind her.

Analogies aside, I wanted to know what had happened. If I had possessed this body, I wanted to know what she'd been doing in that cave and how I'd ended up inside her. To do that, I only had one way to go, but even the thought of going back down into the pit in my makeshift treasure room made me feel sick. The dragon, to my surprise, was even worse. Whenever I thought about the place, I felt waves of anxious dread leak in from her, and I wondered what had happened there to make the proud creature so nervous. Besides possibly being possessed by me, that was.

Exploring the cave would have to wait.

CHAPTER THIRTY-FOUR

Home at Last

I had never really explored the area beneath my mountain. I'd seen it from the air plenty of times, but I was always going somewhere or looking forward to coming home and had never taken the time to get low and look around. I probably should have, but hindsight is perfect.

The land rose slowly here, and the forest climbed high toward the mountains. The farther I got from the coast, the fewer leafy trees there were, and by the time I was getting properly high up, most of the trees were low to the ground and spruce- or fir-like, mixed with somewhat taller ones with bare trunks like small pines. The cool night air smelled wonderful, but there were some scents that made me wary. Besides the various scents I thought of as prey, I smelled bear and something else that made me think of predators—wolves, maybe. Maybe the prey-predator-scent thing had something to do with what they ate. Or, not to be too proper about it, what they pooped. That would make sense, I thought. Regardless, the scent of predators was triggering something inside me, a deep-seated indignation that they had chosen the foot of *my* mountain to hunt on. It was a feeling much like having a harmless bug in your home. They didn't actually affect me, but I knew that they were there, and I wanted them gone!

I sensed that this was going to bother me until I did something about it, but enforcing my territorial rights could wait. The important thing was that I also smelled people. I had become very familiar with the smell of humans who hadn't been able to wash as frequently as they might have liked to. It was . . . distinct.

Anywhere else, I would have avoided them, but so close to home, I needed to know what was going on.

I was no bloodhound, so the fact that I smelled them in the still air meant that they must be close. I couldn't smell any smoke, thought that might mean whoever it was I smelled had the same idea as Herald and didn't want to draw any attention. It took some sniffing around, but I could usually tell where something was by scent, and with some effort, I found them.

It looked like something had taken a chunk out of the mountain, leaving a deep, square, downward-sloping cut in the naked rock. Trees grew almost all the way up to the stone, though, and it would have been hard to spot from above if you didn't know what you were looking for. Within this cut, a party had set up a pretty nice little camp. Three large tents surrounded the cold firepit, where a man with a bushy moustache sat guard, looking into the darkness of the forest. Some tools were stacked neatly between two of the tents, mostly picks and shovels, and two mules and two fine-looking horses slept by a tree.

I wondered if the man could actually see anything, but just in case, I kept hidden and silent as I circled the camp, shifting through the shadows when there was no good cover. There was the beginning of a path worn into the forest floor that led from the camp deeper into the cut, and I followed it down, curious what I might find.

Whoever they were, they had been busy. I wasn't sure how long they'd been there, but judging by their smell and how much dirt they'd shifted, it must have been several days. At the very top point of the cut, they had dug a deep, wide hole, with some rough steps packed into the dirt on the camp side. They had had to have felled a tree to do so, which lay farther up the slope, its roots dug up and left next to it.

Judging by how clean the stone was, they must have brushed or washed away any dirt stuck to the rock. And at the bottom of the hole, where the two faces of the cut met, I could see the perfectly straight-angled top corner of a depression cut into the stone.

I leaned down, curious to see what they had dug out here, and my breath caught. The humans had cleared away the dirt, leaving an empty space between the stone and the dirt about a foot—see, I was practicing—high and just as wide. At the back of that space was a flat stone surface, and on the surface, barely visible and meeting at a right angle, glowed two lines of magical light.

I knew what they had found. I had no idea if that was what they'd been looking for, or if they'd have any idea what they were looking at when they dug it out, but it was clear to me. Here, on my doorstep, almost under my nose, so to speak, was another gate into the mountain. It had been buried for who knew how long, and here was a group of humans digging it out.

I had to get back to my cave. The draw of the safety and shelter it promised was strong, and I had to check on my hoard. But once I'd done that, I knew what I was doing for the next couple days.

Getting up to the cave was both easier and harder than I'd expected. It was easier in that I could shift and move up the side of the mountain as a shadow with not much effort. It was steep, but it wasn't a sheer, vertical face, and it was rough enough that I would have been able to climb it as a human. It was way harder because my cave was, by my estimate, several hundred meters up, and in moving only a few meters at a time, I didn't have a chance in hell of reaching it before dawn. That meant that after climbing for a few hours, I had to spend the rest of the night looking for somewhere I could properly settle in and rest while waiting for darkness to fall again.

This was also by far the longest I had stayed in shadow form, and I felt it. Staying this way for more than a few minutes at a time was draining, and I constantly had to find small ledges where I could shift back and rest for a bit. It clearly used energy of some kind, which must have been recharged by plain old calories, because by the time I found a crevice wide enough to settle into, I was getting peckish. Besides that, it was mentally tiring. I needed to maintain a certain level of focus to stay as a shadow, and now I felt like I'd pulled another all-nighter. Or all-dayer, maybe, since I was sleeping during the days now.

Clearly, I was not going to be able to do this regularly, not unless I could plan for it. For now, though, I had no choice. I'd just have to cut my stay in the cave shorter than I would have liked. I'd check on my hoard, get a good day's sleep down there, and then I'd go hunting. For goats, probably. The high mountain passes were closer to my cave than the forest was, after all, and the humans digging at the foot of the mountain could wait.

My crack in the mountain was definitely in the top three least-comfortable places I had ever slept, but I managed. It was beaten only by the spots I'd once chosen to pass out in after a couple particularly rough nights out. In those cases, I blamed my bad judgment or friends who hadn't been mean enough to keep me moving. In this case, though, I could only blame my own bad planning.

After sleeping away a restless day, I felt a little better. I reached my cave faster than I'd expected, only taking about an hour from the crevice to the ledge, and when I came back together on the sparse grass by the lonely little tree, I felt quite pleased with myself. I'd made one dumb mistake by not paying attention to what was in front of me, and it had cost me a week. But I had made it back, without my wings, using my feet, my sense of direction, and my magic. There was nothing wrong in feeling proud of that.

I looked out across the forest, trying to see where I'd come from. Far in the distance was Karakan on the coast, and north of that, the forest began. I couldn't actually see the edge of the forest, but I could guess where it was. The sea was also invisible, even with the moonlight, but my imagination was enough at the moment.

Having appreciated myself and my achievement enough, I wasted no more time making my way down, following the pull of my hoard. Sliding through the narrow crevice was second nature now, not even comparable to two weeks before, and then I was in. The first thing I saw, of course, was the pit, but I had no time for that and the boatload of bad vibes it brought.

I turned around and could see my hoard, and smell it, and a grinding anxiety that I had only barely been aware of vanished. My hoard was there, whole and safe.

"*Only the girl is missing,*" the dragon whispered.

"Yeah," I answered quietly. I ran my hands over my treasures, spreading the coins a little on the ground, then lay down and relaxed completely for the first time in days. A low, slow rumble started in my chest, completely unconscious but not unwelcome. It felt pleasant. Soothing, even if I was the one doing it.

A little nap would be nice, I thought. I deserved that after what I'd done. Just a short one, as a treat.

Then my eyes snapped open. *Only the girl is missing?* Had I actually heard that?

Nah, just my sleepy brain playing tricks on me. I closed my eyes again and drifted off.

I woke up feeling rested, whole, and absolutely starved. That had been some nap! Or, I admitted to myself, it had probably been far more than just a nap. I slowly got to my feet, not wanting to leave my treasure but knowing that if I didn't go find some food soon, I might do something unfortunate.

As I carefully stretched, I found that a lot of my aches and pains were gone. My chest wound and my side felt fine, and the aching that had built up in my feet in recent days was gone. Even my wing had barely a twinge, though I'd had enough mandatory seminars on sports medicine—and personal experience—to know that I shouldn't rush an injured joint. Other than my stomach, I felt pretty good!

The dragon was happy to be home, but the hunger made her very cranky. She, of course, figured that we should go eat whoever was on guard at the humans' camp, assuming they were still there. I, however, had other plans.

It was early in the night when I left the cave. I wondered if I had sensed that somehow and that was why I'd woken up. Nearby, there was a plateau from where I could walk to the mountain spring that I'd found in my first few days here, and climbing over to it only took about twenty minutes. From there it was a short walk to the spring. There, I filled up on water. Then I started sniffing.

There was a herd of mountain goats that lived here. I'd tried hunting them when I was new to the whole dragon thing, but I never caught one until I found one that was injured and couldn't run away from me. Now I was a little more experienced and comfortable in my own skin, and I'd been practicing thinking like a dragon. I was going to use all my tools, and I was sure that I wouldn't have a problem. Assuming that I could find them, that was.

That's where the spring came in. The goats used it, and they were smelly. It didn't take me long to pick up their scent, and then it was simply a matter of following my nose.

Again, I was not and have never been a bloodhound. Finding the goats wasn't as straightforward as picking up a scent and following it straight to them. I had to go all over the place, losing the scent and backtracking, realizing that the herd must have stopped somewhere and then turned back, and getting way too close to way too many piles of goat crap. But in the end, I did find them. It took well over an hour, but there was plenty of night left.

They weren't all sleeping like I'd expected. Most of them were huddled up together under a rock overhang, but some were walking around, munching on scraggly grass and bushes and apparently not caring at all that it was the middle of the night. Some kind of guarding instinct, perhaps? Whatever the reason, it was lucky for me.

Having some of them separated from the herd made things easier. It meant that I didn't have to grab one from the middle of their huddle, which might have sent the rest running off in a panic. Instead I looked over the loners and picked a smallish one that looked a little rough around the edges. That's what predators were supposed to do, right? Pick off the sick and the old so that the herd stays healthy? Well, these were pretty much my goats, and I wanted there to be a healthy herd of mountain goats here for as long as I was around.

I crept up on the old girl carefully, freezing when one of the other goats stopped and looked in my direction. It must not have seen me, though, and I continued as it went back to eating. Then I waited, watching my target until she got in a good position. My patience paid off as she strolled behind a large boulder, where none of the others would be able to see her.

The last time I had hunted goats, they had avoided me easily, even though I could fly. This time, I wasn't going to give her a chance. Instead of sneaking up on her, I melted into the dark, flowing around the boulder, invisible and without a sound. I became solid right behind her, and she only knew that something was wrong when I lunged for her neck.

That turned out to be a bit of a mistake. Mountain goats have much stronger necks than rabbits, and my plan of biting through it failed. Things got noisy. *Lesson learned.* I did get a great grip, though, which I took advantage of by leaping onto her back and using my weight to bring her down. From there, I shifted my bite to her throat, which cut off her screaming.

After that, it was just a matter of waiting. I was too strong for the old goat to get loose, and with my jaws clamping down on its throat almost all the way to the spine, it quickly went unconscious. I heard some worried mewing from the herd, but nothing that sounded like a panicked rush. Things had gone well.

As I lay there, waiting for my prey to expire, I felt a tiny bit bad. Nothing like the first time I'd killed, though. I'd gotten used to killing animals faster than I would have expected, and that fact made me relieved more than anything else. I needed to eat. It was as simple as that, and if I avoid feeling terrible every time I got a meal, I wouldn't question it.

Once I was sure that the goat was well and truly dead, it was time for the second part of my plan. I didn't just dig in. Instead, I got up and started dragging my kill back toward the plateau near my cave. Ideally, I would have liked to have brought it all the way back, but this would have to do. The goat was heavy, and my neck didn't appreciate the weight, but I got it there, leaving a trail of blood and fur behind me. Only there, close to home, did I eat.

And then, after eating enough that I wasn't hungry anymore, I stopped. It was one of the hardest things I had ever done. The dragon was outraged, not seeming to understand why there was no more meat going down our gullet. When we fed or fought, the dragon became basically feral, and so did I. Unless, of course, I consciously resisted, like I had done now.

"*Food!*" the dragon roared in my mind. All my instincts told me to let go and gorge myself, but I stayed strong. The point here was to see if I could eat enough to feel sated without going into a coma for the next several days. Besides, the air was much cooler up here, and I hoped that the goat would keep for a little while. If not, well . . . I hoped it wouldn't come to that, but I was pretty sure that the dragon, and my body, could handle slightly spoiled meat.

With my stomach full but not filled to bursting, and in defiance of the dragon's outraged protests, I crossed back to the cave. Then I went back to my hoard, lay down happily, and went back to sleep.

When I woke up, I was hungry again, and my wing felt as good as new.

CHAPTER THIRTY-FIVE

Making Peace

I wasn't sure, but I had a pretty strong feeling that sleeping on my hoard helped me heal. That . . . was useful information.

It was like when Makanna had healed me. Last time I slept, most of my injuries had gotten better, and I'd become very, very hungry. Now I'd just eaten a big chunk of a goat, gone in for a nap, and I felt great but hungry. Again. That seemed pretty conclusive to me!

It also seemed to knock me out for as long as necessary. When I left the cave this time, it was, again, not long after sunset. I stretched and flexed my wings, and they felt stiff from not being used properly for a while but were otherwise really good. A few careful practice runs from the end of the ledge to the cave opening confirmed that yes, I could use my right wing without any pain. The relief was incredible. I had missed flying so much! Yes, I had been very proud of my accomplishment in getting home on foot, but walking was stupid. From now on, I was going to fly everywhere I possibly could, which, to be fair, was what I'd been doing until I'd busted my wing.

I celebrated by flying over to the remains of the goat. It was slightly bird-pecked and beginning to get a little ripe, but not nearly enough to put me off. I told myself that it was "aged," trying to put aside my human prejudices, and tucked in.

I finished off about a quarter of the animal, and then, again with great difficulty, I stopped myself. The dragon was no less disappointed than before, and I figured I'd have to make it up to her sometime when I didn't have things to do.

I thought about bringing the rest of my meal back to the cave, but since it had been several days before I'd gotten back, I decided against it. The idea of coming home to a rotting goat stinking up the place was too much, even if the dragon probably wouldn't mind. She was gross like that, but I still had some limits to what I'd put up with.

After filling up on water at the spring and taking care of necessities elsewhere, I sprang up and enjoyed the simple pleasure of flying for a little while. Not for too long, though. First I had some humans to creep on for the sake of my own curiosity and amusement, and then I needed to check the lake. I missed my friends. Well, friend. I missed Herald.

Confident that I wouldn't be spotted against the night sky, full as it was of bright stars, I flew south along the hills. It only took a minute or two before I spotted the angular notch cut into the stone where the camp had been, and I settled down about a hundred meters—or yards, I guess—south of it, then walked back toward it, relaxed and confident in my ability to blend into the darkness.

The camp was right where I had left it. It must have been two days or more since I was there, and it did look a little rougher. There was more equipment lying around, and clothes were hanging to dry on a rope strung between two trees. A different man than the first time was sitting guard, completely bald and with no facial hair. He was no better at spotting me than his predecessor.

It looked like they were settling in for the long haul, and I wondered how they'd handle food. I hadn't seen any signs of them hunting. Were they having supplies delivered? Would there be more people wandering about, clueless to the fact that they were on the porch of a mighty dragon? Only time would tell, and as long as they didn't bring a bunch of adventurers or monster hunters to my doorstep, it didn't make any real difference.

They had gotten a lot of work done on their hole. If the gate here was the same size as the two others I had seen, I'd say that they were halfway down. It looked like they had put a lot of effort into digging out the walls, which were clear and clean for several yards to each side of the recessed gate.

I was pretty sure that these people were archaeologists, or at least scholars of some kind. It was the way the hole had been dug. The walls were clear, clean, and more importantly, completely undamaged. There were no fresh scars that I could see on the stone where a pick or a shovel had chipped it. These people hadn't just been digging; they had been carefully *excavating* the gate and the area around it. Looking for what, though? Murals or rock carvings? If they were looking for the gate, wouldn't they have dug that out first? Unless they had no idea what they'd found. Herald had been shocked at my ability to see magic, so perhaps all they saw was a flat stone surface set into the mountain wall.

These people had me very, very curious. I wanted to know what they were looking for and how they'd known to dig here. Beyond that, I was excited to see what was inside that gate. It led into my mountain, after all. I wondered if they knew. What I really wanted was to have a conversation with them, but it was hard to guess how big of a risk that would be. There was a bounty on me, and I had no good way of knowing who might try to cash in on it. I didn't want to tempt fate, and I would rather not have to kill these people just because my curiosity got the better of me.

The more I waited, the more obvious it became that there was no point in hanging around. Nothing was happening. Maybe I could see how many of them there were, if they each took a shift on guard duty, but I could just as easily come back during the day when they'd be working. So I left the lone guard staring uselessly into the darkness and took off into the night sky, hoping that the bear I kept smelling didn't come around and eat them.

Above the trees, it was just me and the lights of the night. I had the moon ahead of me, to the east. The sky above, almost free of clouds, was so full of stars that it was nearly dazzling. I hadn't paid much attention to the night sky, before or since I came here, but that night, I couldn't tear my eyes from it. There were no city lights here, and with my superior night vision, I could see more stars than I had ever imagined existed. Or maybe there actually were more stars here. Maybe the stars were all different than the ones I'd grown up with. They might've been. I'd never been good with constellations beyond Orion and the Southern Cross, and while I couldn't see either of those, I also couldn't really tell if the stars looked right or not. All I knew was that they were beautiful.

When I arrived at the lake, there was no one there. Not a single lonely tent stood on the campground, and no one waited beneath the tree. But there was a note! In the same place as the first note Herald had left me, stuck with a silver pin, was a piece of paper or papyrus or whatever it was that they used. Only, this time it didn't have any weird letters on it. Instead it was divided into three sections.

The section on the left had a drawing of a tent with a fire outside. Above it were three horizontal lines, stacked vertically.

The center section had two simple drawings. The sun behind the water, then an arcing arrow pointing to the sun behind the mountains. This repeated once below. Two days, I guessed it meant. Above all this were two horizontal lines.

Finally, the section on the right had a crude map of the area, with the city, coast, mountains, road, and lake. Arrows traveled along the road to the lake. Above the map was, unsurprisingly, one horizontal line.

I stared at it for half a minute until I realized that I should be looking at it from right to left. Once I did that, the message, if I interpreted it right, was pretty clear: *We'll come from the city in two days, and we're staying.*

Something struck me then, sitting by the calm lake under a sky full of stars in the silence of the cool night air. I had a safe home and reliable sources of food and water. I had my hoard, which helped me recover both in body and in mind. My last several weeks had been full of pain and anger, but most of all, there had been almost constant excitement in one form or another. And I had friends and acquaintances who, to varying degrees, wanted me around. Enough so that they'd come here and wait for me.

I couldn't even remember the last time I wondered if this all was real or a figment of a damaged brain. I still had no idea what had happened, how I'd got here, but of course this was real. It was as real as anything I'd ever experienced, except I didn't have to worry about work hours or paying taxes or global warming or any of that bullshit anymore. I had a home. Sure, it needed some work, but it was mine. I could sneak and I could hunt, and feeding myself was no longer an issue. I could fight off almost anything I'd come across so far. I could do fucking *magic*.

I could *fly*.

Above all, I wasn't just surviving anymore. I had, in every way that mattered, an actual life. I had one close friend, which was more than you could say for a lot of people and more than I'd expected, and other than her, I had a handful of friendly acquaintances. In that moment, I realized I was happy. Not for any specific, short-term reason, but because I felt generally good about myself and my situation. I was here to stay, and I liked it.

At that revelation, a part of me bubbled with excitement. I was going to see my friends again. Of course, I had no idea when they'd left the note, but the paper was in good condition, like it couldn't have been exposed to the weather for too long. It might be tomorrow, or the day after, or the day after that, but they'd be here, and I would not disappoint them again. They trusted me and wanted me to show up, and this time, I would.

However long it took, when they got there, I would go meet them. And it was going to be awesome.

It didn't work out that way, exactly, but that night, I sat and looked out across the water, and I was at peace.

CHAPTER THIRTY-SIX

INTERLUDE: Herald

In the room that she shared with her sister at the inn Her Grace's Favor, Herald went through her pack one last time. She had spread everything she needed on the too-short bed, and now she inspected each item, making sure that it was presentable and in good condition. The only items not on the bed were the pack itself, which she had inspected, oiled, and set by the door; the tent and bedroll, which were spread on the floor; and her arms and armor, which Valmik had kindly offered to take care of.

Everything was there and in good order. There were the basics, of course: clothes, equipment, dried food, waterskins, and such. Then there was soap, a brush, and other hygienic articles. She was no stranger to roughing it, but she was not staying out for weeks with no possibility of a proper wash or cleaning her clothes. The very thought made her skin crawl. She also had a cheap healing potion for emergencies.

Almost as an afterthought, she included the small cloth wrap containing the chunk of dried skin, scale, and horn that Draka had discarded. She was not sure why she had kept it. It was, objectively, gross. She admitted that. But it was important to her, though she could not quite say how or why. She kept it hidden, but she was not ashamed or embarrassed of carrying it around. She would just rather no one knew about it.

She also had Maglan's letters in a waterproof pouch, along with two books: one intended to help children learn to read and one about monsters, common and legendary. They had cost her a decent bit of silver, but she had spent it gladly. That pouch was one of the most important things she was bringing, together with one containing Draka's money—including her cut of the reward for finding and saving the villagers—the harnessed bag she had ordered, and the firesteel. She must have checked a dozen times that they were accounted for. If she forgot everything else, she would bring those.

She would be leaving for the lake with Val in an hour at most. Mak had finally run out of excuses and leverage to keep her in the city. When they had first gone to meet Draka, four days after parting, as agreed, the others had practically had to drag Herald back. Mak had finally resorted to threats. They had a job. It was a simple one, but the promise to bring Herald along went both ways, and the prospect of being left alone while the others went out had been too much. So Herald had returned to the city, disappointed and worried. They had gone out and cleared a den of monstrous badgers that were raiding a village's livestock. Then there had been meetings with the city authorities, where Mak had brought her as a witness, and a dinner with old friends, where Herald could not be absent for the sake of propriety. Every day, her nerves got more frayed, and her sleep got worse. But now, all that was over.

Mak had not been able to find anything new to tie Herald down. Garal had taken her note with him when he patrolled the forest, promising to pin it to the tree by the lake. And Val, after much arguing and some outright begging, had agreed to follow her to the lake, at least until she got settled in. There was no telling what he had told Tam in order for her brother to accept it, but Val was coming. She would have gone alone if she had to, but she was honest enough to admit that having Val along was a great relief.

Herald had prepared food for a week, but she would supplement it with fishing and hunting. This time, she was staying until she met Draka again. And if Draka did not come, Herald would find her. She did not know how, but she would. Even if they tried to drag her back. Even if she had to face her nightmares and go alone into the forest for the first time in weeks. She knew that she would not be able to relax until she saw that her friend was safe. And if she was not . . .

There was a bounty out for a wyvern. One gold dragon, coincidentally. And if anyone collected on it, Herald would find them, and she would destroy them. Then she would burn the Alchemists' Guild to the ground. Whatever it took. Whatever the consequences.

An hour later, Herald and Val walked down Merchants Street, crossing the central market and turning onto Independence Way. They passed the forum, main temples, and council building, then made for the Forest Gate. Each of them carried a heavy pack, but they were both used to it, and Val had volunteered, or, more correctly, demanded, to carry most of the heavier items. With his strength and endurance advancements, it only made sense, but Herald appreciated it nonetheless.

Two armed and armored individuals leaving the city was nothing unusual in Karakan. Though the city was a member of the Sareyan League, and therefore recognized as cultured and civilized, it was still on the frontier, at the forefront of the effort to reclaim the lands that had been lost in the Great Collapse some hundreds of years ago. Adventurers were a necessary and respected part of that effort.

But no matter how common a sight it was, Herald always drew stares. Some curious, some hateful, many lustful. She did not like it, but she was used to it. Taller than most men and with skin dark enough to mark her as having origins outside of the League, Herald had garnered attention all her life, but especially so since she'd become a woman. During her childhood, it had been fine. People have difficulty telling children's ages, after all, and most just assumed that she was older than she was. But once her body started filling out and she started growing for real, self-consciousness became her constant companion. She had been twelve years old when she grew taller than her brother. At fifteen, she was taller than Val, and she had added a few inches since then.

On top of that, she knew that she was in no way ugly. She was not pretty, like her sister or Lalia, but she was young and healthy and had the same curves most women did. She had had to suffer her share of leers and rude comments, and at not much past seventeen years old, she was already sick of it.

All that was to say that when she walked down a street, especially with her arms and equipment, she turned heads and drew whispers. It was a relief to her when she and Val passed through the gate and into the grassy fields that separated the city from the strip of farmland that preceded the forest.

Out in the open like this, Herald finally felt like she could truly breathe again. The wilds of the forest had been her refuge for many years, a place where she could get away from the looks and whispers. That was not to say that she hated the city. The city had many things that she did not want to live without, like books and good food, music, the theater, and dear friends. It just became too much sometimes, and then she would escape to the forest, sometimes alone, sometimes with Lalia or one of her siblings, or sometimes with one of her less adventurous friends.

Lately, though, even the forest had not felt safe. Ever since she had encountered those two bandits with Draka, there had been a feeling of menace on the roads. Her eyes roved nervously among the trees and bushes, expecting someone to burst from them at any moment. But today she had Val with her, and as they left the farmlands and entered the forest, his presence kept her dread at bay. No one in their right mind would attack Val. Anyone with eyes could see that he was dangerous. Tam was just as dangerous, of course, but he was small and cheerful, not at all like his solid, solemn partner. She loved her brother, and loved spending time with him, but for this, she was glad that it was Val who had come with her.

She may also have had a small crush on Val when she was younger, but that was neither here nor there.

They had not spoken much during their march. Both Herald and Val were comfortable with long silences, content in the other's company but keeping their thoughts to themselves. When they neared the smaller road that would lead them to the lake, however, Val spoke up.

"If Lady Draka doesn't come, what will you do?"

That was Val. Direct and without mercy.

Herald didn't look at him. "I will stay until she does."

"And if food becomes a problem?"

"Then I will return to the city, resupply, and go back."

"How long must pass before you give up? Weeks? Months?" Herald could hear concern in his voice, and she turned to look him in the eyes.

"As long as it takes. Or until despair takes me."

"We worry for you, Herald. You're aware of this."

"I am," she said fondly. "And I appreciate it. But this is something I need to do. I have to know that Draka is all right . . . or become convinced that she is not." At the expression in Val's eyes, she added, "I will promise you this: If you come to the lake, and you find me dying, you may bring me back. But anything else and I will fight you, one and all."

Val searched her eyes for a long moment and nodded.

"Mak won't be happy."

"I know."

"She still doesn't trust Draka."

She sighed. "I know."

"But she loves you and worries for you very much."

"I know," she said again and smiled sadly.

They reached the lake, and Herald inspected the tree as Val began to make camp. With a rush of excitement, she saw that her note was gone. Garal had confirmed that he had pinned it right where she had told him to, and it was unlikely that anyone would see it there unless they were looking for it. Barring some terrible luck, Draka had been here!

"Val!" she shouted as she ran over to where he was setting up the tent. "The note is gone, Val! She has been here!"

"Fortune's with us," Valmik said, his serious face growing brighter at her obvious joy.

"She is all right," Herald said happily as she steadied a pole so that Val could more easily secure the lines. "She is alive, and she is here."

And she has not abandoned us, she added silently to herself. That was another of her fears. Despite her kind parting words, Draka had seemed so angry when they separated, though Herald could not tell why. And then she had not come to the agreed meeting. It was the first time that she had not shown up, and Herald had felt a very real fear that the dragon had decided against cooperating further with her group. And worse, that she had decided against continuing their friendship.

That was a thought she could not abide, and she had quashed it ruthlessly every time it appeared. But like a bad tooth, it would not be ignored, and it had haunted her, in her sleep and other quiet moments.

But now, everything was all right! Draka had seen her note, and she had taken the pin. She would come here, and they would talk. Herald would have her family and her friend, and they had some money now . . . Everything would be good again.

A small, traitorous part of her suggested that the silver-loving dragon might have just taken the pin, but she refused to entertain the thought. *No.* Everything would be all right.

The following days passed slowly. Garal or Lalia stopped by whenever they were on the northern patrol, and Herald and Val had company from another small group one night. The trio was packed heavily, with mules carrying most of their supplies, and was seeking fortune on the true frontier in the far northern woods. It was their third such expedition, and they were certain that it would be resoundingly successful.

To Herald's embarrassment, the three readily assumed that she and Val were lovers. It was a fair enough assumption, since they looked nothing alike and shared a tent, but Herald still could not hide her mortification. Val only waved the suggestion off, though he looked at her fondly as he said, "Any man would be fortunate to win the favor of such a fierce and beautiful young woman. But I think she will not mind if I say that her brother is just as lovely, and it is he who holds my heart."

The conversation faltered after that, and at least one of the three looked at Val with distaste as they left in the morning. In hindsight, Herald thought that she should have known. They were obviously worshippers of the Three, the Father, the Mother, and the Child. They favored doing things in groups of three and considered the third repetition of any act to be especially lucky. But they were also very big on family, preferably with three children. And though Herald knew that not all Three-ers were as hard-line as others, many took a dim view of men who loved other men or women who loved other women. For that matter, they considered any relationship that could not produce children to be unfortunate, even favoring divorce if a couple could not conceive.

Herald did not understand them, but at least they usually kept their beliefs to themselves.

Otherwise they spent their time fishing, hunting, and practicing or pursuing their own interests. Val drilled Herald on her sword work, and she had brought a sheaf of practice arrows, though she had soon broken all of those. Val had a bundle of cheap papyrus that he covered in charcoal sketches of whatever caught his fancy, and Herald read and reread Maglan's letters and the two books she had brought.

By the third day, she was terribly bored. By the fourth evening, when Val had to return to the city, she almost let her resolve fail and went with him. But her desire to see Draka was stronger than her fear of boredom and loneliness. She said farewell to Val, sent her love to her siblings, and stayed.

She amused herself for a while by moving the tent. She could have remained where she was, but as the empty silence dragged on, she became very conscious of the fact that she was a lone young woman, far from help if she needed it. Instead of focusing on that, she set up among the vegetation, camouflaging the tent with young trees and branches for good measure.

Draka still had not come, and fear and insecurity crept in. What if someone else had found the note? Or what if her fears were true, and Draka had just taken the pin? Herald slept poorly that night, alone with no one to comfort her when she woke from her nightmares.

The next day was miserable. Herald had severely underestimated how badly every unexpected sound could startle her, but at least the bursts of fear relieved the boredom. She desperately wanted to pack up and leave, to return to the city and her family, but she could not. She would not let herself. She was stronger than that.

Instead she barely left the tent all day, only going for a quick wash in a nearby stream, and then meeting Lalia when she came by on patrol. Lalia had wanted to drag her back to the city, of course, but Herald had persevered, and the mercenary had finally given up, though she had not been happy about it.

A mix of fear and hope kept Herald awake long into the next night. She stayed in sight of the tree, waiting for Draka to appear, her eyes straining in the dark until she found herself nodding off. Only then did she crawl into the tent and allow exhaustion to finally claim her.

Herald woke with a start. At the very edge of her hearing, there was the rustle of dry leaves and the sounds of long, deep breaths. She held her own breath and reached for her sword, unsheathing it slowly as the sounds circled her tent. Then, by the side of the tent where her pack rested, there came two quick sniffs, and then silence. Nothing.

Herald began to relax and then whirled as there was a quiet snap by the front flaps of the tent. She raised her blade, preparing to thrust—

And her world was set right by one word, said in a soft, familiar hiss.

"Herald?"

CHAPTER THIRTY-SEVEN

It's Been a While

I padded around the hidden tent carefully, not wanting to wake whoever was inside. I sniffed around, hoping to find a familiar scent, but what I found was inconclusive. There was something vaguely familiar there, but it was hidden under the smells of soap and rosemary and, when I reached one corner of the tent, silver. Whoever was in the tent had a decent chunk of change with them.

I heard someone stir inside and froze. Dammit, I was being ridiculous! There was no way I was going to figure out who was in the tent. I would have to gamble.

I focused and shifted into the shadows, moving soundlessly around to the front. I used the few seconds it took to shift back to build up my nerve, and then I whispered.

"Herald?"

I heard a sharp breath and immediately began to shift back, then drifted into the bushes, remaining in shadow to wait and see what would happen.

There was rapid shuffling. The cloth of the tent flaps bulged out.

"Draka?!" Distorted as the voice was by my being in shadow, I was relieved to recognize Herald's familiar contralto as she fumbled hurriedly along the length of the flaps. She finally pushed them open, rushing out on her hands and knees.

"Draka?" she said again as she looked around in the darkness, and her voice had an edge of almost-painful disappointment.

When I focused as hard as I could, it took a little under three seconds for me to shift, and seeing her face when she didn't find me outside made those seconds torture. I stepped forward the instant I could.

"I'm he—"

I barely saw her move. She nearly knocked me down as she took a crouching leap and threw her long arms around me. One went under my wing, and the other down my back, and I was still reeling as she crushed me in a fierce hug. Those reflexes of hers were something else!

"Hello to you too," I said once I got over my surprise.

"I feared that you were gone," she mumbled.

"Yeah, sorry about that. Not showing up, I mean. I kind of got hurt."

Herald released me and sat back on her feet, her face uncomfortably close to mine. I realized that it was too dark for her to really see me.

"Are you all right? Please tell me that you are all right!"

I leant back, wondering why she was so damn intense. "Uh, nah, yeah. Yeah! I'm fine now. I hit my wing pretty bad on the coast and had to walk home."

"Oh, okay." She breathed out a sigh of relief so close to me that I felt its warmth. "Good! That is good. I feared—"

"Hey," I interrupted her, drawing my head back a little. "Do you have a lamp or something? A lantern? So you can see me?"

"Oh, yes!" She turned and crawled back into the tent, then returned with a lantern made of perforated brass. She went through a small door on the side of the tent and did something inside, and the smell of some chemical hit me faintly. Something like kerosene, perhaps. She struck some sparks with a small firesteel and the lantern lit, filling the space between us with a warm, speckled light.

Of course, now I could barely see. The world in my shadowsight filled with invisible patches until I blinked my eyes back to good old, regular, nonmagical vision.

Herald blinked as her eyes adjusted, then looked at me with a wan smile. She looked like she had a million things to say, starting and stopping several times before settling simply on "I missed you."

"I missed you too, kid."

"I am not—" she protested weakly, but I cut her off.

"I know. I know. It's a term of endearment where I'm from, yeah?"

"That is acceptable, I suppose." She sat up a little straighter, then reached out and stroked the left side of my head, rubbing my scar with her thumb.

"You have a small bump here. Perhaps your horn is growing back?"

"Really?" I bent my neck and reached up to feel for myself. Sure enough, there was a little bump under the rough patch of scales there. "Huh, maybe." I wasn't particularly attached to the things, but they probably had some kind of purpose.

"So," I said, "what happened? After I left."

"Well," she began, "we brought the villagers home."

They hadn't been able to leave anyone in the village. It was deserted and ransacked, and the villagers they had with them were still basically sleepwalking. They'd continued to the main road and then to the city.

"Making camp was surprisingly easy. It was only lucky that it did not rain, because we did not have tents for everyone. But they ate when we fed them and drank when we told them to, and then we had them all sleep on the ground in a big huddle to keep the elders warm. A few of them showed signs of coming to by the time we reached the city, but beyond that . . ."

Entering the city had been a circus. They had tried to get the guards at the gate to help them but had no luck. Instead, they marched them up to the harbor district, where the Adventurers' Guild was, and left them in the care of the staff there. All the way, crowds had gathered to gawk and get in the way, and the foursome had a hell of a time keeping people away, whether they looked only curious or were less well intentioned.

"And then, of course, the Guild got the authorities involved. I suppose they had no choice."

"What's going to happen to the villagers?"

She frowned. "I do not know. There were announcements, I know that much, asking for relatives to come forward to take them into their care. For the others, I can only hope that one temple or another might help. The Silent Mercy might."

"And what about the slavers? Have you heard anything that might help?"

"Mak says that she has had to answer many questions about that. We told them as much as you told us, though we left you out, of course. That there was a man with some guards, talking about how his superior had arranged the abductions, but we could not see his face. The questions Mak has had to answer seem to point to many more people disappearing in and around the city than usual, which is worrying. The council sent the Cranes up to clear the place out, though I do not know how that went. Lalia was pretty mad about it, that they did not send the Wolves instead. Anyway, Mak has been called to speak with people from different offices almost every day for weeks now."

"Wait," I interrupted her, "why only Makanna?"

Herald's voice turned a little bitter. "Well, she brought me along a few times, just to keep me in the city. Not like you can say no if you've been called by a Speaker for an office. But of course it is Mak who has been called, since she is the head of the family."

"Head of the family?"

"Well, yes? Since our parents died, she is the eldest. We may not have a name like the proper families—"

"Wait. So she's, like, your legal guardian?"

"That is an odd way of putting it, but perhaps? Mine and Tam's. She is responsible for us, if we commit a crime or some such, and we need her permission for many things. Is that the same as a 'legal guardian'?"

"But you're both adults."

"Yes?"

"And you said before that you can get married and everything without anyone's permission."

"Well . . . I can marry into a family if their head agrees. And I could marry someone and begin a new family with one of us as head. No one could stop us from doing that. But if I wanted to marry someone and bring them into my family, I would need Mak's permission. And if I wanted to buy a property, of course, or take a loan. A legal loan, anyway."

"Why?"

"Who would make an agreement like that with just one person, without the security of their family behind it?" Herald asked back, now slightly flustered. "What if they do not pay? I know that you are not from here, but is it really so different from what you are used to?"

"I mean . . . yes! I don't get it! Why was Tamor the one in prison?"

"What?"

"If Makanna's responsible for you committing crimes, why was Tamor in prison and not her?"

"Oh! Because he would not let her. She tried!"

When I didn't say anything, she started over. "It is like this. We needed a lot of money for Tamor's fine, which we did not have. Thus, we needed an indenture as security while we tried to raise the money."

"Indenture? Like slavery?"

"Almost, yes. Mak tried to use herself, of course, but Tam would not let her."

"But she is the head of the family," I said, trying to get everything straight.

"She is."

"So she makes the decisions."

"She does. So Tam and Val threatened to get married if she would not relent."

"They what?"

"Threatened to get married," she said matter-of-factly. "Then Tam could have been the head of his own house, and it would have been his responsibility. Or Val's, which would have been a whole other fight."

"But . . . why not Makanna?"

"Draka," Herald said slowly, "Tam is a man. His contract would have been bought by some company that needed him for labor. Maybe as a guard. It would have been a few hard years, but indentured servants are not allowed to be used for anything truly dangerous. Mak . . . she is pretty, and she can dance. She might have been fine, but it would not have been easy for her. You understand? And if they found out that she can heal, we might never have seen her again. They would ship her off somewhere, to some estate far away."

"That's legal?"

"No. But who would speak for her? How would we prosecute the holders of her indenture? We will never have the money to go against a rich House. No, Tam and Val refused to take that risk. They would not even let me finish speaking when I offered to take his place. Of course, they said that it was because it was Tam's fault in the first place, and that is certainly true. But Val told me the real reason later."

"That's fucked-up! There's no way to get justice if you're not rich?"

"Can anyone prosecute anyone where you are from?"

"I mean, anyone can report a crime . . ."

"And if the perpetrator is powerful, and the victim is weak, will they be punished?"

I wished that I could honestly say yes.

"So you know how it is," Herald said sadly at my silence. "That is not to say that wealth and power protect you from breaking the law openly, but as long as they are careful . . ."

"Yeah," I agreed. "I've heard that one before."

It took a little while to get back to talking after that, but we managed. They had gotten paid the hefty sum of three hundred eagles, a small fortune, and so they were fairly flush with cash. They had also gone and cleared out some monstrous gophers or badgers or something, though Herald seemed to think that was just so Makanna could keep an eye on her.

That naturally led to Herald asking me to wait a moment, then going back into the tent. She rooted around in her pack for a while, and then came out with a familiar bag. It was the one I had left with her when we went to rescue her people, and it had grown!

"It is all in there," Herald said almost coyly. "Including your share of the reward for rescuing the villagers."

The bag bulged. She held it out, and when I took it in my hand, it jingled, clinked, and tinkled as I hefted it. The thing was, what, a kilo? Two pounds? Relaxed as I was, the smell was nearly intoxicating, even through the leather of the bag.

"How—" I started, then had to swallow. "How much is in here?"

Herald smiled with amusement at my reaction. "Seventy-five or so eagles. And a handful of peacocks."

"That's nice . . ." I told her, my words breaking up as an involuntary rumble began in my chest.

Herald laughed, an almost-girlish giggle, as she took the bag from my hand and hung it by its cord around my neck. "I thought you might like that. The firesteel is in there as well."

"Mmm, thank you," I rumbled, continuing to heft and fondle the bag around my neck.

Then I heard the dragon. "*See?*" she asked. "*This one is loyal. This one adores us. She will not go against us. She is the first.*"

I froze at the words, though my rumbling purr continued. The dragon had been silent for days, and this was what brought her back? Luckily, Herald didn't seem to see anything wrong.

"I think I will go back to sleep," she said. "In the morning, I hope that you will tell me everything that happened to you while we were apart."

"Yeah . . ." I said, distracted by what the dragon had said. "I will."

"Then . . . do you want to come in?" She sounded a little nervous.

"Ah . . . I wouldn't want to crowd you."

"I shared this tent with Val. He sprawls. You cannot take much more space than him."

"Maybe I should—" I looked up into the trees, but Herald interrupted me.

"Please?" she said, and the hope in her eyes was too much for me to resist.

"Yeah. Sure."

I padded into the tent, my bag jingling with every step.

CHAPTER THIRTY-EIGHT

What Are We?

I had slept all of the previous day, but I still managed to nap a few hours in Herald's tent. I thanked my natural draconic laziness for that. Herald, though, slept like a baby well into the morning, smiling and snoring softly, with her arm draped over me and resisting any attempt of mine to leave.

"That," she declared as she stretched in front of the tent once I got her up, "was the best night's sleep I have had in weeks."

I was still thinking about what the dragon had said the previous night. Her words, combined with Herald's somewhat-extreme reaction to seeing me and her eagerness to have me stay near her even while she slept, had me worried. It felt like her behavior was way beyond merely being happy to see a friend after a week or two. Or even a crush, for that matter, which would be kind of weird, but I wasn't going to judge. Was she that starved for someone who'd listen to her and take her seriously?

As bad as it was, I hoped that it was that simple. Because the alternative, based on what the dragon said, was concerning.

"Still having trouble sleeping?" I asked her as she prepared breakfast. She had made a small fire to boil water for tea and soak her hard, dry bread. She'd offered me some, but I'd declined like I always did.

"I have had trouble, yes," she said, poking at the bread to break it into chunks as she added dry cheese and fruit to the water.

"I'd hoped it'd get better after we got your people back."

"Oh, it did," she said with a small sigh, "but then I started having nightmares again. The last two weeks have been quite bad."

"Any idea—" I started carefully, but she cut me off.

"You, you scaly idiot!" she said incredulously, but there was no anger in it. "I was worried about you, of course! Where were you?"

"Right. I promised to tell you, didn't I?"

And so, while Herald ate her weird porridge, I told her about the last two weeks and change. My frustration at not finding the slavers. Hurting my wing and meeting the fisherfolk. I was taken aback at how her face twisted when I told her how they'd tried to collect on that bounty. Anger looked wrong on her somehow, and she was clearly furious. It also wasn't the first time she'd heard about it.

"There were some rumors. About a damaged Barlean fishing boat coming into Karakan with half the crew dead and the survivors babbling about trying to collect the bounty, and how the wyvern had sworn eternal revenge on them. I do not think that anyone took them seriously. They were supposedly mad with thirst or fear."

There was no sympathy at all in Herald's voice when she told me, only that same steady anger, and I didn't feel much myself. Not as much as I would have thought. Mostly, I regretted the deaths, if that was true, as a minor personal failure. I hadn't been trying to kill them, even though they had tried to kill me first. I especially hoped that the younger boy had survived, since I'd kind of made a deal with him.

"It is good that they spoke of a wyvern, even after seeing you," Herald said. "No one should mistake a wyvern for a dragon up close. Still, I think this increases the threat to you. If the 'wyvern' begins to be taken as a serious threat, the council may add to the bounty, and that would attract more hunters. I know that this was not your fault, but you will need to be more careful, if possible."

The bounty had been posted by the Alchemists' Guild, she told me. Apparently, wyverns had many parts that were useful as alchemical reagents, and the skins made excellent leather. Her eyes were smoldering as she told me how she'd checked repeatedly if anyone had claimed the bounty, and I had a strong feeling that she would have done something reckless if they had.

I didn't like seeing her like that, so I pushed on quickly, telling her how I'd been stuck below the cliffs. She brightened a little when I told her how I'd learned about the tides, laughing at my description of waking up with seawater in my nose the second time in one sleep and cheering enthusiastically when I told her how I'd found that I could climb in shadow form.

I glossed over the days in the forest. Nothing much had happened other than me being too late to meet them at the lake. I apologized for that, but Herald waved it off. "I should have waited," she said, "but Mak had accepted a job and—"

"No, no, you don't need to explain yourself. We set a time, and I didn't show. It's totally my fault."

"I felt horrible for leaving. It felt like I was betraying you, but Mak . . ."

"Hey, no! They're your family, and they love you. Don't blame your sister for wanting you around."

"That's not why she does it!" Herald protested, raising her voice. "She just wants to keep me away from you!"

"Look . . ." I paused for a while to consider what to say. Herald's face was a riot of conflicting emotion. Anger, sadness, fear. A plea for me to understand. "Makanna doesn't trust me. Obviously. I wish she did, but she doesn't know me like you do. And I don't think she wants to. So yeah, I think she's worried about you getting attached to me. But I saw you two together in the tunnels. She loves you a lot, you know? I was away with Valmik and your brother for, what, fifteen minutes? And when we came back, she was ready to give you anything just to keep you close."

What I had to say next was difficult and bitter. I was frightened, truly afraid of how she might react. I didn't want to scare her off, but I was honestly worried about what both she and the dragon had said, so I had to put it out there. Herald deserved for me to be open.

"Makanna doesn't want to lose you. And I wonder if she's right to be worried."

Herald looked at me, confusion written on her face. "What do you mean?"

"I . . ." The words stuck in my throat. I tried again. "I'm worried that you might be obsessed with me."

"I do not understand."

"Always siding with me over your sister? Staying here for . . . you must have been here for like four or five days?"

"Six."

"Yeah. Losing sleep over me? The way you greeted me? I'm just . . ." My throat felt thick, but I pushed through, and the words spilled out in an uncontrollable stream. "You're my only real friend here, Herald. I'm so lucky to have met you, yeah? The idea of you getting hurt terrifies me. And I'm scared that this is more than just a friendship to you, that you're idolizing me somehow, putting me on some kind of pedestal where I can't help but disappoint you and hurt you in the future, hurt you for real somehow, and you'll hate me and—"

And I'm afraid that there is something about me, the dragon in me, that's messing with your head. But I couldn't say any more. I couldn't even look at her. I turned my head away, but Herald reached out and put her hands on each side of my jaw, gently but firmly turning my face back toward her. She looked at me seriously for a long while, her mouth twitched, and she smiled wryly, laughing without humor.

"Oh, gods. The arrogance of dragons." There was a hint of tears in her eyes, but she looked serious and determined. "That will not happen. Listen to me, you silly lizard. I am not some child with wild, romantic notions. I am not in love with you, if that is what you are afraid of. I am sorry, but you are not my type."

"Yeah, no dramas. Bit of a relief, really," I said, trying for humor. "No offense, but . . . ew. You're like eight years younger than me."

She very generously forced a laugh. "This is not some misplaced hero worship either," she insisted. "I know that we have not known each other for long. And I will not deny that I am drawn to you. I want to be around you, and I am unashamed of and comfortable with that. When I am with you, I feel safe and excited all at once, and it is a little intoxicating. You are a dragon and a traveler from another world. How amazing is it that I know someone like that? And on top of that, I like you for who you are. I enjoy our conversations and our silences. I feel fortunate beyond measure to know you. Is that so bad? Is it so hard to understand?"

"Maybe not." I still tried to avoid her eyes, but she was a big girl who spent a lot of time shooting a bow, so I didn't have much of a chance. She held my head steady, and turning my eyes away felt ridiculous after a while.

"And what is the alternative? You refuse to meet with me anymore? You would make us both miserable for certain rather than risk it in the future?" I could tell that she was trying to sound stern, but I could see some real worry in her eyes that I might do just that.

I stopped fighting her grip. "No. It sounds pretty dumb when you say it like that."

"Good," she said and relaxed as well. "It *would* be dumb." She gave my cheeks a little squeeze. Then she hesitated before quickly leaning forward and kissing me on the nose. She released my head, her cheeks darkening. "Do not read too much into that. Are we done with this for now? Can you continue the story?"

God forgive me, I still had doubts and worries. It still felt like too much too fast from her side, but I was too weak and selfish to push it any further. If I truly wanted to scare her off, I might have told her about the dragon and how it felt about her and what that made me fear. But I had been so scared to say what I had, and was so relieved at her reaction, that I couldn't handle the idea of making another effort. I would trust her to be mature beyond her years. I would be the best friend to her that I could, under the circumstances, and if she was wrong, I would deal with the pain and guilt when they happened.

For her sake, I pulled myself together and continued. "Yeah. So, there was no one here . . ."

I told her almost everything. I skipped most of the time in the forest, but I told her about the archaeologists and what they had found. I had never told anyone about my cave before, but I told her. I talked about how I'd climbed the mountain and about the cave and the chamber where I had my hoard, and I never felt the least bit of worry about her knowing, neither my own nor from the dragon. I told her about the pit and how I'd never worked up the nerve to go down there, and she was very sympathetic.

I even told her about my new hunting technique, which she approved of.

"You know," she said, "considering your excellent sight in the dark and how you blend into the shadows . . . I would think that you are *supposed* to hunt at night. Like an owl."

"Yeah, in hindsight, it feels kind of obvious." I'd been thinking the same thing but without the animal comparison. "An owl, huh? I'll take it. I like owls."

She was less enthusiastic about my experiments with storing my kills for a few days. I was getting used to it. Sometimes my stomach lurched before I dug in, but I must have learned to suppress it. Besides, it hadn't made me sick so far.

"So, anyway, here's the exciting part," I continued. She was looking a little green after I told her about eating three-day-old goat, and I needed to change the topic before she lost her breakfast. "I told you how I was here and found the note about a week ago, right? Well, I was planning to try to meet you as soon as you got here, but I went to check on the scholars and got kind of trapped. Or maybe 'lost' is a better word for it."

Her eyebrows shot up. "Trapped?"

"Yeah. Not by anyone trying to catch me or anything like that. Those scholars I told you about, the night after I got the note, they finished digging out the gate they'd found. They must have figured out that the sides weren't interesting, because they'd focused on the important part. Anyway, I was bored and really curious. And the gate was right there! So when they were asleep, I, you know. Opened it."

"Did they not have a guard?"

"Yeah, but the camp wasn't that close. And I hope that at least some of them were better at fighting than keeping guard, because they were *not* good at that. I don't think they even heard the gate opening. Or closing. I closed it after I went inside."

"You shut yourself in." Herald was unimpressed.

"I mean, yeah? I didn't want someone to come down and find the gate open."

"Did the doors not leave marks in the dirt? They could see those and know that the gate had been opened."

I . . . had not considered that. "Um . . . well. I hope not. Anyway, there was the same kind of tunnel inside, like where we found the villagers. Long, square, turning. Weirdly dry. This one went up, though. Ended in a big, open chamber, kind of like where we were, but it was a lot more even. It looked almost perfectly round. And there were so many tunnels leading out from it! Every couple yards, there was another tunnel! There was a lower level too, and it was the same thing there. Lots of stairs leading down and a tunnel between every two stairs. Dozens of them!"

"I am guessing that you did not return the way you came?" We had gone back inside the tent by then, and she had settled comfortably on her bedroll, her head propped on a makeshift pillow made of rolled-up clothes.

"Yeah, that wasn't going to happen. I figured I'd be smart, so I went straight across the chamber to the tunnel opposite the one I'd come in through. The opening was bigger than the others, so I figured it would be more important. More interesting, you know? Except that didn't work out so well."

The tunnel had continued upward, just like the one I'd come from, but it wasn't long until it, too, exited into a chamber. This chamber had been very different, though. It was long and wide instead of round, the ceiling far above me. Kind of like a school gym, really, but with a vaulted ceiling. There had been a faint smell in the air, besides the dust, like the ghosts of silver and gold and other lovely things. I'd been understandably intrigued, so I went in and started looking around.

"There were these weird holes in the ceiling. Not a lot of them, and not regularly, just kind of spread out here and there, except for one big square one in the middle. No doors or tunnels on the floor level, just those holes. So I was poking around, and I swear that there must have been silver or gold dust on the floor or something, because it smelled wonderful. But at the same time, I felt a little weird. I was getting anxious, and I couldn't tell why. Still don't know why, but then it hit me all at once, and I had to get out. Like . . . I panicked, and I got the hell out of there!"

"I would love to see it, if you think that you can go back. Now that you know what to expect, it might be easier."

I doubted that. "We'd have to sneak past the scholars, but we could try, I guess. I'd want to try on my own first, though, so I don't run out on you."

What I didn't tell her, of course, was that it was the dragon who had freaked the hell out. She'd been anxious from the moment we entered the second chamber, which had steadily built into a full-blown panic attack. Only, instead of becoming paralyzed, I ran as fast as I could, the dragon screaming *"Out! We must get out!"* and stuff like that over and over and over in my ears until I couldn't think straight.

I could only assume that it was in some way related to the staff of dragon bone that the valkin leader had, though how, I couldn't tell. There was certainly no sign of anything living there or whatever had been there once it was meticulously cleaned out. But seeing that staff was the only other time that the dragon had expressed this kind of fear. Sure, there was the pit in my treasure room, but that was more like a very, very strong aversion.

"When I got back to that first big chamber, I wasn't thinking straight." That wasn't a lie. A massive understatement, perhaps, but not a lie. "I must have taken the wrong door. And then that tunnel branched and merged, and I must have taken a wrong turn somewhere, and I got totally turned around. I must have wandered around in there for . . . how long have you been here? Six days, right? So three days, I think. The bad feeling wore off pretty quickly, but by then, I was hopelessly lost. So I tried to keep going up, and it worked out for me. I finally ended up in a big natural cavern with water and that glowing stuff on the walls and all."

"Glow slime," Herald supplied. She'd been listening to my story with rapt attention, and it was the first thing she'd said for ages.

"Yeah, thanks. Glow slime. Hope it's not toxic, because I drank some of the water. Probably a bad idea. It was salty and tasted real foul." I grimaced at the memory. "I found some gremlins there too, which had me worried for a while. Then I thought maybe I could eat one."

Herald made a disgusted face.

"Hey, I was pretty hungry! Three days, remember? But the gremlins stayed far away from me, and I didn't particularly feel like chasing after them in case they ambushed me or something. Anyway, I was worried because I didn't know how close I was to my hoard, and I don't want those little shits stealing my stuff. But once I was in that cavern, getting out was pretty straightforward. I came out way north of my mountain, but once I was in the air, getting back was easy."

"And the remaining three days?"

"Well, I was in there for three days, remember? And I hadn't exactly had a big meal before I went in. So I hunted down a goat and couldn't really control myself, and then I kinda . . . slept a couple days away. Sorry."

I hadn't heard from the dragon since she calmed down after that terrified scramble through the tunnels, and it had been a silent, lonely search for an exit. I couldn't tell if she was embarrassed or in shock or what, and that had been getting me more than a little worried. She didn't usually stay silent for so long. The first thing I had felt from her was the hunger when I ate that goat, and it had been overwhelming. I'd tried to resist like I'd done before, but this time I didn't stand a chance. Thus my delayed arrival here. It had been a shock when the dragon spoke to me after Herald handed over the silver, especially with what she said, but also a relief. As unhealthy as it might be, I was used to my constant companion, and I didn't want to see her gone.

Herald reached out with one of those long arms of hers and patted me fondly on the side. "You really are just a big lizard, are you not?" she said with a grin.

"You have no idea."

CHAPTER THIRTY-NINE

The Joy of Giving

"I got you some books," Herald told me out of nowhere.

It was a hot day, and we'd been dozing off, me up a dense, leafy tree where I could hide in case someone came, her sitting against its trunk.

"Hmm, what?" I said, not wholly with her and not sure that I'd heard her correctly.

"I got you some books."

I'd heard her right the first time. I snaked my head down to look at her. "That's lovely, but . . . I can't read."

"That is why I got them! I thought I could maybe . . . teach you?"

I grinned. Both because of how thoughtful that was and because she was adorable when she was all shy and uncertain. It was one of my all-teeth grins, and she didn't even flinch.

"I'd love that," I told her.

She sat up excitedly. "Do you want to see them?"

"Yeah, sure!"

I jumped down as she crawled into the tent, coming out with two books bound in leather. I hadn't seen any books here, and it was strange, seeing something so familiar.

She held up the larger of the two. "This one is about, well . . . monsters."

"Like dragons?" I asked, lifting an eyebrow at her.

"Like dragons," she confirmed with a slight blush. "And also wyverns, hydras, advanced animals, and gremlins and goblins and many other creatures. It has a lot of pictures, see?"

She opened the book and flipped the pages slowly. It looked like paper rather than the coarser papyrus-like material she had used for her notes, and there were indeed a lot of pictures. Nicely drawn too, if not exactly realistic. More Roman mosaic than Da Vinci, so to speak, but detailed and nicely colored.

"See, it has a whole section on dragons, different types and what is known about them. But," she said, putting the bestiary away, "we should start with this."

The second book was smaller, but when she opened it, the text was far larger, the pictures simpler and more colorful and, well . . . cute. It was clearly a book for children, the first pages divided into sections with one or two letters and one picture. *A* is for *apple*, *B* is for *banana*, et cetera.

I was not above using a book for preschoolers if it helped me learn the local system of writing.

"All the languages spoken in the Sareyan League . . . That's the league of cities Karakan belongs to. All the languages here use the same system of writing, so if you learn any other languages, you should be able to read those too."

"Oh, I know all human languages, I think," I told her offhandedly while looking at the pictures. "At least the living ones." Herald stopped turning the pages, and when she hadn't spoken for a while, I looked at her. "What?"

She was looking at me flatly, her mouth slightly open. *"I do not believe you sometimes."*

"I mean, I am not sure. But I think that I do."

Her eyes widened a fraction. It took me a second to realize that she'd spoken, and I'd answered, in a completely different language, one full of hard consonants and short, clipped syllables.

Herald shook her head slowly. "And yet you cannot read," she said, reverting to the local language that I was used to.

I wish I could say that I picked it up easily, but no. It was quite different from the good old Latin alphabet. Every "letter" was a syllable, and you tied them together, which changed how they looked, and the pronunciation changed with what came next and whether or not you put little dots next to it and if the dots were above or below or right or left and . . . it was complicated. By the time we decided that we'd had enough for one day, I was proud to have gotten the general idea, and that was plenty. Then we flipped through the bestiary for a while, and I finally truly learned the difference between a wyvern and a dragon.

I understood what Herald meant about them being hard to mistake for each other. Where a dragon was proud, majestic, and had four limbs besides its wings, a wyvern was basically a glorified, long-necked iguana with batlike wings where its forelegs should be. I was almost insulted that someone might think I was one of them, but Herald pointed out that if someone saw me high in the air, all they saw was a flying lizard. Wyverns weren't native to Mallin, but with them being orders of magnitude less rare than dragons . . . well, Occam's razor was a thing anywhere you went.

"So . . ." I dragged the word out as Herald put the books away. "I'm guessing that since you've got all this money now, maybe you want to take it easy for a while?"

"Oh gods, no! Now that you are back, I cannot wait to go and actually do something worthwhile again!"

"Well, in that case, any idea when you guys will be able to go out again? I was hoping you'd come check out the first gate that I found. It's probably too late for the miners, but—"

"If there are valkin there, we should bring the Wolves," Herald said, interrupting me. "Garal has been asking a lot about you. Their commander still wants to see you, so we could probably arrange something. I am sure that they would love to show up the Cranes."

That was good to hear. I'd wondered if they'd written me off when I disappeared on them. "Oh, great!" I said. "That's much better than my idea. Though I figured the payout would be better with just the five of us."

"We will not get paid if we cannot do the job," Herald stated with a small shrug. "Or if we die."

"Yeah, fair enough. So I should talk to the commander, right?"

"I think that you should. But they would not go out completely uninformed. Rallon likes to prepare if possible, and he does not risk his people needlessly. If I let the Wolves know that you would like to meet with Rallon, do you think that you could find something to show them? Some information about what is up there? That would go a long way in convincing him and showing how valuable you could be."

"Probably. I could check the place out on my own, I suppose. But I'd rather have you along."

Herald smiled just the tiniest bit. "I appreciate that. But I would hold you back. You can get there faster on your own, and I doubt that anyone can match you for stealth in those tunnels. I would not be surprised if you could get there, do some basic scouting, and return in the time that it would take me to get back to the mine."

I wanted to argue, but I wasn't going to insult her by pretending that she wasn't right. For all her good qualities, she wouldn't be able to keep up with me, and we would save days if I went on my own while she approached the mercenaries.

I looked up at the sky. The sun wasn't all that close to the mountains yet, but if Herald wanted to get back to the city by nightfall . . .

"Does that mean we should get you packed?" I asked, a little ball of disappointment settling in my gut.

"I suppose it does." She didn't look any happier about it. "Will you walk me to the fields?"

"Of course."

I couldn't help her much other than scattering the camouflage, but Herald's little camp away from camp was orderly, and packing didn't take her long. When she had everything put together, the tent and bedroll strapped under her pack, she turned to me with a leather contraption in her hands.

"Before we go, this is a gift." She turned the thing so I could see it better. It was clearly a bag, with several long straps on it. "The books are inside, and the firesteel. I think your money bag would fit as well, if you want." She looked at me, adorably nervous. "What do you think?"

"What do I think?" I answered, all my delighted surprise on full display. "What do *you* think? I love it! How do I put it on?"

Herald burst into action, my acceptance of the gift triggering some pent-up excitement. "It's made so you should be able to put it on and take it off yourself. You put this over your head, see, and then your arms go through here and here so the bag goes on your chest. Then you tighten this"—she pulled on a strap—"and to take it off, you release it like this, see? No fiddling required. And the bag closes with these and locks with this, so it should be safe for flying. I . . . tested it rigorously. It never opened once."

I wasn't sure what Herald meant by testing the secureness of the bag, so I imagined her flinging it around, spinning in circles and playing airplane with it. A small giggle escaped from me.

"It's great!" I said to cover the very undragonlike sounds. "So I open like this . . ." I fumbled a bit but got it open. I took the money bag off my neck to put it in and paused.

"How much did this all cost?" I was suddenly a little worried. Those books had been full of pictures, and it wasn't like they had printing presses here. At least, I didn't think so. Even with advancements that let someone draw quickly and accurately, either one of these books must be the culmination of several days of work at minimum.

"Do not worry about it," she said, waving it off with the eternal answer of anyone who has spent too much money on a present. "It is all a gift, the bag and the books. From all of us, as thanks for helping us."

"But you gave me a cut of the reward!"

"Yes. But without you, I would not have gotten the others out. Even if I had found the gate, which I would not have known was there, I had no way to get it open. I told the others that I had some things I wanted to get you, and they all insisted on pitching in. Even Mak," she added pointedly.

"But—" I started, then stopped myself. "You know what? Thank you. Really. And tell the others I said thanks too."

Walking back was nice. The bag took a little getting used to, and Herald helped me adjust the straps so that it would sit a little better while walking.

"So what did the bag maker say?" I asked. We were walking the way we usually did, Herald on the side of the road and me among the trees, hiding whenever we encountered anyone.

Herald grinned. "I told her that it was for a large dog. She suggested it should hang on the sides instead, so I had to make something up about the poor thing having sensitive skin. I do not think that she believed me, but she was happy enough to take my money when I insisted."

"If she does custom leather work, she probably gets strange requests all the time," I said with a laugh. "If people here are anything like back home."

Herald's face silently scrunched up in thought for a while before she spoke. "I'm not sure what you mean by that."

"I'll tell you sometime. Just, maybe don't ask Makanna about it."

"Why not?"

"Trust me on this. If she knows what I'm talking about, she won't be happy. She probably thinks that I'm corrupting you as it is."

"Well, that is . . . Now I am not sure that I want to know."

I just laughed.

For the rest of the long walk, we just talked. There had been no news of fighting in the south, which was a big relief to Herald. No new letters, though. She spent a lot of time telling me more about her and her family's friends in the city, and about how Tamor seemed determined to make up for his weeks away by spending every moment he could enjoying their company. He'd been in a constant flurry of outings, dinners, friendly meetings, and parties ever since they got back to the city, and eventually even Valmik had had enough of him, accompanying Herald into the forest for a few days of peace and quiet.

After about an hour in, I realized that Herald had switched to that other, new language, and she gave me a bright smile when I asked her about it.

"It is the language of my mother and father. I rarely get to speak it. Mak and Tam do not like to use it and remember little. And traders from those parts are few and far between. It is just nice to hold a normal, friendly conversation. And it sounds good coming from you."

"Thank you! What parts are those?"

Herald hesitated before answering. *"Tekeretek. An unpleasant place, from all I have heard, and a rival of the League. We do not speak of our origin openly."*

Tekeretek. It meant the City of Rains in their own language. I was curious, but there was an edge of sadness to Herald's voice that stopped me from pushing. She'd tell me more if she wanted to.

The dark moment passed quickly as we moved on to happier topics, which drifted into her beginning to help me think in feet and yards and miles. It came pretty naturally out of us talking about how far ahead things were and her, again, having no idea what a meter or kilometer was. By the time we separated at the edge of the forest I was starting to get a decent hang of it!

Ready to go, Herald gave me a quick hug, then stepped back and looked at me seriously. *"Draka,"* she said. *"Please be careful. This bounty is going to draw out a lot of people who want to try their luck, and I have heard people talking about it. They will be watching the sky."*

"I will. I promise."

And with that, she was gone. We had a plan to meet again at the lake two nights later, with or without the mercenaries.

I watched her go, equal parts happy and concerned. She had waited for six days to meet me. Two of those days, she had been alone in the forest. I would never have asked for that kind of patience from anyone, but she'd simply done it.

I hoped she knew what she was talking about, regarding our friendship. She sure seemed to have given it real thought. I just couldn't shake the feeling that the dragon knew more than me.

Maybe it was time for a long-overdue talk with myself, but it could wait a bit. I mean, I tried but not very hard. I had other things to focus on. It was time to return to the hoard, and while I knew that I couldn't carry my money in there through the crevice, I had a cunning plan.

I had acquired a stick.

When I got back to the cave, I took off my bag and carefully placed it on a high, flat rock near the back of the entrance. I fumbled a little with the straps that held it closed, but I could do it, which felt awesome. Once I had my pouch full of coins out, I closed the bag again, took the pouch and my stick, and headed down.

The crevice was too narrow. Or rather, I had grown too wide to fit through. But dragon or no, I was still mentally human, at least partially, and humans used tools. So I took my stick—from a nicely straight young tree that I'd had Herald chop and strip for me—and carefully threw it into the crevice.

The first attempt didn't go well. I cursed myself as it hit something and clattered to the ground almost out of reach, then got down, reached in with one arm, and stretched as far as I could. I could barely get one fingertip on it and was about to give up and go get another stick to retrieve my first stick when I remembered that I had claws. Once I hooked a claw into the stick, getting it back was easy. The next throw went better, getting it almost all the way to the other side.

The next step was a little trickier and caused me a lot more anxiety, but I had to get my silver to the hoard somehow. So, with a knot in my stomach and my heart in my throat, I gave the money pouch a few practice swings and then tossed it.

It landed on the back half of the stick. *Success!*

After that, it was a simple matter of shadowing in, carefully pulling the stick to myself, with the pouch coming along, and that was it. It worked!

My triumph didn't last long, though. I looked at the bag in my hands. It wasn't big, and it had been a hassle getting it in. Anything bigger may well be impossible. And the ledge was narrow; if my pile of treasures got much bigger, it would start spilling over the edge into that damn pit. Hiding my hoard here had made perfect sense when I understood less of what was going on, but now . . . I was going to have to move it. I wasn't sure where to or how, but I was.

I didn't want to leave my cave. It was home, and it was nearly impossible to get to if you couldn't fly. But with some luck, I wouldn't have to. After all, this was not the end of the cave system. It went deeper. Much deeper. The only reason I'd even had my climbing gear when I came in here was that not much farther in than where I'd found the crevice, there was a sharp drop before the system continued. I hadn't bothered with it since waking up, since it was too steep for me to climb reliably and too narrow to fly along, but with my shadow form, it should be doable.

I didn't even have a day job, and I still somehow kept filling my days with things that needed doing. But this was a little fun, a little exciting. I'd come here *on that fateful night*, as a dramatic person might say, because it had been months since I'd been down there. Now, with my shadow form and my shadowsight, I'd be able to really get around down there, really see the whole place in all its glory!

Yeah, this was going to be fun. When I got around to it.

I happily tossed the pouch on top of my pile and prepared to leave.

"*A fourth minor threshold has been reached,*" came the dragon's voice in my ear. I jumped! There was a decent amount of silver in that pouch, but I hadn't expected anything again so soon, especially on top of her silence lately. It was kind of nice to hear her little mantra again, even if she did sound a little bitter and sulky.

"*How will you increase your power? Strength, to overwhelm your enemies? Greater fortitude, to weather all but the mightiest blows? Physical greatness, to increase the power of your body in all ways at a cost? Charisma, to beguile the weak-minded with your words and presence? Cunning, to plot and see through the schemes of others? Choose!*"

I'd actually been giving some thought to what I'd like to improve, though I never expected to get the chance so soon. I went with strength. Charisma was a new, tempting option, but for now, I needed to be able to fight better. Greater fortitude sounded like it might make me basically invulnerable, but I figured that was no use if someone tried to take me alive, and I did not want that to happen. Besides, dragging around goats had been annoying, and I wanted to be able to carry stuff.

The dragon didn't acknowledge my choice beyond a general feeling of satisfaction. She approved, like I'd thought she would, even if she didn't say so.

I felt the changes wash over me, and my body was left feeling lighter. I took a few steps along the narrow ledge, and my walk felt steadier. I couldn't really try anything else yet, but that didn't matter. It was time to head to the gate.

CHAPTER FORTY

Infiltrator

Sometime after midnight, I was in a valley in the mountains, standing in front of that first gate I had found near the mines. The flight had been faster than I was used to; my new strength advancement clearly affected my whole body, including my wings.

The tracks and marks on the ground that showed the gate had swung open at some point were long gone, of course, and the flat, vertical stone surface sunken into the mountainside showed no sign of what it hid. But I could see the lines, the magical glow that didn't cast any light around them and that, according to Herald, only I could see.

Well, I told myself, *no time like the present!* I had been fighting myself for a long minute by then. Or perhaps it was more accurate to say that I'd been fighting the dragon. She had put two and two together, and she was not happy about going into another of these tunnels when the last two times had resulted in her forcing us to flee in terror. I was pretty sure that she was embarrassed about the whole thing, but there was definitely anxiety as well. But it didn't matter. She wasn't talking, and I had a job to do.

Going in there alone was probably a bad idea, but that was part of the fun. I put one hand on the gate and focused. When I'd done this with an audience, I'd been self-conscious and trying to rush things, but with no one around, I took my time. It came as no surprise that it was easier to focus my will and intent when I didn't worry about anyone judging me, and soon enough I felt a pulse of *something* leave me and enter the gate. The doors slowly swung open, and a soft gust of dry air blew against me as I entered a familiar curving tunnel sloping downward into the darkness.

I considered leaving the doors open in case I needed to make a hasty exit but decided against it. It would be worse if anyone knew that the gate had opened than if I needed to take a few seconds to open it before escaping. I repeated the process, willing the gate shut this time, and the doors sealed perfectly, leaving only a nearly smooth wall where the opening had been and plunging the tunnel into absolute darkness.

Of course, I could see perfectly. Not that there was anything to look at. As I wandered down the featureless tunnel, I wondered how they'd dug the damn thing. I could only assume some kind of magic, because who would bother to cut such nicely square corners by hand? But that only raised questions of what kind of magic could do that and why you'd waste it on a tunnel if magic was as rare as I'd been led to believe. Were all these tunnels the work of one person with one talent they were determined to put to use?

The gates I understood, at least. Secret doors that could only be opened by magic were pretty cool.

I could feel the dragon getting more and more unhappy as I got deeper, but it felt more like anticipation than actual fear. She still wasn't saying anything, though.

When I was returning to the cave after leaving Herald, I had tried talking to the dragon, but despite all her smugness when Herald gave me my money, she wouldn't answer. Not that she often did, but ever since our scare in the heart of my mountain, she had been even less talkative than normal. The only sound I'd had out of her was when she told me the options for my advancement, and after that, nothing. I didn't like it, and I needed to find some way to bring her out.

In the tunnel, all I had was time.

Hey, I thought, *are you listening?*

The few times I had communicated directly with the dragon, I'd usually spoken out loud, but I knew that she could also react to my thoughts.

I know that you're in here somewhere. Or everywhere. However that works.

I waited. Silence.

Come on. We both know that there are things you know that I don't. You keep dropping hints, and it's been invaluable, but it's not enough, yeah? You've been freaking out, and I need to know why.

I kept walking, waiting for any kind of reply. But none came. Well, I had a plan for that. Putting the right tone into your voice to convey a certain feeling could be tricky. But in my head, it was easy. I could put any feeling behind my words in my head, however nuanced I wanted it.

It was time to get petty.

What are you so scared of? I asked, channeling my inner mean girl.

There it was. Still no words, but a feeling, clear as anything. Indignation.

It's okay, I teased, *we all get a little scared sometimes. It's nothing to be ashamed of!*

I had found a button, and it was a big red one. The feeling of indignation flared. The dragon must have known what I was doing. We shared a brain, after all. But she couldn't help herself.

Why don't you just tell me why you're so afraid? I focused my intent to make the thought as condescending as I possibly could.

"*I am not afraid!*" the dragon roared in my ears. "*Dragons know no fear! We cause fear! We are fear!*"

Then why did you make us run and hide like a frightened rabbit? Twice! I asked. That should get her going.

"*We did not flee! Prey flees! We do not! That was . . .*" She actually hesitated. This was a first. "*Those were cunning retreats!*"

Then tell me why! What could be so dangerous, so threatening to a creature like us, that you would force us to retreat from an empty room?

She fell silent again. I hesitated to push; this was the longest exchange we had ever had, and I didn't want to poison it. But I had thrown her off-balance, and I couldn't resist the opportunity to actually get something out of her.

And now you're afraid to even speak to me.

Her reaction was immediate. "*I do not fear a voice in my head! You know that chamber as well as I do! I had to catch the scent to remember, but it is a place we know well. A place of pain and death. We must avoid it!*"

That was more than I had expected, so much more! The dragon knew that place. She had been there long enough to recognize something in the air that triggered her fear.

Something bad must have happened to her there.

And she thought that *I* was a voice in *her* head. That was interesting. I wondered how she rationalized that, considering I called all the shots.

Well, most of them.

What about before? I asked, more gently this time. I could already feel resentment bleeding over into myself and didn't want to push the proud creature too far. *What about the valkin with the staff?*

"*Dragon bone. The bone and tooth of the big one. Old, but I could smell him. If they slew him and took his bones, they can slay us. We must avoid them until we are stronger. And we should not be in these tunnels!*"

The big one? I asked, but there was no reply. *What about the pit in our treasure chamber?* I tried, but again, nothing.

The resentment still burned, and I left her to her sullen silence. I'd learned more than I'd hoped for, really. The dragon had memories of a time before I'd come here. She must have had a whole life, though it sounded like she had some trouble remembering it. The question of whether that was a result of having me suddenly crammed into her skull or something else would have to wait. I'd either need to wait her out or find some better leverage.

There was, of course, a large circular chamber. Like the first of these places I had gone into, this one looked like it had once been a natural hollow in the stone, which had been expanded and smoothed out in places. The tunnel I had come from exited onto a wide floor, with a few other openings, irregularly spaced, leading away in different directions. There was no lower level here, no big wheel, and there were no lights, though there were depressions in the walls where one of those valkin light-balls would have been able to sit comfortably. Instead, the ceiling vaulted high above me, spiky with stalactites, and it made me wonder how the air could be so dry if there had been enough water to create the things at one point.

There was also a wide, staired tunnel that led down from the chamber into depths unknown. Following my instincts, I descended.

There was a whole little complex of rooms down there. Rooms of different sizes, with or without furniture, everything you'd need to house up to a dozen people, if I'd guessed right and the wide, low slabs I found in two of the rooms were beds. Possibly more, if they slept in shifts. The rooms were all empty now, but there were signs of them having been lived in recently, in the form of dried but recognizable vegetable scraps and animal bones on the floors.

The complex had one entrance and one exit. I'd come from the entrance; I left through the exit. It carried me deeper into the mountain, down, always down. It was nowhere near as long as the tunnel from the surface, though it was steeper, and my legs were soon burning from the effort of walking downhill for so long.

This time there was a light at the end of the tunnel. Ahead of me, I saw the tunnel level out and disappear, and as I got farther down and I could see more and more of it, my sight grew slightly dimmer. Blinking my vision back to normal, I was plunged into darkness, except for the faint, pale blue light ahead of me that I knew must be coming from one of those light-balls. Those things needed to be recharged every so often. That meant that where there was light, there were valkin.

I felt my excitement rising, that feeling of doing something I was absolutely not supposed to and being determined to get away with it. I held myself absolutely still. I listened and sniffed the air slowly, trying to catch any sign of the creatures. I thought I caught the faintest whiff, a dry, vaguely metallic scent, but it was hard to be sure. So I did the next most logical thing. I shifted into shadow and moved forward.

I would have been invisible against the blackness of the tunnel, but I needn't have worried. There was a valkin ahead of me, hard to see because of the light-ball next to it. It was probably supposed to be guarding this tunnel, but instead it was sitting with its back to the wall, fast asleep. When I got closer, I heard that it was even snoring gently.

I considered killing it. That would make it much easier to get past, and I was sure that I could do it quietly. I'd simply sit on its legs, hold down its wrists, clamp my jaws around its throat, and wait. Easy. But then, whoever came to relieve it would know that something came this way, and I didn't want that.

The light was too bright to pass through as a shadow. I could have probably snuck by carefully without waking it, but I didn't do that either. Instead, I decided to experiment.

The valkin was fast asleep. For how long, I didn't know, but the light-ball wasn't *that* bright. Bright enough to make it hard to see, sure. Bright enough to prevent me from passing, certainly. But maybe I could do something about that.

With all the shadow of the mountain behind me, I focused. I gathered my will, and I defined and refined my intent until I could see clearly in my mind's eye exactly what I wanted. As I reached the peak of my concentration, a dark light edged with gold left me, and the shadows around and ahead of me pushed. I strained, and they strained with me, stretching forward toward the light. I moved with them, closer and closer to the border, and the pale light retreated from me until the shadow was climbing the walls, long, dark streamers reaching for the ball itself.

My head felt like someone had stuck the nozzle of a compressor through my skull and pushed the switch. I rushed by the sleeping valkin, releasing my focus once I was past the light-ball. I felt the light reclaim the small part of the tunnel and push me forward, but that was fine. I was tired, and I had a headache from straining so hard, but I'd done what I'd wanted to. I continued forward several meters—no, yards, I corrected myself. I had to get used to thinking in local measurements—before I shifted back, then relaxed. I was past it. A thrill went down my spine, and I grinned to myself.

"I'm in," I whispered to no one, pinching an imaginary collar up to my mouth to speak into an invisible mic.

The question I had to ask myself then was: *Now what?*

In the very short term, it was easy. There was only one way to go, and I continued down the tunnel. Not far from the guard, the tunnel was closed off by a wall of stone brick with a wooden gate. I couldn't smell any valkin. I did hear what sounded like distant voices, but nothing that sounded like it was right on the other side.

Holding my breath, I slowly turned the simple wooden latch. It turned smoothly, and there was the barest scraping sound as I pushed the gate open far enough to stick my head in. Light spilled in from a ball set on the other side, but I had stuck to normal sight, and it wasn't a problem. On the other side, only a few *yards* from the door, the tunnel opened into a small, empty room, with open doors set in each sidewall toward the back.

I picked the left side simply because it felt more natural to lean right to peek around the corner, but that way led around a right turn to something like a dormitory where several valkin were lounging. I quickly counted five of the creatures, then pulled my head back before anyone spotted me. Right side it was.

I had more luck to the right. That way turned left, then led to a larger open hall, like the one where the valkin had met with the humans. I entered from one of the short sides, with doors in each of the walls. On a hunch, I took the door to the right and found a long, wide tunnel leading into the darkness. The dust on the ground was disturbed, and I noted it as a possible escape route, then kept exploring.

I spent the rest of my time there moving from shadow to shadow, peeking through doors and sneaking through rooms, in one case using my ability to extend shadows to swiftly move through a room with two valkin having an animated conversation. Or possibly an argument. It was hard to tell.

As a side note, I figured out how they'd solved the problem of getting air down there. Many of the rooms had football-size holes in one or more of their walls, which I had thought were unused places for light-balls. But when I shifted into the shadows and squeezed into one of them while needing to hide from a passing valkin, I realized that it was open at the back, connecting to a vertical shaft. When the valkin had left, I shifted back, and sure enough, there was a weak breeze there if you looked for it.

I didn't know if I could climb to the top, but hey! It was a good place to hide, if nothing else.

My original goal was to figure out how many valkin there were, but that changed when I smelled people.

I found them in a storage room, sitting packed along the walls. I didn't have time to count them, but there were at least twenty people, men and women, young and old, and even a baby held by a glassy-eyed young woman. A small village, in short. Another community sleepwalking into slavery, no doubt waiting to be picked up by the same bastards, or at least someone from the same group, as before. And again there was nothing I could do. There were two regular guards, and I could have probably taken them, but there was also a small, thin valkin with another one of those damn staves.

I managed to suppress the panic this time. Even though I felt the dragon's terror, this time I focused all my will on resisting the moment I saw that staff, and I only felt a wave of fear and nausea instead of the absolute terror of last time. But while I didn't flee, there was also no way I could go any closer. Remaining in place was hard enough, and I was fighting a losing battle. I would have to leave, but on my own terms.

I carefully but quickly made my way back to the empty hall near the entrance. I had good reason to think that the long, wide tunnel would lead me out of the mountain, and the reason was simple: The dust in the tunnel was disturbed by a large number of footprints, many of which looked like they had been made by boots. Valkin didn't wear anything on their feet, but humans did, and all the bootprints pointed toward me.

If the humans hadn't come in this way, I would eat the firesteel that Herald had given me.

I started walking.

Of course it couldn't be as easy as simply walking out. This tunnel was sealed off the same way as the one I'd entered through, only, once I got through the door, the guard was awake and alert. Unfortunately for it, it didn't hear the door open and close behind it.

I couldn't go past it. It would have noticed the light-ball dimming if I tried any shadow tricks, and there was literally no space in the tunnel to hide and try to lure it past me. I had to make it disappear.

There was a short distance between the door and the guard. I prowled forward silently, claws in and tail high, and the guard didn't even realize that anything was wrong until I reached out and grabbed the butt of its spear, easily jerking it off-balance. The moment it turned my way, I let loose with a full, concentrated spray of venom, then wrapped my free hand over its mouth and bore it down, pinning it with my weight. With my new strength, it was easy to hold it down while clamping its mouth shut, preventing it from screaming or even coughing. *No blood*, I told myself. That was important. No blood.

The valkin struggled, of course, but it was mostly blind, unable to breathe, and pinned down. All I had to do was to be patient.

A few days before, dragging a goat a few hundred *yards*—I was getting better already!—had been a struggle. Now I was strong, and dragging a body down the tunnel was easy.

CHAPTER FORTY-ONE

Plan of Attack

The tunnel from the valkins' little complex of rooms was long and, for once, straight. It gently sloped downward, exiting into the morning light in a wooded area of the lower foothills, with only about fifteen yards in front of the gate free of trees. I dumped the body of the guard I'd killed next to a bush and savaged it a little, hoping that it would look like it had just stepped outside if anyone came looking. That should be better than having a guard simply disappear.

The gate wasn't hidden, but no one would have suspected that it was there. If someone who happened to pass by even looked in its direction, all they'd see would be a section of rock that had cracked unusually straight.

There were prisoners in there, and this would probably be the most direct route for anyone coming to collect them. There was no way that I was letting this gate out of my sight for more than ten minutes until it was time to meet Rallon.

I took to the air to figure out exactly where I was, noting which regional and local landmarks I was close to. I'd gotten pretty good at that, and I was confident that I could get close enough to the place to find the gate by simply looking for the glow on the wall.

In my, by then, normal state of hunger and fatigue, I settled into a tall, dense tree with a good view of the gate. I was angry, but it was a cold, satisfying anger. This time they were not getting away.

What followed was almost two full days of mostly sitting still. My activities were limited to sitting in the tree, eating the occasional careless squirrel or rabbit, and dozing with an eye on the gate. I hoped that the dragon was still paying attention, but I didn't bet on it since she seemed to be hiding, or sulking, or whatever she was doing. Instead I had to stay mostly alert when I could, relying on the noise of the gate opening or people moving beneath me to wake me if anything happened while I napped.

Scavengers got to the guard's body pretty quickly, aiding in my cover-up. Toward evening of the first day the gate opened, and two valkin came out, looking around carefully. When they found the guard's body, they seemed annoyed more than anything else, one of them going so far as to kick it a few times before they dragged it back inside. After that, I just had to hope that they'd blame its death on its own carelessness rather than on foul play.

Nothing happened all of the following day, and even with the incredible patience I'd developed, it was boring as all hell. As the sun dipped behind the mountains at the end of the second day, I was reluctant to leave, in case anything actually did happen while I was away, but also very relieved to finally be doing something different.

As I headed for the lake, I took note of where one could exit the road, trying to map as direct a route as I could to the gate. I hadn't been able to find a trail on the ground, but I'd do my best to be able to lead the mercs there by as short a route as possible.

I didn't land directly at the lake, of course. I did my usual thing, settling a decent distance away and then sneaking up on the campsite, staying low and in the shadows the whole time. There was no one there when I arrived, but I didn't have time to get bored.

The group that arrived was larger than I was used to, but I'd expected that. They all came on horseback but dismounted at the campsite and approached the tree on foot. What I hadn't expected was for half of them to be Herald and her family, but considering how close they were to some of the Wolves, it made sense. My guess was that they were there as a neutral party of sorts, not part of the Wolves but friendly with both them and myself and showing that this was intended as a friendly meeting.

Of the other four, I recognized Lalia, of course. Garal wasn't with her, which was a little disappointing, but you can't have everything. There was the older, bearded man, who must be Commander Rallon, and then there were two more, a man and a woman, both around Tamor's age, who I recognized as two of the mercenaries' . . . what? Scouts? Assassins? I was pretty sure these two were among the five who had gone before the other mercenaries at the bandit camp to quietly take care of the sentries. That meant that everyone here was someone who knew about me already, which I appreciated.

Still, those five killers had actually scared me, which was a rare occurrence. I was going to want to keep an eye on the two who were here.

The two I could see, at least.

When I approached the campsite this time, I didn't make a flashy entrance. I wasn't here to impress anyone, and I wasn't feeling petty enough to try to scare Lalia again. Instead I stepped through the shadows into the crown of the lone tree. I climbed out like I'd been waiting there all along. I was feeling antsy about being away from the gate, but I took my time and tried to come across as friendly and relaxed. Looking friendly was hard to do with people who didn't know me, but I made an effort.

Everyone was staring at me, of course, and with a mix of expressions. There was happy familiarity from Herald, there were carefully blank faces from Lalia and Makanna, and there were relaxed smiles from Tamor and Valmik. The two Gray Wolves killers both looked excited, which I hoped was a good sign, and Rallon was the picture of schooled, neutral politeness. He reminded me of many politicians, but I couldn't blame him for it. Even if this meeting was supposed to be friendly, it was still a first meeting, and a negotiation of sorts, so courtesy was in order.

I sat down about ten paces from Rallon, wings folded and tail curled around me. He looked to be in his fifties and was fairly tall, near Herald's height, with a wide face that made his beard a very flattering style choice on him. He looked like he was waiting for me to say something, and I was not sure what to do. Formal introductions had never really been my thing beyond a hi and a handshake. Once again, I had to rely on my entertainment knowledge to help me. I'd seen plenty of first meetings between powerful people, after all. Just because they were on a screen didn't mean they didn't count, right?

"Commander Rallon, I presume." I tried to sound confident. "I am Draka. Thank you for coming."

That seemed to do it. When he replied, his voice was strong and rich. "Lady Draka. Thank you for agreeing to meet with me. I understand that you are interested in cooperating with the Gray Wolves." He paused. "But where are my manners? I am Terriallon Mordo, Commander of the Gray Wolves Free Company and a minor city lord of Tavvanar, though that is of little importance here. Please, call me Rallon, or Commander, if we're to insist on titles. These two are my cousins, her young ladyship Terriallon Rebatia and his young lordship Terriallon Poterio."

His cousins waved enthusiastically.

"You are of course already familiar with Lalia of Karakan, one of my squad leaders—"

Lalia gave me a curt nod.

"—as well as Makanna of Karakan and her siblings, and Valmik of Karakan."

There were waves from them all around, even from Makanna.

"With the formalities out of the way, shall we get to the substance of this meeting?"

"Please," I said, maybe a little more eagerly than I'd intended.

"Very good. Lady Draka, I would like to begin by apologizing for encouraging these rumors about a wyvern. I understand that it has and will continue to cause you some trouble. Know that I do not blame you for defending yourself. Now, per the advice of two of my squad leaders, as well as the testimony of some trusted citizens of Karakan"—he indicated Herald's group—"I believe that we could use your aid in our work to protect the city. I hope that you'll forgive me if we keep this cooperation secret, and understand that I will disavow any rumors as lies and slander if I must. Mallin has suffered under a dragon in centuries past, and it is unlikely that your existence here, or any relationship we might have, would be seen favorably by the council or the citizenry at large. I like to think of myself as being more pragmatic than most, though I confess that I myself became concerned when I first heard of your existence, and I had trouble believing your apparent lack of malice until recently. That said . . . I believe that there was a specific reason that you wished to meet tonight?"

"There is. You've heard about the gates, yeah?"

"I have. Though, again, it was a difficult thing to believe until I heard that the Cranes were sent to clear out some valkin from a tunnel complex hidden behind one such gate. Now, Miss Herald tells us that you can show us another."

"I can do you one better. The gate that Herald told you about? I scouted the tunnels. There is another, way more convenient entrance to the same tunnels, and there are both valkin and human prisoners there. Looks like a whole small village, like last time. If we move quickly, we can rescue them before the slavers come to collect them."

That got their attention. Rallon's cousins started whispering with Lalia, and I thought I heard something about favor with the council.

"They still have prisoners? Are you sure of this?" Rallon said, and I saw a hint of excitement in the glint of his eyes.

"They did two days ago, and no one came to get them. There are a lot of tunnels in there, but with any luck, the slavers are lazy enough to use the ground floor entrance."

"This is an interesting opportunity." Rallon ran his fingers through his beard. "People have been going missing. The council is aware that there must be slavers operating here, but no one has been able to track them. If we could catch them coming to collect . . . do you have any idea when that might be?"

"None at all. But I've been keeping an eye on the gate, and I plan to keep doing that until you all are ready." I thought for a moment. "Couldn't we just get the prisoners out and then wait for the slavers?"

"I'm afraid not. I understand that it might sound callous, but capturing these criminals and hopefully breaking their organization is more important than expediting the freedom of a few prisoners. If we act in haste, the slavers may hear of our rescue operation, and the opportunity will be lost."

I didn't like it, but his words made sense.

"Then, how do you want to handle it? We don't know when the slavers are coming, and if I leave to warn you when they show up, they may be gone before you can get there."

"Quite right," Rallon said, rolling a few strands of his beard between his fingers as he considered. "I believe that we'll have to go with a somewhat riskier option."

"What's your plan?"

"I would ask you to take a small group to this gate. I would also like you to show us where this other entrance is in the mountains so that we may guard it as well. We, the Wolves, will send out few enough of our number to not cause any suspicion, bolstered, if they agree, by Makanna's group."

Rallon looked to Makanna, who in turn looked to the others and then nodded at the Commander.

"I believe that there were six in the slaving party last time," Rallon told me. "Is that correct?"

"That's how many I saw."

"To be safe, we'll assume there are a few more. In any case, I believe that a group composed of yourself, my own squad's scouts, as well as Makanna's group would be enough to kill or, preferably, capture the slavers as they are leaving. We can clear out the valkin at a later date. I don't suppose you found a Nest Heart?"

I shook my head. Then, remembering that the gesture didn't work very well with my long neck, I said, "No."

"I thought not. From the north, most likely. Valkin like to travel. Ah, well. Lalia will take part of her squad as well as another group we've worked with to the other gate, the back door, if you will, and guard there in case anyone tries to go through."

Rallon looked at me, then at the others. "Are there any objections?" he asked, his tone making it clear that he did not expect any.

"Not so much an objection as a question," I said, and Rallon nodded for me to go on. "Why don't we follow them back to wherever they came from? We could break their whole operation that way, couldn't we?"

"Ambitious and too risky. For one, they are unlikely to bring the captives back to the city. They most likely have a handoff arranged, perhaps via one or two ships cruising offshore, waiting for a signal."

Well, shit. I wished I'd thought of that when I was looking for a ship on the beach like an idiot. Of course they wouldn't be waiting right along the coast.

"For another, we can only send a small group, and they may join with a larger force later. No, we'll have to pin our hope on interrogation, I think."

"All right." I'd have to trust him on this. He definitely sounded confident. "And what about the prisoners the slavers don't want?"

"Hmm. The rejects, yes. They did try to dispose of them last time, didn't they? We'll have to strike quickly once the main objective is accomplished. I'll keep a squad in reserve to send out as soon as we hear of your success."

After a few seconds of silence, I realized that he was waiting for me to speak. "That sounds . . . okay, I guess."

"In that case, let us talk about details and compensation. While the company's monthly payments are fixed, I was unfortunately forced to give the council quite a lot of leeway when it comes to compensation for specific actions. That said, I believe that they will be most pleased if we can rescue a number of captured citizens and disrupt a slaving ring before it becomes a widely known problem. I am prepared to offer yourself and Makanna's group twenty percent each of whatever bonus the council pays us, after expenses. Would that be acceptable?"

I had no idea how much that was, but I saw Tamor's eyes bug out a little and his smile grow to a full grin at the suggested share. I took that as a good sign.

"Uh, yeah," I said. "That sounds good."

"Excellent!" Rallon gave me a toothy smile. "That's the unpleasant part taken care of. Now let's get down to business! Lady Draka, I have two requests to make of you. First, to show my two cousins to the gate where we hope for the slavers to appear, and second, to show Lalia to this other gate into the mountain. I understand that this may seem rushed, but would you be able to begin tonight?"

"Well, I can. But don't they need some rest?"

"It will do them some good," Rallon said, looking back at his subordinates. "And without saying too much, they have the tools, training, and advancements to handle it. Thank you for your concern, but there's no need!"

After that, things moved along quickly. I took the opportunity to talk to Herald and the rest, giving them my very honest thanks for the gifts Herald had presented me with a few days before, and Makanna had a talk with Lalia. I saw the telltale glow of magic pass between them, presumably to let Lalia see better in the dark.

"Do you know that you're bigger again?" Herald asked privately before we separated. "Not so much taller or longer as just"—she flexed her arms—"bigger."

I grinned at her. "Yeah, I thought I might be. I got another advancement."

She rolled her eyes at me like this was something I'd done specifically to annoy her.

When we left the campsite, I just told them all to follow the road south, then flew ahead to find the place I'd memorized as the place to turn off. Once they found me, Rallon continued toward the city with my friends, and Lalia, Rebatia, and Poterio came with me. The walk through the woods didn't bring us straight to the gate, but that was fine. I could tell that we were somewhat north of the gate, so we simply followed the exposed rock south until I recognized the place.

We didn't really talk. Lalia wasn't exactly ignoring me, but we didn't exactly have much to say to each other either. The two cousins whispered together, but for all their excitement, they got really tongue-tied whenever we looked at one another. I hoped that we could deal with that, or else we'd have a few awkward days ahead of us.

"This is the place," I told them as we stood in front of the gate.

"I don't see anything," Lalia said, miraculously managing to not make that sound like an accusation.

"You wouldn't, but neither can anyone else. You see how this area is flatter?" I pointed along the edges of the gate. "And the ground here has been disturbed a little. That's how you can tell."

"If you say so. And the one you're taking me to is the same?"

"That one's easier, actually. It's in a kind of trench in the stone, and it's a lot more weathered, so you can see the edges better."

"All right. Rib, Pot, how do you want to do this?"

"I'll stay and keep an eye on things," Rebatia said. "Pot'll take the horses back to the city and bring the others in the morning."

Lalia nodded.

"See you when this is all over, I guess." Then we split up again. Poterio headed back to the road, and Lalia and I went south along the hills.

Just me and Lalia, alone together. For hours and hours.

What the hell had I agreed to?

CHAPTER FORTY-TWO

With an Enemy Like This . . .

Lalia and I went south along the hills to save time. Going back to the road would have been a serious detour, and Lalia wanted this done with as quickly as possible. On that, at least, we agreed.

"Hey, slow down a little," I told her. She'd pulled ahead for the umpteenth time. I'd worried about how the horse would handle the rough terrain, but the gelding must have had a mountain goat somewhere in his family tree, because he moved as easily over loose stone as he did through the forest undergrowth and seemed to have no trouble seeing in the dark. Keeping up with him was not easy to do, especially since he hadn't taken to me anywhere near as easily as Melon had, and even with Lalia's skillful handling, he still obviously preferred to keep some distance from me.

Lalia shot me a look over her shoulder, but she reined in her horse and allowed me to catch up.

"Why do you insist on walking if you can't keep up?" she asked, making no effort to hide her annoyance.

"I told you, there's a bear following us." I'd picked up the scent half an hour earlier. It wasn't strong, but we had the wind at our backs, and the scent stayed with us. The thing was staying close, and considering the monster I'd seen in my early days, I was not going to make any assumptions about its intentions. "I'm not going to leave you here only to have to backtrack to find whatever's left of you."

"Okay, first, most bears sleep at night. We probably just passed a den," she said as if lecturing a child. "Second, I can handle a bear just fine. And third, even if I couldn't, Windfall can outrun any damn bear in any damn terrain. Just fly ahead so we can get this over with!"

Me and Lalia, we didn't exactly get along. She hadn't questioned Rallon's order, but I could tell that she wasn't happy about it. Still, we had gone from outright, open hostility to something more like passive-aggressive sniping, so that was something.

"Yeah, not happening," I told her firmly. "Fourth, some animals are monsters. I've got a bad feeling, and unfortunately there are people I care about who'd miss you. I'm not taking any chances."

She sighed. "Fine. Then how about you go find the thing and decide what we need to do, and I'll promise to shout if something tries to eat me? If it's stalking us, I don't imagine you'll have to go far. You could . . . circle." She gestured vaguely in the air.

And we could both get what we wanted. She could move quickly and not have to be near me, and I could be sure that she was safe. I meant what I'd said. I didn't care much about her myself. I mean, I probably wouldn't just let her die, no matter what. But my few friends liked her, and that made her important to me whether I liked her or not. Besides, it wouldn't look very good to Rallon if I let one of his captains, or whatever she was, get killed during our first joint venture.

"You know what? Good idea," I told her, then leaped into the air. And I could actually do that now. Before I passed my latest threshold and got my strength advancement, getting in the air had always been pretty awkward. The problem had been that I couldn't leap high enough to beat my wings properly without them hitting the ground. Instead I'd jump as high as I could, then make short, furious flaps until I got high enough. Now, though, my legs were strong enough that I could leap to chest height on Lalia, mounted though she was, and with one powerful beat of my wings, I was climbing.

Once I was up there, I started circling. I could glide completely silently. Even when I beat my wings, it didn't make much noise, and I was pretty much invisible against the night sky, which Herald had confirmed for me. Besides that, between my naturally good night vision and my shadowsight, there wasn't much that could hide from me.

Combining all my advancements, I was pretty much a lethal surveillance drone. I wondered how much an invisible, airborne scout would be worth to Rallon.

While I pondered how great I was, I kept an eye on the ground around, and especially behind, Lalia. There wasn't much to see. Rocks and boulders, trees and logs and bushes. Rocks and boulders, trees and logs and bushes. Rocks and boulders —

One of the boulders moved.

I folded my wings and dropped. "Lalia!" I screeched as the "boulder" went from a stealthy creep into a lumbering sprint. "Behind you!"

On the ground, I saw Lalia look up, then behind her. She paused for a split second, then urged Windfall into a full gallop. The gelding was fast, but the bear, somehow, was gaining on them. Fortunately, it was so focused on its prey that it didn't see me coming.

The bear was huge. It might have been bigger than the first monster I'd seen, though I had been a bit smaller then, so it was hard to say. With size comes strength and mass. I might have gotten a little bigger and stronger lately, but when it came to sheer weight, I had nothing on this beast. I turned and hit it from the side after five or six seconds of almost free falling, and I damn near bounced off the thing, tumbling over its back and only barely catching myself before I hit the ground so that I turned a crash into a heavy landing. I'd been hoping to knock it down, but all I managed was to make it stumble, piss it off, and shift its attention to me.

Well, Lalia was safe. Mission accomplished.

I began to right myself to take off again, but had to lunge backward as the monster swiped one giant clawed paw at me. I was durable, but I was not invincible, and the thing looked strong. Even if it couldn't slice through my scales, I didn't doubt that it could break bones, mess up my joints, or at least give me a concussion if it hit me. It kept coming at me, and I kept having to back up, dodging left and right. I tried to spray venom at it, but the damn thing actually *closed its eyes and lowered its head*! It wasn't just way bigger than the average bear, but smarter too!

The thing had me on the defensive, leaving me no time to do anything but stay away from its attacks. That was not going to work. Sooner or later, I was going to stumble or slip up, and once it got one good hit in, it would be that much more difficult to avoid the next one, and it would all snowball from there. If I wanted to get out alive, I had to get past it, or stun it, or make it back off. Anything that would give me enough room to breathe so I could get in the air, or shift, or climb a tree. I had to get out of its reach for more than half a second, and I could only see one way to accomplish that.

The next time the bear attacked, so did I. I bunched my legs and raised my head to draw out a high swipe. When it struck at me with its right paw, I quickly dropped and pushed forward on its left, raking its leg and side with my claws as I went. I almost made it past, and then I was rolling sideways with no idea what had happened.

I didn't have time to think. I was on my back, and the bear was on me in an instant, crushing me with its weight as it tried to bite into my neck. I got a grip on its head before it could bite down, but even with my strength, it was all I could do to hang on and keep its jaws away from me, my claws reaching nothing but thick, loose skin as it dragged me across the ground. I couldn't even kick properly, and I couldn't shift because I couldn't focus on anything except staying alive for another tenth of a second. All the while, the monster was pummeling me with its paws, and though its own claws couldn't get through my scales, they didn't need to. I felt every single blow, and though the actual damage was minor, it prevented me from taking a single good breath.

This is it, I thought, feeling oddly detached from it all. *I'm going to run out of air, and then I won't be able to hold it off anymore. And that will be that.*

Suddenly, two sounds cut through mine and the monster's combined snarling. There was a rising, furious cry and a thunder of hooves, and then they were gone. The bear reared up with a roar, turning and swiping toward its right side, but there was nothing there to hit.

I had an opening, and I took it. I didn't attack. I did not want to bring its attention back to me if I could help it. Instead I flipped onto my belly, took two leaping strides, and practically ran up a tree.

It was not brave, and it was not dignified, but it kept me alive. As soon as I started moving, the bear turned back to me, and I felt it bat my tail as I went. But I was safe.

Or so I thought, until the tree shook and began to lean.

The damn bear wasn't trying to climb the tree. It was too smart for that. It knew that it was too heavy. Instead it was trying to push the tree over, shoving into it, pulling back, and shoving again. And it was working. With every shove, the tree shuddered, and every time the bear pulled back, the tree leaned a little more, a crack appearing in the ground several feet out as roots were pulled out of the soil.

Too damn smart by half.

My body felt like . . . Well, like I'd been pummeled by an overgrown grizzly bear. I wanted to either shift or fly off, but I could see Lalia returning at a full gallop, and the monster was turning to get a look at her. I had to give her an opening.

Bending my neck so I was facing down, I tried to spray. It didn't work well, since bending my neck like that mostly closed off my windpipe, but even though I only managed to produce a dribble, I got the effect I wanted. The bear turned its head to protect itself, and I let go of the tree.

I dropped straight onto the bear's back, digging in my claws and holding on for dear life. The bear went wild, standing on its hind legs, flailing and twisting to try to either reach me or shake me off, but I held firm, biting over and over to both keep its attention and hopefully get some venom into its wounds. I only stopped biting to yell at Lalia as she approached.

Lit by the moonlight, Lalia came charging in with her sword held out to the side. Her eyes were wide, and she came in screaming with her teeth bared, looking equal parts awesome and terrifying.

"Go south!" I shouted as loudly as I could. "Keep going south!"

I saw a flicker of understanding and a nod, and then she passed us, sword flashing and carving a deep cut into the bear's hind leg. The instant it dropped to all fours, I sprang off it and climbed up a new tree, then shifted and moved to another tree, then another before I shifted back, leaping from the tree into the open air and taking to the sky. I stuck around, circling long enough to make sure that the bear demon had had enough and wasn't trying to follow Lalia.

I was hurt, but I wasn't injured. I was bruised and battered, but nothing was broken. I was alive, and so was Lalia.

Most importantly, I was right. Bears sleep at night, my scaly ass.

I caught up with Lalia five minutes later where she'd stopped to wait for me. After she reluctantly admitted that yes, there had indeed been a bear, and I begrudgingly thanked her for not leaving me to handle the monster on my own, we continued on together, and at my pace, though I tried to keep it fairly quick.

"Don't read too much into me coming back for you," Lalia said after we'd been moving for a while. "Rallon wants to work with you. And Herald and Garal like you for some reason."

"Yeah. Right back at you."

The silence was a little less tense after that.

Getting to the mountain gate and back to the road was easy. All it took was time. Lalia snuck past the mining camp, which was occupied again, and I flew right over it with no one the wiser. I guided Lalia to the gate, and she was sure that she'd be able to find her way back on her own without any trouble. She also insisted that she'd be fine to return to the city on her own, but I still kept an eye on her from the sky until she reached the main road.

Only then, with the sun getting high, did I return to Rebatia and the gate in the hills.

CHAPTER FORTY-THREE

Koh-ahp

When I returned to the gate, there was no one there.

Or rather, I couldn't immediately find anyone, but not being seen was part of Rebatia's job, as I understood it. The other part was killing people without flinching. There may be something else to it, but those were the parts I knew of.

I, of course, didn't want to make myself obvious either. Guiding Lalia to and from the gate in the mountains had taken all night and most of the morning, and now it was midday. That wasn't ideal for me, but I was still pretty damn sneaky, and I decided to make a game of it. It would have been better if Rebatia had known the rules, but what could you do?

The game was simple. Whoever got found lost. Now, I could have almost guaranteed victory by shifting. Almost. But Rebatia might already be watching me, and I was in no way ready to let *anyone* except Herald know what I could do.

Staying low to the ground and very still, I disappeared into the ferns and low bushes that even here covered the ground between the trees. I looked and listened, but obviously I didn't pick up anything except the normal sights and sounds of the forest. I could smell a human, but the smell was spread out, and I couldn't sense a direction for it.

I stayed there for a long while just in case something changed, but except for a cat-size squirrel passing through the treetops, nothing much happened. Clearly, I wasn't going to find Rebatia this way anytime soon. While I could have probably waited her out over the next several hours, I was achy, tired, and sleepy. A new vantage point was in order.

Guessing the general area where she was likely to be, I found a good tree. It was a tall pine of sorts, with the kind of dense crown that I liked, and it overlooked my chosen area nicely. I crept along the ground to the back of the trunk, then climbed it slowly, trying to keep myself as hidden as possible. I settled in the way I usually did, finding a good angle for my head where I could watch the gate and look for the scout, and then I waited.

I dozed off but was rudely awoken by the loud "*Koh-ahp! Koh-ahp!*" of some bird. It stopped after a few moments, and after a minute's silence, I relaxed again. The instant my eyes closed, the "*Koh-ahp! Koh-ahp!*" came again, louder and longer this time. That's how it went for the next hour. Every single time I was about to fall asleep, the damn bird would start screaming. I'd look around, fail to see it, and hope that it had finally fucked off. It never did, and after maybe the twentieth time, I had finally had enough. I didn't relax and try to sleep, instead waking myself up and staying alert, waiting for the next time the damn thing started. There was only one way this could go now. I was going to find that bird, and I was going to eat it!

After a minute, the infernal "*Koh-ahp! Koh-ahp!*" started up again, and it didn't stop. It went on and on and on. I hunted around the trees, the bushes, even the rocks around the gate, but nothing. It kept screaming, and I couldn't find it!

Then, suddenly, there she was. Rebatia stood up from behind a rock, perhaps thirty yards to the right and above the gate, and waved at me. Our eyes met across the distance, and despite how tired and frustrated I was, I couldn't help but return the shit-eating grin she flashed at me. It looked like she had not only figured out the game, but she'd won, no contest.

Since the jig was up, I figured I might as well do the polite thing. Looking and listening carefully for a while to make sure that no one was coming—and that Rebatia wasn't looking—I climbed down and crept toward her. I could have flown, but the trees continued up the hillside, and flying around them was pretty annoying if I didn't have to. Instead I tried to find an approach that would keep me hidden.

To my great satisfaction, I got within fifteen yards before she noticed me.

Up close, she wasn't grinning quite as wide anymore. Her slightly wide face was still split by a smile, but there was a touch of nervousness around her eyes, and she kept running her fingers through short, cropped hair as I approached.

"Ah . . . hello," she said quietly, shrinking back a touch as I joined her behind the large rock she'd chosen for her hiding spot. "No hard feelings, I hope? Tam said you can take a joke. Craziest thing. Dragon with a sense of humor! Right?" She had a very rapid way of talking that made me wonder if it was because of nerves or if that was just how she was.

"Hello, Rebatia," I said flatly, speaking with deliberate slowness. Then I just stared at her, putting on my best angry murder-lizard face. Her smile started to fade, and I saw some real concern creeping in, but I couldn't keep a straight face for long. "When did you spot me?" I asked, relaxing my voice and giving her one of my practiced smiles with minimal teeth.

Some of the tension left her and her smile came back, a little easier this time. "Call me Rib, *please*! And . . ." She considered the sky. "An hour and a half ago, maybe. I got lucky and saw you pass through a sunny patch. Since you didn't call out to find me or anything, I figured I'd make you work for it." She showed no hint of remorse. She did, however, look a little embarrassed when she added, "Sorry about keeping you awake. It's a merc thing if we see someone nodding off on guard."

"Yeah, nah, no dramas. I really need some sleep, though. Don't you?"

"Drama . . . ?" She blinked rapidly, then shook her head and fished out a vial half-full of clear liquid from a belt pouch. "Won't need rest for a while yet. I'm running on these for now. Good stuff! I'll be fine until Pot comes back with the others."

Some kind of stimulant. That might explain the quick, jerky way that she talked. I hoped it wouldn't be a problem.

"Pot," I said. "That's Poterio, I guess. He's your brother?"

"That's him. And we're cousins, like . . . second once removed? Big House, the Terriallons." She paused and put the vial back in her belt. "Might as well be siblings, though. Same age, grew up together and all that. Like him better than my real brothers, pack of pricks that they are."

I was too tired to try to follow *that* up. "Well, Rib, I really need that nap," I said instead. "Are you good to watch the gate?"

"Good as gold," she said, patting her belt pouch. "Have a good one."

I didn't just curl up and sleep. Rib felt trustworthy, but she was new. Instead I headed back to the tree I'd come from and settled in. There I drifted into a nap, mercifully free from birdcalls.

When I woke, the nap had turned into a full day's sleep. It had been some time after noon when I'd curled up, and now a sea of stars sparkled through the breaks in the tree's crown.

As I stretched a bit and began to look around, there came a *"Koh-ahp!"* and I nearly fell out of the tree. It hadn't come from the hillside, though, and when I looked around, I spotted an unfamiliar man with long hair and a goatee in a neighboring tree. He waved at me silently, then pointed to the left of the gate. I gave him an uncertain thumbs-up, which I remembered too late didn't mean anything at all here, and he looked at me in confusion before gesturing again and going back to watching the path leading to and from the road.

Between the man's gesture and his lack of urgency, his meaning seemed clear enough. I climbed out of my tree, padded over to the gate and then up the hillside on the left. A few dozen yards up, in a hidden dip behind a cluster of rocks that rose sharply out of the sloping ground, I found a small camp. There was no fire, of course, only a couple of low tents and two figures sitting guard. I recognized Herald immediately and Poterio—Pot—shortly after.

They both looked up as I crested the rise, hands on their weapons, and relaxed when they recognized the only dragon on the island.

"Evenin'," I said softly as I got close. "Did Lalia make it back all right?"

Herald gave a short, barking laugh before smothering it with her hand. "I am sorry," she said, also keeping her voice down. "I can hardly believe that the first thing out of your mouth was to ask about Lalia's well-being!"

"Yeah, well . . ." I looked at Poterio instead. "So, did she?"

"She did, though she was half-blind when she came in. Wouldn't tell us why either. Embarrassed about taking too much potion, I'd guess."

If he didn't know, I wasn't going to tell him. "And you all? You make it here all right?"

"There was no trouble," Herald said. "Pot has a perfect memory for landscapes and locations, and we took a covert route here just in case. Rib is sleeping, as are Mak, Tam, and Val. The rest of the scouts are"—she gestured vaguely to the forest—"out there."

"I saw. Well, one of them showed himself and pointed me here. I'm guessing Rib told him what birdcall to use?"

Pot grinned. "She thought you'd recognize it."

He got a little huff for that. "Yeah. What kind of horrible bird makes a noise like that, anyway? I hate it!"

"Are you sure that you want to know?"

"Why?"

"You won't like it."

I sighed. "Just tell me."

Pot gave me a big smile, the same smug fucking grin as Rib had, and said, "The koh-ahp."

It was four days before anything happened. Apart from being silent death on two legs, the scouts turned out to be good people. A bit odd, maybe. I wasn't sure if the weirdos were encouraged to become scouts or if being a scout turned you into a weirdo over time, but they were a nice and friendly weird, not a creepy weird. Rib and Pot, despite being full-blooded how-much-could-a-banana-cost aristocrats, shared love of absolutely filthy ballads and shanties. They promised to show off their repertoire once we were done and could finally speak above a whisper, and I accepted happily. Not that I'd ever been into that kind of music, but I'd take what I could get out here. They even tried to rope Makanna into it, and she actually smiled and said that she'd think about it.

Boot, real name unknown, was the guy in the tree with the hair and the goatee. In his thirties, he was the oldest and most experienced of the scouts. He was also the one of the scouts who was most wary around me. But Rib covertly told me that Boot had a weakness.

Boot loved boots, and he warmed up considerably when I, being a dragon and thus naturally ignorant on the subject, asked him to tell me all about them. He could, and did, spend a whole watch talking about the merits of different styles and materials for different parts, depending on the purpose, surface, and season the boot was intended for. He was also completely unashamed of his particular love of boots on women, though, mercifully, he didn't dwell on that for long.

If you needed advice on properly maintaining your boots, Boot was your guy. He was also the scouts' unofficial cook and owned the first piece of enchanted equipment I'd seen, which he happily showed me on the second night.

"See," he said, holding it so I could get a better look at it. It was a flat, round metal disc with a middle part and an outside ring that could rotate, a complex design covering the whole surface.

"You turn it like so," he said, holding it by the center and turning the outer ring so the design lined up, "and then you just drop it in your water!"

He dropped it in the pot he'd filled with water. There was a quick hiss, and then the thing sank. After a few seconds, the first small bubbles rose to the surface, and after a minute, the whole thing, over a gallon of water, was boiling gently.

It was fascinating. One moment it had just been a fancy piece of metal, but when he'd turned the ring so the pattern lined, up it had glowed all over with magic. Even after he'd dropped it in the pot, I could still see it shining through the liquid, growing dimmer little by little.

"And there you are! It'll keep going for a good while before it runs out. I usually have to fish it out. Doesn't stay hot if it's not in water. Wish I had one for oil, but it's not like I can fry stuff out here anyway, is it?"

"And then what?" I asked, peering into the bubbling cauldron. "Once it runs out, I mean. How do you make it work again?"

"Easy! I just wash it off, turn it back, and then it'll be good again in a few hours. About five if it runs out, less if I fish it out. Draws ambitent—"

"Ambient," Herald corrected from where she was sitting.

"Thanks—that, yeah. Draws magic from the air. Little Herald here can tell you more than I can. She's always loved this enchantment stuff."

Herald rolled her eyes at the "Little" part, but I could see her smiling behind her book.

I never saw much of the remaining two scouts, Arlal and Med. For one, they had the same sleep schedule as me, sleeping the days away. For another, they didn't seem to like being around us very much. Not like they actually disliked people, or me, for that matter, but more like they each just wanted to be alone as much as possible. They'd come in, report, eat, exchange some jokes and a few smiles, and then sleep. Then they'd wake, eat, talk a little, and head out. I'd have liked to get to know them a little, but they seemed happy enough, so who was I to interfere?

I took a couple of shifts watching the gate like anyone else, but other than that, I was free to do as I pleased. I talked to Tamor, Valmik, and even Makanna when they were awake, but they slept during the night and watched during the day, so we didn't have a whole lot of overlap. I spent most of my time with whichever of the scouts was in the camp and, of course, with Herald.

When I realized that Herald had switched her sleep schedule to match mine, one of the first things I did was to head back to the cave to fetch my books. The sight of me returning with my "chestpack" amused Rib to no end, and I think that anyone who saw us was amused by the sight of Herald helping me with my letters. I couldn't blame them. Seeing a proud and mighty dragon struggling with a children's book, under the patient guidance of a seventeen-year-old girl, must have been something. The few sessions we managed to cram in when the moon was bright enough really did help, though.

In the early hours of the fifth night, we were alerted by the hooting of an owl. I didn't think anything of it at first, but Boot stopped greasing the seams of one of his boots and listened intently.

"That's Pot," he said and waited. The hooting came again, and again, a little different each time. "Enemies approaching. Nine of them. Wake the others. This is it."

CHAPTER FORTY-FOUR

A Moment of Clarity

When the slavers approached, it was, of course, only the beginning of more waiting. They had two long, heavy crates with them, and I idly noted that they were all men, same as the last group I'd seen. It felt like there must be a reason for that, considering female adventurers weren't uncommon, and it looked like about one in four of the Wolves were women. Not that it mattered at the moment, but I thought that it was odd.

The slavers stood in front of the gate for a while before it opened from the inside. I didn't see any kind of signal, so the timing had probably been prearranged. They entered, ushered inside by two valkin, bringing their crates with them. The gate was left open. When Pot came into the camp from a long, circling route, he told us that they'd left three of their number behind just inside the tunnel. That made setting our ambush marginally harder, and in hushed voices, we quickly changed some plans.

I suggested simply killing the sentries, but, as Valmik pointed out, that might make the rest of them cautious about leaving the tunnel. No one wanted to get into a stand-up fight in a tight space with an unknown number of enemy reinforcements.

"Could we do a repeat of last time?" Tamor suggested, then explained to the scouts, "Draka here is pretty much the element of surprise incarnate. You stealthy folks can hide in the trees, and we four stay above the gate. Draka hits them from the air going only the Sorrows know how fast, and then we all come in while they're trying to figure out what's going on."

"What do you think?" Pot said, speaking to Boot.

"Could work, if she"—he nodded at me—"can hold her own for a few seconds against two or three men. We don't know how strong they are, but they should all be fighters. Could be risky, but it always is, isn't it? Rib?"

"Lots of unknowns, yeah. But that was always going to be the case. Gonna need to hit them right outside the gate. We don't know for sure which way they'll go. Might have some valkin behind them. Mak and all, can you hold the tunnel?

"Herald can provide ranged support from up here," Makanna said with a slow nod, "and the rest of us will make sure there's no one behind us before we move on to the slavers."

With our plan of action worked out, there was still the problem of not knowing how long we'd have to wait. That meant that everyone had to get into position and then wait there, alert, until it was showtime. That didn't sound like a big problem to start with, but half of us hadn't slept for anywhere between sixteen and twenty hours, and if the wait dragged on, the risk of someone falling asleep was very real.

Rib had a solution for that. She pulled out enough of her little vials to give one to anyone who wanted it, telling them to take small sips when they started feeling tired, and nothing else.

"I drank a whole vial in one go once," she said. "Makes you feel like a fucking god for about ten minutes. Doesn't really mix well with plans and ambushes. Unless the plan is *Run in, kill three of them, then die*. And the crash if you take too much at once is vicious."

Then, with everyone in position and properly stimulated, we waited.

An eternity later, Tamor, closest to the gate, signaled that something was happening. I had posted myself about sixty or seventy yards up, where I could get a good run but still see my companions. Human figures slowly began appearing from the side of the hill, stopping and waiting outside the gate. I counted four. I'd kept the anger at bay while we were staking out the gate, but ever since the slavers had shown up, it had been flaring again, and I was itching to go. But I had to be patient. We needed them all outside, where we could cut them off from the tunnel. And since I was the signal, I couldn't go off half-cocked or I'd make a mess of things.

I gathered myself, digging in my feet and preparing to leap, confident that at this distance and in this darkness, I was invisible. Two more slavers came into view, along with a short procession of people in simple, everyday clothes. They shuffled out, walking carefully in the darkness. Whatever the slavers used to see in the dark, they clearly hadn't shared it with their prisoners. Even at a distance, it was easy to see that these were the kids and younger adults, an even dozen of them. *The valuable merchandise*, I thought, my disgust churning. *Not long now*, I reassured myself. *I don't need to hold back for more than a moment.*

The foremost slavers were among the trees, but that was fine. As long as I built up enough speed and prepared myself, I'd be able to hit any of them, even with my wings folded.

The last three of the party came into view, making the full nine with the two sentries. If I could see them, they were already a couple of yards in front of the gate. By the time I got there and the slavers knew that something was wrong, they'd be a couple of steps farther ahead, and with any luck, they'd rush forward when a big, scary animal attacked one of their members at the front. That should be plenty for Tamor and Valmik to cut them off.

Time to go.

I leaped into the air. I didn't go straight toward them. Instead I flew north then banked sharply to the left so that I had the whole procession lined up. My wing beats were almost silent, and no one had so much as looked around. I had three beats to choose a target and pick up speed before I'd have to fold my wings to avoid the trees. I couldn't tell who the leader was, so I picked the biggest of the four in front.

They never saw me coming.

As I tore through the air above the procession, I gave a roaring screech, emptying my lungs before impact. The big bastard didn't even have time to turn. I had no idea what kind of skills or advancements he may have had, and it simply didn't matter. When I slammed into him, feet first, I felt bones break and squishy things pop inside him even before he slammed into and skidded across the ground. I'm not going to pretend that it was a comfortable experience for me either, but I'd healed from my bear-inflicted bruises over the last four days, and I was a hell of a lot more durable than any human. I rolled once, the limp man going with me, and then I was on my feet and facing the rest of the scum.

To their credit, they reacted quickly. The night erupted into noise. Orders went out from one of the three remaining at the front, and they spread out around me. Unfortunately for them, they were completely focused on me, just as we had planned. Now all I had to—

A short sword thrust at my neck with such speed that I dodged just enough to avoid being impaled. The thrust skittered across my scales, then turned into a slash, and though I leaped back, the tip still caught me under the chin. Jesus, Mary, and Joseph, this guy was little, but he was quick, and that stab had some force behind it! As I backpedaled from a flurry of attacks, the other two were closing in from the sides, and my allies were nowhere to be seen.

Well, shit. I'd been hoping to keep them distracted until the others could disable some of them, but I wasn't going to let myself get stabbed. Or chopped. The big guy on my left had an axe. That brought back some unpleasant memories of how I'd lost the horn on that side, and if I didn't want a repeat of that experience or worse, I'd have to go on the offensive.

The little guy was devilishly quick, and I wasn't confident that I could catch him with my claws. So the next time I dodged back and he came forward, I sprayed him with venom. He tried to dodge it, but I spread it pretty wide, and his eyes reflexively squeezed shut. At that point, it was too late. I felt the dragon stirring, finally, when my subconscious went from seeing the guy as a threat to seeing him prey. I had a strong urge to finish him off, but he was no longer such a danger to me. Instead I immediately lunged to my left, going for the big guy with the axe.

I didn't have a plan. It would be a moment before I could spray again. I had no training, hadn't even thought much about fighting when I didn't have to, and I only had a little bit of experience. My strategy for this guy only had two parts: (1) *go in hard, trust in your awesome body, and do more damage than you take*; (2) *try to get the big guy between you and his buddy.*

As I prepared to try to dodge around the big guy, he raised his axe to chop, but neither of us got a chance. He was wearing some kind of leather armor—I really needed to take some lessons in identifying arms and armor—and when he lifted his arms to hack at me, Arlal suddenly appeared out of the darkness behind him.

Arlal stabbed the guy viciously through the armpit with a long, thin dagger five or six times in barely a second. The big slaver brought his arm down and turned to try to defend himself, but Arlal had already vanished back into the gloom. I still rushed forward to get past the guy, knowing that I had his friend behind me, and as I passed, he seemed to realize what had happened. He tried to chop at me—a sad attempt that I easily avoided—as he dropped to one knee with a weak, gurgling groan, then collapsed to the ground.

I turned and looked at the remaining man. He had what I would consider a normal-size, slightly curved sword in his hand and was looking at me warily. His small eyes flicked to the dying man next to me, then to my first victim, to the small man wheezing and rubbing at his eyes on the ground, and finally to me. For a second, I expected him to run or surrender, but then he . . . I wasn't sure what he did. He closed his eyes, mumbled something, and relaxed. I didn't see any magic happening. Perhaps he made peace with his gods or something. Whatever it was, he came at me.

His sword whirled and danced, but he was nowhere near as fast as the small man, and his attacks seemed to rely on cutting rather than stabbing or chopping. I doubted that attacks like those could do much damage, and the dragon was out now, her lust for battle burning bright, which made me aggressive and careless. So instead of scrambling backward, I went straight for him.

If I had been anyone, else I would have died right there. The guy was surprised, sure, but not too surprised to lay his sword on me and draw its entire length across my throat. The damn thing even went up under one of my scales, though it caught on its neighbors, and while I felt it cut my skin, the wound was shallow. Still, my attack worked out. That was the only chance he got, and he hadn't made it count. I pinned his arms with mine, bit down across his throat, and tore it out with a vicious jerk. As his blood poured across my tongue and down my throat, I nearly swallowed the chunk of flesh and gristle before I realized what I was doing and flung it to the side.

As that hit me, I looked up and saw Rib staring at me from the darkness, dagger out and poised to help. Or I hoped so, at least. She stared at me with what I could only interpret as a mix of terror and awe before shaking her head and disappearing into the back of the fight.

I left the blinded man wheezing on the ground and followed her. Our rescuees were standing around calmly, remaining right where they'd been when I struck, oblivious to the carnage that surrounded them. As I passed them, I saw Pot tending to Med, who was propped against a tree with a vicious gash in his leg and a dead man in front of him. Nothing a potion couldn't fix, I hoped, because there was nothing I could do. I kept going.

This was the first time I saw an actual fight between humans trained in and specialized for combat. Ahead of me, Valmik was locked in a duel with one of the remaining slavers, Valmik constantly pressing, the bandit constantly falling back up the hill but never actually disengaging, tying Valmik up while saving his strength and maneuvering. Their swords were a blur in the air, and Valmik's shield rang constantly, while their footwork was practically choreographed. Meanwhile, one single bandit was holding off Rib, Boot, Arlal, Tamor, and Makanna while simultaneously avoiding Herald's arrows.

The man was nothing much to look at. He would have had a completely forgettable face except that he had a scar running across both lips, like they'd both been split at the same time. Still, he stood out from the others by how neat he looked. He was clean-shaven with short, well-kept hair and dressed in simple travelers' clothes, though his looked whole and tidy compared to those I'd seen on the road. He had a curved sword in one hand, much like the one of the man I'd just killed, and a long dagger in the other. He was surrounded, fighting five opponents, and it looked like he was slowly winning.

Makanna's spear was broken, cut through right behind the point, and she had her sword drawn. Herald's arrows littered the ground, and she was going to run out soon. The three scouts couldn't get close. The man was in constant motion, and anytime they tried to get close with their daggers and short swords, the slaver's dagger was there to parry, his curved sword forcing them back. Tamor, with his longer sword, should have had an advantage, but the gulf in skill and speed was enormous.

At first, the slaver seemed to have the same problem that Valmik had against the gremlins. He was holding everyone off, but he couldn't commit to an opponent or he'd open himself too much to the others. But it looked like he wouldn't have to. As I approached, Tamor lunged in with a thrust, and the slaver's dagger was there, knocking the blade aside easily while the curved sword licked out. By sheer luck, Tamor stumbled and only got a cut on his arm instead of losing a hand.

And all this, people moving, swords and daggers slashing and thrusting and parrying, happened at a speed that I could only barely follow.

Tamor stumbled back with a hiss. His wasn't the first wound either. Both Rib and Boot had shallow cuts, bleeding but not as bad as Tamor or Med. Still, the fact was that this one slaver was slowly wearing them down while his companion kept Valmik busy. Something needed to change.

I tried to decide where to attack, but the decision was made for me. It suddenly clicked for me that the man Valmik was fighting was not just falling back and keeping Valmik busy. He had gradually but inexorably been making his way toward Herald, who was too focused on the man fighting her siblings to notice. This guy could hold Valmik off while maneuvering toward a new target. Herald wouldn't stand a chance against him.

I couldn't fly, not yet. I had to get out of the trees. I ran a few strides and saw with horror how the slaver reached Herald. She saw him at the last second but barely got her sword out. In one dashing move, he stepped under her swipe, grabbed and twisted her sword arm behind her with his free hand, and forced her to her knees with a kick, her weapon falling from her hand. It only took a moment, and then the slaver was facing Valmik, his sword at Herald's throat.

"*The arrogant worm!*" the dragon growled as I broke from the trees, her anger fanned into full, incandescent rage. I leaped above the heads of the circle of fighters and beat my wings twice, landing on the hill above the standoff.

The slaver looked at me, his eyes widening for half a heartbeat before he spoke in a low, cold voice. "Call it off," he told Valmik. "Call it off and let us leave with the slaves, or the girl dies here and now."

The sound of fighting below us had stopped, and I could see the others looking up, awaiting the outcome of our situation. Valmik hesitated. "You'll release her if we let you go?" he asked, his voice trembling with anger.

"We'll keep her until we're satisfied that we're safe. If you don't do anything foolish, you'll get her back in one piece."

I prowled left and right, growling with fury. "*He would take what is ours,*" the dragon raged in my ear. She itched for us to throw ourselves at him, but I understood the threat of his sword at Herald's throat in a way the dragon clearly didn't. "*He would steal away our treasured servant. Look in his eyes. He will never return her.*"

And I could see it. The cold arrogance, the spite. This man looked like someone who would go back on a deal simply to hurt us, no matter the consequences. I had no doubt that if we let them take Herald, we would get her back in pieces, if at all.

They were not leaving with her.

"*Listen carefully,*" I said in the language of Tekeretek, the language of Herald's parents. I saw her eyes lock on me when she heard me.

"Stop the damn thing chittering," the slaver said, glancing at me, some nerves breaking through his cold mask.

"*When you hear me hiss, I need you to close your eyes, hold your breath, and push the sword away. Whatever it takes,*" I continued.

"Draka!" Valmik said, his tone pleading. *Right.* He probably didn't speak any Tekereteki.

Herald looked deeply into my eyes, then gave the smallest nod. When I saw her free arm bend slowly upward, I struck.

I hissed and gave him all the venom I had. The moment I did so, Herald, with her glorious reflexes, closed her eyes and mouth, brought her free hand up, and pushed away on the edge of the sword at her throat while letting herself drop.

The slaver's face twisted with fury for a breath before he got a face full of venom. It didn't stop him sawing his blade sideways, though. I never thought I'd be relieved to hear Herald scream, but in that moment, I was. It meant that the sword had only cut cruelly into her hand instead of her throat.

As the thieving bastard's eyes squeezed shut against the venom, I was already moving. I struck him high on the chest, and we went down the side of the hill together, Herald tumbling after us before the slaver lost his grip on her arm. His sword had vanished somewhere along the way, but he still tried to punch me or pry me off as we rolled. It was useless. I had the claws of my feet dug in under his armpits as my claws fought for purchase around his head.

"Thief," I hissed at him as we rolled. "Filthy fucking thief!" I couldn't tell if it was me or the dragon talking at that point. I wasn't thinking anymore. We came to a stop, and the man gave off a muted scream and clutched my talons as I got a nice, firm top-down grip on his face, digging my claws in under his jaw. He kicked and thrashed, and then I released my feet, bent my body to dig them into his shoulders instead, and *pulled*.

He screamed through his teeth, his jaw being pulled shut, and his struggles grew more frantic, kicking, bucking, beating desperately at my talons and my forelimbs as the pitch of his scream rose higher and higher into a muted wail. There was a crackling *pop* that I felt through my talons, and he jerked and went silent and limp, except for a few spasmodic twitches. Then I really put my back into it, and with a wet, tearing *squelch*, the bastard's head came off in a burst of blood, trailing wet tubes and dangling bone.

I would say that I didn't know why I did that, but that would be a lie. The truth was that I did it because I could, and because simply killing him wasn't enough. Not nearly. He had to die horribly, and he and everyone else had to know that there was *nothing* he could do to stop me. They had to understand that if they tried to steal from me, there would be consequences.

I would say that that all came from the dragon, but that would be a lie too.

We had come to a stop a couple yards from the still circle of fighters. As I got up, I looked into a dozen horrified eyes, and then I did the only thing that made sense at the time: I threw my trophy at the last remaining slaver and started prowling forward, blood dripping off me as I went.

"I surrender," the slaver said loudly, throwing his weapons to the side. I wasn't really interested, though I noted that there was no fear in his voice, but quite a bit of urgency. As I kept slowly stalking forward, he dropped to his knees and looked at me directly. "I surrender," he said again, looking me in the eyes. Again, there was no fear, only a calculating kind of hope. I honestly don't think he would have cared if I killed him. He merely preferred that I didn't. It was infuriating.

I passed between Rib and Boot. The first backed off a healthy distance as I approached, and the other looked at me with the same awe that I'd seen before. The savaged head was in my path and I kicked it forward so that it hit the kneeling man's leg, and I stopped before him. The fury that was bubbling inside me was almost overwhelming. I wanted this man to die. I wanted him to know that he was going to die and to know despair before I tore him apart. That's all that held me back. He hadn't broken yet. My claws raked the dirt as I flexed them, and I pushed my face right up into his, growling as I looked into those too-calm eyes. I got some satisfaction as I saw blood and spittle spatter his face, and he blinked painfully as some got in one of his eyes. The moment his gaze left me, I tackled him hard, and he fell backward onto the ground with a grunt.

I was going to enjoy breaking him. And not because of the slaving. Not because he'd hurt Tamor and my new friends. No, his worst crime was that he was associated with that bastard who'd tried to take Herald. And since that bastard was dead, I'd go for the next best thing. He wasn't afraid right now, but everyone had a limit. I was going to find his.

Then I heard a soothing voice next to me.

"Draka," Herald said, her voice tight. I looked at her, and she was a mess. Pale and sweaty, her nose running, she was standing next to me, cradling her wounded hand. Blood ran freely down her arm.

"We need at least one alive, Draka," she said, taking a step closer.

I looked at her. "*Your hand*," I growled at her in Tekereteki. It felt somehow natural to speak that language with her, especially now.

"*It will heal*," she answered in the same language, swallowing her pain. "*With care and time.*" She reached out with her good hand and put it on my neck. "*Please, Draka.*"

I looked at her, then at the others. I saw wariness, outright fear, even awe. *Ridiculous.* We came here to fight, didn't we? What difference did it make if you did so with a blade or with claws and teeth? I was sure I'd killed fewer people in my life than most of them had. Valmik could have killed that man far more efficiently; he just didn't get the opportunity. And if he had, no one would have stared at him like a . . .

They wanted to fight side by side with a dragon. What did they think that meant?

And I'd been naive, hadn't I? That little idea of mine to be one of them, to be part of a team—that had been absurd. I would never be one of them. I could see that now, looking at their faces. It had been fine while we were lying around waiting for something to happen. There had been a respectful wariness, sure, even from Rib and Pot, who seemed to like me, but mostly I'd been treated as a welcome stranger. I'd even started to think that the threat to me was overstated, that hiding myself might be unnecessary in the long run. But now that the claws were out . . . Fear and awe. That was how humans regarded dragons.

But I saw none of those emotions from Herald. She wasn't judging me. Her hand was a mess, I was covered in gore, and all I saw on her face was concern. For me or for the plan, I couldn't tell, but her presence and touch calmed me a little.

I looked back at the slaver and snorted with disgust. It occurred to me that he had both seen me and knew that I could talk, but I'd trusted Rallon and his people this far. I'd have to trust that they'd make sure he wouldn't be telling any tales, and I didn't care what that meant for him. *"They can take him. There is another survivor in the front of the prisoners,"* I said and moved off. *"Take care of your hand."*

"Where are you going?" she asked as I headed toward the hillside.

I looked at the open gate, a handful of valkin corpses strewn around it, plus one human. I felt a grim satisfaction at the two arrows in his chest. I was pulling ahead, but Herald was doing her best to keep up.

"I have some anger to vent," I told her. *"Let your sister help you. Do not follow me."*

CHAPTER FORTY-FIVE

Let It All Out

padded as quickly as I could through the long, straight tunnel that led to the valkins' complex. We had won the fight against the slavers and rescued the captured villagers. We even had captives of our own. But the violence had been nowhere near enough to calm the fury raging inside me.

The slavers had intended to sell those kids and their barely adult siblings into a life of misery. They had discarded the older prisoners to be disposed of as if they were defective or damaged. That was what drove me alone into the darkness, together with my anger at myself that I hadn't been able to rescue the "desirable" prisoners from the first group we'd found. Not to mention the miners, who were surely long gone by the time we even knew what was happening.

On top of that was the lingering outrage at how that slaver had been planning to take Herald away as a hostage. *My* friend. *My* Herald. I knew how possessive those thoughts were; I could be honest with myself. In the heat of the moment, I had called the man *thief.* Not *slaving bastard* or *piece of shit* or anything else that was certainly true about him, but *thief.* He had tried to take something, someone, that was mine.

I knew how I felt, and I had denied it to myself for weeks now. I would never agree with the dragon's view of her as a "servant." That was insulting and outrageous. But I certainly did treasure her. I would never coddle her or try to tell her where and when she could or couldn't go. I would never try to hold her back. But I would never let anyone keep her from me, or me from her. It was time I accepted that.

For the moment, though, all my murderous rage had to go somewhere. There were still around a dozen prisoners in here, guarded by somewhere around ten to a dozen valkin, and I was not going to lose another group of prisoners just because Rallon wanted to be cautious.

I could move at about the speed of a human jogging while hardly making a sound. It was far from the gate to the complex, and when I saw the guard post up ahead, it became clear that the guard had heard nothing of the battle outside. With the light-ball beside it and the darkness behind me, the guard didn't spot me until I was close enough to forget about stealth and break into a sprint. Even then, it barely had time to scream before I was on it, tearing it to shreds.

Killing the guard didn't help. My anger didn't cool. It just became more focused.

I picked up the light-ball and threw it back the way I'd come, watching it bounce and roll down the slight incline. As darkness filled the tunnel, I approached the door a little ways up and waited.

Twenty or thirty seconds later, I heard steps and voices approaching. The door flung open, and the three valkin on the other side, spears at the ready, were greeted with a spray of venom. Their choking screams echoed through the tunnels as I barreled into them, ripping and tearing anything in front of me.

I found the two long boxes in the hall where the tunnel met the complex. They'd been opened, showing that they were filled with swords, spears, knives, and more mundane metal tools like hammers and small axes. That was the worth of two dozen human lives to these creatures: a few tools. Some weapons.

Perhaps that was fair. The lives of the valkin were worth less than nothing to me, especially at that moment.

I couldn't say in detail what happened after that. I've heard about seeing red, and I've been blackout drunk, and the next several minutes were a bit of both. I stalked through the corridors like a monster out of a horror movie, hiding in the shadows, picking off valkin in ones and twos as they desperately tried to figure out what was attacking them. They finally rubbed their two shared brain cells together and gathered in one room in an attempt to protect their leader, and some measure of clarity returned to me as I burst in. They had flipped some tables to cower behind, but they never saw me until I was among them. I drove the shadows before me, crashing through their makeshift barricade and scattering them throughout the room as the leader raised his staff. I saw magic gather and flow into the staff, and pain like someone driving their thumbs through my eyes shot from my head and down my spine.

The dragon whined with fear inside my mind, but she couldn't reach me through the pain and the rage. I rushed the leader who, wild-eyed and still screaming, swung its staff at me with desperate strength. It caught me on the right hip like a sledgehammer, and the pain shooting from my head throughout my body was joined by one shooting from my hip down my leg.

With a roar, I grabbed the staff, trying to wrestle it from the valkin. Its grip was strong, but its body was light, and instead of wrenching the staff free I threw the creature sideways and into the floor. It let go when it bounced off the stone.

Like a raging ape, I lifted the staff in both hands and tried to bash the valkin's brains out with it. It was a stupid, useless, *human* thing to do. Swinging anything was extremely awkward for me, and the valkin rolled to the side at the last moment, the staff smashing hard into the stone instead. There was a loud *crack* and then a blinding flash as the bone staff snapped and the fang at the top shattered, throwing fragments around the room.

The pain in my head vanished, and the valkin leader let out a long, mournful moan, reaching out to gather the shattered pieces of the staff as I tried to blink away the yellow and purple flashes in front of my eyes. I tried shadowsight, and it was no better, but when had I ever needed to see properly to fight? In this room, there was only me and my enemies, and half-blind or not, I threw myself at them, clawing and biting wildly, focusing on whatever my talons found until it stopped moving. It was a bloodbath. The valkin had spears and shoddy daggers while I had scales like armor, razor-sharp teeth, and claws that cut through meat like paper.

When the search party returned to help, they found a room spattered with gore and a dragon growling at them, and they turned and ran. Even on three legs, I was faster angry than they were scared. None of them got far.

I was in a small room, pacing back and forth, trying to get myself under control. I didn't know how long I'd been there. It couldn't have been that long. My hip hurt like hell, and I limped with every step, but the pain was good. It helped me think. All my enemies were dead. I was sure of it, and the evidence was all around me, the floor, walls, and even ceiling spattered with black in the pale blue glow of the light-balls. I had turned this place into an abattoir, and the anger still wouldn't abate. So I paced.

There was, hopefully, a group of prisoners deeper in who needed to be brought outside, but I was angry at them too now for getting captured in the first place. It was cruel and irrational. I knew that. But that didn't make my anger any less real. So I paced, because I didn't trust myself to approach them, because I was afraid that the anger and the smell of blood that filled this place would be too much, and I would do something terrible.

I stopped my pacing when I saw Valmik.

"Draka," he said, "are you yourself again?"

His bald head shone with a thin layer of sweat in the pale light. He held his shield relaxed at his side, though his sword was sheathed, and he looked apprehensive. Not afraid, exactly, but ready to run or defend himself if it became necessary.

I began pacing again, though slower this time, and never got closer to him.

"What are you doing here?" I asked, and when I saw the confusion on his face, I realized that I had spoken to him in Tekereteki. "I told you not to follow me," I said in Karakani.

"I would have followed sooner. There were wounded, Tamor among them. They needed tending first." He looked around the room at the scattered remains of the last valkin I had run down. "I arrived while you were still fighting."

"Why didn't you join me?" I asked, though I didn't really care about the answer.

"Battle frenzy is well known among my people. I have seen it before. Friend and foe can become difficult to distinguish."

"You think I would have killed you?" I asked him. Even suggesting it myself left me feeling insulted.

"Perhaps. Or perhaps not. I thought it better not to test it."

"So why are you here?"

"There was much worry, Draka!" he said, throwing his hands out in exasperation. "Fresh from battle, you threw yourself in here with an unknown number of enemies! We feared for you, and we were right to. You're hurt! And if that means nothing to you, Herald feared for you! She was beside herself and wanted to go in herself!"

I kept limping, keeping my eyes on him as I turned. "She didn't try to stop me."

"She would no more try to stop you than you her. She has spoken much of you to me. It seems clear that both of you would rather mourn the other than try to hold each other back." He sighed. "It is admirable, I think, but it does not lend itself to helping each other make good choices."

I thought about that. It sounded harsh, but he was probably right. If Herald wanted to fight a pond full of crocs, I'd jump in with her, but I wouldn't stop her. "So why you?"

"The others are injured, or exhausted, or they fear you. And there is the captured slaver. A great impression was made tonight by your display, though I do not now know what Rallon will think of it when he hears."

I chuckled darkly to myself. "It got the last guy's attention pretty good."

"So it did. The battle is won. The prisoners are rescued. What of the remaining captives in here?"

"I don't know. I thought it would be better if I didn't see them."

"You mean if they did not see you?"

"No, I meant what I said," I told him. He was silent for a moment, then nodded.

"If you wish, you can leave, and I can lead them out. Though where they are is unknown to me."

"That's probably best," I said. Then, after a pause: "How are the others? Herald, Tamor? I saw Med had a nasty cut on his leg."

"They'll be fine," he answered, and I felt some relief. "Though I think Makanna's magic is revealed to the others. She was not very covert when she healed her siblings."

"It was going to come out sooner or later, if you keep working with Rallon."

"You're probably correct."

I described how to get to the room where I'd found the prisoners and then left for the exit. I even felt magnanimous—or possibly ashamed—enough to recharge two light-balls for Valmik. It took some trial and error, but it was easy enough when I knew what to focus on, and he promised to bring me one when he got out.

To my great and undeserved surprise, talking had actually helped. I hadn't even talked about what made me so angry. But simply talking, trying to put some rational thoughts into words, had cooled me off enough that I didn't feel like I was a danger to people around me anymore. And though I was still annoyed with the dragon, I'd been feeling her presence more and more in the short time since destroying the dragon-bone staff. She felt more like her regular self, with subtle pulses of smug pride and satisfaction bleeding through whenever I thought about my short, decisive fight with the valkin leader. I had to admit to myself that having her back was a relief.

I limped my way down the straight, sloping tunnel, back toward the outside.

CHAPTER FORTY-SIX

Coming Down

Outside the gate was a scene of barely contained chaos. Children were crying, their piercing wails cutting through the night, while the older rescuees were talking all at once and trying to handle the kids while dealing with their own fear and confusion.

Adding myself to the equation could not possibly do any good, so I remained in the shadows at the end of the tunnel. Besides, I didn't feel like enduring the stares of the scouts until I'd had a wash and some good sleep. It would be some time before Valmik came with the older people we had freed inside, and I should be able to get out unseen through the shadows if I really had to. I would just rather not risk revealing what I could do, even here.

Two young people who looked like the oldest of the rescuees were shouting at Pot, who was fighting a losing battle in trying to calm them down.

The woman was right up in Pot's face, though it might have been because she could barely see in the dark. There were a few lanterns and improvised torches spread around the area, but the light was pretty dim. Either way, the woman looked like she was close to violence. "You can't seriously ask me to leave without my daughter. I refuse!" she snapped, her voice trembling with anger. At the same time, the young man waved his arm at the group of kids, where the older children were trying to care for the younger ones while the raised voices just made things worse. "And you can't expect the children to sleep out here!" he shouted. "With no tents, no blankets? Why can't we just go back to the village?"

The young woman couldn't be any older than eighteen. The young man was the only one of about the right age to be her husband, if she had one, but by the way they stood, I didn't think that he was. Probably a sad story there, one I would never know and couldn't do anything about.

"Please!" Pot said, his hands up. "I understand that you're upset, but we have to take you back to Karakan! The council—"

"The council doesn't have children as young as two to keep safe and fed!" the man interrupted.

"Or a baby girl not three months old still in the clutches of those monsters!" the woman added and advanced on Pot, who took a step backward.

"I'm sorry, but we don't have the people to escort you at night!" Pot protested.

Meanwhile, the captured man knelt by a tree, his arms and legs bound behind him, with a spiteful smile on his face. Only him, though. I might have overdone it with the venom against the little guy, but . . .

I focused and shifted. Flowing out from the tunnel, I first headed for the nearby stream to wash off the gore I'd collected. It didn't bother me, but I was pretty sure it would put the others on edge. When I returned, I looked around until I saw Herald, sitting with her siblings a little ways away from the chaos. Makanna was slumped against a tree, asleep, while Herald and Tamor sat close, talking to each other.

Not wanting to risk being seen, even with the darkness surrounding me, I made my way among the trees. I made sure to have several trunks between me and the crowd before shifting back and limping over. Herald and Tamor both started when I got close, then relaxed when they recognized me.

"Mercies be blessed," Herald said, reaching out to place her hand on my neck, as though to convince herself that I was real. "What happened to your leg?"

"Got hit."

"Hard enough to hurt *you*?" Tamor said.

"They had a magic user." I didn't want to elaborate. "How are you two doing?"

"We'll be fine," he said and waved to his older sister. "Makanna is spent, but she is good at what she does. She's saved us a fortune in potions over the years."

"She would not let me go after you," Herald grumbled.

"Valmik told me. Don't tell her, but for once, I'm glad that you listened to her."

Herald scowled at me, but she didn't look like she meant it.

"Valmik," Tamor said. "He's—"

"Fine. He came in after I . . . finished up in there. He's bringing the rest of the people out."

"The valkin. You killed them all?" Herald asked.

"Yeah. One or two may have gotten away, but I don't think so."

"Good," she said, dragging her fingers over my scales as she looked toward the children. There wasn't a trace of pity in her voice. "I suppose you must have done something in there. Last time, the prisoners took days to wake up. Now you went in, and a short time after . . ." She waved her hand vaguely. "This."

"You remember how the valkin leader had a staff last time?"

"The one with the fang on top?" Tamor suggested.

"I never saw it," Herald said, "but, like Tamor said. The bone staff with the fang?"

"The valkin here had one just like it. I smashed it. I'm guessing that undid whatever was controlling these people."

"A magical focus, then," Herald said. "That would do it." She went silent for a moment, then pointed at the gate. "Look! The others are coming out!"

So they were. Led by Valmik, a procession of the older villagers left the tunnel. Though, in fairness, only two or three were actually old. Most looked to be in their thirties to fifties, which was apparently enough to be discarded as undesirable. There was a commotion as the younger crowd saw and ran to greet their elders, and then a joyous scream of "Elva!" as the young woman I'd seen ran to collect a small bundle from one of the older ladies.

As far as I could tell we'd saved everyone. There were tears, hugs and kisses all around, and all in all, it was pretty damn heartwarming. It was sweet enough that the last of the fire went out inside me.

I'd hoped that once the anger was gone, it would be replaced with pride and satisfaction. There were hints of that, though they may have been leaking through from the dragon, and mostly I felt emotionally . . . flat. Empty. I was just tired and in pain.

It was a familiar experience, though it had been a while. Running on adrenaline is just another kind of high, and with every uncontrolled high, there's an inevitable crash. Usually, the ways I got my adrenaline highs meant that there would be a dopamine rush, but even that would pass sooner or later. In my case, the crash usually took the form of an emotional emptiness, and that night was no exception.

I lay down heavily, letting the cool ground sap the last of my energy.

Herald kept silently stroking my neck. *"You have done well, my friend,"* she said in Tekereteki as softly as was possible in such a hard language. *"These people are safe thanks to you."*

"It was pure luck that I found them," I objected wearily.

"Luck also well," came Tamor's unexpected voice. *"Do never . . .* Umm, negations are hard . . . *Not to disparage luck?"* He looked at his sister. "Did that sound about right?"

Herald smiled at him. *"Well done, brother. But you need more practice."*

"I didn't realize you spoke Tekereteki," I told him. "From what Herald has said, it sounded like you and Makanna would rather leave the old country behind you."

"Mother, Father teach. Childhood. Talk then, now . . . to forget? No using." Tamor grimaced. "You're not far from the truth. From the things our parents told us about Tekeretek, and from what I've learned since they passed, there is nothing I want

from there. But kitten here never stopped. She kept our parents' language alive, speaking to sailors and merchants' assistants. Despite our best efforts," he added with a smile. "And here you are, speaking it like a native. I'm pretty sure you even have a noble accent."

We watched the freed villagers for a while. The mood was much improved now, especially with a bunch of parents, grandparents, aunts, and uncles to look after the kids.

"What'll happen now?" I asked.

"Well," Tamor said, "we don't have tents or anything for all the people, so we'll probably have to make a bunch of fires and have them huddle up to keep warm until morning. Once Rib and Arlal come back from hunting our missing slaver—"

"Missing?" I interrupted, lifting my head from the ground a little to look at Tamor. Herald's hand stopped petting me for a moment before it continued.

"I am sorry," Herald said, looking crestfallen. "The man you told me about before you went in. He is missing."

"Well, shit," I said, but my heart wasn't in it. I laid my head back down on the ground. I was too tired to worry. "Don't know what you're sorry about. It's not your fault. I should have killed him or hamstrung him or something. You think he'll try to rescue his friend?"

Tamor snorted. "These bastards? I doubt they have any loyalty to each other. No, I think he'll try to make it to either the drop-off or the city to report what happened. Or he might try to escape south or across the sea if his boss doesn't tolerate failure. Hard to say, but hopefully Rib and Arlal will get him. They're very good at their job."

"They didn't do so well against our prisoner." It was uncharitable of me, but it was true.

"No, but if they end up in an actual fight, something has gone wrong. Their job is to find hidden people, or ambush them, and dispose of them *without* a fight. You don't need to be a duelist if your opponents never see you coming." Tamor looked over toward our captive. "That guy . . . I wonder how far along he is. Wouldn't be surprised if he's at his first or second high minor, and all or most of them combat related. And that's on top of him being skilled and well trained. Valmik would have turned the fight in our favor, though. That's why the other slaver focused on tying him up."

"Until he came for me," Herald grumbled. "The worst thing is that I saw him coming. I tried to fight back, and there was nothing I could do. He was stronger, faster, and better than me." She looked at the palm of her free hand, the one that had been cut. "Fucking embarrassing."

"It worked out," I said from the ground. My exhaustion was catching up to me. I'd been pushing my shadow magic too hard, and if not for my hip I might have fallen asleep already. "And you got one," I added, thinking of the slaver she'd shot down in front of the gate.

"I suppose," Herald snorted, still caught up in her own perceived failure.

Tamor watched us, me lying flat on the ground, Herald stroking my neck. I couldn't read him. After a while he pushed himself to his feet and walked over to Makanna.

"What's important is what we learn from this, right?" he said as he tried to coax his sister back to wakefulness, at least enough to walk. "Come on, you all. I want to be doted on by the man I love, Herald should probably do some guard duty, and you two," he said, looking between Makanna and myself, "need to get somewhere warm to rest. The morning is going to be rough, and we still need to watch over all these people until then."

"Can't let 'em see me," I mumbled, getting my feet under me through a titanic effort.

"Keep the light between you and them and they won't even see a shadow," Tamor said, forcing some encouragement into his voice. Right. He was probably tired too. And sleepy. He'd been awake since this morning, and it was well into the small hours now.

I ended up sharing a tent with Makanna, she in her bedroll and me curled up on the ground. It might have been uncomfortable, but she was barely awake when Tamor helped her get her boots and armor off, and I was too tired to care. I shuffled around until I finally found a position that was tolerable for my leg and fell asleep.

I woke to an incredibly high-pitched, though quickly strangled, squeak. My eyes flew open and I looked around, searching for a threat. I wasn't in my cave, and I was on the ground. I never slept on the ground!

Then my groggy brain caught up with the situation and I relaxed.

"Morning, Makanna," I said.

She was sitting up, covering herself with a blanket while slowly rubbing her face. "I'm sorry," she said. "I didn't expect to see you first thing in the morning. Don't you usually sleep in a tree?"

"I got hit last night. My leg's hurt. Didn't want to try climbing." I didn't tell her that I probably could have shadow-climbed a tree. For one I was keeping those abilities under wraps, just in case, and for another, I'd frankly been too tired to try. Besides, sleeping in a tent had sounded like a nice idea.

"You're hurt?" Makanna asked, and I saw some genuine concern on her face, which was more than I'd expected from her. "Do you want me to try to do something about it?"

"Thanks," I said, meaning it. "But no thanks. I just need some rest, and you need your energy to walk back to the city."

She shrugged but looked a little relieved.

"Last night really took it out of you, didn't it?" I said.

"Yeah. Tamor was lucky. His cut wasn't bad. Herald, though . . ." She shook her head. "She was putting on a brave face, but that blade went to the bone. Flesh, tendons, everything. It takes a lot of focus and effort to fix things like that, but the alternative was for her to lose almost all use of that hand, so . . ."

I was briefly stunned. I hadn't realized that it had been that bad! And rolling halfway down the hill with that . . . Herald must have been in agony while she talked to me.

"Thank you," I told Makanna softly. "I know that she's *your* sister, but . . . thank you. And I'm sorry."

"Why?"

"It was my fault, wasn't it? At least part of it."

She shook her head. "I saw the same thing you did. We couldn't risk them taking her. Perhaps we could have freed her some other way, but if we'd thought for too long, it would have been too late. You gambled. You won. I'm happy that you did, so don't be sorry. If anything, accept my thanks, and let's leave it there."

"Sure." I still felt some guilt, but it was good to have had a positive exchange with Makanna, especially after the previous night. If she was satisfied, I didn't want to push it.

Half an hour later the camp had been struck, the bodies having been buried during the night. Most of the nine fighters were trying to bring the rescued villagers to some kind of order before marching them back to Karakan. The exception was Herald, who was keeping me company in the hidden depression behind the hill, where the camp had been. I was helping by not being seen.

Rib and Arlal had returned around sunrise, without the missing slaver. Herald told me that Rib was unhappy, to put it mildly, and I'd heard her ranting and swearing up a storm down below until some responsible soul managed to shame her enough to spare the children more of her extremely colorful language.

Perhaps I should have killed the man. If nothing else, a dangerous criminal was still free when he could have been put out of everyone's misery. But we had needed prisoners, and when you need to make a snap decision, it doesn't matter how good your hindsight is.

I said my goodbyes to the scouts out of sight of the villagers and the prisoner. We made it quick. They were polite enough, but there was still that wariness. The camaraderie that had started to grow was gone.

"*We will be leaving soon,*" Herald said when she joined me. She looked tired, between the magical healing and being awake during the day, a time when she'd normally been sleeping as of late. "*I do not suppose you will be coming with us?*"

"*Normally I would shadow you from a distance, but my leg hurts too damn much for me to walk that far. I need to return home and rest. Sorry.*"

"And I am sorry to leave you, but it cannot be helped," she said with a tired smile. *"And we will meet again soon. I am sure that Rallon will want to talk with you, and there is the reward, of course."*

The gleam in her eye was impossible to miss. If anyone loved silver as much as I did, it was this girl. Although she was pretty free with spending it, whereas I . . . wasn't.

"Speaking of rewards, I have a request to make." I'd been thinking a little, and I wanted to try something. *"When you receive my share, I would like as much of it as possible in gold."* I was planning to move my hoard, and the less physical volume, the better. *"Also"*—and here I had to steady myself. It was hard to say, or even think, but I fought through my instincts and prejudices, and after a long silence where Herald began to look concerned, I emerged triumphant. *"Could you spend some of it for me?"*

CHAPTER FORTY-SEVEN

Rewards and Recreation

The council was most pleased," Rallon told me after we'd gotten through with the pleasantries.

This was my first real outing since returning to my cave three days earlier. I'd had a quick trip to check the tree and grab a goat, which I'd brought back to the cave. Other than that, I'd been sleeping and healing on my hoard.

We met by night in the usual place. There had been some people at the camp, but Rallon's people had "encouraged" them to stay away for a while. It made me think that I needed a new place to meet people. I'd been using this place out of convenience, but anyone could tell that a literal campsite near the main road was not a good place for secret meetings.

"Criers have been announcing the rescue of two dozen citizens every morning for a few days now," he continued. "Not that anyone knew that they were gone. With a small hamlet like that, it might have been weeks before anyone realized that it was deserted."

I'd seen the remains of deserted settlements before. Usually, only some stone foundations and possibly a few decaying walls would remain. I'd asked Herald about it, and she'd pretty much shrugged it off. Bandits, monster attacks, blood feuds—who knew why a small collection of houses might be abandoned? These things happened, and if it was small enough and in an area that wasn't well traveled, a hamlet might spring up, exist for a few decades, and vanish without ever existing in a record or on a map. The only reason we'd heard about the nameless village in the mountains was that a few of them had left for the city before the valkin struck.

"Did you get anything out of the guy we captured?" I asked.

"Unfortunately not. We questioned him—"

"*He is dead*," Herald, standing next to me, added bluntly in Tekereteki.

Rallon looked at her with annoyance, straightening and tensing slightly. "Though I do not speak the language, I have some guesses as to what Miss Herald just said. As I was saying, we questioned him quite thoroughly, and unfortunately my interrogator may have become too enthusiastic. The man expired without giving us anything useful. If we could have handed him over to the council's experts, perhaps they would have been more successful, but . . ."

"Neither of us would want that," I finished for him.

It was too bad. I'd hoped that we could have found out who the slavers worked for. On the bright side, the man being dead tied up a loose end. There was still the problem of one that got away, but he didn't know that I could speak. Best case he'd think that he and his crew had been attacked by the infamous wyvern, and that the human attackers had taken advantage of that. Maybe he'd think that they were controlling me. Either way I hadn't said a word in front of the man, so I wasn't too worried about him. The council's investigator apparently had some hope of tracing the weapons, but Rallon didn't recognize the maker's mark and thought it more likely that they'd been brought in from outside.

We finished our conversation with mutual reassurances that we wanted to continue working together. The terms were simple. If I found anything that threatened the people of Karakan or might otherwise be of interest to the Wolves, I'd get in touch. Even if I didn't get involved directly, I'd still get a finder's fee of at least ten eagles to make it worth my time. On their part, if there was something I was uniquely suited to helping them with, they'd get in touch with me, and we'd discuss compensation depending on what they wanted.

The whole arrangement felt comfortable and lucrative. And to drive home the point of just how lucrative it could be, Rallon asked Herald to hand over my payment for this first job we'd done together, which she'd been holding for me.

Herald opened up a deceptively small pouch and poured its contents into her hand. In the lantern light, I saw the shine of maybe two dozen silver coins and the beautiful gleam of seven smaller golden ones, enough that she could only barely hold them in one hand without spilling.

"The council paid us a bonus of fifteen hundred silver eagles," Rallon told me. "Since there were no significant unexpected expenses, and since you, Lady Draka, secured the safety of the unwanted prisoners on your own, I thought we could forget about the whole 'after expenses' clause of our agreement. So there is your share. Seven gold dragons and twenty silver eagles."

I was glad that I had enough of a sense of shame that I didn't just bury my face in Herald's hand. That, and I didn't want to embarrass her in front of Rallon. Still, I couldn't wait to get my new treasure back home. I think Rallon noticed how distracted I was, because he bid me farewell right after that, returning to his people to wait for Herald and me to finish. Thankfully, I managed to control myself, and didn't start rumbling until he was out of earshot. I had an image to maintain, and purring like an overgrown house cat was not part of it.

Wait. Something was wrong. I looked at the coins in Herald's hand. There were seven dragons and twenty eagles, just like Rallon had said. I looked at Herald. *"You did not spend any of it,"* I scolded her. *"Yet I notice that you have a large sack with you."*

Herald looked away with an embarrassed smile. *"I wanted to make it a present. To show my gratitude."*

"How much did it cost?" I asked sternly.

"There is no need to worry about that."

"How much?"

"Twenty-four eagles," she admitted.

"Herald," I said after doing the numbers in my head, *"that is a third of your share!"*

"I know, but I wanted to—"

"My friend," I said to her, though I had to force the words out. *"Please take the money out of my share. Helping me buy these things is thanks enough, if you need it. Spend your money on yourself. You have a bow to save for, remember?"*

"But—"

"Herald. Please."

She looked at me, then relented. *"Fine,"* she said with a sigh. She put my money minus a dragon in the bag, then counted out the difference from her own purse.

Money taken care of, Herald was eager to show me the purchases I'd asked her to make for me. *"I will confess that it was amusing, shopping for such things for a dragon,"* she said with a wry smile, *"but who am I to question a lady's desire for comfort?"*

Herald opened up the large bag she'd brought, carefully emptying it for me. First came a folded tarp-style sheet, which she opened up partially on the ground. On top of that, she placed a nicely carved wooden chest, from which she took out two thick blankets of dyed wool. Finally, four square pillows in different colors came out of the sack.

"Thank you, Herald," I said happily. *"This will do nicely."*

"Now that you have begun to decorate, when will I get to see your home?"

"As soon as I figure out a way to get you up there safely." I'd been thinking about it off and on, but my most realistic idea so far was to just grab her and fly. I might be strong enough, but there was no way that I was going to risk dropping my best friend in the world a thousand feet if I was wrong.

"Until then, perhaps we could bring you into the city? There is much that I would like to show you."

"I would love that," I told her, squishing one of the pillows. They were soft and must have been stuffed with some kind of fiber. Wool, maybe. *"And getting in would be easy. It is remaining unseen that worries me."*

"We will think of something. Now, let me pack this back up for you."

She put everything back neatly in the sack along with the money pouch, folding the sheet so that the dirty side wouldn't touch the pillows. The sack had a drawstring to close it and a sturdy strap sewn onto it, letting me hang it around my neck for extra support. Now I had two different ways of transporting things depending on size and weight, and both were thanks to Herald.

"I hope you do not mind that we did not sell the illumination orbs," she said as she packed. *"They are far too useful, and since we have some money now . . ."*

"Not at all." I liked having the one that Valmik had brought out for me as well. Darkness wasn't a problem for me, but I needed light to see any kind of color. Or to be able to read, for that matter. I couldn't see any letters with shadowsight for some reason. Besides, I'd discovered, after some trial and error, that my intent when I charged the light-ball let me change the temperature of the light. Now I could have my cave bathed in a nice, warm glow whenever I wanted.

"What will you do with your share of the reward?" I asked Herald as I got ready to go. I was mostly putting off leaving her, and I knew that, but I was genuinely curious. *"Are you not fairly rich, now?"*

Even in the lantern light Herald's smile was radiant. *"We are all quite well off now, yes. We talked briefly about buying a house, actually. But none of us is of a particularly domestic nature. We would need one servant at least, so we rejected the idea. Besides, we can live well at an inn for over a year on what we have. No, I think that I shall be buying myself a nice new outfit or two, and a fine bow. Perhaps a new set of armor if I find a good one that fits."*

She suddenly looked shy. *"And I think if I grease the right palm I might be able to get a letter to Maglan. The officers can still send and receive mail, and I know some people. I couldn't justify the cost of the bribe before, but now . . ."*

Right. Maglan. For a while, I'd forgotten that he even existed. I wondered briefly if that made me a bad friend, but it wasn't as if Herald brought him up very often.

"Good luck with that," I told her, trying to be sincere. *"I hope you get a reply."*

"As do I." She paused. *"I have been thinking about what you said. While we were going to rescue the others, I mean. How I need to figure out how I miss him? And I really do miss him. Miss his company. I keep reading his letters, and, you know, I miss what we did. Before he left."* She blushed and cleared her throat. *"But now that I have not seen him or heard from him for months . . . I just want to know that he is safe."*

"There is nothing wrong with that. But if you do get a letter to him, be clear. Do not let him think that you will want to marry him or something like that when he comes back."

She sighed sadly. *"I suppose I should. I am not looking forward to writing this letter, though."*

I gave her a sympathetic bump on the arm with my head.

"Well," she said. *"I think I have held the others up long enough. Do you want me to get you anything else for next time? It is no trouble."*

"Thank you, but nothing right now. See you soon?"

"I hope so."

After that, I sent my greetings to the others, and with a quick hug made awkward by the sack I was carrying, we were both off.

Carrying the sack worked well. Between the strap around my neck and my arms gripping it, I never felt worried about dropping the thing, and my strength let me fly with it without any trouble. It was a huge difference compared to when I'd hauled my loot back from the bandit camp.

That brought my thoughts back to the bag I'd brought home that day, and it made me think. That bag had contained more gold and silver coins than I'd been paid today, as well as a significant amount of precious metals in the form of items, which made no difference to me. Getting paid was definitely nice. But hadn't I earned that loot as much as I had what I'd been paid tonight?

Of course, that way of getting more treasure meant that I needed to find someone who deserved losing their loot and possibly their life. I was going to have to think more about that.

Ever since I'd woken up in this world, a lot of the things I'd done, and the habits I'd settled into, had been out of convenience or immediate necessity. My choice of meeting place at the lake was one, though it was objectively not a good place for secret meetings. But now I was starting to really look toward the future, and part of that was tying up loose ends, dealing with things I'd been putting off, and settling in in a deliberate way. I had a mental list of things I wanted to do—to which I added *get some dragon-appropriate writing materials*—and the things Herald had bought for me were essential for item one: making a home.

So far, "home" had just been the cave and the place where I'd put my hoard. But it wasn't homey or comfortable or even very convenient. It was time to change that, and I arrived at my cave eager to get started. I didn't think that it would be a huge job, but I'd wanted to lay down the groundwork before I got started. I didn't want to just dump my stuff on the ground the way I had been doing.

I was making a nest, and I was making it nice.

The place I'd picked was not far from my hoard's current location. Only a little deeper than the crevice, before the vertical shaft that led into the depths of the cave system, a turn in the passage bulged into a chamber. Even better, a line of narrow columns separated the bulge from the passage, creating the effect of a room. Sure, water trickled down the walls onto the floor, but that was what the tarp was for.

But I wasn't throwing that straight on the floor either. I had work to do. I unpacked everything from the sack near my old sleeping spot at the cave entrance, and then I headed back into the forest.

The sack was large, but it still took multiple trips and what was left of the night to gather what I needed. When I was done, though, the floor of my new nest was covered in a thick mat of fir boughs, and on top of those I spread the tarp. Or sail cloth, or whatever it was. It made a wide, dry surface to sleep on, and when I completed it with my pillows and blankets I was pretty damn satisfied with my work. My books went in the chest, and then I was done with the heavy work for the night.

I spent the last bit of time before sunrise sitting at the cave entrance, trying out the firesteel. This was really item six on the list, but it was easy to slot in when I had time. I'd found a piece of flint that I could hold, and I'd gathered a bunch of dry grass and twigs and such. Herald had shown me what to do, so I made a little ball of grass, practiced with the flint and steel until I could reliably make some good sparks, and then I got to work.

By the time the sun rose, I had a cheerful little fire burning, and I was very pleased with myself.

I should have slept like a baby that day, but when I woke up, late in the afternoon, I was a bundle of nerves. This night I'd be moving my hoard, and a deeply rooted part of me was very anxious about the whole idea. It was doable, I knew that much. The problem was the risk. The tiny, tiny risk that something might be lost on the way. I told myself that it was irrational. That my plan was pretty much foolproof, with almost no chance of anything going wrong. But it didn't help. The idea of a single coin being lost on the way was intolerable, and I had the feeling that I'd have to power through and live with the anxiety until everything was collected and accounted for in my new nest.

The plan was very simple. I had some bags and a pole. The same way that I'd recently gotten some silver in, I could get everything out. It took a couple of nerve-wracking trips back and forth, and I did end up scrabbling madly to recover the pouch once when it landed almost exactly in the middle of the crevice, but after an indeterminate amount of time I had everything collected in the sack.

I learned something interesting about myself that night, and that was that I knew immediately when my hoard was lacking. Sure, I knew that I was removing things and transferring them, and I could see pretty clearly that the pile was shrinking, but it wasn't that. It was deeper, an instinctive knowledge every time I saw the pile that something was missing, without necessarily knowing what or how much. Together with that was a growing need to find whatever had been lost, to recover it and return it to the hoard, and to utterly and horribly destroy whoever was responsible. Thankfully this didn't lead to any self-destructive ideas. On the other hand, I was constantly fighting an urge to return everything to the pile, an urge that grew stronger with every bag I moved.

The dragon was hardly unaffected, either, though she seemed to understand what I was doing and why. Her contribution to the whole process was to urge me to be faster and more careful. Repeatedly and frequently. Sometimes several times per minute.

I also learned that I had no idea about what would actually be considered a hoard. While the pile was shrinking, I still recognized it as my hoard. Even when the pile was gone and everything was gathered in a sack, it didn't become my hoard. No, my hoard was gone, lost, on the move, and potentially in the hands of thieves. It was one of the worst experiences of either of my lives, and the panic only went away once I emptied the sack among the pillows and blankets and fell onto the carpet of precious metals, emotionally exhausted. At that point, everything seemed to shift, and I felt whole again. My hoard was safe. What my eyes and my mind told me were true. My hoard was in a different location, but it was whole, and it was safe.

I still had to take a nice long nap on it to fully convince myself, but by the time I woke up, everything felt fine.

Item one on the list was done; I had made myself a home.

CHAPTER FORTY-EIGHT

On the Road Again

Item two on the list was dealt with a lot faster than I would have liked.

The next night, after taking care of food—some slightly ripe goat, which improved a lot when I grilled it—and water, I went down into the depths of the cave system. Unfortunately, it was nowhere near as exciting as I'd hoped. It was still gorgeous; it was just that it was exactly the same as I remembered it. No glowing ponds, no ancient murals or secret chambers, not even a gremlin. It was just a cavern, and I'd seen lots of beautiful caverns lately.

At least this one was mine.

Since that had taken all of an hour, thanks to me being able to move around down there with impunity in my shadow form, I moved on to item three. The reason I would have liked item two to take longer was that item three was the Trauma Pit.

The pit where I'd first woken up was maybe four yards wide and fairly deep. There was a passage leading from it that I really, really should explore, especially now that the scholars had dug out a gate at the foot of my mountain. But I couldn't do it. Even thinking about going down was enough to give me vertigo. So I did the only reasonable thing: I put it off. I put the pit out of my mind the best I could and moved on to the next item on my list. *Item four: getting rid of the other predators in my territory.*

After a short nap in my nest, I went to look for the wolves and bears that I'd smelled around my mountain. It wasn't a rational need, and I knew it. But the idea of other predators in my territory was intolerable. It had been bugging me for weeks, and every time I smelled them, it was like an itch that I couldn't scratch. Sooner or later, they had to go.

Of course, finding the damn things was impossible, no matter how I sniffed around. I could only assume that they could smell me at least as easily as I could them, and they were smart enough to stay out of my way. Relying on my nose wasn't going to cut it, and after hours of fruitless hunting I gave up, accepting that it was going to have to be a long-term project. It was starting to get light anyway, and I was getting tired.

Luckily, I knew someone who was at least a competent hunter. Or so she said. I didn't expect Herald to lie to me, but she had her pride, and she might have exaggerated her prowess a little. I had no way of contacting her myself either way, and so I pretty much took the next few days off. I checked on the scholars' camp, but they were gone, and of course I visited the tree by the lake every day, but otherwise I just lived. I hunted, I flew, and I slept. Sometimes I practiced reading, flipping through my bestiary. I could read some of the descriptions now, though I would still need help with the more complicated passages. If ever a writing system had needed reform, it was this one.

That was my life for a few days, and it was good. There was no anger or anxiety. Nor was there any fear. The dragon remained silent, but I could feel her contentment, and it reassured me. I did have to dodge the occasional lone hunter or group of them, some of whom were looking for the "wyvern," and I had a near miss with an arrow that came flying up at me from among the trees, but otherwise I remained happily unbothered.

After several days, I found a note on the tree. *Job to the north*, it read, simple words in a careful hand, then in a quicker, hard-to read-scrawl to the side, *Should be fun!* The first hand was Herald's. The second I didn't know, but I'd bet my remaining horn that it was Tamor's.

I met the gang two nights later. They were packed for a longer outing, and had a mule with them, heavily packed but looking unconcerned. His name was Stalwart, and much like Windfall he was not a fan of murder-lizards. But Valmik kept him calm, and while he never really warmed to me, he at least got used to having me around.

"What are you all doing, going out on a job?" I asked after the hellos and how-are-yous. "I thought you'd be living the good life for a few weeks!"

"Like any of us could sit still for more than a few days!" Tamor said cheerfully, to Herald's and Valmik's smiling agreement.

"You, if anyone, should know that one can never have enough silver," Makanna said. Her tone was serious but there was a glint in her eye when she said it. "And this opportunity was too good to pass up."

"So what are you doing?"

"Did Herald tell you about the Three-ers she and Val met?" Makanna asked me back.

"A little. Sounded like a bunch of assholes, honestly."

"They can be, yeah. The important thing here is that those three haven't gotten back yet, and their congregation is worried. So they put out a job, and we took it."

"I'm guessing they want their people back?"

"That's right. Or proof that they're dead."

"And they're paying well?"

"Right again."

"Three dragons minimum!" Tamor said happily.

Makanna gave her brother an annoyed look before turning back to me. "Like Tam said. Three dragons if we can show that they're dead. Minimal work. But if we can bring any of them back alive . . ."

"Then we get a share," Herald said dreamily.

"A share of what, exactly?" I asked, looking between their greedy smiles.

"Much treasure is to be found in the northern ruins," Valmik said. "The Three-ers were treasure hunters. Some old letters had been found from previous expeditions long ago, and they thought they knew for certain where to find the villa of a very rich family."

"And if you bring them back you get a share of the treasure?"

"Exactly," Makanna said. "And even better: they gave us the location, as best they know, that the three were going to. If they're dead, or if we don't even find them, there may still be a whole treasure there, untouched!"

"And we want you to help us find it!" Herald picked up where Makanna stopped. Makanna gave her a sidelong glance that left no doubt about who exactly had insisted on bringing me along, though she didn't look all that unhappy about it herself. "It is all dense forest up there, so finding ruins is a real slog. But if *someone* could get a dragon's-eye view, they would have a real advantage. And of course they would get an equal share of the spoils. Do you know anyone like that?"

I grinned. "You really know the way to a girl's heart, don't you?"

The gang stayed at the campsite overnight, of course. I returned to my cave to get my harness and the bigger sack, just in case. Who knew if there was any treasure to be found at all, but I wanted to be prepared. I also grabbed the light-ball, because it was too useful not to carry around.

I rejoined the others before dawn. Makanna had the last watch and greeted me as I approached out of the dark.

"Morning, Makanna," I said softly, not wanting to disturb the others.

"Draka," she said with a nod.

"What, no *madam*?"

"I think we're past that," she said, scratching at the dirt with a stick. "Not very ladylike to pull a man's head off. But don't worry. I think us commoners have more fun."

"Maybe," I said. Then, after a short silence: "So, how did you guys end up with this job? It sounds like every adventurer in Karakan should be fighting over it."

"They would have been. But it was only offered to a few. The Three-ers are picky. They needed a group with a good reputation. It would be easy to betray them."

"Kill the three missing ones and make off with the loot, you mean?"

"Just so. While we're not the most famous group by a long shot, we do have a reputation for honour and reliability. Especially now, after freeing all those villagers. Which we have you to thank for."

"Yeah, no worries."

She gave me a small smile that didn't reach her eyes. "Besides that, they're superstitious. The fact that we are three siblings was apparently considered very auspicious."

"But there's four of you in the group."

"True."

"And I thought they didn't approve of Tamor and Valmik."

"Also true, for a lot of them. But they can be very pragmatic when it suits them. There's also the fact that they refused to pay up front, which reduced the number of willing candidates to us and . . . one other group, I think." She gave me another mouth-only smile. "Most groups can barely afford to outfit themselves for an expedition like this without an advance. But since we are heavy with silver at the moment, it was no trouble for us."

I snorted. "You know what? I don't think I mind the rich getting richer when it happens to people I like."

This time, her smile was genuine.

For all my flying I'd never gone more than a few dozen miles north of my cave. Perhaps it was because I'd been so focused on humans, and that was where the small specks of light in the night ended, along with all other signs of human habitation. And yet there was apparently a whole lost civilization up there, abandoned and fallen to ruin after some cataclysmic disaster. As we travelled I tried to learn something about it, but it was so long ago that most of what was known was half myth and half legend.

"We do not know who the old Mallineans were for sure. We cannot even read the texts they left," Herald told me sadly. "They left plenty of scrolls, but the few that do not crumble to dust as soon as you touch them are covered in writing that no one can read, completely different from our script. And even if we could read it, we do not know which language it might be in." More brightly, she continued, "They left plenty of mosaics and murals, though! Mallinean art is extremely durable and highly prized among the very richest all around the Sea of Sareya."

"Paints beyond belief," Valmik said wistfully. "Still vivid after centuries. The loss of their making is a tragedy."

Tamor patted his shoulder. "Perhaps one day . . ." he said indulgently to his partner.

"We can but hope," said Valmik.

"They spread around the sea, though." Makanna picked up where Herald left off. "They weren't the only people to fall during the Collapse, but their cities are found all over. Same architecture, same writing, same art. Their biggest city was here, though, on the northern part of Mallin."

"That's why you call them Mallinean?"

"You'd think so," Makanna said. "But really it's because Mallin is the only island where no other ruins have been found but theirs. Every city and major town on Mallin is built on top of a reclaimed ruin. Even then, taking back the island has been slow going. There's a reason we passed the last village yesterday, and why the road is becoming so bad."

"That reason being . . . ?"

Makanna gave me a secretive look, then laughed. "As much fun as it would be to tell you that you'll see when we get there, I suppose that you deserve to be prepared. Goblins, valkin, the monstrous bears and boars and everything else that plagues the reclaimed lands, they all come from the north. It's . . . background magic or something. I don't really know. But it turns animals into monsters, and it lets Nest Hearts form. And it's a process that feeds itself. The more monsters there are, and the longer you leave the nests, the faster they're created."

"Wait, so the mountains are full of monster nests up there?"

"Oh, not just the mountains," Tamor said happily. "The forests too. Gremlin nests only show up in caves, but goblins, valkin, trolls, stuff like that? They can pop up anywhere!"

"Like Tam says," Makanna went on, "you can find nests anywhere. And the north has more of them than the south ever did, for whatever reason."

"One popular theory is that the Mallineans were cursed, and that is what caused the Collapse," Herald added. "Another is that they had a truly massive enchantment that went wrong."

"I can see the problem, though," I said. "The more monsters you have, the more you get. And the only way to get rid of them is to get rid of *all* of them."

"Just so," Makanna said. "And this is also why we're being paid three dragons just to walk there and back. As I'm sure that you can guess, this is far from the first group of adventurers and treasure seekers to disappear in the north."

"Aren't you worried, though?"

All I got for a while were embarrassed smiles. Then Tamor said, "At the risk of sounding like we're taking you for granted, we kind of assumed that you would want to come along. And between the five of us we should be able to handle anything we're likely to face."

"Especially after what Lalia told us about that bear you fought," Makanna added.

"It's not like I killed the thing," I said.

"But you survived long enough for Lalia to come to your aid, and with no lasting injuries. Even that is remarkable. And between the two of you, you could have killed the thing in time, I'm sure."

"Well, if you put it like that," I said bashfully. This was high praise, coming from her. "Speaking of bears. When we get back . . ."

It took us five days to reach our destination, and they were good ones. We talked—though Makanna kind of kept her distance—laughed, hunted, and gathered as we went. In the evenings we told stories and sang by the fire. I even pitched in, doing my best to quickly adapt half-remembered Brothers Grimm stories and movies to something that would make sense to the others. My attempts at singing went fine, I suppose, but translating songs so that they'd still work required a better lyricist than me. At least they liked "The Wayfaring Stranger." Score one for my dear old dad.

We first went by road. In the south it was good and solid, a proper paved affair, though covered with a layer of dirt, but as we got farther north that became more and more degraded until it was easier to go by paths. Finally, we were breaking a trail through old growth forest, with me taking to the air every so often to confirm that we were heading the right way. Even with hunting, foraging, and the terrain going to hell the way it had, Valmik estimated that we'd covered more than eighty miles in those five days. That was pretty respectable, even if I could have done it in a couple of hours by air.

Monstrous creatures became more common once we left the human settlements behind, and what struck me most was the variety. I'd only seen a few changed creatures in my many weeks on Mallin: a boar, a couple of bears, possibly a squirrel, though I wasn't sure what that thing had been. And I'd heard about a whole den of giant badgers from the others. Here, I understood that anything could be changed. I sometimes shared the sky with some enormous bird, but those that saw me gave me a wide berth. The thing about enormous birds, though, is that even if you make a sparrow a yard long from beak to tail feathers it's still a sparrow. It's still a prey animal by nature, and so were most of the other giant birds I saw, except for the occasional hawk or crow or whatever they were. They were too clever to try me either way.

The same went for animals on the ground. I saw overgrown mice and rabbits, but even a one-hundred-pound bunny is going to run when it sees four humans and a dragon. A three-ton bear, on the other hand, goes wherever it wants. That might explain why I'd seen the creatures I had in the south. The ones that made it that far were the ones that just didn't give a damn about humans unless they presented themselves as a convenient snack.

Even the forest itself was monstrous in a way, noticeably wilder and more savage than in the south. Few people had tried logging or foraging here for several centuries, and the whole place was a maze of massive trees and grasping undergrowth. I asked how they expected to find the Three-ers, but it became clear pretty quickly that this was very much secondary; their goal was the villa and its supposed treasures. Herald always kept her eyes open, but she was very honest about the chances of finding any trace if they hadn't passed close to the villa. And finding that was primarily my job, since I was the one with wings.

On the fourth night, as I ranged ahead, I found the overgrown ruins of a building complex, right where it should be. What had taken me minutes by air took hours to cover on foot, and it was well into the afternoon when we approached. Still, it was better than scouring the forest for days, which is what they would have had to do without me.

"Here," Herald called from where she'd stopped ahead of us. She'd found some possible signs of people passing earlier, and now she was proven right. She'd found a camp.

It had been set up in a small clearing behind a hill, and it was a mess. It hadn't just been abandoned, but torn apart. The two tents were trampled, the packs shredded and the gear strewn about. It didn't take long to figure out that there was nothing edible and few things made of metal left.

"Well. Any bets on what did this?" Tamor asked as Valmik began to set up their own gear. Stalwart the mule looked nervous, and I could smell an earthy musk in the air.

"No need to wonder," Herald said softly, coming down from the hill with a sour face. "Keep your voices down, and go up that hill and take a look. You can just barely see the remains of the walls from there. We will not be digging for treasure uncontested."

"Way to build suspense," Tamor said with a roll of his eyes, before jogging up the hill. It took him a little while to get back. Presumably his eyes weren't as sharp as Herald's.

"Well, shit," he said emphatically as he returned. "That explains our missing Three-ers."

"Not you too," Makanna groaned. "Just tell us!"

Tamor gave us a wan smile and simply said, "Trolls."

CHAPTER FORTY-NINE

Trolling

The discovery that our destination was infested with trolls did surprisingly little to dampen the mood. We packed up and moved back about half a mile and ruled out any possibility of a fire that night. Otherwise my companions kept on talking and laughing, just in lower voices.

"Only once have I hunted trolls," Valmik explained, his eyes wistful and faraway. "They are big and strong, but they are only just cunning enough to be stupid. They can take much damage, but they die like anything else if you do not let them heal. And we have a big advantage: They will make dens together but hunt alone. And we stick together. One by one, that is how you kill a troupe of trolls. It is only a shame that we are not prepared. Their blood draws a fair price from the alchemists."

Once darkness fell, I volunteered to scout the ruin. They knew about my excellent stealth skills, though I still held back about my shadow magic; despite the trust and camaraderie we'd built, I still didn't feel comfortable telling anyone but Herald. Her I trusted implicitly, and I knew that the ever-pragmatic dragon approved.

With secrecy in mind, I put some distance between myself and the camp before I shifted. Being almost completely undetectable was obviously a huge advantage, but I also wanted to see if I could improve my endurance, letting me stay shadowed longer without becoming exhausted. And besides being good practice, it was honestly a lot of fun. As I drifted through the forest I made spooky sounds in my head, like some kind of demented ghost. And once I reached the ruin, there was nothing stopping me from going wherever I wanted. The trolls didn't use any fires, and their den was even darker than the forest, which was perfect for me.

The ruin itself lived up to the name. The foundations were fairly intact and indicated that the main building had been large, with a footprint like a suburban McMansion. The surrounding buildings were smaller, but there were half a dozen of them to make up for it. Partial or whole walls stood in many places, but there wasn't a single room that wasn't open to the sky, with bushes and other low plants dominating the site. There were even trees growing in some places, though fewer than I'd expected.

I found the reason for that in the trolls' den. They had dug, or possibly expanded, an entrance into what was clearly the villa's cellar, as evidenced by the regular layout and the stone walls and ceiling. Most of it was intact, though roots hung down between the stones in places. Of course, no dirt meant nothing for the roots to draw nutrients from, which severely limited any tree unfortunate enough to try to grow above the den. And it probably didn't help that some of the roots looked broken off or gnawed.

The trolls' den was, of course, full of trolls. Not that there was a huge number of them—I counted five, one male and four females—but they had a way of filling the space. Not only were they big brutes, but they sprawled in a way that seemed intended to cover as much area as possible.

The den filled one large room of the cellar, along with one smaller one through an open archway that may or may not have contained a door, once. The floor was filthy, and the trolls had dragged in branches and brush to make sleeping spots. Much less refined and comfortable than my own nest, I noted with some satisfaction. And much poorer. These creatures collected baubles in the form of stones and bits of metal, but it would be an insult to compare anything they had to my hoard. If they weren't eight or nine feet of hulking monster I'd have pitied them.

The den contained three more notable features, none of which was a Nest Heart. The first was a collapsed stairway, which must have led up into the villa. The second was a closed and intact door, made of what still looked like sturdy wood banded with metal. I placed a lot of hope on that door.

The third was a refuse pile, or possibly a horrid storage area. There I made a macabre, but not unexpected, find. Along with the bones and spoiling parts of various animals, large and small, it contained the unmistakable remains of humans. It was such a mess that I couldn't count them, but I'd be surprised if there weren't three.

I would have preferred to find the Three-ers alive, but finding what I assumed to be their remains didn't bother me a whole lot. They'd known the risks, coming up here, and more importantly they'd been utter asses to Valmik. They still hadn't deserved to die.

There was a very real temptation to throw myself at one of the sleeping trolls and see how much damage I could do, but it had little to do with the dead Three-ers and much more with testing myself. Common sense prevailed. I had no idea how strong one of these things were compared to myself, and we already had a strategy for dealing with them. Instead I left the den, keeping my shadow form until I closed in on the camp. When I shifted back I felt my mind relax, and a mental fatigue washed over me. Keeping it up for nearly twenty minutes had been a real workout.

Makanna was on watch when I returned to the camp. She must have heard me coming because she was turned in my direction, spear in hand, but relaxed when she recognized me.

"How did it go?" she asked softly. "Did you see any trolls?"

"I got a head count. They've got their den in a cellar below the ruins. I snuck down. There's five of them."

Makanna's eyes widened. "You entered the trolls' den? Alone?" she whispered harshly. "I can't tell if you're incredibly brave or incredibly stupid!"

"Brave." I ignored her tone. "And extremely sneaky."

She ran her hand over her face. "This is . . . Draka, please be more careful! What if they'd woken up?"

"I would've fought them or ran." Not that there was ever any chance of them noticing me, but I wasn't going to tell her that.

"You could have been killed! I know how tough your hide is, and how strong you are, but trolls can tear through armor and survive injuries that would make *you* sick to see. What if they'd caught you? We rely on you! Herald . . ." She trailed off.

I actually felt a little chastised by that. I hadn't thought much about how the gang would be affected if I got myself hurt, or how Herald would react if I, against all odds, got killed. Again, there had been no risk, but I couldn't blame Makanna for worrying.

"I'm, uh . . ." I said. "I'm sorry. I didn't consider that. But the risk really was very small. I can be extremely sneaky when I need to."

"Yeah, I know. And I'm sorry for snapping. But please, try to think about these things in the future." She sighed and looked to one of the tents. "Herald adores you. She has friends, but I can't remember her ever having one that she was so . . . taken with, as you. I don't want to see her get hurt, all right? I can heal most wounds, but I can't do anything about grief or a broken heart."

"Yeah. Again, I'm sorry. Honestly. I've gotten used to doing things on my own."

"I get it. Dragons are solitary, right?"

"Right," I said noncommittally. "Hey, do you want to turn in? I'm good at keeping watch, and I don't mind."

Makanna was about to say something, hesitated, then considered for about two seconds. "Sure. Thanks." She got up and moved to the tent she shared with Herald, then turned back.

"Draka," she said apprehensively, "did you tell Herald something about, ah, specialty leather goods at some point?"

I looked at her innocently.

"How do you even know about that?"

"G'night, Makanna," I whispered as I settled in.

She gave me a tiny smile. "Dammit. Good night, Draka."

I woke with the others when Tamor, who'd had the last watch, decided that it was time for breakfast. I went off for water while the others ate, having finished off a haunch of venison the night before. With everybody satisfied, it was time to gear up and head out.

I got the feeling that Herald had really splurged. She didn't have any new armor with her—she'd ordered a set modified for her, but it hadn't been ready in time— but she did have a nice new bow, longer and heavier than her old one, and the same went for her sword. Her old sword, while fine, had apparently been too short for her to capitalize on her long arms. Makanna had a new spear, of course. It had a foot of head with a cross guard, and metal reinforcement for another several inches below that. She clearly didn't want a repeat of her last fight. Tamor and Valmik didn't look like they had anything new, but they'd been doing this for longer than the sisters and were probably happy with their gear.

Stalwart the mule, of course, came along. We were not about to leave the poor thing tethered to a tree with no one to watch over him, not when even a fox might be big enough to take him on, never mind the trolls.

We started in a position overlooking the ruin. It paid off; after a while, we saw one of the trolls emerge, its skin mottled green and brown in the sunlight. Some noises came behind it, and it turned back to roar into the den. The noises were just about regular enough to be some kind of rudimentary language, but that might have been me anthropomorphizing the creatures. Our target, one of the females that I decided to call Camouflage, or Camo for short, took off northward, and we followed.

Makanna, Tamor, and Valmik stayed well back initially, while Herald and I stayed closer, using her eyes and my nose to track Camo. We didn't just want to attack when she was alone; we wanted her to be busy. Distracted. Vulnerable. We followed her for half an hour before an opportunity presented itself. Camo had found some carrion, and was inspecting it carefully. But as Herald fell back to tell the others to hurry up, something distracted Camo, who took off to the east, her prize in hand.

I had to rush back, tell the others, and then rush forward and after Camo with Herald the best we could. Thankfully the troll had a pretty distinctive, earthy smell, and was fairly easy to follow. We found Camo in a glade and realized that Camo and I had something in common.

Camo had found a rabbits' nest and was trying to get herself some delicious little bunnies. While the others closed in, I finally got to see those large hands in action. The trolls had wide, thick nails on their large hands, and Camo put them to good use, digging out dirt by the armload. The others reached me, and we quickly decided on a plan of attack.

Distracted as she was, Camo didn't notice me before it was too late. I had leaped into the air and came at her on the wing. But I didn't go for the kill. I didn't crash into her, trying to bring her to the ground the way I usually did. Honestly, it probably wouldn't have worked. I was probably somewhere north of two hundred pounds, while Camo looked like she must have been half a ton at least, with a sturdy, stable build.

Instead I came in just close enough to rake her with my claws, hurting her and grabbing her attention. It worked as well as one might expect. Camo roared with pain and anger at me, though I was long gone. Once I'd whirled around and came back toward her, I could see that she'd left the burrow and was standing ready, waiting for me to come back. So they had some shred of intelligence. What had Valmik said? Just clever enough to be stupid?

I swept in above Camo, and saw her prepare to leap when she realized that I was too high. She was too slow, never even coming close, and when I looked back I saw her following me on the ground, stumbling about in a rage, waving her arms and roaring at me. I led her around for a while, swooping on her to keep her attention, and when she started slowing down I did my best to maneuver her closer to the trees, then turned her around.

The others began their part. As I came back in I saw a long arrow slam into Camo's back, and she roared and threw her arm around her chest, feeling for whatever had hurt her. Among the trees, I saw Herald readying another arrow, and Camo set off for her. Herald calmly loosed, then vanished into the trees. Camo stumbled, indicating that she'd been hit again, but didn't slow.

I landed behind Camo and ran after her, but it was mostly up to the others now. I had enraged the troll and tired it out. Now the others would wear her down until we could all go in together for the kill. As Camo ran there was a flash of reflected sunlight, and Makanna's spear lashed out from among the ferns to take her in the back of the thigh. Camo turned toward the tiny woman, trying to slap the spear away, but the spear tip kept the troll at bay while Makanna menaced her with feints and aborted stabs.

There was another rustle, and Valmik came in behind the troll, stabbing for a kidney before falling back. I was getting close now, and I saw the wildness in the troll's eyes as it realized that it had enemies on every side. Camo started turning, flailing wildly, and when I got close enough and she faced me, I sprayed her in the face with venom. She roared, wiping her face with one shovel hand, blinded but otherwise seemingly unaffected. Still, it effectively ended the fight. She was slowing, blood loss taking its toll, and blinded. As she stumbled and flailed, Makanna moved in and, with one determined strike, drove her spear up to the guard into Camo's throat before withdrawing it and dancing back.

Camo gave a gurgling moan and fell to one knee, but the fight was not gone from her yet. She still lashed wildly around her, trying to reach us until finally Tamor came in behind her. He focused, poured magic into his blade and, with one cut, severed Camo's head. Amazingly, her body stayed on its knees, continuing to flail for a full five seconds before it slumped to the ground, jerked a few times, and stilled.

There were cheers all around. Herald grumbled a little about the arrow that had broken under Camo's collapsing body, but it was obviously theatrics.

We had just started talking about how to proceed when there was a roar, a loud crash of breaking branches, and a second troll threw itself at us at almost-point-blank range.

CHAPTER FIFTY

It's All Fun and Games . . .

Herald was, of course, the first to react. Almost the moment I heard the crash, she had already begun to draw an arrow, and by the time I heard the roar, she was bending her bow. When I saw the troll, it already had Herald's arrow deep in its gut, fired from a powerful bow only yards away.

That didn't slow it in the slightest. It was the male, at least ten feet tall, and it was berserk at the death of one of its mates.

Next to move was Makanna. The troll came in behind Valmik and Tamor, and before they could start moving, Makanna was there, her long spear stabbing at the troll's face to try and keep it back. "Fall back!" Makanna screamed. "Stick together and fall back!"

The boys started moving, but at the same moment, the troll slapped Makanna's spear so hard that it jarred it out of her hands.

Another arrow sprouted from the troll's side, and it turned toward Herald, not fifteen yards away.

I moved. With a spray of venom that did nothing, I leapt at the huge creature. Even leaping as high as I could I only dug my front claws in halfway up the troll's side, using its ribs as rungs to hang from. My feet found purchase above its hip, but as I tried to climb, to get closer to its neck, it swung one mighty elbow back with the inevitable force of a landslide. Next thing I knew, I was flying, tumbling, crashing into a tree, my whole side a single mass of pain. I shook my head, trying to clear it. I could hear shouts, screams, and roaring. When I finally forced my eyes to focus, I could barely follow what was going on.

The boys had entered the fray. Seeing them together in a real fight, not the slaughter that had been our ambush of the valkin, was quite a sight. They barely said a word, only throwing each other quick glances and nods, but they moved together almost like one creature. When Tamor seemed to leave himself open, drawing the troll in, Valmik would be there cutting at its legs or flanks. When

Valmik got just close enough for the troll to swing at him he somehow rolled the blow past himself with his shield, and Tamor used the opportunity to open a nasty gash in the creature's back. All the while they maneuvered so that Makanna would be able to retrieve her spear and left a lane open for Herald to fire a second, third, then fourth arrow into the thing.

It had been tempting to see myself as the linchpin of the team. Seeing them dismantle a brute as big as all of them put together was humbling.

Until it all fell apart.

As I got to my feet and approached the melee the maddened troll abandoned all thought of self-preservation, throwing himself at Valmik. Valmik was tough, but he was the slowest of the group, and while he avoided being grabbed or bitten he couldn't avoid a blisteringly fast swing of one of the troll's long arms. It caught him on the shoulder, and I thought I could see that whole part of his torso deform before he went flying, rolling on the ground.

"Val!" Tamor screamed desperately, redoubling his efforts, but the troll ignored the cuts he gave it, lumbering after Valmik who lay still on the ground.

I could barely run. I don't think I could have jumped. But as the troll reached down to grab Valmik's leg I did the only thing I could. I threw myself forward, latching on with my teeth, then claws to his arm and hoping that I was strong enough to take the pummeling I had just invited.

The troll roared. He pulled his arm toward his chest and tried to bite me, but I released my jaws and roared right back. I planted my feet on his torso and held on for all I was worth, straining to keep him from getting me close enough to his mouth to put those horrible teeth to work. I tried to spray him in the face but only managed a dribble, and while I instead snapped at him with my teeth, he swung his other arm around, smashing me against his chest. It knocked the wind right out of me and hurt like hell, bruising my bruises, but I didn't think anything got broken. When that didn't detach me, he instead grabbed me around the base of the neck, his hand big enough to go nearly all the way around. A sledgehammer pounded in my brain as he squeezed, closing off my veins and forcing blood into my head. I could have sworn that I felt my eyes bulge out of their sockets.

All I could do at that point was to hold on and fight against the pain. If I let go with my hands or my feet the troll would be free to go for Valmik, or to use his free hand or teeth to do something horrible to me. I couldn't turn my neck to bite him anywhere vital, and instead I sunk my teeth into his upper arm, using them to help control the limb.

Black and purple started creeping in at the edges of my vision. I wouldn't be able to hold on for much longer, and I felt myself weakening as the troll squeezed and jerked at my neck, trying to remove me. I couldn't win, and I couldn't get out. It was the bear all over again.

Then we were both falling. The troll toppled to the ground with an angry, confused scream, letting go of my neck to break the fall with its arm. I took the opportunity to let go, pushing off and rolling on the ground before getting to my feet, then stumbling and falling between Valmik and the troll.

Makanna was trapped under the haft of her own spear, but its point was buried in the troll's left knee. It must have cut something vital, because the knee had buckled, bringing the troll down almost all the way to the ground. I could see a half dozen arrows in its back, and Herald coming in behind it, sword in hand and with a wild look in her eyes.

I couldn't muster the strength to move. The thing righted itself and reached for me, but before it could grab me a glowing length of steel swept down, cutting into its forearm and lodging in the bone. As it snatched its arm back with a roar, Tamor screamed right back and wrenched his sword loose, then raised it and hacked and hacked and hacked. There was no technique there, nothing of the swordsman that I knew he was. There was only fury and desperate strength. He hacked and hacked, putting everything he had into it, first finishing what he'd started and severing the arm that the troll threw up to block, then the other, then biting in where the troll's neck met its shoulders until his sword clove first through the troll's collarbone and then its spine. At that point the troll's body gave up on it. With a mournful groan it toppled over, tearing Tamor's sword from his grasp as blood gushed onto the ground.

The three left standing didn't bother to finish the troll off. As soon as it was incapacitated, they all scrambled over to where Valmik and I lay.

Tamor was still wild as he reached Valmik, tears streaming down his face. "Val!" he pleaded. "Stay with us, my heart! Stay with *me*!"

Valmik groaned weakly, a horrible, wet sound and the first sign of life from him since the troll hit him. His face was pale and covered in sweat, blood bubbling at his lips as he took slow, shallow breaths, and his shoulder . . . I could best describe it as an innie, which is not something a shoulder should be. I didn't need to know anything about medicine to know how bad this was. The fact that he was even still alive was a small miracle.

"Oh, thank the Mercies," Tamor whispered, leaning down to kiss Valmik's forehead. "He's alive." Then he went flying with a surprised cry as Makanna tackled him.

"It's all right, Val. It's gonna be all right. Herald! Where's that damn potion?" she shouted as she loosened the straps of his armor, then slid her hand in under his tunic, skin on skin. She breathed heavily but regularly, then slowed, forcing herself to focus. I saw the magic gather in her, then continue gathering as she kept drawing on whatever its source was, even as she mumbled, "Heal, damn you. Heal! It's not time to go with the Traveler just yet," and the light flowed from her and into Valmik. I had to turn away as his shoulder visibly shifted back out of his chest and into its normal position. It was both amazing and nauseating to see.

His breathing became a little less shallow, a little more regular. Then Herald reached him, a small, very nice bottle in her hand. "Here," she said, holding his head steady with one hand while holding the vial to his lips with the other. "Drink."

She poured a little of the contents into his mouth, then immediately covered it with her hand as he coughed weakly before swallowing. She repeated the process until the whole bottle was empty, right around the point where Makanna's eyes fluttered closed and she fell sideways, her hand still on Valmik's shoulder.

Tamor caught her, laying her down gently. "There, sister," he muttered. "I can't . . . Thank you. I'll get you some food and drink. You just rest."

Makanna was knocked out from exhaustion. Valmik was already looking better, but was unconscious from a combination of trauma and two forms of magical healing. I was a mess of bruises, and Tamor was a nervous wreck as he made a small fire to prepare something he could feed his lover and his sister as they recovered.

"Well," Herald said, breaking the long silence with forced levity. "That went better than it might have!"

"Better than . . . ?" Tamor said after a stunned silence, and for a moment, I was genuinely worried that he was going to snap and explode at his little sister. But that just wasn't him.

Instead he wiped his eyes and laughed nervously. "Better than it might have!" he tittered. "That's certainly true. Gods, I was so scared."

"I know," Herald said and put her arm gently across his shoulders as he worked. She looked at me and said, "Me too."

I stalked through the forest surrounding our temporary, makeshift camp. Once I'd had a chance to breathe for a couple of minutes I'd felt okay to stand and move around, which I'd taken advantage of immediately. I'd given the excuse that someone needed to keep an eye out for threats, which was true, but mostly it was because the siblings had been getting more emotional than I was comfortable with, and I wanted to give them some space. It would be hours before Makanna was in any state to do something about my pain, anyway, so I might as well walk it off.

I was getting pretty used to being a walking bruise. Perhaps I should reconsider my lifestyle. Only pick on things my own size.

Nah. This was much more exciting.

I returned after my patrol to find Makanna half-awake, propped against a tree and being very unhappily spoon fed by Herald. Someone had gone and brought

Stalwart from where we'd left him before engaging the first troll, and Tamor had cooked up a big batch of their gross porridge of dried meat, dried fruit, and hard bread. At the edge of the camp sat the heads of both trolls, long ears drooping, both of the gruesome trophies staring at me as I approached.

Makanna looked unsteady and confused, not just sleepy but something more, and then something clicked in my head. Using magic made you tired and hungry. What else makes you tired and hungry? Among other things, a drop in blood sugar. Blood sugar is used to replenish the . . . *a*-something, the little bits that actually store the energy in your cells. Get your blood sugar too low and your brain turns to mush until the situation's fixed by breaking down fat and protein and glycogen, or until it starves to death, whichever comes first.

Hah! I learned something in biology after all!

"I can feed myself," Makanna said unconvincingly, sounding not all there.

"We tried that, Mak," Herald told her patiently, scooping up another spoonful of mush. "It didn't go well." She pointed downward with the spoon, and I saw the mess that *someone* had made of the front of Makanna's leather chestpiece.

"Oh," Makanna said as she looked down. Herald used the opportunity to stick the spoon in her open mouth.

Herald barely finished feeding her the contents of the bowl before Makanna was back asleep.

Valmik, who probably needed food even more than Makanna, was still in a deep sleep. His color and breathing were better, and there was no more blood when he breathed and much less when he occasionally coughed. He lay on his back, his head resting in Tamor's lap while the latter gently ran his fingers over his bald head.

"Draka," Tamor said softly. "You put yourself between an enraged troll and Valmik. I won't forget that."

"Nah, that's—"

"No. On my life, I swear that I will find a way to repay you."

"All right, yeah." He looked so earnest that I couldn't very well dismiss his promise. "I'll remember that." I hissed with pain as I settled in on the ground.

"So, what do we do now?"

"About what, exactly?" Herald asked.

"We've taken care of two of the trolls. And, by the way, nice little display at the edge of the camp there—"

Herald grinned. "Glad you like it. Hacking the big one's head off took some work."

Bloodthirsty girl, I thought approvingly, and continued. "But that still leaves three more. We can't leave Makanna and Valmik alone, and I'm pretty banged up. I can fight, but not at full capacity. If one of the remaining trolls finds us, we're in trouble, aren't we?"

"Yeah," Tamor said. "Honestly, we never expected trolls in the first place. One or a pair might wander this far south, but a whole troupe of them . . ." He shook his head ruefully. "And that male coming on us right after we finished the first one? It's like my luck's fucking turned on me."

"At least the biggest of them is dead now," Herald said. "And Valmik will live. Makanna will be on her feet again tomorrow, and Valmik . . . I do not know. He should be awake and able to take care of himself tomorrow, then able to fight in two days, maybe. Three at most. And it is not like we can travel until they've recovered anyway. This is a delay, that is all! I say we get these two back to camp. We feed them until they hate us, keep an eye on the remaining trolls, and then finish the job!"

"Is this the same girl who was reportedly nervous about going into the gremlin mines not three months ago?" Tamor asked with a small grin.

Herald stuck her tongue out at him. "I did not come all this way and commit to fighting trolls for . . ." She thought for several seconds. "A fifth share of three dragons?" she finished and looked at me.

"That's, uh . . . twenty-four eagles."

She smiled at me fondly. "Without a counting frame or anything. But you see, Tam? The potion cost more than that. We need to see what we can get from that ruin, and that means getting rid of the trolls. We cannot risk going in there and having them return. Fighting a troll in a cramped space like that would be a nightmare."

"You know," Tamor said, "Valmik would give me the silent treatment for days if we withdrew because of him. I'm with you. But what about the boss?" He nodded toward the softly snoring Makanna.

"Do not worry about her," Herald said, swelling with confidence. "I am sure that she will see reason."

CHAPTER FIFTY-ONE

Two Down

Absolutely not!" Makanna hissed, her hands on her hips. She was still a little wobbly on her feet but she wanted to make a statement, I suppose. "Val almost died—"

"But he did not!" Herald protested.

"Half of your arrows are gone—"

"It's less than a quarter!"

"And we used our good potion! Besides, Draka's hurt!"

That made Herald visibly hesitate until I spoke up. "I'm not that bad," I said. Makanna didn't reply, but the look she gave me screamed, *Not helping!*

"Please listen, Mak," Tamor said. "What happened here was a fluke! You saw how easily we took down that first troll. Just because we had some bad luck—"

"You don't have bad luck!" Makanna shouted at him. "We fucked up!"

"Just because we had some bad luck," Tamor repeated stubbornly, "doesn't mean that we should give up entirely! Yes, the biggest, baddest bastard I've ever seen came on us when we weren't prepared! Yes, Val got hurt, and that haunts me! But the troll is dead, and Val is not, thanks to you."

"If anything luck was on our side. You think it was bad luck that let one stab of your spear ruin that troll's knee?" I asked Makanna. She scowled at me. "Or that let me reach the troll right before he grabbed Val?" I glanced at Tamor. "Maybe luck can only get you so far, but fortune favors the bold, right?"

"Oh, I like that," Tamor said under his breath.

"Focus!" Makanna said.

"This is what we do!" Herald said, and Makanna spun to face the renewed threat of her sister. "We take risks, and we get rich! We cannot give up every time there is a minor setback!"

"A minor—" Makanna sputtered.

"We've seen what they can do now, and it's five against three," Tamor pressed on. "The chance of fighting two of them one after the other again is minimal!"

"Two of us—" Makanna said, whirling back toward her brother.

"You know, I could watch the ruin from before dawn and make sure we get one that's wandered off far from the others," I said. "I blind it, Herald peppers it with arrows, and then you finish it off. We might even be able to do it *without* Valmik."

It took a few more salvos, but eventually we wore her down. In the end Makanna's pride and greed were stronger than her caution. The finishing blow came when Herald alluded to some horse that Makanna had apparently had her eye on, and which she might be able to buy guilt free if we got a good haul from the ruin. She agreed to stay and fight on, on the condition that we plan every engagement meticulously.

"The Herald was right," my dragon said out of nowhere. I hadn't heard from her in what felt like ages. *"Her sister did see reason."*

I committed fully to keeping Makanna onboard. The rest of the day and most of that night I alternated between napping at the temporary camp and patrolling the area. An hour or so before dawn I made my way to the ruin, confirming that all three remaining trolls were there. They'd taken the loss of two members in stride, having each claimed a larger area of the den for themselves.

The trolls woke up before dawn, the first one waking the others by simply being its own loud, unpleasant self. A small scuffle broke out, the two that had been woken being very unhappy about the fact, but once that was settled they all left the den and headed out into the forest. They went roughly toward the points of a triangle, covering the maximum area either by cunning or instinct, so I followed the one whose direction took it closest to my companions.

This was the smallest of the original group, so I called the hulking beast Tiny. She was not only shorter, not quite topping eight feet, but thinner as well. I guessed that being smaller made her easy for the others to bully, which meant less food for her from the larder/refuse pile, which meant that she stayed smaller, and so on.

Tiny made up for her size by being sneakier and cleverer than I'd seen from the others. She didn't just lumber around. I followed her until she spotted something and watched with interest as she held up one hand, considering the wind then carefully sneaking around to keep herself downwind from her prey, which looked like some kind of land-dwelling beaver. While she stalked the beaver, I watched her, curious about what she'd do.

With great care, Tiny searched the ground, then very quietly dug out a large rock. She found a spot she liked in some bushes, next to a narrow trail, and hunkered down. But she didn't throw the rock at the beaver-thing, which was happily gnawing on a thick, exposed tree root. Instead she threw it in an arc, sailing high above the creature and crashing down on the opposite side of it from herself.

The beaver leapt into a run, right in Tiny's direction. When it got close to Tiny's hiding spot, the troll crashed out, wrapping her arms around it and squeezing until something crunched. Well done, Tiny!

Tiny had to die.

Trolls were already nightmares with their size and the amount of punishment they could handle. A clever troll this far south was unacceptable, not because it was a threat to every human it might come near, but because it might wander into my territory. I didn't like the idea of a *bear* wandering around my turf, and Tiny was infinitely worse.

Before I knew it my attitude had gone from following Tiny to actively stalking her. It was a bad idea. I knew that it was a bad idea and I did it anyway, with Makanna's words the other night about being more careful either ignored or forgotten.

Tiny chowed down immediately. She ate quickly and messily, probably out of hard-won habit, and while she didn't have my sharp teeth she more than made up for it in sheer strength. Human me would probably have thrown up, but as it was I watched with a sort of horrified fascination. I wondered what I looked like when I ate. I knew that it wasn't pretty, but it couldn't be this bad, could it?

A memory flashed of me tearing off the lower leg of a goat and swallowing it whole, skin, hoof, bone, and all. No wonder the others always looked away "politely" when I ate.

I hoped that Tiny would choke on a bone or something, but that, unfortunately, didn't happen. A little after finishing she did, however, become visibly drowsy, probably something similar to how I went into a torpor after a large meal. And so, I hatched a plan.

Since Tiny was far from my companions and not heading in their direction, I risked leaving her for a while. I still needed to keep a general idea of where she was, but if I lost track of her it wouldn't be the end of the world. My goal was simple: find something fairly large and kill it.

I decided on a combination of my old strategies. First, I sniffed around until I found a trail. Then I climbed a nearby tree and hung out there, invisible among the branches, until I heard something walking along the ground, not quite crashing along but not sneaking either. Looking down I saw a decently sized boar passing by, stopping to root around among the leaves every so often.

It didn't stop right in the shadow of my tree, but it was close enough. In quick sequence I shifted, forced the shadow to deepen, then glided up until I was no more than a yard away from the pig. I couldn't see it, since it stood in the light, but I could still hear it rooting around.

There was no sound when I shifted back except for the soft crunch of leaves under my feet, but that was enough for the alert boar to look in my direction. It saw me just in time to get a face full of venom. With a loud squeal it took off running blindly for a dozen yards before it crashed head first into a tree so hard that the branches rustled. It got up, wheezing, stumbled a few steps, then collapsed.

Very pleased with myself, I walked up to the dying boar and tore its throat out with my claws. Part one of my plan was done, and the blood that spilled on the ground was the beginning of part two. I grabbed the pig with my jaws and one hand, happy to have something between my teeth to bite down on as pain shot up my bruised side, and then began dragging the carcass in Tiny's general direction, trying to keep downwind of where she should be.

I found Tiny again some time later. She'd spent what must have been a whole lot of effort digging out some kind of burrow, but had nothing to show for it. Don't worry, Tiny, I thought to myself. You'll have a whole pig to yourself soon.

With Tiny still busy I dragged my catch around so that I'd be upwind of her. Hopefully, she wouldn't smell me and be spooked, but that was a risk I'd have to take. I found a location I was happy with, and then I set up my ambush.

It was simple. I left the pig's carcass in the sun, upwind from Tiny. Then I quite messily disemboweled it, only snacking a little before spreading the guts out in front of the pig. That done, I posted up in a tree and waited. Fortune was clearly on my side, because soon a breeze blew through the trees, bringing the scent of free pig in Tiny's direction.

I didn't have to wait long. Tiny came sneaking up to the small clearing, sniffing and looking around suspiciously. The fact that she never even glanced toward my tree suggested that I either didn't smell strongly enough for her to notice me, or more likely that I was so covered in the smell of the pig that I was indistinguishable from the strong aroma that hung in the air.

Seemingly satisfied that she was both safe and lucky, Tiny rushed forward, shoving some of the pig guts into her mouth and then dragging the rest of the carcass into the bushes, where she began to feast with a sound like a chicken going through a garbage disposal. I waited patiently, wondering if there'd be anything left when she was done. She was a big girl, after all, even if she wasn't big for a troll.

It was afternoon when she finished. It had taken Tiny a little over an hour to polish off a whole pig, but polish off a whole pig she did. My mind again drew some unflattering parallels between her and myself, but a bit of unpleasant self-reflection was worth it. Soon Tiny slumped down in the sun and propped against a tree. I could see her fighting to stay awake, but it was a futile struggle. After several rounds of her eyes slowly closing and then popping open, they stayed closed, and soon I heard a soft snoring.

She snored less than Herald, which was hilarious.

One thing about trolls that I was reminded of very quickly was just how tough they are. I did my thing, sneaking down and spraying venom in her face. I even waited until she inhaled for maximum effect. Then, before she had a chance to react, I gave her a good slash in the neck with my claws, which got her bleeding pretty badly. Of course, because she had her eyes closed in sleep she wasn't blinded, and neither did she wake up in the confusion I'd been planning to use to put some distance between us. Instead she woke up in an immediate, berserk rage. Her eyes popped open wide, and she took a swipe at me that was just barely too slow to catch me on the head. I threw myself back with a hiss, managing to spit rather than spray a spatter of venom that didn't do more than make her blink.

Still, she was bleeding heavily from the neck, and I could hear her wheezing. Time was on my side. I jumped back a bit to give myself space, then turned to leap up the nearest tree. If I could only—

I felt a painfully strong grip around my tail, and with a yank that made my hips pop, Tiny reeled me in. I felt her other hand on the base of my wing, and when she pulled I had no choice but to scrabble back or have my wing dislocated or broken. As she pulled me close I whipped my head back in pure desperation, and got a good look at her ugly mug coming down to bite me. Reflexively, I bit her instead, right across the face. My upper jaw on one cheekbone, my lower jaw on the other, and dozens of sharp teeth digging into her flesh, I bit down for all I was worth.

Tiny howled. Or she would have if she could. Instead all that came out was a piping wheeze. She jerked her head around, but all that did was to rip my teeth around in her flesh. When that didn't work, she released her grip on my tail and wing, leaving me hanging from her face by the strength of my jaw.

Then she punched me.

One moment I was hanging from her face. The next, I was on the ground, my vision white as I tried to understand what had happened. That was the second time a troll had hit me, and they were two for two in nearly knocking me out. I had a brief chance to gather myself before she kicked me away from her, into the shadow of an old, leafy tree.

I panted on the ground, desperately trying to orient myself. Looking around I found Tiny, grasping at her ruined face with one huge paw. Blood ran in sheets down her cheeks, her neck, and her chest, making the malevolent stare she gave me all that much more horrifying. As she started advancing on me I felt truly afraid for my life for the first time in . . .

Well, shit. Since yesterday, I thought. Probably not a good pattern.

I acted on pure instinct. I couldn't get my feet under me fast enough to get up the tree, so instead I pushed at the shadows with all that I had, and began to shift the instant I felt the resistance of the light recede. I shifted just in time, and felt a moment of *wrongness* and disorientation as her huge paw passed through where my head should have been. Giving thanks to God, Baby Jesus, Thor, the Mercies, and anyone else who might possibly be listening, I flowed straight up the tree, as far as I could go, before shifting back.

I hung there, more tangled in than lying among the branches, panting and alternatingly cursing and congratulating myself. I'd added to my bruises and my head was still ringing, but I was alive and, again, nothing felt broken. Though that might be shock setting in, a treacherous little voice that remembered my first aid training said.

Tiny raged down below, smashing the tree with her fists, but she was weakening noticeably by the second. Soon she slumped to the ground, gasping and wheezing shallowly. A little after that, she stopped making any sounds at all.

I felt . . . ashamed. For a moment, I wondered why I'd killed her. She hadn't done anything to me. She wasn't anywhere near my territory or anyone I cared about. She was in my way, that was all. She'd looked like she'd had a rough life, but she'd been smart . . . for a troll, at least. Maybe she'd had potential that other trolls lacked? Maybe she could have been something more. And I'd taken that away. Snuffed it out.

Then the feeling vanished. She *was* in the way. She'd probably eaten at least parts of the Three-ers. That was a pretty big deal. And she had been a terrible threat. What if she'd found a new male, and spawned a whole tribe of clever eight-foot monsters?

No, I'd been right to kill her. Maybe I should have waited, so that we could have done it more safely, but one less troll, at least here, was a good thing any way you looked at it.

After catching my breath, I shifted, flowed down the tree, and shifted back. I didn't even want to think about climbing with the way my sides hurt. I looked at the dead troll. My guilt was gone, but I still felt a kind of preternatural kinship with her. If I didn't have the advantages that I did, with flight, being extremely stealthy, and then my shadow powers on top of that, would someone have killed me in my sleep by now? I was a monster by most people's standard.

But then that feeling went away as well. There was no point in worrying about that. I needed to get back to my friends and rest. There were still two trolls out there, and then, hopefully, a treasure to dig out.

"Sorry, Tiny," I said. Then I dug my way inside her rib cage and ate her heart. I was hungry, and it felt like a weirdly respectful thing to do.

CHAPTER FIFTY-TWO

Two to Go

When I stumbled into the camp, Makanna was the first to see me. She dropped the piece of wood she'd been whittling and said, "Mercies! What happened to you?"

"Fought a troll," I groaned. The two batterings I'd received were really catching up to me once the adrenaline high was gone. "I won."

By then, Herald and Tamor had arrived and started fussing over me, directing me to a spot to lay down.

"How did that happen?" Makanna said, the concern in her eyes now clouded by suspicion.

"I saw an opening and I took it." I was too wrung-out to try to keep her happy.

Makanna's face thundered over, but before she had a chance to say anything, Herald preempted her, eyes shining.

"You cannot say something like that and not tell us the story! I want a blow-by-blow!"

I was tired, but how could I refuse her when she was so excited? Fighting down the pain, I gave them a somewhat-abridged version, only leaving out my shadow magic. I still felt vaguely guilty about that. When I'd finished Makanna looked almost defeated. She slumped where she sat, looking as tired as I felt.

"Dammit, Draka!" she said, but there was as much concern as anger in her eyes. "Of all the irresponsible—"

She caught a hard look from Herald and swallowed whatever she'd been about to say.

"You know what?" she said instead. "I'm sorry. You took a big risk, but it paid off. You got rid of a threat, with no risk to me or the rest of my family. So thank you for that. I keep forgetting what you are."

"How do you mean?" I asked her, worried that something nasty was coming.

"You're . . . you can do things like that. Fight a monstrous bear and survive. Kill a troll by yourself—"

"A small troll."

"Fine, yes. A small troll. You killed a small *troll* by yourself while you were still hurt from our last fight. My point is that I can't think of you like any other member of my team. I can't worry about you the same way. But that's easy to forget, because despite"—she gestured at me broadly—"you speak and often act like you were just some foreign woman five years my junior." She sighed. "I'll try to do better."

I wasn't sure what to say. "You worry about me?" I managed after a long moment.

"Of course I do! We may not be close, but you're a member of my team and my sister's closest friend. What did you think?"

"I don't know? I guess I never thought you cared much either way." But of course the team mom would care about me on some level. "When you put it like that . . . sorry, I guess? I'll try to be a little more careful."

"I'd appreciate that," she said with a small, tired smile. "Keep on being you, just please don't try to fight any more trolls on your own."

"No risk of that." I lay down properly with a groan. Tamor insisted on washing the blood from my head. And neck. And shoulders, a bit. I'd really gotten in there.

I still patrolled during the next few days and made sure to keep an eye on the ruins when the trolls left in the mornings, but I didn't want to move too much if I couldn't set the pace myself. Valmik was up and moving carefully by the evening of the day that I killed Tiny, and we returned to the original camp. He was doing some slow exercises with his arms the day after that, and felt fighting fit on the third day. Fed on a steady diet of meat hunted by Herald, his recovery was amazing to see, even after what I'd seen from Garal and Makanna. I asked Makanna not to waste her strength on me out of some kind of self-flagellation, but she badgered me until I caved.

One night, as the others slept, I told Makanna, "You were right."

"Hmm?"

"You were right. The thing with Tiny? The troll, I mean. Fighting her on my own was irresponsible, and I knew it. I don't know why I did it."

"Pride, probably," Makanna said matter-of-factly. "You're like Lalia in that way. Overestimating yourself." Then she snorted. It was a surprisingly cute sound, coming from her. "Though in this case, I guess you estimated yourself very accurately."

"Like Lalia, huh? I'll take that as a compliment, Makanna."

"It was. And call me Mak, would you? Makanna isn't even my real name, it's just what's on the census rolls."

"Uh, yeah, sure, Mak. But really? How come?"

Mak poked at the ground with a stick for a while, then said, "You know how we came to Karakan, right?"

"Kind of. You were . . . refugees, I guess?"

"Pretty much. There wasn't a Tekereteki community here. There still isn't. Except for some people passing through, the three of us are it. Our parents wanted us to fit in as well as we could so, when we were officially allowed to stay, Makanarata became Makanna and Tamotonoro became Tamor. Sounds similar to the local names, you see."

"Yeah, sure. I've heard of similar things. What about Herald, though?"

Mak smirked. "There's a tradition among our people that when a new colony is established, the birth of the first girl marks the true beginning of a community. Since we were it for the Tekereteki in Karakan . . . it was supposed to be symbolic, I guess. She heralded a new, better time for us, something like that. I always thought it was dumb, but Herald doesn't seem to mind."

"Makes it hard to give her a nickname, though," I pointed out. The first syllables of her name in Karakani, on their own, meant something . . . well, *rude* was one way to put it. "Unless she'll be okay with everyone calling her 'kitten' like Tamor—Tam—does."

"It's your head, if you want to try."

A little later, she said, "About this whole job, or expedition, or whatever it is now. Are you sure you're satisfied with a fifth share?"

That caught me completely off guard. "Where did that come from? Why wouldn't I be?"

"When we dealt with the slavers, you got the same share as all of us four combined," she pointed out.

"Sure, yeah. Rallon offered and I accepted."

"And you're a dragon. Your . . . kind, if I may be so crude, are supposed to have a fondness for gold and silver."

"I fucking love gold," I said, dreaming myself away for a second. "And silver. Doesn't change anything."

"I don't think that we could deal with the trolls without you. And you killed one on your own. Are you *sure*?"

"Mak, what's going on? Are you trying to argue me into demanding a larger share? I won't. I *like* you guys. I want to see you all rich and happy, and I'm not going to try to screw you out of treasure that you all worked damn hard for." I meant it. I was there for the companionship more than the treasure, though the promise of treasure was a very, very nice bonus. "And I'm not going to come back and demand anything later either. I promise you. And if that's not good enough, we can wake up Herald and I'll promise *her*."

Mak turned her face from me, looking guilty, and played with her stick some more. "I believe you," she said after a while. She *sounded* sincere, so I took her at her word.

"Besides. *You*, personally, probably saved my life when you brought that troll down."

"What?" Mak looked honestly surprised. "Did I?"

"Yeah," I said, remembering the fight with a small shudder. "You probably couldn't see, but he was choking me out pretty good. I don't know how much longer I could have stayed conscious, and then . . . I dunno. He'd have probably bitten my head off. So, you know. Thanks."

"I truly had no idea."

"Would it have changed anything?"

"No."

"Then it doesn't matter if you knew or not, yeah? You still saved my life. So, thanks."

"You're welcome, I suppose," she said. "I'm glad I could stop a troll eating your head."

I snorted. Mak didn't joke much, so I appreciated anything I could get. "All right," I said. "If that's settled, do you want some sleep? I can take over."

"No, you go ahead," she said. "I have some thinking to do."

Even after Valmik felt ready, Mak still insisted that we wait until the following morning before we went after another troll. After Camo, the big male that I had posthumously named Big Boy, and Tiny, the last two went down easily. Or they were no harder to kill than the first, but since I'd made sure that they were far from each other when we struck, there was no sudden extra troll to deal with once the first one went down. We killed one in the morning, and the other in the late afternoon. I didn't even bother to name them.

I wondered if they even understood what had happened. They hadn't seemed to act any differently after first Camo and Big Boy disappeared, and then Tiny. Maybe members of their group disappearing was completely normal and expected. Or maybe they just didn't care. In any case, if they'd banded together after the first two they would have been safe. We never would have dared to go after three trolls at once. But they didn't, and so four humans and one relatively small dragon killed five giant monsters. Teamwork makes the dream work and all that.

After killing the last troll we went straight to the ruin. We made good use of the light-ball I'd brought, and the one that they'd had with them, though I had Mak charge them rather than doing it myself. They already knew that I could do something magical, since I'd been the one to find and open the gates, but I didn't feel like Mak trusted me fully yet, and I had some vague hope that me trusting her with little things like that might help.

The others reacted far more poorly to the trolls' den than I did. My primary reaction to the smell of death and decay was interest. The others reacted as you'd expect a human to react to the stench of old blood and rotting meat in a hot, humid cellar, and together with the heavy aroma of troll they were effectively forced to stay outside until they'd foraged some strong-smelling herbs to make odor-blocking masks with. Once they made it inside we all had to dig through the various heaps of "treasure" and refuse, which were sometimes hard to tell apart, and my poor companions had to return outside frequently to take some deep breaths and recover. We found some items of minor value: a few rings, a belt buckle, a knife still in good shape, and of course some coin. But we kept looking until we'd found three identical pendants, each made of three interlocking triangles.

"Ugh," Tamor said. "Well, that's our proof of death, at least."

"Couldn't you just get three of these somewhere and pass them off as the real ones?" I asked him.

"You could try. But when we report back we'll have to swear before a Guild controller that we truly believe that they are what we say they are, and the controllers are extremely good at detecting lies and half truths. Our reputation would be ruined if we were found out."

"Oh, right." Of course they'd have human lie detectors! Despite everything, I still sometimes forgot that this place basically ran on magic.

There was a great deal of excitement when I showed them the heavy wood-and-metal door. It wasn't in perfect condition by any means, with the wood being weathered and the metal corroded, but it had still stood up to the test of time far better than it had any right to. It also seemed to have swollen and twisted over the centuries, wedging it in tight in the stone arch of the doorway.

But no matter how well it was constructed, and how impressively it had lasted, it was still a door made to keep out thieves in the night. It was never designed to stand up to four determined adventurers with axes, pry bars, chisels, and hammers, and their magically supercharged dragon companion. It took hours. We ended up working our way through the stone around the hinges and the bolt, and then prying the whole damn thing out, fraction by fraction of an inch until it fell into the cellar, nearly crushing Tamor's toes as it came. But open it we did. And inside . . .

Nothing. Bare stone and bare shelves.

"Sorrows be damned!" Mak exclaimed, striding into the revealed chamber holding one of the light-balls. "There must be something here! A loose stone in one of the walls, maybe?" She looked back at the others, who gazed in with open disappointment. "Come on!" she ordered impatiently. "Get in here and start looking!"

While they all hopped to do as Mak said, I took it slower. I had the feeling that she was right. Even over the death and the troll, I could swear that I smelled silver. Not gold, unfortunately, but definitely silver. I could do silver. You usually got a lot more of it than with gold, and quantity, I'd heard, has a quality of its own. If nothing else, it spread out nicely for sleeping on.

I sniffed around the walls, pushing the others away if necessary, but I couldn't find anything. We tore out the rotten shelves to get better access to the walls, but it didn't help. I kept smelling that silver, though, and the more people moved around, the stronger the scent got.

It was only when Herald tripped on something that I looked down.

On the floor, one of the stones was slightly higher than the others, rising out of the thick layer of dust that had accumulated. And I could swear . . .

I brushed around the stone with my hand. There! Faint but unmistakable, I saw the glow of magic. It ran in a straight line, and I brushed along it, revealing more. Then a corner, and more line, and another corner and so on until I'd revealed a group of stones outline in a faintly glowing square.

"Guys," I said, but they were too busy searching to pay attention. "Guys!" I said it louder, to no effect. In irritation, I roared.

Everyone stopped. Not just that, but everyone went for their weapons, until they realized where the sound came from.

"Now that I have your attention, could you all back off from this square I've outlined? Or better, step out of the room. I have no idea what's going to happen when I try this."

"Try what?" Herald said.

"I'm going to open it. Like one of the gates."

"What? Oh. Ooh!" Mak looked at the floor and back to me before she started herding the others out of the room. "Out! Everybody out!"

I put my hand on the stones inside the boundary. The only real similarity between the square on the floor of the cellar and the gates was that they were stone, and outlined with magic. But there had to be a connection. How could there not be? I focused my will, and commanded the patch of stone to open.

Nothing happened. Of course, I hadn't announced my attempt, so as far as the others knew I hadn't failed. I tried again, and again nothing. I frowned in annoyance and looked at the square. Some of the stones were raised . . .

I commanded the stones to rise. I made myself see it, how they'd slide right up as though it was the most natural thing in the world, the only possible outcome of my will. I looked, visualized, focused, and commanded.

Something left me, and with a slow grinding noise, the stones began to rise. They rose and rose, and a thick, square plate of stone cleared the floor revealing four narrow stone pillars. It all kept rising, until before us stood something like a display case holding a red lacquered lockbox, finely carved and inlaid with silver forming a minimalistic mountain scene, reminding me of old Chinese or Japanese art. It was a treasure in itself, never mind whatever might be in it. The box was about a foot on each side and six inches high, the ornate legs not included. The wonderful aroma of silver lay thick around it, and the artistically inlaid lines shone golden to me.

"Take it," I said hoarsely.

Valmik quickly entered the room, reached out, and lifted the box with some effort. "Heavy," he commented expectantly. "Seventy, seventy-five pounds." He tilted it experimentally, and something clinked and jingled inside.

"Open it. Open it! Crack it open!" Herald said, vibrating with excitement as she hung over Valmik's shoulder, wide-eyed and grinning wildly.

"Patience." He inspected the box from every side. "It is beautiful, is it not? Destroying it would be a crime!"

Herald looked nearly manic in her excitement. "So break the lock or the hinges and leave the rest!"

"There is no lock. Look, no keyhole anywhere."

"Don't you dare damage that box," I said as Herald, becoming impatient, brought out a dagger to try and pry the thing open. "Put it down, Valmik. Gently."

Valmik set the box down almost reverently, Tamor having the presence of mind to spread an empty sack on the floor. As the others crouched around it, Mak holding out the light-ball, I pulled in my claws as hard as I could and put my hands on the sides of the box. I focused. I willed it to open.

There was a click.

CHAPTER FIFTY-THREE

Ten Good Days

An enchanted lockbox," I said. "What do you all think that might be worth?"

The others said nothing as Mak reached out slowly, her hands trembling as she opened the lid. Silver glinted inside. Lots of silver in little coins that were only barely tarnished by the centuries that must have passed since the box was last opened. Tamor reached out and buried his hand, lifting a palm full of the beautiful little discs.

"You beautiful lizard," Mak said, coming around and putting her free hand on the back of my neck. She grinned at me. "You beautiful, reckless lizard!"

"I still mean what I said," I whispered to her, and she grinned wider.

"There must be over a thousand of them," Tamor whispered. "More than two thousand, even. Each of them a little larger than an eagle."

"There are five Old Mallinean silver coins to six eagles by weight, as a rule," Herald confirmed. She brushed the coins aside to reveal a gray-brown surface. "What's this?" she said, carefully digging the item up and lifting it. It was something boxy, wrapped in fine leather.

With trembling hands Herald began to unwrap it. "If this is . . ." Her breath caught. Inside the package was a thick stack of perfectly preserved paper pages. Herald flipped a few. They were all covered in unfamiliar writing and vivid illustrations of landscapes and buildings.

"A whole . . . a whole book . . ." Herald's voice trembled, and she thrust the thing away from her. "Someone take this! I will cry. I swear I will cry. This is . . ."

"That is our fortune," Tamor finished for her, taking the treasure from his sister and wrapping it again. "The box, the coins . . . they're nothing compared to this. A preserved Old Mallinean book. Almost unheard of. To the right buyer . . ."

"Thousands," Mak said. "Thousands and thousands of eagles. Enough to set us all up for life. Enough to make us a House! Even *if* we share it with the Three-ers!" She looked at us each in turn, then sighed. "Are we sharing it with the Three-ers?"

"I mean . . ." Tamor said slowly. "They gave us the location. But we did all the work."

"All they did was fatten up the trolls a bit," Herald scoffed, and the others all turned their heads to look at her with shock while I sniggered.

"What? They were real asses after they found out about Val and Tam. But I see why we might want to. It would look extremely bad."

"Unfortunately so," Valmik said. "Also, selling the book at the most advantageous price would be difficult without help. If the Three-ers had a stake, they would surely try to secure the best deal possible for us."

"But we are splitting the coins ourselves, right?" Herald said, looking around the group.

"Oh, yeah." "For sure." "That goes without saying," the group replied all at once, then everyone glanced at me.

"Gimme," I said, and we were in agreement.

Needless to say, we were all in a very good mood when we packed the next morning. All except poor Stalwart, who had to carry an extra hundred or so pounds of treasure. Befitting our triumphant mood we went slower on the return trip and took more rest, taking six days in total to cover the same distance. While we were excited to return and enjoy our spoils, there was also no need to rush. On the way north there had still been the hope and possibility of finding the Three-ers alive. Now we could enjoy ourselves.

While three of the four humans were city folk at heart, Herald being the exception, they still all enjoyed the outdoors, especially in one another's company. While we still had to be alert for monsters, most of the time was spent messing around, pointing out interesting things, and talking about old memories and hopes for the future. It was a heartwarming thing to be a part of, and with every day that passed I felt more and more like a part of the group. Even Mak was warming to me, casually asking for help with little things, making conversation, and joking around. Tamor and Valmik, having noticed me using the short form of Mak's name, insisted that I do the same for them. Apparently they both thought that I kept using their full names out of formality, rather than the reality of me feeling awkward using the short, familiar forms without them asking me to. In return, there was a very short period of Tam calling me Drak, but it mercifully didn't catch on, and he dropped it after less than a day, to everybody's relief.

They say that money can't buy happiness, but it sure brought me into the group. There was no discussion about whose credit it was that we'd found the treasure, and they were all free with their gratitude to the point that I asked them to stop out of pure embarrassment.

We had plenty of time to count out the coins on our way south, and by the time we separated I had just over five hundred of the slightly larger Old Mallinean coins in my harnessed bag, weighing in at something like fifteen pounds of only slightly tarnished silver. Together with my light-ball, the bag was pretty much fully loaded, if not in volume then in weight, and Herald helped me check and double-check the straps before I left.

"We will have much to do in the coming days," Herald told me. "But if I cannot go to the lake myself I will have someone I trust bring a message to the tree. I will come see you as soon as I can, all right? I haven't forgotten about those bears you were talking about."

"See you then," I said. She leaned forward and I stretched up, wrapping my neck around her shoulders in a hug. That still felt weird to do, but it was nice, so whatever. And that was the end of our adventure in northern Mallin. Two weeks of travelling, hanging out by the fire, fighting, almost dying, and finding treasure together. It had been, for the most part, awesome, but everything has to end sometime. I said my goodbyes to the others with smiles all around, and then we went our separate ways, with me flying back to my nest and them heading down the road to Karakan.

The cave felt oddly empty after spending so long with my friends, but the feeling was quickly washed away as I reached my nest. I quickly took off my harness and undid the straps of the bag, then poured the contents onto my blankets. Five hundred is a lot of coins, and I watched them pour and roll, the clinks of metal on metal coming so quickly that it turned into a rustling sound, with the shattered clonk of the light-ball landing on top of the mat of silver signaling the end. I ran my hands over them, spreading them, feeling them, then threw myself on top of them with a squeal of glee. It wasn't a catnip-like situation, but the mat of cool, smooth coins felt wonderful. I curled up with a happy rumble in my chest. Life was good.

I wasn't disappointed to not have reached a threshold. I hadn't expected to. This was a significant addition to my hoard and there was more to come once the others found a buyer for the book and possibly for the box. We hadn't decided if we wanted to sell that yet, in part because it was so useful, and also because it was, quite frankly, beautiful. Val, especially, loved it. Despite not getting an advancement, though, I did hear the dragon, who'd been almost completely silent for the whole adventure. She spoke up as I was drifting off into a much-needed nap.

"That was good, and enjoyable," she purred. *"It will bind the humans closer to us."*

Nothing like bleeding and getting rich together to really build team spirit, I agreed dreamily. *You don't mind us taking an equal share with the others?*

"Their willing cooperation will be worth much more in time," she said. *"And once they are all ours, it will not matter."*

"What's mine is mine and what's yours is ours . . ." I mumbled to myself, and then I was asleep.

I didn't go back to working on my list that night. I went hunting. My more varied diet on our adventure had made me realize that I was pretty tired of eating mountain goat for every meal, and for both that reason and as a test of my strength, I grabbed myself a small deer from the forest instead of a goat, flying the whole thing up to my ledge without too much effort.

It made me think that I might already be at the point that I could bring Herald up there—Mak or Tam would be possible for sure—but I was sure as hell not going to risk her life on *mights* and *probablys*. Still, it was good to know.

After eating the bits that would spoil the quickest and dousing the rest in venom, which I'd discovered kept the bugs off, I went to check on the scholars' camp. They weren't there, but the camp looked different than the last time I'd seen it and more of the mountainside had been exposed. Though they hadn't gotten the gate open as far as I could tell, finding something obviously man-made had clearly made them want to come back for more. If I was them I would have probably attacked the gate, trying to get inside, but maybe they honestly didn't know what it was, or they were reluctant to damage it.

They were definitely doing something around the site. Thin wooden poles had been driven into the soil here and there, with numbers painted on them in narrow, careful strokes. Some of them were around the gate, and some along the mountainside. When I looked closer I could see that the wall was straight and might have been flat in places, marked on each edge by poles. I couldn't see anything on the stone surfaces, but maybe the scholars had found something after all.

I was just going to have to wait until they came back so I could listen in to their conversations. Unfortunately, the two, a man and a woman, who I'd identified as the scholars of the group, seemed just as excited by pieces of rock as they were by the gate, so knowing when it was worth listening was not entirely easy.

Whatever. They weren't there, and there was little point in hanging around until they came back. Instead I went for a long, circuitous flight, taking me across the forest to the coast, south along the cliffs, where I'd had my run-in with the fisherfolk and past Karakan. I skimmed low over the waves as I passed the city and the ships that lay at anchor there, a million lights in the night. There were more ships in the harbor than before, and I wondered if that meant that the tensions in the south had gotten better, worse, or if it was completely unrelated. Maybe I should head far south one day and see for myself. Going north had made me want to see more of Mallin, and the idea of exploring further excited me. I didn't even know how large it was!

South of the city, I turned west, crossing the fields and pastures and the uncountable small farming communities that lay nestled among them. Even seen from hundreds of feet up high up, the farmland extended to the southern horizon, a hundred miles at least, with villages and towns dotting the landscape and the coast. I wouldn't be surprised to learn that Karakan, as large as the city was, produced enough food to not only support itself but export it as well.

Fields gave way to rolling hills, and I kept heading east as they climbed into the mountains. Soon all I could see were rocky peaks and steep-sided valleys, but I still pushed on for almost an hour until the mountains dropped off and I could see another vast forest on the other side. The range must be forty or fifty miles wide where I'd crossed, and I couldn't see anything even hinting at a human presence on the other side. No lights, no regular breaks in the trees indicating fields or roads. Nothing. It was another wilderness, another frontier, and I wondered what secrets of the Old Mallineans may be hidden there. If a single villa in a place that was already being explored by adventurers had netted us so much treasure, what might we—or I, on my own—find in a completely untouched place?

As I continued north along the western edge of the mountains, crossing peaks, valleys, and rivers, the possibilities ahead of me seemed endless. But I was in no hurry to plan any new adventures. I could take some time and enjoy what I had, and continue securing my mountain. It was truly my home now, no longer out of necessity, but because I felt happy there. It was convenient, comfortable, and above all, safe. Sure, there were some curious humans poking around, and some predators intruding, but those were minor things that I would deal with in the coming days or weeks. The only real problem was the pit. It haunted me, and I needed to deal with it. But not immediately. There was no rush. I could afford to take some time to work up my nerve.

For the time being, I had beautiful weather and a clear sky full of stars that belonged to me and me alone. I spread my wings over an unexplored world, full of monsters to fight and treasure to claim, and grinned into the wind, screaming my joy to anyone who cared to hear. Then I turned, setting a course for home, where I would rest, count my treasures, and look forward to what tomorrow would bring.

About the Author

AvaritiaBona is a proud nerd whose biggest joy in life is to turn tea into words. His stories are about friendship and not being quite right. He lives in Sweden with his wonderful wife, surrounded by supportive friends.

Podium

DISCOVER MORE

STORIES UNBOUND

PodiumEntertainment.com